LA VIE EN ROSE

LIFE IN PINK

LYDIA MICHAELS

BAILEY BROWN

LA VIE EN ROSE: Life in Pink

First E-book Publication: © Lydia Michaels 2015
Print ISBN: 978-1-957573-25-0

Romance | Women's Fiction | New Adult

DEDICATION

*This book is dedicated to the unshakable
Yvonne Gattelli whom I reserve the right to hug
whenever the mood strikes. Yvonne, you always have
a smile—even in a classroom full of eight-year-old
maniacs. Thank you for being such a beautiful
person. You inspire me.
Love,
Lydia*

Book Soundtrack

Stand By Me by Ben E. King
Pictures of You by The Cure
La Vie en Rose by Daniela Andrade
Just Breathe by Pearl Jam
Mad World by Gary Jules
Send Me On My Way by Rusted Root
Hero by Family of the Year
*The Guy That Says Goodbye to You is Out of His
Mind* by Griffin House

**Lydia Michaels also spent a great deal of time
researching goats on YouTube.**

And, yes… she laughed every time.

PART I

Pretty little ribbons…

True beauty, for all its enchantment, fades.
It is not timeless in appearance, but in experience.
Recognize life's beauty and those memories will
never die.

CHAPTER 1

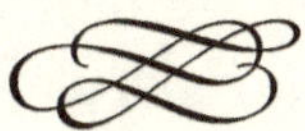

Riley's lips twitched as soft ebony curls ghosted over his bare stomach, lower and lower, tickling his hips and teasing that tight strip of flesh just below his bellybutton. A deep, satisfied growl rumbled in his chest like distant thunder as anticipation teetered on impatience—but it was a good, burning sort of anticipation. Holy fuck, was it good. Stretching, he gave Curls the access she needed and—

"So I'm thinking we're going to settle on coral with deep navy blue accents for the main theme. That should complement the nautical look Becket wants."

Why was his roommate's voice in his dream?

Shaking off the distraction, his palm lowered, fingers gently knotting in the satin ringlets to better direct the ebony waves going down on him. His body hardened as soft kisses teased his happy trail and she got to work. *Yes...*

Rolling his shoulders, he stretched his hips and drew in a slow breath. Heaven. The first true sensation of tongue-to-tip had his toes pointing as the heat of her pouty lips—

"Whatever you want, toots. It's your day."

Oh God, no! What the hell was his sister doing in his dream? *Get out, Rarity! Get out!*

The ethereal weight of the dark haired woman's touch faded. No, no, *no!*

There was a soft girlie sigh. "I can't believe it's actually happening. I'm going to be Mrs. Becket Grayson."

Emma, his roommate, was definitely there too. Damn it! They were ruining everything. This was his time. Not their time. Dream blowjob time! The anticipation of sin and sex paled, as Emma's voice carried on about champagne toasts and processionals. His roommate's incessant wedding planning was officially intruding on *everything*.

The loft used to be a sanctuary. The day Emma got engaged their living situation took a turn for the worse as girlie crap slowly corroded every square inch of his life—even his fantasies. Passing out on the couch was a dangerous gamble, leaving him widely susceptible to wedding babble bullshit when he could've been enjoying some nice fantasy head.

"Will I be wearing coral or navy?" his sister asked then mumbled, "Say navy. Say navy."

Emma did that tiny chirp she claimed was a laugh. "You can wear navy, but there's nothing wrong with coral."

"You know how I feel about pink," Rarity reminded.

"Coral's not pink."

"It's in the family."

"Fine. You'll wear navy, but you're wearing a dress."

Rarity groaned with resignation. She'd always be the brother he never had. "Fine, but Lexi's wearing a tux."

"Look at these carnation balls I found in this issue of *I Do*. My florist can make them in the coral."

It was as if he were invisible. They just kept yapping and yapping.

"They look pink to me," Rarity said.

He growled obnoxiously. "That's it! Do you two mind? I'm trying to sleep!" *And I lost fantasy girl!*

A throw pillow smacked him in the face. "Then don't use the couch as your bed, dumbass. It's noon. Go to your own room if you want quiet," his sister snapped.

"Sorry, Riley. We'll be more quiet," Emma apologized then whispered, "We could use navy ribbons to hang the balls off the white chairs we're renting for the ceremony."

Their loft was spacious. Did they have to stage these womanly talks right on top of him? They could have at least moved to the kitchen ten feet away—or better yet, parked this prenuptial symposium all the way down the hall in Emma's freaking room.

The wedding plans carried on ceaselessly, as

they had since Becket proposed to Emma six months ago, and Riley once again considered how much happier he'd be renting his own place. Sharing a loft with two girls, one being his sister, hadn't been a bad setup until that damn ring and all those girlie magazines came along. Before the dawn of the bridal apocalypse everything was kosher.

They lived in the hipster section on the posh Upper West Side of New York. He liked his home, loved the industrial feel and the exposed brick walls. The raw space, exposed ductwork and battered moldings were just aged enough to qualify as vintage. Splitting the rent three ways afforded them some square footage, but things were getting a little cramped lately, with Emma's new obsessions.

His sister, Rarity, exhibited a tolerance for girlie crap that surprised him. Rarity was seriously chill, like a pretty guy that peed sitting down. She didn't cry or squeal like a valley girl or do that needy drama shit girls tended to do. She was easily the coolest chick he'd ever met. And being that she was a lesbian, they had plenty of shared interests.

Never giving a damn about clothes or purses, Rarity appreciated the finer things in life, like good beer, decent music, a nice set of tits, and red meat. Her unarguable beauty and confidence pulled men in from miles away. And for years he enjoyed watching his little sister turn every last one down. She was his best friend and Emma was hers.

The only girlie thing Rarity couldn't live without, apparently, was Emma.

Rarity was uniquely striking, with dark shorn hair and high arched brows, but it was her dry wit and endless sarcasm that could make any man second-guess his worth—a neat parlor trick to watch. Emma, on the other hand, was compassionate with soft blonde curls, dimpled cheeks, and eyes that pathologically betrayed her, eyes too full of innocence to hide her inexperience.

Emma was the quiet, sweet type that never got in the way. But lately she'd really cranked up the fem-meter and was driving him insane—which made him a horrible person, because he was going to shoot her if she didn't shut the hell up.

All this wedding talk *had* to be getting to his sister. Riley was ready to duct tape Emma's mouth shut. How in depth could a discussion about linen be? The texture, the hues in natural light versus candlelight, the thread count—bullshit conversations like that went on for days. He was amazed Rarity hadn't reached her limit and freaked yet.

"I can't wait until my dress gets here!" Emma announced, clapping like an excited child. "I'm *dying* to try it on."

Riley groaned. It was as though no one could see him at all. Screwing his eyes shut and jamming a pillow over his ear did nothing to drown out her voice. *So much for dream sex.*

"You already tried it on," Rarity said.

"That was in the store. Once I get it to the

loft, I'll be able to really appreciate it. Then, when you get your dress, we can try them on together. It'll be so much fun!"

"Sounds mind-blowing." Rarity's sarcasm was so expected it didn't phase Emma.

The doorbell buzzed and Emma screeched—literally screeched. *"It's here!"* The chair skidded against the hardwood floors as she catapulted out of her seat.

Yeah, he wasn't going back to sleep.

Groaning, he twisted and cracked open his lids as she sprinted down the hall toward the main entrance. Craning his neck in the direction of the chair, he peeked at Rarity, who wore a disinterested expression as she paged through a wedding magazine.

"There's something wrong with her," he grumbled.

"Yup," she agreed.

"This isn't going to stop until she gets married, is it?"

"Nope."

"When's the wedding again?"

"We have nine more months of this and the closer we get the worse she's going to be."

Shifting, he sat up and frowned at his sister. "You're surprisingly calm."

"She's my closest friend and she really wants me to be a part of this. I can do the maid of honor thing as long as she doesn't expect me to throw her some hideously pink party where girls drink cosmos and act like prissy hyenas, while being the pole for some male stripper to rub his scabies all over."

She sighed and turned the page. "Plus, I smoked a fat joint the second she pulled out the wedding binder. You could probably cut my leg off right now and I wouldn't put up much of a fight."

"Nice." He stared at the front door waiting for Emma to come racing inside at any second carrying the legendary dress. "She's not gonna walk around in a wedding dress for the next nine months, is she?"

Rarity shut the magazine and tossed it on the table. "Don't let her hear you call it a dress. It's a *gown*. I've been corrected twice. And I have no idea. I wasn't born with the bride gene. None of this shit makes sense to me."

At least he wasn't alone. Rubbing a hand over his jaw he yawned. "You're bringing Lexi to the wedding?"

"Yup."

He chuckled.

"What?"

"You realize Mom and Dad will probably be invited."

"They won't go," Rarity said, matter-of-factly.

"What makes you so sure?"

It shouldn't matter anyway. His sister was twenty-four years old. She and Lexi had been a couple for over a year. It was absurd to hide that she was gay from their parents. Who cared what they thought?

"It's the Devonshire's fortieth wedding anniversary. They'll pick that over Emma's wedding. You know how they feel about her."

He grunted. His parents—mostly his mother—had always been weird about Emma. Though he and Rarity were nothing like the people that spawned them, they were still blood, so his and Rarity's liberal attitudes were often overlooked, but that didn't mean their parents would abide the same socialist standards from others.

Their parents were proud black card members of the upper crust society that summered in the Hamptons, went yachting on the weekends, and dined on ridiculously hard to pronounce small foods like *Foie Gras*.

Riley was once grounded and accused of being a 'recalcitrant activist' because his friend Jake came over in a PETA T-shirt and asked if he wanted to play Frisbee. To his mother's way of thinking, that was a gross and barbaric display of uncouth trash.

He and Rarity were generationally wealthy trust fund babies. No matter how much they survived off their independently earned incomes, *Mumsy and Daddy* would always be there to bail them out if needed. It was their shared goal in life to *never* need their parents in such a way.

Their wealth should be comforting, but it felt more like a noose around Riley's non-conformist neck. The entire white pants, polo-playing, fracking-investing group of peers was repellent to him.

Emma didn't have a house in the Hamptons or an au pair as a child. She had parents that worked nine to five and wore—*gasp*—denim. Her association with the Lockhart's was the result of her grandmother's trust fund, which included scholarships to the same schools he and Rarity attended.

Once, while walking the topiary garden with his mother as she sipped a crushed Valium cocktail, she referred to Emma as 'that new money filth having a bad influence on Rarity'. It was clear then that his mother would never approve of Emma, which quite possibly could have permanently cemented the girl into Rarity's life.

Emma's fiancé, Becket Grayson, wasn't a guy he or Rarity would voluntarily hang out with, but he made Emma happy. The Graysons were paying for the wedding, of course, so it was nice she was finally getting a fantasy she never expected. That was why they let her carry on about linens and bows and whatever the hell a nosegay was. Because she was nice.

"What's wrong?" Rarity's voice broke the comfortable silence.

Riley glanced at the door and scowled. Emma stood, trembling. Big brown eyes, rimmed in red, shimmered under a sheet of unshed tears, as she stared at them.

"Did they send you the wrong dress?" he asked stupidly, then corrected, "Gown."

He never saw her upset. It was filling him with all sorts of uncomfortable emotions, feelings he didn't know the names of. He wanted her to stop being upset that instant so he could have his manly emotions back. Dear God, it was like staring at a helpless basket of kittens floating down the river.

"Emma, say something," Rarity insisted.

"It wasn't the delivery from the bridal boutique. It—" A stuttering breath intersected her words. "It was Becket." The heel of her palm swatted away the tears as they quickly fell. "We —*oh God*—we broke up."

Silence.

This was bad. How long was an appropriate length of time before someone could say something in situations like this? And why hadn't he gone to his own room when he had the chance? Now he was stuck there, smack dab in the awkward—

"He *what*?" Rarity snapped.

Emma blinked, sending big crocodile drops unchecked down her round cheeks. "We aren't getting married," she croaked. "We're through." She spoke as though she was still convincing herself.

"What do you mean, *you're through*? You just ordered ugly invitations with stupid anchors on them. Becket insisted on the anchors!"

Her head crooked as she blinked those big innocent eyes at his sister. "You thought my invitations were ugly?"

"*Who cares what I thought?* What happened?"

Shuffling to the living room without shutting the door, she delicately sat on the edge of the overstuffed chair. The picture of the carnation ball was still in her hand, drawing his attention to her enormous engagement ring as it winked in the sunlight.

"He was supposed to be in class," she whispered.

Rarity scooted to the edge of the chair and removed the crumpled magazine page from her grip. "Toots, look at me. *What* happened?" she asked again, slowly.

Drawing in a shaky breath, Emma shook her head. "He said he couldn't marry me. He said he's…in love with someone else."

"What?"

Emma sniffled. "Her name's Goldie."

Rarity drew back and made a face like she tasted vomit. "Goldie? What is she, a retriever? Who the hell has a name like Goldie?"

"Good question, *Rarity,*" he chimed in. *Goldie Hawn's hot. Don't mention that now.*

His sister's evil stare snapped to him. "Shut up, dick."

Yeah, he'd better stay out of this. Figuring now was a good time to escape, he gripped the arm of the couch and—

"How could he do this to me? I'm so humiliated!" Emma burst into tears again.

Riley dropped his head to the back of the couch and shut his eyes. This was going to take a while.

~

SIX HORRIBLY UNCOMFORTABLE days later things hadn't improved. Emma had planted herself on the couch and only got up to use the bathroom, but never for bathing. Riley never saw her eat, but someone took his ice cream, a conundrum that had consumed him. Her hair had inflated to three times its usual size and her eyes were vacant pools of pink.

There could only be one explanation for such a drastic change. She was in some sort of zombie chrysalis stage and he was scared.

"Shouldn't we do something?" he whispered anxiously to Rarity as he lurked in the hall by her bedroom, never completely taking his eyes off what used to be Emma.

His sister shrugged as she folded a shirt and placed it in a vintage Pendleton bag. "Maybe she just needs to feel this right now."

"Who wants to feel something like that, Rarity? Rejection's awful. And she's hogging the couch. There's snotty tissues all over the place and I'm pretty sure she ate my ice cream." *I know she ate it.*

Sending him a sidelong glance, she rolled her eyes and went back to packing. "Is this about your concern for Emma or the fact that she's monopolizing the common area of the loft?"

"I'm concerned."

"About your ice cream." She closed her bag and tied a red flannel around her waist. "If it's bothering you, say something to her."

He frowned as she hefted the bag off the bed. "Where are you going?"

"I have a shoot this week."

"A far away one? Where? How long will you be gone? What about Emma?"

"Calm down, Riley. I'm only going to Saratoga Springs. It's the yearling auction."

"You're abandoning your best friend in her time of need to go take pictures of stuffy blue-bloods throwing down millions at a *horse auction?*"

"It's one of my best paying gigs. I can't miss it. Emma knows that. I'll be back in a week with my BFF-Got-Dumped checklist."

His brows lifted. "Is there really a list for that?" It might be helpful.

"Shut up."

He grabbed her arm as she shouldered her way out of the room. Sometimes having a sister short on feelings was an issue. "She's upset, Rare. I don't think you should leave her. She's all drippy and making puppy sounds—I'm not versed in that language."

She arched a brow. "And you think I am?" Peeking through the hall they stared at their sniveling roommate. She was sobbing into a tissue and hugging her wrinkled gown, which showed up an hour after the groom dumped her. Irony—the bitch—had impeccable timing.

His sister sighed. "Look, there's nothing I can do for her at this stage. When she gets to the angry stage I'll jump in the game, but she's days away from that, maybe weeks. She's going to be sad, Riley, and she's going to cry. Emma dreamt about getting married since she was a little girl and Becket crushed her. Let her mourn."

He shifted and scuffed his shoe over the wood floor. "Can I leave?"

"No, you can't leave. Someone has to keep an eye on her!"

He scoffed. "You're so full of shit, all your talk about grief and necessary feelings. You're bailing, because you don't want to see her this way. Well, she's your best friend, Rarity. I'm just the roommate. It's not my job to babysit—"

"No one said you have to babysit her. Just make sure she doesn't do anything stupid, like contact Becket or beg him to come back. The man is scum."

"Oh, like I'm qualified to stop her if she wants to call the guy."

"Just run interference and stop being such a pansy. Now move, I have to be there by seven."

"You're a… pansy," he muttered, unable to think of a better insult as she went to the kitchen and grabbed an apple from the bowl.

Rarity went to the couch and kissed Emma's head. "This too shall pass, toots. I'll be back in a week. Riley's here if you need anything and I'll have my phone on me. Don't text him. Love you."

Emma only nodded, made an ugly crying face, and a high pitch hum like a teapot. The door closed and they were alone. Great. Sticking to the perimeter of the loft, he crept to his room and quietly shut the door.

Riley avoided the common area as long as possible. Eventually Emma's tiny whimpers stopped and she slept, some British romantic comedy playing softly in the background.

It was his night off and he didn't have plans, but he couldn't stay there. Her depression was suffocating him. Sneaking into the kitchen, he swiped his keys off the counter, the nearly silent drag of metal over granite having the effect of a tray of dishes toppling to the floor.

"Riley?"

He cursed his luck and rotated, pasting on a fake smile. "Hey, Em. How's it going? I'm lovin' the new do."

Frowning, she lifted a hand to her hair and patted down the nest of blonde frizz. "Are you going out?"

"I…uh, yeah. Out."

Her shoulders shook as the puppy whimpers started again. He drew back at the awful, high-pitched whines. It wasn't a natural sound for a woman to make.

"O—kay," she stuttered. "Ha—have fun."

Oh, for the love of fuck. He tossed his keys on the counter and trudged to the couch. It would be cruel to leave her like that.

Sighing, he pushed her legs out of the way and dropped to the sofa. "Come on." He held open his arms. "Let's hug it out."

Startlingly, she collapsed into his hold and proceeded to wail.

"There. There." What did that even mean? There where? He dragged a hand down her back and inelegantly blew away the straggly snarl of hair sticking to his lip, as her arms wrapped around his waist and squeezed.

He couldn't remember ever hugging Emma

before. As Rarity's best friend, she was in the no touch zone by default. It was strange touching her now. He never realized how short she actually was. Like really short. How did she drive? Or look a bank teller in the eye?

"Thanks for staying with me," she whispered.

Staying? Had he said he'd stay? Definitely didn't remember agreeing to that. "Um…no problem."

If he wasn't making a clean escape that didn't mean he was on the soggy hug shift. Something had to give. Her arms tightened and he panicked.

He could be a friend, but not this kind. He'd keep her company, but crying made him uncomfortable. She'd have to toughen up if she wanted him to stay. And he needed to eat. "What do you say to ordering some food?"

"I'm not hungry."

Damn women and their ridiculous bird appetites. This was exactly why his sister was a cool chick. She'd throw down a T-bone steak and chase it with a tray of garbage fries. She never played the *I'm not hungry* game. And for a girl who wasn't hungry, Emma sure ate the shit out of his ice cream.

"How about a milkshake?"

"No, thanks. Just order something for yourself. Don't worry about me."

Was this one of those things where a girl said she wasn't hungry then ate all the guy's food? Because he wasn't down with that. It was the first meal of his 'day', coming off nightshift. He wanted to eat and wasn't in the mood to share.

He'd order her whatever she wanted, so long as he had enough to fill his own belly.

"What about a pizza?"

"No, thank you. I'll just have a can of soup if I get hungry."

It was useless. Fishing his phone out of his pocket he speed dialed the pub around the corner.

"Hair of the Dog."

"Hey, is this Jasmine?"

"In the flesh. Who's this?"

"It's Riley."

"Oh, hey, Riley. When are we gonna go out again? I had fun last time."

He chuckled. Yeah, she did.

"That reminds me. I think I lost an earring at your place. You didn't see it lying around, did you? It's gold with a topaz stone."

"No, but I'll keep an eye out."

"Thanks, hon. What can I get'chya?"

"I need a porchetta, heavy on the *au jus*, an order of Old Bay fries, and—" he glanced at Emma who was still hugging him like she was choking a pillow. "You sure you don't want anything?"

She shook her head, her messy hair snagging on his five o'clock shadow.

"And put aside a six pack of Brawler for me."

"You got it. I'll see you in twenty."

He ended the call. "Uh, Em...my arm's falling asleep." His stomach was also starting to sweat, which was weird.

"Sorry." She eased back and sort of crumpled

into the sofa, pulling the wedding dress over her chest like a blanket.

"What do you say we put the dress away for a while? It's getting all wrinkled."

A derisive laugh puffed past her lips. "Like that matters. Do you know that this gown is a Martina Liana? It was the wedding gown I dreamt of since I was sixteen. It's *the* gown. And now it's ruined. Tainted."

"Maybe if you stopped wrinkling it and dripping on it—"

"It's not ruined because of tears! It's ruined because it'll always remind me of him and I'll never have the chance to wear it. I'll have to get married in some other stupid gown that isn't perfect and I'll look fat and ugly. Not to mention I'm out three thousand dollars!"

He clearly wasn't getting the dress from her. "When I go pick up the food do you want me to grab you something? Beer? A bottle of wine?" *A tranquilizer?* He remembered she liked some sort of pink drink. Maybe if he gave her enough she'd relax and let go of the dress.

"I can't drink."

He paused. "Why not?" *Please don't be pregnant. Please don't be pregnant.* If she was knocked up with that guy's trust fund progeny, he was definitely calling Rarity. Talk about being underqualified to deal with a situation.

"Because if I drink I'll call him and I can't do that."

Huge relief. "Well, in that case I could just take your phone."

She sniffled. "I don't know."

"Tell me what you drink and I'll pick up the stuff when I get the food." Soggy Emma was getting old. His only solution was giving her copious amounts of alcohol and hoping for the best. She needed to dry out, cheer up, and maybe pass out for a day or seven.

"Really?"

"Yeah. Why not?"

She shrugged. "We never drink together."

"There's a first for everything. Besides, it's not like you and Rarity haven't hung out at the inn while I'm working. That's sort of the same."

"I guess." She shrugged. "I like Malibu bay breezes."

He tried not to gag. That sounded about right. "Delicious." Standing, he grabbed his keys. "You have my number if you think of anything else. Can I trust you not to call Grayson?"

"Yeah." She snuggled into the dress.

Step two was peeling that satin nightmare away from her. "I'll be back."

By the time Riley got the mixers and booze to make Emma's drink, his food was cooling. Starved, he raced up the steps to the loft. Those Old Bay fries were getting seriously violated the second he opened the door. And that porchetta—

Oh shit. Not good.

Emma lay on the couch, much like he'd left her, only now she was *in* the dress. "Uh… you changed."

She shrugged. "At least I got to wear it. Believe it or not," she quietly wept, "it sort of makes me feel better."

"Better is good." He shut the door and cursed his sister again. "I'm not real sure about your sanity at the moment, but better is definitely good."

He dropped his bags on the coffee table. Time for part two of his plan. "Hand over the phone and I'll make you a drink." With all that lace, fluff, and bad hair, she had a dumpster version of Glenda the Good Witch going on.

Taking the phone was silly, but, according to Rarity, he was supposed to be on guard. Still, if she asked for it back he'd hand it over.

Grabbing a cup he mixed the drink. It might not be to his taste, but as a bartender in the Upper West End it was his business to know every froufrou concoction to ever exist, so he made her a good one, lime rind twist and all.

"These fries are delicious."

Riley stilled. *Mother of God.* Pivoting, he mentally prepared for what he might see. *She better not be eating my food. I asked four times if she wanted food. I swear, if she's—God fucking damn it!*

He forced a smile. "Oh… you found my fries. They are good. That's why *I* ordered them, because *I* wanted them. Remember when I asked if you wanted anything?" His shoulders drooped. She wasn't listening.

She hummed with appreciation and sucked the seasoning off her fingers. "Wow. What else did you get?"

How about a can of soup? "A sandwich."

Clenching his teeth he continued to smile. "Want half?" *You better say no.*

"I don't know. I feel bad eating your food."

He hated girls. Seriously hated them. Sighing, he turned, and mumbled, "I'll get a knife."

Carrying two plates, a knife, and her cocktail back to the living room, he shoved her dress out of the way. The skirt was everywhere, like a frothy nightmare.

He divided the food, not caring that it was a seventy-thirty split, heavy on his end. By the time he cracked open a bottle of Brawler and bit into a fry it was cold.

"So it's just going to be us this week," she announced, letting a good amount of the *au jus* drip from the sandwich. She was ruining it. If she couldn't properly respect the sandwich she shouldn't eat it.

Looking away before he lost his temper, he responded. "It's not like Rarity hasn't gone away on a shoot before." His sister wasn't a homebody. She often slept at Lexi's and frequently traveled for work.

"Yeah, but I took a leave of absence from my job, so I'll actually be home when you're home. Usually we keep opposite schedules."

Dread knifed down his spine and he tried not to panic. He couldn't be the designated tissue dispenser all week. If this weepy shit carried on much longer he'd drive to Saratoga and haul his sister's ass home, high paying horse auction or not. "Cool."

Chances were he'd be sleeping when she'd be

awake and vice-versa. Maybe he could grab an extra shift or two at the bar, nothing against Emma, but bonding was not on his agenda.

She nudged him with her shoulder, the netted material of her gown rustling loudly. "We might actually be more than roommates by the time the week's over."

His mouth stilled mid-bite. "What?"

"We might end up friends." She smiled, with those big eyes as trusting as an unseeing doe with a rifle aimed at its six. "Don't look so shocked, Riley. You and I both know we aren't close. I mean, we live together, but you're my friend's brother and I'm your sister's friend. That's where our connection ends. I really don't know any-thing about you."

Why did girls talk so much? He finished the last fraction of his sandwich, still hungry and searching for a distraction.

His fingers peeled at the label of his beer. "What do you want to know?" Why did they have to know anything about each other? As long as she knew he was going to make his portion of the rent their relationship should be complete. No other details necessary.

"I don't know. What made you want to be a bartender?"

"I'm good at making drinks." He'd give her a few impersonal facts and she'd likely move on.

"What about the people?" she asked, a fanciful smile curling her lips. "I bet you meet some fasci-nating people bartending at the inn."

"Not really."

"Do you have any funny regulars, like a guy who hates going home to his wife or a know-it-all social misfit everyone finds annoying?"

"It's the West Inn, Emma, not *Cheers*."

"Oh." Her posture sort of deflated. Maybe she was looking for a distraction from her own problems.

He could humor her. "How about you? What made you want to be..." Shit. "What do you do again?"

"I'm a personal assistant at Phibbs & Grayson."

"Grayson as in Becket Grayson?"

"Yeah. I should have never taken that job. Now I'll have to see Becket's dad every day. I'm so humiliated."

"Is he your boss?" That would suck.

"No, Donald Phibbs is my boss, but he's Mr. Grayson's partner so we see each other often. That's why I took a few weeks off. I'm too embarrassed to face them right now. I'm a laughingstock."

Wiping his fingers clean, he tossed the napkin onto his plate. "Hey, what do you have to be embarrassed about? Becket's the one who did something wrong."

"It's demeaning. He cheated on me. That tells the world I wasn't satisfying his needs, that some girl named *Goldie* is better than me."

"No, it says you're better than him. He probably knew it all along. Maybe this Goldie chick is more in his league. He did you a favor, Emma."

Her chest lifted and light reflected in the tiny

pearls sewn into her dress in neat little rows. "Thanks. That helps."

Snatching her drink, she slouched back on the couch and latched onto the straw like a baby calf to an udder. He grabbed his beer and joined her, digesting in the welcomed silence.

"Did anyone ever cheat on you, Riley?"

Even silence had a shelf life.

"I've never dated anyone long enough to give them the opportunity."

The rattle of ice being siphoned up a straw accompanied her slurping. "You've never been in love?"

"No."

"That's sad," she said, matter-of-factly.

"Not really. I'm fine with it. I mean, look at you. You were in love and now you're sitting in a wrinkled wedding dress with Bride of Frankenstein hair and tearstains on your face. I don't see the appeal."

"It's a gown, not a dress."

"Whatever." He sipped his beer.

She rustled around and gathered her puffy *gown* as she stood, swishing to the kitchen. He silently observed as she mixed another drink, not commenting when she annihilated the recipe, adding way too much rum.

"I would have made a good wife," she enunciated the statement with a swish of her glass.

"And someday you will."

"That's right," she decided, her enthusiastic agreement taking him by surprise. "Some guy will be lucky to have me." She sipped her pale drink, never removing the straw from her lips as she spoke.

"Damn straight."

"Because I'm fun and honest and nice and I can bake the fuck out of a batch of cupcakes!"

"You're a modern day Betty Stewart," he agreed.

"Yes—" She frowned. "Who?"

"The lady who calls everything a good thing." *Betty Stewart? Martha Crocker? Aunt Jemima?* It was on the tip of his tongue.

She snorted. "You mean Martha Stewart."

"Whatever." Like it mattered. She got the point.

"Well you're damn right!"

He jerked back as her voice abruptly got louder. She swished in a cloud of crinkled ivory across the room, one hand holding her drink, the other choking the bottle of rum.

"And let me tell you something else, Riley Lockhart."

"I'm listening." This was turning into quite a show. Apparently Emma couldn't hold her liquor.

She kicked the trash off the coffee table and climbed on top, her bare feet perfectly proportioned to her miniature size. "I *never* cheated. Once there was this guy who asked me out and I said, 'No way, José! I have a boyfriend.' Well, I should have said yes—that's what I should've done."

"Should've."

Finishing her drink, she unscrewed the cap of

the rum and dumped more over the ice. It was coconut rum so it couldn't be that strong, but Emma was rapidly getting wasted.

"Well, let me tell you a bit of news, mister." Her fist holding the bottle lifted. "As God is my witness, I'll live through this and when it's all over, I *will* have sex again!"

Her recovery, though drunk, was to be admired. "You go, Hester Prynne."

She wagged a finger, her eyes droopy. "I was doing Scarlet O'Hara."

"Right."

"And next time, I'm going to do it with the lights on and maybe even topless."

He frowned. What kind of sex was she having before?

"I just have to find a sexable guy. Oooh! Or maybe a girl! Wouldn't that be fun to make Becket think he turned me gay. If Rarity wasn't with Lexi I'd totally have sex with her."

"Ew." He quickly erased the image of his sister in any sort of sexual context.

"What? Your sister's hot, Riley. Do you know how many guys hit on her when we go out? Like seven."

He had to laugh. "Seven?" Was that in total or per outing?

"Yeah." She sipped, this time right from the mouth of the bottle. "And do you know how many guys hit on me?"

Probably more, especially if she was drinking. "How many?"

Her brows drew together as she pegged him

with her doe eyes and her mouth lost all anima-
tion. "None."

Her arms lowered, hands weighted by rum
and ice. "No one ever sees me. Not the way they
see your sister or other girls."

When she looked at him again his heart
pinched for the desolate longing in her stare and
he wished he had the words to comfort her.

"Why is that, Riley?"

Shaking his head, he gave her honesty. "I
don't know, Emma."

Lowering herself to the surface of the table,
she bunched up the layers of ivory lace and sat
cross-legged like a child. The white bottle lifted
and she took a long swig. "Do you think I'm
pretty? Be honest."

He laughed. "You're very pretty, Emma. Today
you just look like Courtney Love on a bender,
but usually you're adorable. If guys aren't paying
attention to you it's because they're intimidated.
That's all. Don't make what Becket did anything
more than it has to be."

She slouched. "You're smart, Riley. You know
what to say."

"I think you're drunk. I'm not even sure if
what I said makes sense."

With her head down, she raised her gaze and
grinned. "Drunk s'okay. I deserve drunk."

He held out his beer. "To drunk."

"To drunk." She clanked her bottle of rum to
his Brawler and sighed. "I don't want to hurt
anymore, you know? It just hurts so damn bad
and I can't make it stop."

"I believe in avoiding the tough feelings at all costs."

"Yes," she agreed, nodding heartily. "Screw feelings. They're heavy and messy and make you fat."

"I know you ate my ice cream."

She smirked and met his stare. "I'm not even sorry."

He gasped. "You bitch."

"It was spectacular, all those pieces of toffee and chocolate fudge clumps. I hurt that ice cream."

"You're not right."

She laughed. "Do you forgive me?"

"No. That was my ice cream." Strangely, he wasn't pissed about it anymore. At least she appreciated it when she devoured it.

"I wanna think like a man," she slurred, easing her back to the coffee table and staring at the ceiling.

"I'm not hooking you up with my sister, so forget it."

"No. Rarity's in love with Lexi. I'd never take that from her. I mean, I don't wanna feel all these girlie things anymore. I don't wanna care."

"But you're a girl, Emma. You do care. That's what makes you, you."

"Tell me how to be someone else then. Just for a little while. Please."

Though she was a far cry from her usual, put together self, she was still in there somewhere. Emma was a special breed of woman. She was soft and naturally feminine. Delicate. He didn't pity her, because she was above being pitied. However, he sympathized with her.

"Don't be someone else, Emma. All the someone elses in the world can't compare to you. You're a dying breed."

"I feel like I'm dying," she whispered, keeping her gaze on the ceiling, a tear sliding into her hair.

"Hey." Leaning forward, all joking aside, he nudged her shoulder until she faced him. "We are who we are in this life. Pretending to be someone else never solves anything. Trust me. I've tried it."

"I'm not sure who I am anymore. I mean, look at me, Riley. I'm lying on a table in my wrinkled wedding gown. I haven't brushed my hair in days. My legs are hairy. There's something sticky on my neck and my burps smell like Old Bay and coconut. No wonder Becket didn't want to marry me."

"Becket's a douchebag. I'm not sure what you saw in the guy, but I never saw you get half as excited about him as you did over cake frosting or linen samples. Maybe all this disappointment really isn't about him. Maybe it's about not getting the perfect wedding or wearing the perfect dress."

"It's a gown." She sniffled. "It's really sweet of you to say all that—I think—but it's also really sad because you might be right. What does that say about me, if I'd marry someone I didn't even love just to have the perfect wedding? What kind of person does that make me?"

"You're a product of our generation. We're

screwed up. It's drilled into our heads that we need extravagant parties and SUVs with heated seats and coats that coordinate with each outfit. We are living in a material world and you are a material girl."

"Are you blaming Madonna?"

"No. She just nailed the truth. The world changed before we were born and those who changed it blame us for meeting the standards they set. We're messed up because of their rules. Everything has to be fancy and fast, but sometimes the simpler things in life are what make it beautiful. It's crazy what things have become priority and how much of it is fake, superficial bullshit. You're not the first girl to plan a big wedding with a man you're not meant to marry."

She pouted. "You're right. It's like I became obsessed overnight with things I never thought twice about. And for what? To marry someone I don't love? It's all so fake."

"Yup," he agreed. "The amount of money people waste on imitation is mindboggling. When did it become logical to spend a hundred dollars on a knockoff purse?"

She chuckled. "Yeah, you don't need a purse after that, because you don't have any money left."

"And they're spending that on the knockoffs. Quality's a thing of the past. Everyone's willing to settle for an impression of good, instead of waiting for what's actually good. People get so caught up with what's trending they all start looking identical. Everyone's chasing the same fake bullshit."

"Hair dyed to look like someone else's natural color."

"Exactly. New furniture that looks old." It drove him nuts how people defeated the purpose of individuality, living like one big oxymoron.

She grinned. "Sunscreen for tanning beds."

He laughed. "Medals for all the losers."

"Ripping out half your eyelashes by gluing on fake ones."

"Women do that?"

"Yeah."

"Why?"

"I don't know. What were we talking about?"

He laughed again, the beer catching up with him. "I have no idea."

Turning her head on the table, she grinned at him. "You're a nice guy, Riley. Thanks for hanging out with me tonight."

As much as he dreaded being exposed to her heightened emotions, he was actually enjoying himself. "You're not so bad yourself."

"I don't want to be the loser that gets a medal. What happened to me was real. My fiancé dumped me. That's a big deal, but I don't want to sit around and cry about it either."

"Good for you." This was an attitude he could get onboard with. He was all about encouraging the Anti-Cry Act. "Fuck Becket."

"Fuck him," she repeated, raising the rum bottle high. The liquid sloshed, announcing how much she'd drunk. "I'm not ashamed. I was a good girlfriend. Yeah, my fiancé dumped me. So what? He's gonna wish he had me back some day. And you know what, Riley?"

"What?"

She rolled to her knees, nearly fell, stood, wobbled, and steadied herself like she was riding a surfboard. "He can't have me, because I don't want *him.*"

Her shoulders jerked as her neck did a strange pelican thing and she burped. Uh-oh. "You okay, Em?"

"I'm…" She did the hairball heave again and held up a dainty finger like she was at a British tea party. Her brows pinched as her mouth pursed.

"Emma?"

"I just… wanna say…" Hiccup. "You and I are officially frien-zuh—" The last word was cut short as she recovered her cup and vomited into it, quick and as feminine as puke could get. She pouted. "Ew."

He drew back. "Yeah. Ew." Girls throwing up equaled totally disgusting. "You okay, tiger?"

"I *am* a tiger! *Rawrr*—" Her roar was interrupted by another dry heave.

"Uh…maybe sit down for a minute. You want some water? Maybe a cracker?"

Lowering herself to the table again, she looked at him with glassy eyes and placed her cup aside. He tried to forget what was in it.

"I'm done caring now. I'm done worrying if I'm good enough to visit the Grayson's country club or if my knockoff shoes are passable—because *yes!* I'm one of those losers that spent money on a knockoff." She slumped to the left and pouted. "And the stupid strap broke."

She held up a stern finger, her expression turning harsh. "Don't you judge me, Riley Lockhart. That was the old me. I'm done. From now on, I'm gonna do what I want, when I want, because I'm a good person and anyone who doesn't see that doesn't deserve to have me in their life. You get what I'm sayin', Ri?"

"I'm smellin' what you're steppin' in. Go on."

"I'm done," she said, stabbing a finger in the air. "I'm going to forget Becket Grayson. Erase him from my life and move on. If it was meant to be, it would be, but it's not gonna be so I'm meant to be somewhere else or something. You know?"

"Absolutely. Why don't you lay down on the couch for a few minutes?"

"Well, okay."

He stood as she rustled her way from the table and collapsed on the couch. Everything smelled like coconut.

"Promise me you'll shower tomorrow. You're getting a little rank."

"That's not nice," she mumbled and shut her eyes. "But okay. I'll do it for you, Riley Lockhart. Because we're friends."

He pried the nearly empty bottle from her fingers and covered her with the afghan. "Because we're friends," he agreed. "Goodnight, Emma."

CHAPTER 2

*E*mma neatly tucked a sprig of basil beside the omelet and placed two pats of butter on the warm, golden toast. *Perfect.*

Lifting the tray, she nudged into Riley's bedroom and carefully navigated her way around the laundry piles and numerous cassette tapes covering the floor. She wasn't sure why he collected something as dated as cassettes, but it had something to do with the fact that people gave them away for free and he didn't see the sense in wasting perfectly good music. The man didn't own a single CD and forget about an iPod.

Fitting the tray of food on the nightstand was no easy task, with all the books and empty bottles. Once she had her hands free, she lifted the blinds and let in the early morning sunlight, bathing the dark space in immediate brightness. "Rise and shine—"

"What the hell?" He covered his face and

rolled over as if he were a vampire. "What time is it?"

She frowned. "It's nine." Nine was an acceptable time for breakfast. She'd been awake for hours.

"In the *morning?*"

"Yeah." Why was he so angry?

"Emma," he said as though he were taking extra care not to freak out. "I have work ten hours from now. Why the hell would you wake me up this early?"

Didn't he see the lovely breakfast she made him? "I just thought we could hang out."

"I went to bed two hours ago. The only thing I want to hang out with is my *pillow!*" he snapped and she stepped back.

She hadn't realized he was up so late. "I'm sorry. I'll let you get back to sleep." Guilt-ridden, she shut the curtains, and backed out of the room.

Damn it. She was such an idiot. The crushing sense of rejection locked around her heart again. She was being stupid and needed to go somewhere private—fast. Her vision blurred.

"Emma. Wait."

Riley cursed and she winced, making a quick escape to the kitchen. Busying herself with the dishes, she tried not to get upset. She was annoyingly sensitive at the moment. Waking him as a distraction was inconsiderate and selfish. They weren't close like that. She'd have to find something else to keep her preoccupied. It wasn't Riley's job to babysit her.

A door creaked. "You made me breakfast."

"It's nothing. I just wanted to say thanks for last night." Shutting off the faucet, she waited for him to say more, but didn't turn around.

"You're not wearing the gown."

"It's just a dress." She had to keep telling herself that. Otherwise, that beautifully tainted dress would only symbolize her failures and barren future.

"Emma…"

Bracing herself and locking away all emotion, she faced him with a smile. "It's okay. *Really.* I'm not going to break."

He nodded and disappeared into his room. A moment later, he returned, carrying the tray of food. "Let's eat."

Touched by his easy forgiveness, she grinned, fought the urge to hug him, and walked to the living room.

"Hey, you cleaned up."

"Step one of recovering one's dignity: destroy all evidence that it was ever lost."

He eyed her as he chewed on a slice of toast. Butter crumbs clung to his full lower lip as his mouth cocked to one side in a half grin. "I'm proud of you, Em. I wasn't expecting this sort of transformation." He took a sip of fresh squeezed orange juice.

"When I said I was done caring, I meant it. Today I'm going to look for a new job and tonight I'm going to have sex with a perfect stranger—" Orange juice sprayed from Riley's lips, startling her to her feet. *"Oh God!"*

Dragging the back of his hand across his mouth, he cleared away the dribbles of juice. *"What?"*

"You got juice everywhere."

"Emma, you cannot have sex with a stranger."

She frowned, retrieving a paper towel from the kitchen. "Why not? Guys do it all the time."

"Guys are different. We're emotionally detached. You're built differently."

"Rarity's had plenty of one night stands."

"With *women*," he argued.

"I'm a woman."

"She's different. She thinks like a guy. You're not like that. You'll sleep with some asshole and wind up getting hurt. I think it's great you wanna get out there, but don't rush into anything until you find your sea legs again."

"My *sea legs?*"

"You know what I mean."

She laughed. "Riley, do you think of me as some sort of virgin?"

"No." Fidgeting, he seemed incapable of eye contact. "I'm sure you and Grayson had plenty of cardigan sex."

"*Cardigan* sex? What the hell is cardigan sex?"

His shoulders undulated and he grimaced. "You know…tender."

"Tender?"

"Stop repeating everything I say!"

She hid a smirk and shoved a fist on her hip. "You think I'm prissy."

"No, I don't."

Unbelievable. "Yes, you do. You think I'm one of those girls your parents wanted Rarity to be."

"My parents definitely didn't want Rarity to be like you." The words fell clumsily out of his mouth, cutting off her humor.

"What?" Mr. and Mrs. Lockhart weren't her biggest fans, but he made it sound like they hated her.

"Nothing." His attention focused on the plate of eggs.

Her fingers closed over his wrist and stilled his fiddling. "Your parents don't like me?"

"My parents don't like anyone, Emma. It's no big deal."

"It's a big deal to me. Is this a new thing or a since grade school thing?"

"It's not a thing. Look, maybe you should talk to Rarity about this—"

"She isn't here right now so I'm asking you. It's not a hard question, Riley. Give me an honest answer."

There are moments when a stare becomes so penetrating it hurts, that slow burn of exposure that heats until it's so acute one reflexively flinches away. It's the piercing sting of unspoken truth. Not everyone has a high threshold for brutal honesty.

She wanted to flinch away as he stared at her, the truth blatant in his pitying eyes, but she wasn't a coward. If the Lockharts had an issue with her she deserved to know, that way she wouldn't break her neck going out of her way to impress them.

The unease of another approaching rejection filled her heart with ice, but she didn't back down. "Tell me the truth."

"No," he whispered. "They don't like you."

The pain was anticipated and therefore slightly blunted. Still, it hurt. "Has this been forever?"

"They never have. But they're assholes, Emma, and what they think shouldn't matter. You're a—"

"Good person. I know." Wow. Her opinion of Riley and Rarity's parents wasn't great to begin with, but their disapproval still cut deep. "You're right. It doesn't matter what they think."

All the times she went out of her way to make a good impression ran through her head. They must have laughed at her pathetic efforts, judging her behind her back.

"Hey." Riley's hand brushed her arm. "People suck. If there were more people in the world like you, less people would turn mean."

"Thanks." *I think.* She couldn't wait until Rarity got back so she could ask her more about her parents. What exactly had they said? Was it that she didn't come from a wealthy family? Did they think she was holding their children back from something?

"You're still thinking about it," Riley interrupted her fixated thoughts.

"No, I'm not."

"Liar." He glanced at the clock and sighed. "I can't believe I'm up this early."

"I'm really sorry I woke you up." Their opposite schedules weren't something she thought about, because they never really hung out. "It was quiet and I started thinking about Becket. I needed a distraction."

"Well, now you have one. What are we doing today?"

"We?" Was it that easy? "Um, I was going to get a mani-pedi at some point."

"What is that? Can you eat it?"

Laughter bubbled up her throat. "No, it's a manicure and a pedicure."

"Like a foot rub?"

"It's feet and hands. You wanna come? Guys get them too." The unexpected idea of going to the spa with Riley was fascinating.

"Do they have those massage chair things with the feet hot tubs?"

"Yup. And they rub all these oils into your skin and massage up to your knees."

He wrung his fingers like they were arthritic. "Hands too?"

"Hands too." He was going. Her mouth twisted, as she tasted victory.

"My tinnitus has been really bothering me."

She silently chuckled. "Riley…"

"Yeah?"

"Tinnitus is ringing of the ears."

He ceased wringing his hands. "I knew that."

"Do you want to come get a mani-pedi with me? I won't tell the other boys."

"Can we go to Brooklyn for lunch? I want to catch Smorgasburg before summers over."

"What's Smorgasburg?"

His eyes widened. "Are you kidding me? You live in New York and you don't know what Smorgasburg is?"

"In all fairness, I didn't grow up in the city—"

"I don't care!" he cried as he fell back on the couch. "Unacceptable, Emma. Get your stuff. We're leaving in five." Bounding to his feet, he went to his room where drawers opened and snapped shut.

"What about the mani-pedi?"

His head popped out of the doorway. "We're doing that too. Four minutes."

She grinned and went to find her flip-flops.

~

IT WAS AMUSING how the girls on the subway watched Riley. Emma supposed he was above-average handsome, but since he was Rarity's older brother she never looked too hard.

Now, seeing him in his element, riding the subway in a Pet Shop Boys T-shirt, jeans, and battered chucks, she recognized what the other women on the train were seeing. Riley was hot.

His brown eyes were so clear they shined as though they were blue. Sloppy chestnut waves curled in perfect careless disarray, complementing his naturally tanned olive skin. He even had the five o'clock shadow down to an art.

Scanning the surrounding female passengers, she counted six of them gawking at him, begging with their eyes for him to glance their way.

Amazing. The pheromones could choke a prostitute.

Skimming the male passengers, she frowned. Not a single one was looking at her.

What if *she* was Riley's girlfriend? They were standing close enough, but the other girls didn't seem to notice her at all.

She rolled her eyes. *Invisible.* Meanwhile, Riley scratched his nose with his thumbnail—it was practically a casual pick—and three of the six leering women sighed as if he read a verse of poetry. *So unfair.*

"Wait until you taste some of the food there," he whispered in her ear.

Her chest filled with warmth as his voice sent a thrill of excitement tearing through her belly. It wasn't sexual. It was what being feminine was all about. Who cared what he said? He was talking to *her*; the guy every other girl was drooling over was talking to her. And in that moment, the other women finally registered her presence. Every stink eye she got was so totally worth the thrill of attention.

Ha! Not only does he talk to me, he lives with me. I've seen him in his skivvies. Take that, ladies.

As the ride continued, her pride mended with each spiteful glance tallied in her favor. Not used to this catty need for attention, she chalked it up to recently being dumped. It was against her nature to behave like a clingy girlfriend, but with Riley it was all make believe, a temporary tonic for her battered ego.

Sometimes it was nice to be seen, though a

great deal of her life had been conducted as a wallflower. Perhaps her affability gave her fiancé the impression that she wouldn't mind him delving into another woman's panties. Or maybe he'd already lost interest…maybe she wasn't good at sex. Oh dear God, was she vanilla? A wallflower in bed?

Again, the emphasis she placed on other people's perception concerned her. Riley didn't care what anyone thought and people loved him. Even when they were in school, he was always a popular guy. Teachers loved him, jocks loved him, and, of course, women adored him.

Rarity was popular by default, because she was Riley's sister. Publicly kissing girls promoted her to a novel level of cool only genuine lesbians could achieve in high school, but she'd always been cool by proximity first.

Emma was drawn to their energy like planets to the sun. No one was immune. They were simply attractive people. And as the permanent sidekick that existed in the cool guy's sister's shadow, it felt nice to have a bit of Riley's innate popularity rub off on her as they stood together on the subway.

You're pathetic. Those girls only know you exist because you're pretending to be something you're not. Oh, well! Self-esteem is in the gutter and pretending is helping.

She arched a brow at one of the gawkers.

"What are you grinning about?" he whispered.

Her attention jerked to his smiling russet eyes. He was almost a foot taller than her. Should she tell him? Would he laugh at her? Deciding she didn't care, she whispered, "You're inadvertently inflating my ego."

Confusion tightened his brow so she tipped her head at the other passengers. Shockingly, it seemed the first time he noticed the other women.

"They all assume I'm with you. They hate me."

He glanced at the other women, each glare transforming to a seductive pout the moment his attention fell upon them. With his hand gripping the rail above her head, he leaned close. "And them hating you is a good thing?"

Didn't he get it? "They're jealous of me. Not many people are."

The train rattled and slowed. People got off as new passengers climbed on and settled into seats as it whistled back up to speed.

His scrutiny heated her cheeks as he unabashedly studied her. "I can play that game," he whispered.

"What game?"

Rather than answer, his mouth hooked in a half smile and he winked. She flinched as he dragged his curved knuckle down her bare arm, making the fine hairs rise in its wake. His fingers laced with hers and she watched, amazed, as every female followed the motion.

Her belly tightened with the thrill of exhibitionism. Her feet pointed toward the aisle. His pointed to her, his hip angled at their audience. Shifting a step closer, still holding on to the bar above, he spoke loud enough for the others to hear. "I caught you."

Her eyes traveled past his lips, no longer shaped in a smile, and landed on those dark eyes. Her brow knit in confusion, unsure what he was doing.

"Looking at me," he clarified. "You know how that makes me crazy."

Oh, my God. She should have never told—

"It's like this morning, when we were spooning in bed, my body pressed tight against yours, flesh to flesh, belly to back, nook to cranny. Everything was fine until I pressed that one kiss on the back of your neck right here."

Her body tensed with awareness as his finger touched an extremely sensitive spot behind her ear. She couldn't remember anyone ever touching her there.

"The second I kiss that spot you turn to liquid in my arms, soft and wet, and I can't help but drink you up, taste every square inch of you on my tongue. My lips. Everywhere. When I catch you looking at me like that, it's my kryptonite, *my* secret neck kiss."

She swallowed and glanced at the women watching them. They were literally gaping, some even appeared to be quietly panting. Holy crap he was slick. "Um…"

Thank God he didn't let her say anything. She didn't have his skill. "Next time you look at me like that…" He tucked a curl behind her ear as chills raced over her shoulders. "I can't be held responsible for what happens." His fingers squeezed hers tightly and the train hissed and whined to a stop. He winked. "Let's go. I'm suddenly ravenous."

He tugged her off the train and into the loud subway. Musicians played for coin and people bustled through the underground world, racing to get where they needed to go. She saw it a thousand times before, but now it was brand new, her senses overstimulated and raw.

As they climbed the stairs to the street her heart pounded wildly. Wafts of traffic, people, and city food greeted them under the August heat. Voices and motion mingled into a cacophony of commotion until she was standing above sea level, fighting to catch her breath. What the hell had he done to her?

Laughing, he released her hand and turned—a totally unaffected grin on his charming face. "That was fun."

"Y—yeah." It wasn't fun, it was thrilling and telling, and in some secret way, quite embarrassing. He'd been toying with those women, putting on a show, yet in those few seconds of phony attention, his artificial reverie trumped every *real* experience she had. She needed to get a grip.

Demanding her emotions go back into the shadows, she focused on their purpose. "So where's this Smorgasburg?"

"Can't you smell it?" He breathed deeply and grinned as his chest expanded, raising his broad shoulders. Weird. She didn't want to keep cataloguing his every masculine trait, yet she couldn't stop. "Ah, it's just past the bridge. Let's move."

The snap of her flip-flops put a melody to their strides. As the impressive Brooklyn Bridge stretched before her, she had one of those out of body moments that reminded her she lived in one of the coolest cities on earth. "I don't appreciate New York the way I should."

Walking beside her, a pleasant set to his mouth, he sent her a sidelong glance—not bothering to disagree.

"Becket and I never walked around like this. Once he took me to Tiffany's, but we were in and out. I'm not even sure what he was picking up." Probably something for his mistress. "He never stopped for street meats or pretzels. We only dined at restaurants that held reservations."

"You can't plan New York through a concierge. It's meant to be experienced. It's alive, pulsing, like an animal. We can only observe it and let ourselves be led by its verve. The minute we try to control it we miss something spectacular, like with nature. It really is the world's largest organism. There are so many people setting its rhythm, better to experience it organically."

"I never thought of it that way." The scent of ethnic faire grew thick in the air; tempting her appetite out of hiding and drawing her steps toward the mouth-watering aroma of succulent meats grilled over open flames.

Voices traveled, rising in volume as they stepped into a mass of people patronizing what appeared to be a market of New York's cleverest food venders. How had she not known about this event?

Riley rotated, a phenomenal grin on his face as though he'd entered man heaven. "Where should we begin?"

"You're my captain. I trust your instincts."

Canopies and makeshift booths formed long aisles for people to wander. Steam clouded the various sites, eliciting attention with each peculiarly pleasant aroma.

Chefs acted as street performers, enchanting patrons, drawing them near with careful explanations for pairing fermented spices and specialized condiments with seared meats. It was a sort of live gallery, showcasing the artistry of New York cuisine.

Servings were sometimes dainty, offering a sampling of what could be the world's most eclectic menu. The selection was endless, filet mignon sliders, fresh pecan bread sold by the slice, doughnuts the size of grapefruits, and even specialty booths for vegans and other diets she'd never heard of before.

"Oh, we have to start here," he veered to the right and she followed. When the walkways became clogged with people, he reached through the crowd and pulled her to his side. "Watch this, Em. This is how meat *should* be treated."

It was indeed a performance. The vendor tossed a steaming brisket onto the wood surface and unwrapped the charred foil covering. Juicy morsels of fat were trimmed away to unveil perfectly cooked, tender, pink beef. As the peddler made a show of slicing the meat in precise portions, it fell apart and her mouth watered.

Riley's voice turned gravelly. "Oh my God, we are so eating that."

She grinned at him, loving the glazed lust in his eyes. Only men got that way with meat. She supposed beef and pork were to a guy what shoes and purses were to most women.

As the chef prepared their sandwich, Riley asked questions about the smoking process. The vendor was very friendly and informative. "You want everything on it?"

"What's everything?" Riley asked.

"Cheese, pickles, hot peppers, sweet sauce."

He glanced at her. "You afraid of hot?"

"No." She wanted to taste the sandwich the way the creator intended it.

Riley grinned. "Give us the works."

The man dressed the small sandwich until it was bursting with meat and dripping with sauce. Riley paid and she followed him to the side of the booth where coolers held the vendors' supplies.

"Are you ready for this?" he asked, eyes set with excitement.

"You taste it first." She wasn't sure what would be more enjoyable, watching his exhilaration or actually tasting it for herself.

"You sure?"

She nodded as he carefully held the messy sandwich and took a bite, bits of cheese and meat falling from his fingers. "Oh my God," he moaned over a mouthful. "You have to try this." She reached out, but he shook his head, still chewing. "Just open. It's too messy."

Opening wide like a ridiculous baby bird, she

let him shove the corner of the sandwich in her mouth and bit down. "Oh my God!" she echoed.

"I know, right?"

An exquisite blend of flavors burst over her tongue. "It's amazing," she mumbled, holding her fingers over her lips so food didn't fall out.

"I could eat twenty of these." He took another bite.

"We so should." She opened as he held the rapidly shrinking sandwich out for her again.

They didn't waste time talking for the next few minutes as they devoured the most delicious sandwich she'd ever tasted. When they finished, Riley snagged some napkins and passed her several to wipe her mouth.

As they journeyed onward they sampled maple bacon cupcakes, Bangladeshi street cuisine, and even shared a pumpkin spiced S'more cooked under the flame of a blowtorch. It was an incredible festival of food.

"Do you like oysters?" he asked as they approached a merchant standing before a bowl of crushed ice.

"I don't know." She'd never tried an oyster before.

"Wanna try one?"

"Sure."

As the chef sliced open the rocklike case and revealed an opalescent inner shell, she tried not to be revolted by the goopy booger looking mollusk inside. He shucked the blob loose, leaving it resting on half a shell, and placed it in a bed of crushed ice.

"What do they taste like?" she asked.

The chef continued to shuck. "Briny, like the ocean. If you're virgins I can dress them in a mignonette sauce to soften the taste. I have a nice ginger cucumber one."

"What do you suggest?" Riley asked.

"I'm a purist, sir. I like them with a bit of pepper and lemon and that's it."

Riley glanced at her.

"I think I should try it with the sauce." The more she stared at the little glob the more unappealing it became. These were considered delicacies? If she was remembering correctly, they were also aphrodisiacs. She didn't see anything sexy about them.

"Ready?" Riley asked, holding his lemon oyster while offering her the one dressed in the ginger sauce.

Timidly, she reached for the shell.

Their eyes met and he counted off. "One… two…three." His head tipped back and her mouth filled with—

Oh my God. What the fuck is in my mouth?

"Not bad." Riley grinned then started laughing. "Are you okay?"

She shook her head, booger mollusk sliding around her tongue, and desperately searched the table for a napkin. *You gag and it's all over.*

"Swallow it!" he shouted, laughing at her.

The vender passed her a napkin.

"No, don't spit. Swallow!"

Oh my God, she was going to kick him if he didn't shut up. People stared as they walked by and she spit the disgusting thing into the napkin and balled it up.

Riley shook his head. "Oh, Emma, I'm disappointed. Good girls swallow."

"Shut up," she snapped, her face burning.

He laughed and nudged her, tossing a few dollars on the table and directing her into the crowd.

"That was disgusting. Now I can't get the taste out of my mouth."

He stopped and ordered a cup of cranberry Brooklyn soda. "Here, you big tissue."

"I'm not a tissue. I tried it."

"Let's sit for a while." He led her to a stout cement barricade along the jetties and they sat facing the East River.

They'd walked miles in a matter of hours so she was grateful for the respite. The short wall was warm from the afternoon sun. "Today was really fun, Riley. Thanks for bringing me here."

"I had fun too. It's nice to waste a day taking advantage of everything the city has to offer. We can get immune from living here."

She smiled, her cheeks tingling under the moist wind off the river. "There's so much I've never experienced. I've never even been to the Empire State Building."

"*What?*"

She laughed at his shock. "I know. I'm the worst New Yorker in the world."

"You gotta get out more, Em."

"I want to." Letting out a deep breath, she relaxed. "I'm so sick of being me. It's so tedious, always doing what everyone else thinks I should do."

He frowned. "What do you mean?"

"I think you were right. I don't think I loved Becket."

"Conceivable."

"Was it that obvious? Because if I'm being honest, I'm still getting over the shock."

"Don't hate me, but Becket was a prick. He didn't bring anything to the table. You guys were always running off to meet *his* friends or attend functions at *his* father's law firm."

"Well, I do work there."

"Exactly. You work for *his* family. When was it about Emma Sanders?"

There wasn't an excuse at the ready. "I guess it never was."

"Yeah, that's not love. So when you say you don't think you were in love with him, I can believe it."

"You're a pretty deep guy, Riley. Not a lot of men are like that."

He shrugged. "I'm comfortable with you. I can just say what I feel."

"Yeah," she agreed, her mind drifting back to Riley as a tousled child in grass stained corduroys and wild curls. Although they knew each other since braces and bike rides, this was the first time they actually hung out alone. It was strange they never talked about personal things before, because she really was extremely comfortable around him.

"What do you say we head back and go get that mani-pedi?" he asked.

Her feet were killing her and the idea of a pedicure sounded divine. "Okay."

He glanced down at her flip-flops and tsked. "I'm not sure they can help those stank walkers."

She gaped at him. "There is nothing wrong with my feet!"

"Whatever. Where's your baby toe?"

"It's right here!" She lifted up her foot.

He leaned forward and squinted. "You can't call that Darwin freak show a toe."

"If it's not then what the hell is it?" Her toes were perfectly normal!

"That's a nubbin."

"Whatever." She stood.

He rose as well. "You think you can manage on your deformed hobbit hooves? We got a hike back to the subway."

She stomped away. "Jerk." And just when she was starting to think he was nice!

"Wait up," he called. "Don't be like that. We don't have to wee-wee-wee all the way home. It was a good day at the market, piggy."

She held up her middle finger and prodded on—laughing under her breath.

CHAPTER 3

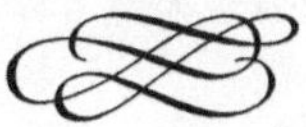

Riley didn't get home from the bar until almost five in the morning. When he woke up sometime the next day, the loft was quiet and he took full advantage of the unusual privacy.

After a lengthy shower and a silent cup of coffee, he settled in with an old, battered copy of *Great Expectations*, refreshed and ready to start the day. But his focus was continuously interrupted by curiosity. Where was Emma?

Tossing the book aside, he went to her bedroom door and knocked. "Emma?"

The door glided open and he stilled, certain it was bad roommate etiquette to visit a roomie's room without an invite. "Em?"

Glancing around the empty area, he slowly pivoted. Whoa. This was definitely not common area loft space. Her bed, which was made, sat against the exposed brick wall, dressed in vibrant floral prints. Why had she made it? Was she expecting company?

Pictures of girlie shit like birdcages and pearls were everywhere. She had fresh flowers on her nightstand. Who took the time to buy fresh flowers? *Unless they're from Becket.* He scowled at the flowers.

Cracking open the closet, he noted how orderly all her dresses were hung. Emma wore a lot of dresses, not the trampy kind, but soft cotton ones that smelled like sunshine and came in Easter colors. They reminded him of that laundry bear that giggled and bounced on fluffy towels.

In the back of her closet was *the* dress, still wrinkled and hanging like a forgotten dream. He gently touched the delicate beadwork at the hem.

Becket was an asshole.

Riley hadn't realized how cool Emma was until recently, but he hadn't asked her to marry him. Becket had to know the cool girl he was giving up.

Shutting the closet and checking to make sure everything was as it should be, he left her room and wandered into the kitchen. The front door opened and he immediately smiled. "Hey, stumpy. Where you been?"

Emma's steps slowed and she pursed her lips. "What did I do to you that you have to call me the most insulting nicknames?"

He scoffed. "They're terms of endearment."

"So far you've called me Stumpy, Piggy, Ma 'goats, and Tiger. How flattered should I feel?"

She was in a feisty mood today. "You're short. There are too many compact names I never get to use. I'm trying them out, sugar pants."

"Sugar pants?"

He took in her short white shorts and blue striped shirt. Her hair was tied back in a white cotton headband. "Where were you?" *Yachting?*

"The roof. I came down to grab more sunblock. Wanna join me?"

"Sure. You have music?"

She disappeared in her room and returned a moment later lathering sunscreen on her shoulders and neck. "Only my iPod, but I'm not into music right now. Everything's a love song and most songs remind me of Becket."

"You're listening to the wrong genre. I'll grab my boom box and meet you up there."

After selecting some cassettes he went to the roof. Emma lounged on a sunny yellow chair in her shorts and a red bikini top. *Nice jubblies.* Stripping off his shirt, he popped in *The Cure* and collapsed on the blue chair beside her.

"How was work last night?" she asked, her face veiled by her oversized Jackie O. sunglasses.

"Work was work. The inn's always busy on Sunday nights, so I made good tips. You enjoying your sabbatical?"

"Yes. I found two places looking for PA's. I'm going to apply to both of them."

"Good for you."

Her brow wrinkled above her sunglasses. "What are we listening to?"

"The Cure."

"I said no songs about love."

"Ah, but this is classic 80's, a time where love was deep and real, not the shallow impression we accept today. Embrace it. Learn from it, grasshopper."

"Were you even alive when this was written?"

"No, but that doesn't mean I can't appreciate it. Now stop talking. You're spoiling The Cure."

The warm August air heated his skin as he shut his eyes and breathed in the moment. The entire first side of the album played and when the cassette needed to be flipped neither of them seemed eager to get up and do the job.

Silence settled over them as the hum of far below traffic drifted in a hushed whisper to their ears. It was a comfortable backdrop.

"That's the problem with vintage," she said. "Who's going to flip the tape?"

"I will in a minute." He released a deep breath, relaxed and at peace with the calm surroundings.

"Riley?"

"Yeah?"

"Do you think you could fix me up with one of your friends?"

Calm feeling gone.

Lifting his glasses, he peered at her. "Seriously?"

She shrugged. "Why not? You have plenty of them."

He groaned. "But if they're an asshole to you I have to cut them off. You're my little sister's best friend. That puts you in sister territory and the same rules apply."

"But I'm not your sister. I'm your roommate."

"And as roommates, we sometimes have to witness the aftermath of breakups—example, couch zombie bride. I don't want to see you crying over something my friend did. It puts me in a bad position."

She was silent for a few moments. "Fine. I'll just find someone on my own."

Relieved she understood, he agreed, "Good." She seemed disappointed, but he had valid reasons. "Wait, where are you going to find someone? There are a lot of douchebags out there, Emma."

"Which is exactly why I asked you to fix me up with someone you know."

Grumbling, he contemplated his selection of friends, ticking each possibility off in his mind. "No, they're all douchebags too."

Her palms slapped the arms of the lounge chair in humorous frustration. "He doesn't have to be perfect. I'm just looking for…a rebound."

Again, he faced her. "Sex?"

"Maybe."

"You want me to set you up on a booty call?"

The pink on the bridge of her nose traveled to her cheeks. "Well, I wouldn't want you to put it to your friend in those terms, but yeah. I don't like having Becket as my last when Goldie was his."

"Who cares about what or who Becket's doing? We've already established he's an idiot. That's not a reason to sleep with someone. You're not cut out for casual sex."

"Why not?"

Giving the topic the respect it deserved, he sat up. "How many people have you slept with?"

"Three."

Huh, he'd actually been expecting her to say Becket was her first. "Okay, who were they to you?"

"Well, you know Becket. Before him was Matt Sinclair from high school, remember we dated for a while after I graduated? And then there was Tim Jones, who I lost my virginity to."

"And how old were you when he punched your V-Card?"

"Can we not call it that? I was eighteen. It was senior prom."

He shot his finger at her. "Bingo."

"Bingo what? I'm not innocent if that's what you were trying to prove."

"You lost your virginity after prom, Em. How much more cliché can it get?"

"So? Would it be better if I slept around in high school?"

"No, but most girls get more experience than that. You were an adult."

"Again, so?" She sat up and propped her glasses on top of her head. "Maybe if I hung around with a different clique I would've been more high profile in the sex department, but my best friend's gay and we spent our time going to concerts and traveling. I don't see that as a reason to penalize me now when I want to be a little adventurous."

His blood pressure started to rise. It was like

he was dealing with Rarity only his sister never encountered these issues.

"I'm just saying you shouldn't rush into anything. This is your body you're talking about. What happens if you pick some guy based on looks and wind up getting pregnant and he turns out to be a total dipshit."

"Oh my God, forget it, Riley. I asked you as a friend, not because I needed a lecture and a chastity belt. I'll wait until Rarity comes back and she'll go out with me."

"Fine." He didn't want that sort of responsibility anyway. Emma was too sensitive for casual sex. She was delicate and the marrying type. He understood she wanted to push her limits and break out of her comfort zone, but having sex with a total stranger could break her.

She gathered her sunblock and book. "I'm going in."

As she abruptly stood, he shook off his thoughts, putting all logic aside to understand her very illogical mood shift. "Wait, are you mad?"

"Of course not." She snatched up her top and towel. "You don't think I'm good enough for any of your friends. Why would that make me mad?"

"That's not what I meant! It's them that aren't good enough for you."

"Whatever," she carried her stuff to the stairwell door and let it slam behind her.

"Damn it." *Women.*

She can be mad. I don't care. I'm not going to

follow her around like some puppy just because her feelings got hurt from hearing the truth.

Grinding his teeth, he glared at the silent radio. His foot tapped as he stewed. "Son of a bitch."

Leaving his crap where it was, he followed her. When he found her she was in the kitchen at the counter making a sandwich—looked like a BLT.

"You know, Emma, friends look out for friends. I'm not going to fix you up with some scumbag who's going to use you and never call."

She shoved the frying pan onto the burner. "If they're scumbags then why are you friends with them?"

"Because I'm not in it for their values on monogamy. They're my guy friends. Their credentials include an ability to provide beer, remark judiciously about superior tits and ass, have access to sports channels, and being available to do nothing at a moments notice."

"Are my tits not remarkable?" She held out her arms, still in her bikini top, as bacon sizzled on the heated pan.

He turned away. "Whoa! Don't do that!"

"Why? I'm a girl, Riley. I have breasts and feelings and urges."

The bacon snapped as he held out a pleading hand, but kept his eyes averted. "Look, I really don't want to discuss your *urges.* Could we please talk about something else? And put a shirt on before the grease hits you."

Her tongue clicked against the roof of her

mouth. "My God, you can't even look at me. I'm sorry you find the fact that I'm a living, breathing woman with adult impulses so distasteful."

This was why he hated girls. "You're twisting everything I'm saying around to make me out to be a jerk."

"You make me out to be some desperate sleaze because I want to meet someone. I was just *dumped* by the guy I expected to marry, Riley. Do you have any idea how that makes me feel?"

"No!" He had no clue why he was yelling.

"Horrible. I feel ugly and unattractive and dull and sexually stunted. I just want to feel like a woman. Is that too much to ask? I'm not looking for fiancé number two. I'm only looking for enough attention to erase the memory of my last sexual encounter and possibly repair some of my broken pride. I want someone to make me feel pretty and good enough for one measly night."

"Shit," he muttered, now understanding why this was so important to her. How could she think she wasn't good enough? She was *too* good. "I'm sorry, Em."

The bread popped from the toaster, but she didn't move to grab it. "I just…hurt. It hurts knowing the person you trusted picked someone else over you. I know a one-night stand isn't real. I've had enough reality lately. Maybe that's why people act fake, because the real stuff makes them feel too much. I'm only looking for an escape. One night of being put first. I've never had that and I want it—even if it's gone by morning."

Yeah, he could understand how that might

help her ego after being sacked by a guy like Becket. If she were one of his guy friends he'd advise her to get laid and move on. Fair was fair.

"Fine. You're off for the next few days. Come to the inn and hang out at the bar. My friends are there all the time. If you see someone that catches your eye… I'll introduce you."

Her smile was slow, but so worth the wait. "Thank you."

"Now, you're making me a BLT too, right? I mean, that is the going rate for pimping out friends these days."

"Mayo?"

"Does a bear shit in the woods? Yes, mayo. Lots of it."

CHAPTER 4

The West Inn was a swanky, upscale establishment Emma would never typically visit if not for her roommate tending bar there. The restaurant served overpriced fare that drew in snobby foodies from all over the tri-state area. Sometimes Riley brought home leftovers from the kitchen that smelled spectacular, but he rarely shared.

Once he left for work, she started getting ready. Who knew what the night would entail? After a long soak in the tub and a thorough exfoliation and shave, Emma rummaged through her closet for the perfect one-night-stand ensemble. When she spotted her wedding gown she punched the lace and shoved it deeper into the shadows.

She wanted to look attainable, but not desperate. Settling on a slinky, pale gray strapless dress, she bit her lip and debated accessories. In the end, she settled on four inch cream sandals and a necklace made of clunky ivory roses.

Grabbing her clutch, she locked the apartment and fidgeted the entire walk to the inn. The evening heat was refreshing against her neck and she was glad she'd pinned up her curls for a change. New woman, new look.

By the time she stepped through the heavy glass doors of the inn she was desperately in need of a drink. How did people do this? The idea that she might actually be having sex in a couple hours with someone she'd never met made her stomach slosh around like a plate of runny eggs on a tilt-a-whirl. There was a great chance she might throw up.

When she spotted Riley she let out a sigh of relief. Having him as her wingman definitely added to her courage.

Seeing he was busy with other customers, she slid onto a stool at the bar and waited. His head turned and he did a double take. His jaw unhinged, but he recovered with a grin. Noting his reaction, her confidence bolstered and she sat a little taller. She could do this.

Traveling to her, his gaze still crawling over her attire, he spoke before he fully reached her. "Holy shit, Emma, you look incredible."

"Really?" Not used to being on display, every bit of his reassurance helped.

"Really. Can I get you a drink?"

Self-esteem strengthened, she relaxed. "I'll take a bay breeze, but not a strong one."

"You got it, Lothario."

She shook her head. Him and his nicknames.

Scanning the crowd, she wondered if anyone there was a friend of Riley's. He placed her cocktail on a napkin and slid it close.

"So do you know anyone here?"

"Is that going to be your opening line?" he asked.

She frowned. "No, I'm asking *you*. Are any of these people your friends?"

"Oh. No."

She deflated. "You told your friends to come here, right?" She'd thought they'd reached an understanding.

"Yeah. Yeah. Your mission for French happiness. I'm on it."

He was acting really strange and hyper. "What's French happiness?"

"You know…" He curled his fingers in the air like he was twirling a mustache. Pinky up, he spoke in a terrible French accent. "Ah'penis. Happiness. Ah'penis. Get it?"

"Are you okay?"

He dropped his hand and went to take an order. While Riley was tied up making drinks a man in a suit took the stool beside her. "Hi."

Trying to calm her smile, she bit her lips and took a deep breath. "Hi."

"I'm Warren."

That was a nice name. "Nice to meet you, Warren. I'm Emma."

"You from around here, Emma?" He was cute. Dark skin, bald head, thick lips, deep voice, all things momma liked.

"Actually, I have a loft a few blocks from here."

"My place is on the east side, but I'm also local. What do you do, Emma?"

She twisted, pointing her lady parts in his direction. "I'm a personal assistant at a law firm."

"Really? I'm prelaw myself."

Her enthusiasm staggered. "Oh."

"Do you have an issue with lawyers?"

No, she didn't think she did. Except for the fact that Becket was preparing to be one and he was a big, fat, cheating liar. "My ex was prelaw."

"Really? When did you break up?"

She laughed nervously. "Last week. He dumped me, actually. When the bell rang I thought it was going to be my wedding gown, but nope. It was him, there to rip out my heart and shit on my dreams. But don't worry. The dress came later that afternoon. Just. In. Time."

Warren's expression was blank and she realized she just turned into crazy girl.

"Oh." Shaking her head with regret, she explained, "I'm *really* sorry about that. I hadn't meant to dump all my drama on your lap. I mean, God, talk about diarrhea of the mouth. *Blah!*" She laughed. "I'm really not crazy. I'm just not used to this."

Warren's face was unreadable.

Riley approached and she grinned, relieved. "Ask him. He's my roommate. He can vouch for my sanity."

"I'm set." Warren tapped the bar and walked away.

She winced as he fled.

Riley stared at her, eyes wide. "What the hell was that? Did I hear you use the word diarrhea?"

She folded her arms on the bar and dropped her face into darkness. "I suck at this."

"Diarrhea is never a sexy word, Emma. Come on, you know better."

Nodding, she sat up. "Can I have a refill?"

"Sure." He replenished her drink and went to check on the other customers.

A guy in a slate gray shirt with a deep V collar sat beside her. "Is this seat taken?"

"No."

"I'm Mark." He held out his hand and she turned to shake it. *Well, hello Mark.*

He wasn't as distinguished as Warren, but he also wasn't hard to look at. "I'm Emma."

"You look like you've had a rough night. Can I buy your next drink?"

She glanced behind him, about to agree, but hesitated as Riley waved his hands and shook his head mouthing *no*.

Trying not to be obvious, she smiled at Mark. "Sure."

He turned and flagged over Riley, who now stood with his arms at his sides. "I'll take a Strong Island Ice Tea and whatever the lady's having."

"A what?" Riley was usually so cordial to the customers, but at the moment he looked like he was preparing for an enema.

Mark chuckled and sent her a sidelong glance like they shared a secret. "It's a Long Island with double the kick, if you get my drift."

"Loud and clear, champ." As Riley mixed their drinks he scowled at the man. He returned and slid two glasses forward.

"Thanks, bro." Mark nodded and slid a twenty across the bar. "You go ahead and keep the change."

Riley rolled his eyes and walked away.

"I always like to tip a little extra," Mark explained. "Help out those working their way up the ladder."

She grinned without showing teeth, omitting that Riley was her friend and, although his longer hair and shadowed jaw made him look like an ordinary civilian, his lineage was practically American royalty.

"Let's you and I get a table and talk."

Was that a question? "Sure."

She followed him to a small booth in the corner. "So tell me a little about yourself, Emma."

Cautious not to spill her guts again, she spoke slowly. "Well, I'm newly single and I'm sort of just looking for something easy and fun right now."

"Right. Right. Do you work out? You look fit."

Feeling a bit exposed, she shifted and sipped her drink. Was that a normal date question? "Not particularly."

"I'm at zero percent body fat right now. That takes dedication, but that's the kind of guy I am. I know what I want and I go for it. Hardcore. Always closing."

Forcing herself not to laugh, as he was clearly

devoted to these ideals, she considered how much bacon she ate on a regular basis.

He said something about his car, but the sunglasses around his neck momentarily distracted her. It was dark out—put the glasses away.

"Tell me something about yourself, Emma. What's your five year plan?"

Was she interviewing for a pyramid scheme? "Um… I'd like to find a new job."

"Good. It's important to push for more, always strive to be at the top of our game. Losers wait for motivation. Winners make things happen. Doesn't matter what you do as long as you get out there every day and crush it."

He was more exhausting than a preschooler, but if she looked hard enough, she could see his nipples through the cotton of his shirt. "Um… what was the question?"

"What are your goals?"

Finished with her drink, she stifled a giggle. Given the choice, Mark might ask to see her resume before her boobs. "I'd like to someday own a car less than a decade old."

His brow lowered. "What?"

This was simply too much. "Look, Mark, I'm not in the market for anything serious right now. I do, however, think you're cute. I'm just getting out of a really long relationship and the only thing in my plan is a guy capable of making me forget my ex for one night. Do you think you could be that guy?"

His expression was priceless, a cross between

shock and fascination. "Do I…you want…me and you…I should…"

It was sort of fun being the aggressor in this instance. "Sex, Mark. I'm asking if you're interested in having sex with me."

A garbled string of chirps escaped his throat, sort of like a sentence of hiccups. "Y—yes." He cleared his throat and dropped his voice an octave. "Yes. I would very much like to have sex with you."

He was definitely more attractive when he was silent. "Good. Why don't you order us each a shot and clear the tab? I'm going to freshen up and then we'll head back to my place."

"O—okay."

She slid out of the booth and hid a smirk. The new her was ballsy. She liked it.

After using the ladies room and washing her hands, she gave herself a mental pep talk. Mark was perfect one-night-stand material. His personality was long-term repellant, an insurance that would prevent any attachment issues from unexpectedly cropping up. Plus, he was pretty and she was very interested in counting his abs with her tongue.

Stepping out of the ladies room someone snagged her arm and forced her to an abrupt stop. "What the hell do you think you're doing?"

"Riley. Jesus. You scared me!"

"You can *not* go home with that douchebag. He keeps checking himself out in his phone."

She yanked her arm out of his grip and tsked. "I'm not going to marry the guy, Riley.

And he's got reason to check himself out. He's hot."

His face scrunched up. "Ew. Come on, Emma. I feel violated thinking of him in our home. You can't honestly be considering letting him in *you*."

Her mouth unhinged as her cheeks burned. "Riley!"

"What? Look at him. He has a neck tattoo of a dollar sign."

She shook her head. "You're such a hypocrite. I've seen some of the women you've brought home. Talk about double standards—"

"Yes, Emma, it's a double standard. Tough shit if you don't like it. This guy's a total piece of shit. He's a condescending, superficial narcissist. I'm not telling you to give up on finding a hookup, but for Christ's sake, raise the bar above a crawl and let someone better than that snake get by. Oh, and by the way, your big tipper doesn't leave a dime when he's alone."

Glancing around the corner, she watched as Mark silently practiced schmoozing to himself. She deflated. "Fine."

Riley seemed surprised she'd conceded. "Really?"

"Yeah. But I already told him it was a sure thing."

"I can take care of that for you."

"No." She sighed. "I don't want to embarrass him. I'll do it." He was already embarrassing himself enough, using the camera on his phone like a narcissist's mirror app.

Pursing her lips, she returned to the dining

room. Mark beamed, waving a hand over the shots he'd ordered. "All set?"

"Yeah, it's not gonna happen, Mark. I'm sorry."

"But…" His expression crumbled. "I thought…"

It was like giving a kid a new toy then snatching it away. "I'm really flattered that you would… but… I don't think we're the right fit."

His head lowered in disappointment and guilt swamped her until his gaze lifted and all cocky signs of bravado returned. Brow quirked, duck lips out, and a penetrating smolder zeroing in on her, he cajoled, "Come on, Emma. You know it would be great. We have this incredible connection and—"

"Get out."

They both turned and she stomped her foot. "Damn it, Riley!"

"You know this guy?" Mark asked, confused.

"We live together," Riley answered before she had a chance. "Now, beat it."

Mark stood, his eyes drifting from her to Riley and back to her. "Emma?"

"I'm sorry."

Finally, he huffed and left the inn without much of an argument, which was mildly disappointing.

She glared at Riley. "That was unnecessary."

He shrugged and strode to the bar. "I'm over it."

"I could have been under it."

His steps faltered as his face twisted. "Gross."

"Serves you right." She reached for the shot and tossed it back, unprepared for the burn of turpentine. "Son of a bee sting! What the hell is that?"

Riley shook his head. "Look at you. You're not ready to have sex. That was schnapps." He let out a long-winded sigh and walked away.

She placed the empty glass on the table with a snick and scoffed. "What do you mean I'm not ready to have sex? I am too ready to have sex. Don't you walk away from me, Riley Morgan Lockhart. I'd have sex right here, right now if I saw any doable men, but all I see is you and you're just a cock-blocking killjoy."

He continued to shake his head as he returned behind the bar. "Are you done now?"

She scooted onto the stool. "No. Maybe. Yes. Ass."

"We're going to have to work on your insult repertoire."

A man approached the bar and cleared his throat. "Excuse me, miss. I couldn't help over hearing you were in the market for some company—"

"*Get out of here!*" she and Riley yelled at the same time and the man took off.

Unreal. She faced Riley and rolled her eyes. The entire predicament suddenly seemed hopeless and hysterical. Her palm covered her mouth as a fit of giggles escaped. His head tipped back as laughter barked out of him.

When they finally got their amusement under control, Riley passed her a soda. "I'm pretty sure you can have your pick of any man here—now that they all know sex is on the table."

She snorted. "How sad is it that I've never had sex on a table?"

"Not what I meant, but good to know. Here's a lesson on men, leave a bit of mystique. We like a challenge, the thrill of conquering. If you let them know sex is guaranteed, they're sold, but they're not gonna work for it. Even the unavailable assholes can sign up for a sure thing."

"Gross. I'm not that desperate."

He wiped away a spill. "You don't have to be any level of desperate, Em. Just be you and eventually it'll happen." He crossed his arms and leaned on the bar. "You don't want to sell yourself short and miss the best part."

She arched a brow. "Which is?"

"That moment where all the desire builds into this bullet of need aimed to one target and then…pow." He drew in a slow breath. "Chemical explosion. Lust. Need. Hunger. All those intense senses come into play and make…" He shrugged. "Ecstasy."

She swallowed. "I don't think I've ever felt ecstasy."

"You will, but not with some douchebag you search out at a bar. The connection has to be authentic."

Massaging her forehead, she growled. "This is so hard. It never used to be this difficult."

"It's not that complicated. Stop trying so hard and just wait for it to happen. You're so worried about selling yourself you're overpitching."

"But no one sees me if I don't put myself out there."

"They see you. You *are* out there. You're here, in a bar, looking beautiful. That's the appeal. Constant declarations of self-worth scream insecurity. Have faith in yourself. Being you is enough."

Ashamed her insecurities made a spectacle of her first evening on the prowl, she decided to call it a night. What was she doing anyway? This wasn't her.

Plucking the earrings from her lobes, she slouched forward and sipped her soda. "You're pretty knowledgeable when it comes to women." It freaked her out how in tune he was with her flawed logic. He knew her better than she knew herself in some cases.

"I get people. It's part of being a bartender." He rested his elbows on the counter. "I watch them, Emma. The women that come in here and lay it on thick, they're as transparent as glass. Sure, they get plenty of company and free drinks, but that's because they're selling guarantees. They're still paying. It's a trade, their body and pride for a shallow impression of affection. They get exactly what they ask for, but nothing more. You deserve the more."

"What's the more?"

"Respect. There are ways to keep it casual and respectful, but you can't rush into it."

"You're right. I should probably thank you for saving me from that guy."

"Yeah you should. He was a tool."

"Thank you," she grumbled. Scooting off her stool, she grabbed her earrings and tucked them in her purse. "I think I'm heading home."

"You sure?"

"Yeah. The only guy I want to be with right now is Colin Firth."

"Who?"

"He's a British actor. I'll see you at home."

"Hey, Em…"

She turned. "Yeah?"

"I got more ice cream. One for me and one for you. They're hidden in the back of the freezer behind the corndogs."

Her face softened, as her opinion of him climbed another notch. Ice cream was exactly what she needed. Ice cream and maybe a good ugly cry. "Thank you, Riley."

He nodded. "See you at home."

CHAPTER 5

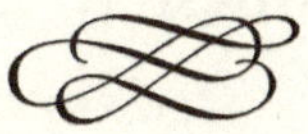

Joni Mitchell's voice crooned from the television as she and Riley crammed onto the couch, foot to foot, sharing the comforter from her bed while watching her favorite movie of all time, *Love Actually*.

Her heart pinched as the scene unfolded in a memorable display of treachery and neglect. Hearing a sniffle from the other side of the couch, she glanced at Riley. "Are you okay?"

"She's just so stoic. How does she do it, knowing he bought the necklace for the other woman while she's home breaking her ass trying to raise his family?"

She wiped her eyes. "I know. It's a great movie."

The scene cut to Liam Neeson's character. "Oh," Riley groaned. "And then there's these two. This boy's ripping out my heart. Why did you make me watch this? I'm delicate!"

"Wait. It gets better," she promised.

Since embarrassing herself in front of a bar full of people, she decided to spend the last of her vacation doing things she truly enjoyed. Riley was sucked into her plan of absolute laziness sometime mid-Wednesday during the second *Bridget Jones* movie.

Turned out, he had a soft spot for romantic comedies, so it was only right for her to introduce him to all her favorites. After this they were watching *The Princess Bride.*

As the movie played her mind wandered. This was not where she expected to be. Her calendar was crammed with appointments she wouldn't keep, consultations, tastings, dance classes and more. She'd been so consumed with planning a wedding, she'd forgotten who she was before she got engaged. The real her was in there somewhere, but lost.

"Do you believe in God, Riley?"

She hadn't expected him to answer anymore than she expected to ask the question out loud. He was so engrossed in the movie, but it was a quiet scene so he did. "Sometimes, but I think I'm wrong. My God's a cross between St. Nick, Jesus, and Zeus from the Disney version of Hercules, but not as tan."

This made her smile. "You believe in a Santa God?"

He chuckled. "Yeah, sort of. I imagine him sitting on a throne like the Abe Lincoln monument, but holding a trident and surrounded by clouds.

But I know that's not what it's really like. It's just what I imagine when someone says God."

She grinned, finding his version of Deity charming. "Do you think God has a plan for us, like everything happens for a reason?"

"I don't know, Em. If he does and you find the cheat sheet he's only going to change it to smite you."

She also wasn't sure the real God smote people. Maybe God wept with them and steered them toward something better, but if they made too much noise or moved too fast they'd miss the purpose of the struggle. "I think God's a woman."

He was quiet for a long while. "You're probably right."

She decided there was a bigger reason Becket was removed from her life. She just didn't know what it was or if she'd ever find out.

After the movie was over and they had themselves a nice cry—which Riley swore was allergies—he insisted she watch some stupid online clip about screaming goats.

"I can't believe I agreed to this."

Riley jumped onto the couch like an excited tween and opened his laptop. "I dare you not to laugh. As a matter of fact, I *bet* you crack up."

"At a goat? *Puh-lease*. Put your money on the table. I will take that bet as fast as I'll take your money." She straightened her shoulders and focused, not caring that it was four in the afternoon and she was still in her pajamas.

"Fine. How much? Keep in mind, if you lose,

which you will, I'm taking your money. Don't expect sympathy."

"Twenty bucks."

He reached in his pocket and pulled out two tens. "Where's yours?"

"I'm good for it."

"Nope. Get it, because when I take your money I'm ordering food with it. None of this IOU garbage."

"Fine." She went to her purse and dug out a twenty. Slapping it on the coffee table, she returned to the couch and crossed her legs. "This is going to be the easiest money I've ever made."

"You aren't kidding," he snickered. Once the clip was cued he hit play.

Oh dear God. She hadn't expected goats to look like that. She saw goats before, but never ones that looked so ridiculous. These were not the ones Mother Goose talked about. The poor creature had drooping ears that curled at the end like Pippi Longstocking's braids and lips that looked like they'd been sucked into a vacuum for days.

The first threat to her composure came as one goat mumbled in what honestly sounded like a human voice. That wasn't how goats sounded, was it?

Biting her lips to keep them sealed, she stared as the camera cut to a different breed. Oh the horror! The teeth and the floppy tongue, it was just too silly to watch with a straight face. Someone operating the camera started to giggle and contagious mirth slid into the slippery pit of her stomach where laughter was born.

She silenced each tiny burst of snickers, refusing to let him win, but the longer the clip played the harder it became. Her eyes started to water as thick laughter clogged her throat.

No! You are taking his money. Don't you dare laugh!

And then it happened. A goat, with bug eyes and a long messy beard, looked right at the camera, parted its bucked teeth, and screamed. She was done.

"Yes!" Riley shouted, leaping off the couch and snatching the money. "I knew you wouldn't make it."

As he danced around kissing her twenty-dollar bill, she collapsed on the couch, holding her stomach in a fit of laughter. One goat after another screamed into the camera. They weren't in pain. Apparently, these were the sounds goats naturally made. How had she never known they could baa like that?

Their screams grew more ridiculous and her laughter turned into pure hysteria. Tears, she was in tears! A cramp formed in her side and she moaned, but couldn't stop laughing. For two solid minutes she struggled to breathe as this absurd compilation of goat shrieking went on.

And then, there was a new sound.

Riley froze. "Oh. My. God."

She stilled, eyes wide, not a single breath moving through her lungs, her laughter completely gone. *That did not just happen.* The clip stopped and the room silenced.

"I can't believe you just did that," he whispered, face set in stunned amusement.

Her skin heated to a scorching burn. If he were anything close to a gentleman he'd pretend nothing happened. She waited for him to change the subject, give her a mulligan. Friends did stuff like that.

His head fell back as laughter erupted from his chest and he pointed. *"You farted!"*

"Shut up! It was an accident! Those stupid goats made me laugh and it just slipped out!"

He collapsed onto the chair and held his stomach. "You should totally give me another twenty for that. Not only did you laugh, you released the Kraken!"

That was it. She stood, grabbed her cup of water and dumped it on his crotch.

"Hey!" He continued to laugh.

"You, Mr. Lockhart, are no gentleman." She stomped to her room where she slammed the door.

"Oh, come on, Emma! Don't be mad. Friends don't let friends fart and walk away angry!"

"I hate you!" she shouted, but laughed silently.

Eventually she'd get over her embarrassment. She'd have to face him sooner or later, but at the moment she was hiding. Stupid goats.

~

The following morning when Emma awoke she found a surprise in the kitchen. There was a lily, like the ones that grew outside of the inn, sitting in a beer bottle on the counter. He was a pain in the neck, but he kept her smiling.

Dear Ma'gotes McHobbit Toes,
 Roses are red, violets are blue,
 You farted.
 You can't hide in your room forever.
 Let's have a Ferris Bueller day and go sightseeing.
 Wake me up at noon.
 #GoatFartsForever
 -Ri

And just like that, she got over her embarrassment.

The idea of a day wasted on the sights of New York sounded awesome. She dressed in a navy blue skirt and a white tank, taking an extra few minutes to rub sunblock into her shoulders. As she tossed the lotion in her purse, her phone rang. Reading the screen she smiled.

"Hey stranger!"

"Is that you, toots? How are things?" She hadn't realized how much she missed Rarity until hearing her voice.

"Things are wonderful. How's the shoot?"

"The shoot's fine. Lexi surprised me and came to the hotel last night, so that was awesome."

"Cool." There was definitely something to envy about Rarity and Lexi's relationship.

Her friend laughed, but her next question was cautious. "You…you sound really great, Em. Did something happen with Becket?"

She scoffed. "No, screw him. I've just been enjoying my time off and hanging out. Not taking life too seriously as I try to figure out where I go from here and who I want to be."

"Um…what?" She laughed, sounding dumbfounded. "When I left, you were a puddle of emotions fused to the couch. I thought I'd have to set it on fire to get you up. What the hell happened?"

She didn't know how to explain her rapid transformation, because even she was surprised by her resilience.

"Well, Riley got me drunk one night, I put on my wedding gown, and gave a few undignified speeches I'm glad no one else witnessed. I puked, hit an all time low, came to terms with the fact that Becket's scum and I'm too good for him, went to Brooklyn, almost had sex with a douchebag, watched a lot of Colin Firth movies, applied for a few jobs, and today I'm going sightseeing."

Silence.

"Rarity?"

"Yeah. I'm just…shocked. You've been hanging out with Riley?"

Reservations clouded her upbeat mood. Rarity asked the question as though the idea of Emma and Riley being friends was the strangest part of everything she disclosed. It seemed more monumental to Emma that she'd come to terms with Becket leaving her.

Did her friendship with Riley make Rarity uneasy? That couldn't be right. Rarity had two best friends, her brother and Emma, all three of them being close made convenient sense.

"We've only been hanging out when he's not working. Is that not okay?"

Rarity's laughter was hollow. "Of course it's okay. Why wouldn't it be? I'm glad you're not fused to the couch. It's all good. Anyway, I gotta run. I just wanted to call and check on you. I'll be back Saturday, okay?"

"Okay. Miss you."

"Miss you too, toots. *Mwah*."

"*Mwah*."

Emma dropped the phone in her purse and replayed the conversation in her mind. Was it so weird that she and Riley were finally getting to know each other? They'd met almost two decades ago and shared an address. It was bound to eventually happen.

The sound of Riley's phone vibrating caught her attention. Following the soft tremble, she paused outside of his room.

"Hey, Rare." His voice was gruff and raspy from sleep. Rarity was calling him now? Why?

"What? Wait. Slow down." Covers rustled and Emma slowed her breathing to listen closely.

"It isn't like that, Rarity. We're friends. Give me a little credit. I wouldn't treat her like that. I don't shit where I eat."

Emma drew back. Shit where he eats? What

did that mean?

"I know she's your best friend. I'm telling you, you have nothing to worry about."

Emma grimaced. She didn't need Rarity looking over her shoulder like she couldn't take care of herself. What made her the expert on life? Rarity had never been engaged or cheated on. She didn't know what that did to a person. And Emma just told her everything she needed to know. Why did she have to call Riley?

"Rarity, I'm not discussing this with you. I told you it's nothing and I meant it. We're just friends."

He was quiet for a moment and then she heard his steps approaching the door. *Abort!* Panicked, she ran to the couch and jumped into the center, grabbing the book sitting on the arm. His door opened and he walked straight to the bathroom wearing only his briefs.

It wasn't the first time she'd seen him in his underwear. When you lived with someone those sorts of things happened. But suddenly everything seemed wrong and inappropriate in an under-the-microscope sort of way. Damn Rarity for getting in her head and stirring up drama that didn't exist five minutes ago.

The toilet flushed and Riley reappeared, pausing when he spotted her on the couch. "Oh, hey. I didn't see you there."

"Yup. Been here all morning. Just hanging out. Maxin' and relaxin'."

He frowned. "You okay?"

"Me? I'm totally fine. As a matter of fact, I'm

so fine I was thinking about handling some errands I've been avoiding, so I don't think I'll be able to have a Ferris Bueller day with you after all. But thanks for the offer."

He eyed her suspiciously. "Is this about the goat fart?"

"Oh my God, please stop calling it that. And no. I just have some errands to run."

"Okay." He didn't appear overly disappointed that she wouldn't be spending the day with him and for some reason that smarted.

"Okay then." She grinned and tossed the book aside. Sidestepping to the door, she grabbed her purse. "I'll see you later."

"See ya."

The door closed behind her and there she was, standing in the hallway with no place to go. She was pissed things got weird and they wouldn't be sightseeing. The only errand she'd been putting off was the trip to Becket's to get all her stuff. She didn't *need* to do that. She could walk around for a few hours until Riley went to work.

Her mind was a cluster of confusion, phrases like *shit where you eat* and *Ferris Bueller days* running through her head, the sound of Rarity's concern ringing in the background of every thought.

Emma rolled her eyes. First of all, guys like Riley never went for girls like her. They were two different species. Second, they were just friends. This was about Rarity's insecurities, not their behavior. She'd see once she got home—everything was platonic and fine.

Good, you figured that out. Now what?

Pacing the hall, she debated facing her ex versus continued procrastination in all tasks deemed icky. Seeing Becket could derail her progress and send her back to the couch. Ugh, back to the gown.

No! She would not give him that sort of authority. She had to be tough. Maybe dealing with this was a good thing—get it over with. But maybe avoiding it and building back some added strength was wiser. Eventually she'd have to face him.

How did the saying go? It's not the bang, but the anticipation of the boom? The anxiety and fear of facing her ex was eating at her. Maybe she should get it over with so the anxiety would be gone.

Finally, after much pouting and pacing, she texted Becket.

Hi. It's Emma. I guess you know that. Anyway, would today be a good day to pick up my stuff? You have my good sneakers and I left my flat iron at your place, plus some clothes and DVDs. Let me know. Thanks.

Send.

Oh, God, she was going to throw up.

The door opened and Riley bent to pick up the paper—still in his underwear. "Emma? I thought you left."

She sighed. This was stupid. She should just

talk to him about what Rarity said. That way it wouldn't be awkward and—

Her phone buzzed.

*H*EY, *Baby. How are you? Yes, of course you can come by. You're always welcome. Why don't you come over now and join me for breakfast. I miss you, baby. Xo*

H*ER* H*EART* TH*UNDERED* SO F*AST* her throat seemed to be vibrating. What the hell kind of reply was that?

"Em? Everything all right?"

She laughed, sort of outside of herself. Holding up her phone, she made a face of absolute bewilderment. "It's Becket. He wants me to come over for breakfast." Talk about mixed signals.

"*What*? Did you call him?"

Why was he so concerned? "I texted him, but only to ask if I could swing by and grab some of my stuff."

"What did he say?"

"He said yes and called me baby and said I was always welcome. He said he missed me." Did he really miss her? Did she miss him? What about Goldie? What did this mean?

"Shit."

She looked at him in question. "Why are you upset?"

"Because it was my job to make sure you didn't call him."

"Your *job?*"

He waved a hand. "You know what I mean."

"No, I don't. Did Rarity tell you to babysit me? Is that what this week's been all about?"

"No." He scoffed and she suspected he wasn't being totally honest. "She just asked me to make sure you didn't call Grayson. Everything else was a result of me having nothing better to do."

His words came like a kick to the chest. She stepped back. "Wow." This morning was really taking a turn for the worst.

"That didn't come out right. I meant to say I was hanging out with you because I was having fun. I liked being with you this week. I wasn't doing it for my sister. I was doing it for me. I had fun with you, Em. Please don't get mad at me. It makes me feel all guilty and blah inside."

Her stomach tightened uncomfortably at the anticipation of more rejection. She didn't want to look at him.

"Emma…" His words were whispered, his expression genuine. "We're friends."

The pain in her chest gradually unknotted. She didn't need people lying to her. "You really think of me as your friend?"

"Yes. You're cool as shit. This week was one of the best weeks I've had in a long time. I don't have that sort of connection with most girls, but you're also different than my guy friends, because you don't judge me for unwinding to some Cyndi Lauper after a long day or for biting my nails and spitting them across the room—"

"Totally gross."

"But you don't say anything. You don't make me feel bad about who I am and I like that."

She laughed. "You do love Cyndi Lauper."

He hardened his expression and puffed out his chest. "It's a heavy like."

It was impossible to stay mad at him. Her frown gradually faded. "I feel like I can be myself around you too."

"You can." He held out his arms. "Friends?"

She walked to him and sighed as his hold closed around her, comforting and secure. "Friends."

"Thanks, Hobbit Toes."

She tried to knee him, but he grunted and quickly blocked the assault. "Riley?"

"Yeah?"

"Will you do me a friend favor?"

"Sure."

"I seriously do have to get some things from Becket's. The longer I put it off the more the idea of facing him freaks me out. Will you come with me so I don't do anything stupid?"

"I'd never let you go alone."

She smiled. "Thanks."

~

When they arrived at Becket's Manhattan high-rise, her courage abandoned her.

"Do you want me to go get your stuff?" Riley offered as she paced on the sidewalk, mumbling to herself.

"No. I want to be able to get it myself. I don't want him to have this effect on me."

"What effect are we talking about, exactly?"

She paced. "I don't know. I feel crazy unbalanced right now. Like in one breath I might tell him to go to hell and in the next I might cry and beg for him to take me back."

"Is that what you want, to get back together?"

"No!"

"Good."

"But I also don't want to come second choice to some girl named after a collie."

He jumped in her path, causing her to jerk to a stop. "Hey, look at me. You are *not* coming second. *You* are putting yourself *first*. Screw that yuppie. Maybe you should tell him to go to hell. Why are you afraid to hurt him after he hurt you? Stop protecting him, Emma. The only person you need to protect is yourself."

Theories about burning bridges frightened her when she thought of lashing out at Becket. Even though she knew she didn't want him back and didn't love him the way she should have, there was some sort of safety net in keeping things polite.

"I don't know why I'm like this with him."

He studied her for a moment, his eyes heavy with concern. "You know what I think? I think you're scared. I think you're afraid to be mean, because he might eventually want you back. Don't be his backup plan, Emma. You're a plan A girl. Leave the plan B slot for someone not so nice. Hold out for a guy that puts you at the top and knows that's where you belong, a guy that never makes you question your worth."

His insight surprised her. So did his kind words. The tension in her shoulders eased, as a bit of her nausea dissolved. However, she was still human and that meant she knew her imperfections better than anyone. Sometimes great people spent their lives alone.

She was hovering close to ordinary, miles below remarkable. "But what if that guy never comes?"

"He will. Trust me."

Riley didn't have the authority to throw out guarantees like that, but she appreciated him bluffing straight to her face. Maybe that's how things got done—bluffing. The only way to get through something this uncomfortable was to push through it—stupidly fearless and full speed ahead.

She nodded. No more pussyfooting around. "Let's do this."

She hyperventilated for the majority of the elevator ride. Riley rubbed her back and kept quiet, never making her feel stupid for having such reactions to her ex.

When they were in front of Becket's door she wanted to turn back. Riley gave her shoulder a slight squeeze and stepped to the other side of the door where Becket wouldn't see him. But she saw him and that was all the support she needed.

She knocked and the door opened. Becket looked impeccable with his Armani reading glasses and pressed Polo shirt. Crisp, all the way from his strategically tousled hair to his seersucker shorts.

The breath actually seemed to knock out of her at the sight of him. Oh, the pretty babies they would have made.

"Hey, beautiful." He grinned, arousing nostalgic sensations she'd assumed were dead.

Suddenly weak, her insides melted as his gaze softened, wreaking havoc on her ovaries. Her girlie parts were under fire.

"H—hey, Becket." Damn the dreamy tenor of her voice. *He cheated on you!*

"Want to come in?"

He affected her like a delicious opiate. "Sure—"

Riley tipped his head and sent her a stern look, reminding her of his presence. Right. In and out.

Shaking off the effect Becket was having on her, she refocused. "I actually have somewhere I need to be. If you could just get my things I'd appreciate it."

"Oh, come on, Emma. Don't blow me off like that. I haven't seen you in over a week. How have you been? You look great. I didn't expect you to look so…"

Slighted, she scoffed. "Great?"

"Recovered." He grinned, that sly lawyer charm dripping from every pampered pore.

She laughed without humor. "Well, I am. I just need my stuff back so I can keep on truckin' or whatever the saying is." She made some corny motion with her arm, sluggishly screwing her fist in the air, and then folded her hands behind her back before she further embarrassed herself.

If she could survive this with a shred of dignity that would be wonderful.

"Come inside," he cajoled.

"No."

"Please." He excelled at the persuasive pout, which was exactly why he'd eventually make a great attorney.

Feeling played, she firmed up her defenses, letting a touch of snark into her expression. "Where's Goldie, Becket?"

"She's at class. Come inside."

She stepped back as he reached for her hand. "I don't think so."

"It doesn't have to be like this, Emma. Goldie's a demanding woman. She expects certain things. She isn't as agreeable as you. Just because the wedding's off that doesn't mean we still can't be…friendly."

Her mouth fell open. He did not just say that. "Define friendly."

"Come in and I'll show you. I promise you'll enjoy it."

He reached for her again and Riley stepped in front of her, causing Becket to take a startled pace back. "That's enough. Fun time's over. Emma, go wait by the elevator. Grayson, go get her stuff."

"Who the hell are you?"

Crap. Emma peeked around Riley, who, next to Becket, suddenly seemed twice his normal size. "Becket, you remember Rarity's brother, Riley."

Becket eyed him from his wavy dark hair to his wrinkled white T. "Why is he here with you?"

"Why are you asking so many questions? Get her stuff. Now." Riley snapped, frustration clear in his voice.

She wasn't used to seeing him so short-tempered. It was impressive and unexpected.

"I really don't think this is necessary, Emma—"

"You know what I think?" Riley cut him off. "I think you have a hearing problem. I also think your parents misled you with too much ass kissing and caused you to believe you're a lot more important than you actually are. You know what you really are, Grayson? You're nothing. You're a dime a dozen, prelaw punk, who's gonna nurse off his father's tit as long as possible. I hope that Goldie chick really loves you, because being an asshole is eventually going to catch up and outweigh your preppy, bullshit charm. Now, I can't help you with being an asshole, but I can work with you on the hearing problem." He leaned forward and shouted, *"Go get her fucking shit!"*

Becket jumped and shut the door. Riley peeked over his shoulder and grinned. Dumbfounded, she just stared. Who was this guy?

A minute later the door opened and a box of her crap was tossed into Riley's arms. "I want you to leave now," Becket said, his voice lacking its usual steadiness.

Riley chuckled, his laugh sounding distant with a touch of menace. "She didn't want to stay in the first place, dick." He turned to her. "Let's go."

Her breathing was shaky as they took the elevator to the ground floor. She couldn't stop staring at him. The man she just witnessed was Riley, but not the Riley she'd known since childhood.

Seeing this hard, protective side of him did strange things to her. Whatever effect Becket had on her girlie parts didn't compare to what Riley's act of authority just did.

"Do you wanna take a cab back to the loft to drop this stuff off? It's sort of heavy."

Licking her dry lips, she nodded. "Sure."

She didn't say a word the entire way home. Riley didn't seem fazed by what happened. On the contrary, he appeared his ordinary self, commenting on his never-ending appetite and contemplating when he'd eat next.

Although it was still early and they had hours before he needed to be at work, Emma didn't think spending the day together was in their best interest. Maybe they needed some space.

Things were a little claustrophobic and she needed some time to herself to get a grip on reality. The trick was coming up with a place to go that Riley would never follow.

"Once we drop this stuff off, wanna grab something to eat?" he asked as they neared the loft.

"I can't."

"Why not?"

"I have… an appointment."

"You do?"

"Yes."

"Where?"

Crap. Just lie. Quick! "With my…gynecologist."

He winced. "Oh. Okay."

Content that he wouldn't follow, she secretly breathed a sigh of relief. Now to figure out where she could go while at the imaginary gynecologist.

~

EMMA DIDN'T RETURN to the apartment until late afternoon. Riley might still be home, but she was getting tired of walking around and had consumed way too much coffee. As she turned the key in the apartment door, she braced for anything.

"Hello?"

Silence.

Relieved, she put her purse on the table by the door and collapsed on the couch. Her flip-flops dropped to the floor and she groaned.

Rarity wouldn't be home for two more days and she'd eventually have to see Riley again. It was stupid to feel different about him. He was still the same guy she lived with last week. This new awareness was Rarity's doing. If she hadn't said anything—

The front door flung open. *"Emma!"*

Startled, she bolted upright. "Riley?"

A stampede of furry motion plowed through the entryway, knocking over chairs and bumping into bookshelves. Jolted into action, she sprang off the couch and landed in a Daniel-san pose, armed with a flappy flip-flop. *"What's happening?"*

A flash of brown knocked into the coffee table, shoving it across the carpet, as a long, furry tail beat at her legs and a cold, wet nose sexually assaulted her.

"We got a dog!" Riley proudly cheered, perching his hands on his hips like Peter Pan.

"Whose dog? Get away from my crotch!" The enormous, heat-breathing beast licked at her knees a mile a minute.

"She's ours."

Her eyes went wide. "Riley, we can't have a dog." Seriously, she was being licked to death. Carefully nudging the slobbery animal back she said, "Please stop doing that."

Soft brown eyes looked at her as the dog panted and somehow smiled, long tongue drooping clumsily to the side. *Don't look at it or its cuteness will suck you in.*

"Why not? There's nothing in our lease about it, just an extra fee of twenty-five dollars a month. I'll pay that. Look at her, Em. How could you turn her away?"

He dropped into the chair and the dog trotted to him, snuffling his chest until she was lapping at his chin with that big ham tongue. Her face twisted as she watched the slimy display of affection.

Riley praised the animal in a high-pitched

voice she never heard him use before. "Oh, who's the most beautiful girl in the whole wide world? You are! Yes, you are. Like a big, brown princess."

"It's a girl?" She didn't have much of a feminine figure, sort of stumpy and fat.

He hugged the dog's enormous head away from his face, but the thing kept pushing to lick his chin. "Well, I didn't see any guns or roses, so I'm thinking she's female."

It looked purebred by its dark chocolate coat and Labrador build. Dogs like that didn't just appear. "Where did you get her, Riley?"

"Funny story. I was grabbing a coffee on my way to work and she came out of nowhere and sat on my foot. So I gave her half my muffin—"

"You'll share food with a dog, but not people?"

He shrugged. "I like dogs. Anyway, I gave her half my muffin and she followed me. I can't take her to the inn, so I brought her here."

"Well, she can't stay here either." They weren't ready for a dog. They never had food in the fridge and barely kept a routine schedule. Dogs required love and time and care.

"I say she can."

"You know how Rarity is about her things. Dogs chew and leave hair everywhere. She'd never agree to a dog."

"Ah, but she's not here right now. I just have to get you to agree and then Rarity will be outvoted. Come on, look at that *punim*." He lifted the dog's gigantic head. Its floppy jowls showing pink at her gums. Two brown persuasive eyes stared at her as that long tongue unraveled like a carpet.

"How could you not wuv her?"

"Oh, for Pete's sake."

Riley smiled. "Can we keep her?"

"For a very short trial period—"

"Yes!"

"—But if she misbehaves, she's gone. And we're putting up signs in case someone's looking for her."

"You won't regret this." He jumped up and surprised her with a hug, the heat and scent of his body overwhelming her.

"O—oh, okay, we're hugging."

"Thank you, Em."

"You're welcome. But Riley, she probably belongs to someone. We have to let people know we found her and keep an eye out for posters."

"Maybe they didn't want her anymore."

She glanced at the adorable lab. How could anyone not want that beautiful creature? "Maybe."

Pulling back, he grinned at her. "She might be hungry and she could probably use some water. I've been calling her Stimpy, as in 'Ren and'. Here's fifty dollars if you feel ambitious and want to take her to the pet store for supplies, but if not there's ground beef in the freezer you can heat up—"

"Whoa! You're leaving her here with me?"

He frowned. "I told you I can't bring her to work."

"What the hell, Riley? I didn't sign up for dog sitting. What if I have plans?"

He pursed his lips. "Do you?"

"That's not the point!"

"Please, Emma. She's a good girl. Look at her."

Turning, she watched as the oversized puppy licked the chair cushion. "She doesn't seem too bright." She was an adorable dog though. Sighing, she agreed, "Fine, but leave a *hundred* dollars. If I'm dog sitting you're buying me dinner. And we're not naming her Stimpy."

"Stimpy's a cool name."

"Stimpy was the cat, Riley. No."

"Fine." He tossed another fifty on the table. "I gotta go. I'm already late."

Turning, he placed a smooch on the dog's head. "There's my cute baby. Be a good girl," he crooned. The dog's tail flopped happily, drumming on the wood floor. Who didn't love an idiot?

At the door Riley paused. "Oh, how was your girlie appointment? Everything okay with the old wizard's sleeve?"

Everything inside of her stiffened as her eyes went wide. "Um…are you asking about my vagina?"

He, too, appeared rather surprised by the conversation shift. His feet crept closer to the door as his mouth turned down in a Robert De Niro grin. "Yes. Yes, I am. Is that a problem? We could talk about the general health of my penis if you want. It's good, by the way. Strong." He paused to flex. "Cat like reflexes—"

"Get out."

"Yeah, I'm gonna go." He edged into the hall. "We won't mention the subject of your juice box again."

Stone faced, she asked, "My what?"

His hand curled around the knob. "Penis…fly trap?" It was like he had some sort of Tourette's.

"Stop talking now."

"Bajingo?"

Even the dog was staring at him, judging him. "There's something wrong with you."

"The down stairs?"

She was done responding.

Easing out the door, he guessed, "The bunny tuft?" The door closed and he yelled, "The Pink Mink!"

She faced the dog and shook her head. "That's your new owner. I won't let him name you after an ugly cat, don't worry."

Her tongue lulled out and she panted, which Emma took as gratitude.

As it turned out, pet supplies were wildly expensive and addicting. Half the items in her bag were probably unnecessary, but didn't Marla—that's what she named her—need a matching pink, bedazzled collar to go with her bedazzled leash?

By the time they returned to the loft Emma was in love. Marla was an enormous cuddle bug, who thought she was the size of a kitten. It was like having an endless supply of affection available. With very little respect for personal boundaries, they immediately became close friends.

When Emma used the bathroom, Marla scratched at the door and barged in, squeezing into the small space so they could be together for all things. If Emma went to the kitchen to grab a drink, Marla followed.

It occurred to her that she should probably have some ground rules for the dog, like no climbing on furniture, but she was so at home Emma didn't want to discourage her from settling in. Marla did prefer Rarity's bed to all the others, though, and that was going to be a problem. She continuously shut the door to Rarity's room, but Marla, being a solid eighty-pound chocolate lab, plowed right through that barrier.

They'd figure it out later. When Emma decided to call it a night, Marla was sprawled out on Rarity's bed sound asleep. She smiled, thinking having a dog wasn't such a bad idea after all.

Once washed up and changed into her pajamas, she climbed into bed and settled. Two seconds later the soft ticking of Marla's nails on the wood floor followed and the enormous dog bounded into bed with her, rocking the mattress like a life raft in a typhoon.

Warm and soft, she curled into Emma's side and let out a contented snuffle. Emma smiled. She hadn't expected to love again so quickly, nor had she expected a dog to be the focus of her affection. If anything, Marla was loyal and *that* was something Emma could appreciate—something that deserved love.

CHAPTER 6

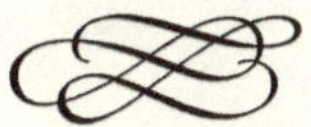

The afternoon sun warmed his face as he relaxed on the picnic blanket. Voices carried over the soft breeze as people wandered across the grass. The dog appeared quite happy to learn there was a park so close to her new home.

Emma sighed. "I've been thinking we should put signs up with Marla's picture in case her real owners are looking for her."

Riley watched as Emma played a slow game of toss with the dog, which was now called Marla. They'd left their number with the local vets and pet store, but hadn't heard anything. "That's probably the right thing to do." But imagining someone taking the cuddly brown animal away wasn't easy. One sign should do the trick, one sign, hung upside down on a payphone, by the far East Side.

"Marla, fetch!" she tossed the pink tennis ball

from where she sat on the grass. Everything the dog owned was pink, which made the morning walks a test of masculine security. But Emma was happy and, strangely, that made him happy.

"I don't see what was wrong with the name Stimpy."

"Stimpy was ugly."

"And you named her Marla after…"

"Marla Hooch from *League of Their Own,*" she mumbled.

"Oh, and she was a looker."

"Shut up. Her name is Marla."

He grinned.

There were so many hidden parts of Central Park. It was nice to take the time to enjoy the open space. Having a dog gave them an excuse to lounge around in the grass and sun and still believe they were accomplishing something, because dogs needed exercise.

"My sister comes back tomorrow."

"I know. She's going to freak out when she finds out we have a dog."

He worried Emma might forget about him when Rarity returned. "Do you think things will be different when she comes home?"

"What do you mean?"

He shrugged, trying not to appear overly concerned. "I don't know. Us hanging out, you and Rarity doing your thing."

"We could all hang out together."

"Sure," he agreed, but that wasn't the same.

Once Rarity returned, Emma would have her best friend around for all her little adventures and feats. She'd confide in Rarity and sooner or later he'd just be the roommate again.

Marla returned, dropped the saturated ball on the grass, and collapsed beside them. Emma filled a tiny pink travel bowl with bottled water.

"There you go, baby."

The dog panted and lapped up the entire offering then nestled beside them on the quilt.

He eased back and made a pillow of the dog and Emma did the same. Clouds drifted overhead and there was a quiet moment of peace shared between the three of them.

"That one looks like a sailboat." She pointed to the sky.

"This is what our conversations have reduced to, cloud watching?"

Nose wrinkled, she grouched, "What's wrong with cloud watching?"

"Nothing. It just means we have nothing else in common to talk about. It's sad really, the death of intrigue between new friends."

"Aren't you in a dark mood."

"No, I'm not. I'd just prefer more stimulating conversation than 'Oh, that one looks like a dinosaur'."

"Fine. What's your greatest fear," she asked and he grinned at the challenge.

"Ice age. Era not movie."

"An ice age, really?"

"Yes, really. And don't roll your eyes. More are coming. They decapitate mountains and cover the earth in sheets of ice eight times the height of the Empire State Building. You'd never survive one."

She laughed. "And you would?"

"I'd have a better shot than you. It's just the nature of the beast. I'm a survivor. You'd be in a heap on the floor watching Hugh Grant movies while hugging a pillow."

She smacked his arm. "I should probably be insulted."

"But?"

"You're probably right."

He chuckled. "Now, a zombie apocalypse, *that* you might have a shot at surviving."

"Because it's totally improbable?"

"Oh, zombies are real and when they come, I'll be ready. Get yourself a crossbow and some sturdy boots and I might let you join my regiment."

"You're a moron."

He faced her. "What's your biggest fear?" Her eyes were closed, the sun painting her cheeks in a soft gold hue.

"That I'll never be enough."

His brow creased. She'd lost him. "Enough for what?"

"Someone's love… trust, loyalty… everything that's worth anything. I want to be worth something."

"You are." He scowled. How could she believe she was worthless?

"I mean, by just being myself. I'm so tired of pushing to be more than I actually am. We have to be so much. It's a lot of pressure and I always feel like I'm coming up short no matter how hard I try. I wish it was enough to just be me."

"That's ridiculous."

"You're afraid of zombies and ice ages."

"Touché." He studied her for a long moment. "I think you're just fine the way you are, Em."

"It's only natural to want to improve."

"True, but work with what you got. Don't go trying to redefine everything you are. You're an awesome person. If you change too much, people will miss the real Emma and she's something great."

She turned and their eyes locked. Something tightened low in his gut as everything inside of him insisted he look away, but he was trapped there, under her close, compelling stare. The breeze passed overhead, intensifying the scent of grass and her delicately perfumed hair. She always smelled so clean, like cotton and sunshine.

"Are you hungry?" she whispered, but her eyes seemed to be saying something different.

He swallowed. "Yeah. I could eat."

"We should eat."

The sudden urge to lean close and take a nibble of her plump lower lip took hold of him and he jolted upright, his body sending all sorts of haywire signals to his lower regions. Shit.

Where the hell were these urges coming from? Rubbing his face roughly with his palms, he groaned and thought of the unsexiest place to get food in the city. "Wanna go to Flushing and grab some Chinese? They sell gizzards on sticks."

"Queens?"

"Yeah."

"Sure. But I'm not eating gizzard." She sat up and the dog lifted her head. "We should probably take Marla back to the loft first. She's tired."

Nodding, he stood and busied himself with gathering the blanket and dog toys. Emma fumbled with getting her shoes on and he stilled, transfixed by her pudgy little toes.

Dear God, he was chubbing up—chubbing up over Emma—which was abso-freaking-lutely not okay. Turning away, he stuffed anything and everything into their bag.

As soon as he had their stuff packed he started walking at a clipped pace toward home.

"Riley, wait up. I have shorter legs than you."

He shut his eyes as his mind filled with images of her little, curvy legs. Christ, even the thought of her deformed baby toe was doing things to him.

"I have to use the bathroom," he lied, deciding that was the best excuse for walking ahead of her.

"Are you sick?"

His mind was definitely playing sick tricks on him at the moment. "Yes. Sick."

"Okay, well, you go. Marla and I will catch up," she yelled from several yards behind.

He didn't need any more encouragement. The entire way home he jockeyed his way through crowds of pedestrians and practically sprinted over crosswalks and through alleyways. What the hell was wrong with him?

It was like a switch was flipped and he could

no longer separate Emma his friend from Emma the delicious little cupcake he wanted to nibble. When he made it to the loft he tossed the bag of dog toys on the floor and went to the bathroom.

Staring at his sweaty reflection, he grit his teeth. "Knock it off."

His breathing gradually slowed as he stared at himself, degrading every baser instinct he possessed until the storm finally settled and he was back to normal. Then the front door opened.

"Riley?"

His gaze dropped to his jeans. "Damn it," he hissed. "In the bathroom." He quickly locked the door.

The dog's nails scrabbled along the wood floor. He couldn't go out there like this. Emma tapped on the door. "Do you need anything?"

His eyes closed as his head fell back and he silently groaned. "No. I'm good."

"You're sure? I have antacids and some stuff for cramps."

He laughed without humor. "No, I think I'll be okay." His dick just needed to chill.

"How about some tea?" That voice... "I can put some ginger in it—"

"*I'm okay, Emma!* Just...give me a minute. Please." He shouldn't have snapped.

"Okay. I'm right here if you need anything."

Did she have to be so damn nice? Maybe a cold shower would help. Swallowing, he let out a long breath and turned on the water. After stripping off his clothes he climbed under the icy spray and gasped. "Fuck, that's cold!"

He adjusted the taps, unable to withstand torture below a lukewarm seventy degrees, and glowered at his rock hard cock.

Grandma. Grandma in a bikini. Grandma in a bikini eating tapioca pudding without her dentures. That was working.

Suddenly the image flipped to smooth ivory skin and a familiar birthmark in the shape of a strawberry. That was Emma's birthmark. He noticed it when she was in a tank top. Sometimes her bra strap covered it, but every once in a while he'd get a peek at it.

Fuck. He was hard again.

Taking matters into hand, he pumped his fingers over his flesh. He needed to get laid, that was all. He squeezed, almost painfully, trying to think of any woman besides Emma. It was impossible.

Soft, blonde curls that smelled like summer wind clouded his mind. Those naturally pink lips, pert and smooth. Those big brown eyes so full of trust and innocence. He imagined all of it, damn him.

He violated their friendship so severely in those passing seconds, imagining his fingers knotting in her hair as those full lips closed over his flesh, those big, virtuous eyes staring up at him.

He cursed, bracing his arm on the slick tile of the wall as his release shot from his pulsing veins and his entire body shuddered under the force of temporary relief. Panting hard, he tried to remember a time he was that turned on. It didn't matter that he'd masturbated to completion. He was still twisted in knots, raring to go. He wanted her. "Fuck!"

Rinsing off, he stood in the cooling steam a while after he shut off the water, shivering. Mind over matter. Whatever this was, it would pass. He'd ignore it, because Emma was his friend and he didn't want to ruin that. Plus, if he crossed that line his sister would castrate him. Yes, there would be absolutely no fornicating with Emma.

He'd been in the bathroom for an embarrassingly long time, which worked in his favor. Explosive diarrhea—imagined or otherwise—was about as far from sexy as one could get.

Climbing back into his clothes, he buffed his hair dry with the towel, and prepared to face the music. Cautiously, he turned the knob and stepped in the hall.

She stood up from the couch. "Are you okay? You were in there a really long time."

His heart pounded and his blood thickened. There was no hope. "I'm…sort of having a problem right now." It was unbelievable. Nothing like this had ever happened before. Why now? They were fine an hour ago.

Noticing his discomfort, she took a step forward.

He held out a hand. "Stay back! It might be contagious."

"Do you need a doctor? Something from the pharmacy?"

His hand trembled. "Just…stop. For the love of God, stop…talking."

Taken aback, she stilled and he regretted his choice of words, as her expression turned wounded. "I'm only trying to help."

"I know." He shut his eyes and pinched the bridge of his nose, facing the wall so she wouldn't notice his *situation.* "That's the problem."

She scoffed. "Fine. I won't help."

Glancing to his left, he tried to say something, but his words got distracted when he looked at her. She no longer wore shoes. The bottom of her thighs peeked out beneath her little white dress. He could have a hundred fantasies about that tiny dimple above her knee.

Jesus, what was wrong with him? Taking a deep breath, he pulled his attention away from her legs.

His mouth went dry as his stare focused on her breasts. Soft and round. He bet her nipples were the same deep peach as her lips. Oh, and what color would her other hidden parts be? He swayed as dizziness came over him.

"Riley?"

Shit. He was going to explode if he didn't get out of there. "Emma…"

She took a few quick steps toward him. "Are you sure you don't need a doctor? You're sweating." She tsked. "I'm calling the doctor."

"Wait!" Trembling, he released a shaky breath. "I…" Forking his fingers through his hair, he squeezed his eyes shut. "I'm not sick."

"Well, something's wrong with you."

"Definitely. Emma, don't hate me…"

"Why would I hate you?"

She touched a hand to his arm and he whimpered. Giving up, he blurted, "I'm having really inappropriate thoughts about you right now and I can't make them stop!"

Everything stilled. The apartment fell into utter silence, the ticking of the living room wall clock tapping with the subtlety of a hammer.

"What?" she croaked.

"I'm sorry. It came out of nowhere. I'm totally freaked out and trying not to think of you that way, but I can't stop."

When she didn't respond, he chanced a glance at her. Her breath was labored, but slow, each pull of air lifting her breasts against the cotton fabric of her dress. He looked away.

"You're...having fantasies? About *me*?"

"I'm sorry."

"Like what? Maybe we should talk about it."

He really wanted to undo the top button of his jeans, get some breathing room. "I don't think that's a good idea."

"Why? We're adults. We're friends. We can talk about...that."

Visions of holding her plush thighs open as he dragged his tongue up her pink flesh filled his mind. "No," he said, voice strained. "Talking would definitely be bad."

She tsked and laced her fingers with his, tugging him toward the living room. "Don't be silly, Riley." A thousand volts of electricity shot up his arm as she pulled. "Come sit down and—"

He yanked her back and pinned her to the

wall. "You're not listening, Emma. I don't want to talk." He ground his hips into her soft belly and she gasped. "Feel that? That's what talking to you did to me. I'm telling you, I think we should put some distance between us until *things* settle down and go back to normal."

Her gentle brown eyes went wide as she stared up at him. Slowly, she licked her lips. "Riley," she rasped.

He groaned. His name on her lips was an unfinished caress that ended in private pain. She didn't understand the affect she was suddenly having on him. "Emma, you don't—"

"You're turning me on."

Every good intention vanished. Nostrils flared, he breathed in her feminine scent. "What?"

Her lips parted as she breathed, staring up at him with dark, lust filled eyes. "I'm aroused. The moment you said you were thinking about me that way, my body just—" His mouth crashed over hers, silencing her ramblings as he stabbed his tongue deep between her lips and tasted heaven.

Sweet, like coconut, her kisses were the perfect blend of temperance and lust. She gripped the side of his face, pulling him closer and he growled, unable to get enough. They were frantic, unstoppable, raw, desperate. No kiss had ever been so frenzied.

Her small form cushioned his body as he pressed her into the wall. Frantic need took hold of him, burning hot and fast like brushfire.

Everything inside of him demanded he move and move fast.

"Let me take you to bed," he whispered over her lips, giving voice to everything he wanted in that moment.

"Yes." Her fist tightened in his hair. "Please."

Her legs lifted to his hips and he cupped her sweet little ass, excitement tunneling through his veins. Oh, he and that ass were going to be good friends by the end of the night. Her mouth detoured to his neck as he toddled them to his room. Opening the door he frowned at the clutter.

Recalling her crisply made bed, he pivoted and headed to her bedroom, not stopping until he was dropping her on the floral comforter and catching his weight above her.

She smiled, her hair a wild spray of mad curls. God, she was beautiful.

"Are you sure about this? There's no taking it back," he warned. *Please don't ask me to stop.*

Not a glimmer of concern showed in her eyes. Reaching down, she grabbed the hem of her dress and lifted until it slipped off her shoulders. "No going back now," she whispered.

His breath caught in his throat. Emma was naked, naked and lying beneath him in nothing but her bra and undies. The intensity of the moment hit him and he froze. This was different from every other sexual encounter.

"Are *you* sure?" she asked when he hesitated too long.

Slowly nodding, he swallowed. There was no

doubt he wanted her. The depth his wanting traveled frightened him. "Yeah. It's just… You're different, Emma. You're important. I don't want to ruin anything."

Her smile was warm and comforting as she cupped a hand over his jaw. "You won't ruin anything, Riley. I promise."

He glanced down. She was lovely, like some sort of centerfold for vintage lingerie, in her plain Jane white cotton bra and panties. Something about the simplicity of her undergarments undid him. She was so no-frills, so unquestionably stunning in her own right, more delicate than any lace, and softer than any bow, she was the real thing.

His hands shook with the magnitude of the moment. Once he touched her body it could never be undone. He needed her to understand how important she was to him, that he never got this nervous with other women.

He tried for something romantic. "You take my breath away, Emma. I think you're really… great." Not quite what he imagined, but he wasn't a poet.

Her face softened as her lashes swept low. "Riley… I've never been with anyone that knows me the way you do. This probably should feel weird, but I'm totally comfortable with you. I'm not afraid."

She should be. Lowering his head, he pressed his lips into the wing of her collarbone and breathed. He was greedy for her scent, suddenly aware of how long he'd refused this desire silently building inside of him.

His hunger was so potent it seemed impossible that it stayed hidden for so long. Letting it out was the best feeling in the world.

She made the most girlie sigh as she arched into him, pressing her breasts against his chest. He wanted to feel her skin against his.

"Take off my shirt."

Reaching for the hem of his T, she pulled, gathering the material until it lifted over his head and she tossed it away. Sliding an arm under her back, he raised her to him so they were chest to chest. Her heated flesh pressed to his in an intoxicating burn.

His mouth kissed down her shoulder as he dragged the strap of her bra away. Nestling his knees in the space between her legs, he took his time kissing the swell of her soft breasts and tracing the edge of her bra with his tongue.

Her breath turned sharp the more he teased, her hands needing his arms, as her tight nipples beaded against the cotton. They were lost in a rhythm so natural yet rare, every caress fueled their yearning, but never did they stumble, never did he overthink what he was doing. Instinct drove him like never before.

Her fingers sensually combed through his hair. Easing back, he looked at her, committed her image to memory, finding her the absolute definition of beauty. Hair tousled, cheeks rosy, lips parted, eyes dark with desire, she was suddenly a threat to all of his control.

She was stunning.

He pulled back the cups of her bra and two petite peach tinted nipples hardened. His body throbbed as his mouth watered. She was perfect.

Shoving the bra to her ribs, the straps slightly pinning her arms to her sides, he massaged her breasts, plumping them in his palms and rubbing the tips with his calloused thumbs. "Does that feel good?"

"Yes," she breathed.

"You have amazing tits, Emma."

Her eyes flared and he wondered if he should have called them something else, something a bit more delicate. Breast wasn't a word he typically said unless describing chicken. But they were tits and they were lush and full and he couldn't quite think beyond getting them into his mouth at the moment.

"Are you uncomfortable? Do you want me to take off your bra?"

"No. I kind of like it like this."

Appraising the way the garment held her arms in place he raised a brow. "Really?"

She nodded. He was fascinated by the steady rise and fall of her breasts as she breathed.

Scooting up her body, he moved his legs to the outside of her hips and unsnapped the top button of his jeans. Using both hands, he pinched her nipples. "Do you wanna see me?"

She licked her lips. "Yes."

He pulled at the tips of her breasts, stretching her delicate nipples until they were dark and engorged. "Do you want me in your mouth, Emma?"

She swallowed, her breathing audible. A tinge of rose darkened her cheeks. Eyes wide, her lips parted as she gave a subtle nod and whispered, "Yes."

Well, Christ. Releasing her nipples, he unzipped his jeans and wrapped his hand around his length. He pumped leisurely and slid a hand behind her neck until she was sitting up. "Open for me."

Her lips parted and he eased the tip into her hot mouth. Sweet Jesus, the heat and suction was incredible. *Innocent Emma's sucking your dick.*

He shivered and nearly exploded. Not wanting to overwhelm her, or himself, he made a few quick dips, and eased back.

Slithering down her body, he caught a pert nipple in his mouth and pulled. She nearly jackknifed off the bed, and he had to press her back down. "You like that?"

"Yes." She panted as he moved to the other nipple, teasing and playing, flicking the tip with his tongue then nibbling and pulling until she cried out.

His hand slid over her panties and settled above the heated crease between her legs. Her arousal had left the cotton damp and he massaged her through the material as he sucked on her beautiful tits.

"Riley, please."

"Please what?"

"I want more."

Dirty, dirty girl. He chuckled, never expecting this sort of sexual verve from a girl like her. "I'm going to kiss you there, Emma. And I'm going to make you scream."

"Oh, God."

He slid lower, peeling her panties away with exquisite slowness. Distracted by the dimple at her knee, he spent a few moments kissing it. "Your legs turn me on."

"They do?"

"Oh, yeah. Even your weird little toes. I wanna bite them."

Dragging his palms up her outer thighs, he savored the last moment wondering if she'd be shaved, waxed, or soft with a natural nest of blonde curls.

Curls it was, neatly trimmed into a tidy strip of gold. He teased the fine tuft with the back of his knuckle and groaned.

Seeing her arms were still twisted in the bra, he pulled the material lower and freed her hands, leaving the cotton around her nipped waist. She had a great body. It wasn't boyish or bony. It was petite, but womanly, all compact feminine curves, soft and rosy, swelling at all the right places, and responsive to his touch.

He bit the little pouch of softness below her belly button and she yipped in surprise. Nestling his nose against the soft patch of curls, he breathed her in, sharp and tempting, he couldn't wait to taste her.

Sliding back, he parted her thighs and—soft shades of pink. It was everything he'd imagined.

Something inside of him shifted. His desire melded with implications and responsibility.

So exposed, so vulnerable, he felt every ounce of trust she'd laid on him. He'd never forgive himself if he hurt her.

Reaching forward, he gently parted her folds and teased her sex. "Are you sure about this, Emma?" Crossing this line was bigger than perhaps either of them realized. "We can stop if you want. It doesn't have to be weird."

Her brow knit with confusion as she turned to her side, closing her legs and shutting him out. "You don't have to go any further, Riley. It's okay."

Frowning at the dejected tone of her voice, he reached for her chin. "Hey, what are you talking about? I want you. I just want it to mean something if we do this and I don't want you to regret anything."

Her chin trembled as his words sunk in, relief evident in her eyes. Biting her lower lip, she whispered, "It means something."

"Good." Dragging a hand under her hair, he pulled her mouth to his and kissed her. Her warm body curved around his as his hands explored and teased.

She clung to him, arms wreathed around his neck, breasts smashed to his chest, as he eased her back and parted her thighs again. This time he wasn't stopping.

Gliding his touch to her center, he gently slid a finger into her heat. She arched and breathed against his neck as he delved deep, swirling in and out.

"Riley," she whispered as her grip tightened over his shoulders.

Easing her to the pillows beside him, he dragged his mouth down her throat to her breasts as he continued with his fingers. Soft mewing sighs filled the room as she crested and her sex contracted in what was likely the most delicate climax he'd ever witnessed.

He smirked. If that slight tremor was what she was used to, he was about to blow the doors off her house. Withdrawing his fingers, he brought them to his mouth and stole a taste. Heaven. Her eyes flared.

Leaning over, he kissed down her soft tummy and parted her thighs, exposing her sensitive pink folds, caressing gently as she trembled.

"Easy..." He lowered his mouth and she gasped.

Sliding his middle finger into her sex, he closed his lips over her and sucked as he thrust his finger, deep and firm. Her hands knotted in his hair as her knees curled around his shoulders. Those soft little cries transformed into breathless sobs as he drove her higher and higher.

Slipping another finger inside, he pressed deep as his mouth pulled tight, sucking her engorged bud hard, barely probing, and she shattered. Her cries broke like a wave of diamonds, shattering every bit of calm in a blinding display of beauty. Her body twisted in his grip as she came undone.

Tipping back her head, she cried out his name. He swallowed, finding her response indescribably sexy. Soft ringlets clung to her throat as dew coated her skin.

He licked at the perspiration between her breasts, pulling her onto him as he rolled to his back, wanting to hold her as she came back to earth. As she curled into him and shivered, he realized he needed to hold her as much as she needed to be held, perhaps more than he needed his own release.

Time passed in immeasurable beats where he simply kissed her ear and played with her hair. When her mouth pressed into his shoulder he knew she was coming back to him.

Her hand drifted over his abdomen and fit its way into his pants. He shifted, giving her room as her gentle fingers wrapped around his engorged flesh.

She fondled him for several moments, her head resting on his shoulder as if it were the most natural thing in the world to touch him that way. Shutting his eyes, he luxuriated in the weight of her caress, the awareness that it was actually Emma's hand making him tremble.

Releasing him, she shifted and kneeled between his legs. "Let's take these off." She smirked as she gave his jeans a gentle but firm tug.

He lifted as she stripped him. Tossing the pants to the floor, she settled between his knees and appraised his body. "You're a big man, Riley."

He grunted with amusement. What guy didn't like hearing that?

Her dainty fingers curled around his flesh, burning in the most delicious way. "I'm not really good at this, so be patient, okay?"

Those eyes. They were his undoing. Unable to form words, he nodded and watched as she stared up at him. Her lips parted and she guided him deep. Wet heat closed around his flesh as his hips reflexively lifted.

She watched him as she lowered her mouth, gently taking more and more. His spine tingled and the soles of his feet prickled as fire rushed through his veins.

Gently brushing the hair away from her eyes, he simply stared as she sucked him off. The unintentional eroticism of her stare would haunt him forever. It wasn't about making him come or taking him deep. It was about the connection, and he felt it more in that moment than he ever had with anyone else.

Her hand leisurely glided up and down beneath her lips. Saliva slicked her way as her motions turned bolder.

"That's it, Emma. You're doing amazing."

His encouragement seemed to register as she tightened her grip and took him deeper. Her eyes closed and he immediately felt their connection sever.

"No." He rubbed a finger down her cheek. "I like when you look at me."

Her lashes lifted and her focus intensified. Deeper and deeper she took him, making him mad with need and lust. Her eyes sparkled as she watched him and he loved knowing she saw the moment he came apart, the moment she drove him to the edge of reason.

Not wanting to shock her, he nudged her back as his climax erupted. She was breathing roughly, her awe-struck gaze focused on his hand as he trembled through that moment of ecstasy. It was as if she'd never seen a man come before.

Reaching to the nightstand, he snagged a few tissues and hissed with lingering sensitivity as he quickly cleaned up the mess. Slightly self-conscious, he looked around the room, unsure what to do next. He was going to need a few minutes.

Chancing a glance at Emma, he sucked in a jagged breath. The sight of her sitting naked with that plain cotton bra still twisted around her waist hit him like a bolt of electricity. His insides tightened as a rush of excitement left him dizzy.

Her lips compressed in a tight smile. "I can't believe we just did that."

Fear snuffed out his excitement. "Are you sorry?"

Slowly, she shook her head. "No."

Thank God. Relieved, he blew out a slow breath. "Do you have a condom? I'm going to need a few minutes, but...we should probably have one on hand."

Her cheeks flushed a deeper shade of rose than what she already wore. "I have some in my purse."

"You travel with condoms?" This surprised him.

"I'm a new woman, Riley. You never know

what the day might bring." She laughed. "I'm also overly optimistic as the box hasn't been opened."

She climbed out of bed and he swatted her plump little ass. "You better bring that ass right back, because I'm far from done with you."

Her smirk bloomed into a full smile, her upper teeth pressing into her full lower lip. "Okay." She pulled the sheet free and wrapped it around her like a toga.

"Emma."

She paused at the door. "Yeah."

"Leave the sheet. You don't need it."

Her stare drilled into his as her smile froze. Carefully, she uncrossed her arms and let the covering fall away. Sweet, curvy hips jutted and nipped into a pert little waist as the sheet fluttered around her ankles. Her breasts hung like ripe fruit and he wanted to sip their nectar for days.

"You're exquisite."

Her gaze lowered to the floor as a flush worked its way down her throat. It wouldn't always be this private in the loft, so it was fun taking advantage of their seclusion while they had it. As a matter of fact…

Riley followed her into the living room and snuck up behind her. She gasped when he wrapped his arms around her waist and pressed his naked body to hers from behind. Sighing, she relaxed into his hold as he kissed the back of her neck and he whispered, "I wanna fuck."

She stilled and he worried his words had upset her. Pulling out of his grip, she turned and faced him. The flash of royal blue foil pinched between her fingers caught his eye.

She stepped back, sauntering deliberately, and lowered herself to the big chair in the living room. Draping one leg over the arm, she slid the ottoman out of the way with her foot, giving him a clear view of how aroused she was. "I'm all yours."

His jaw literally loosened from its hinges. Who was this girl? Her breast bore the rosy mark of his stubble and her delicate folds were still swollen and wet from their play.

His body hardened as she raised her arms overhead and stretched. Her tits lifted, her nipples hardening and darkening as blood filled the tips.

He swallowed. He couldn't blink. "You're a dirty girl, aren't you, Emma?"

She giggled. "Not usually."

That made it even better. "Just with me?"

Her arms returned to rest on the chair. "Apparently."

Things just got interesting. "Is there anything you won't do?"

"I don't know."

He grinned, a breath of laughter slipping past his throat. "Let's find out. Touch yourself."

A mischievous smirk teased her lips. "Only if you do it too."

Not even a question. He grabbed himself and stroked, watching as she traced a slow finger down the side of her breasts. "Touch yourself."

Her hand stilled, her gaze dropping to where his hand deliberately stroked.

"Please," he rasped.

Her fingers dragged over her belly and settled between her legs. She teased her outer lips.

"Is that how you masturbate?" he asked, still caressing his own flesh.

"I don't really masturbate."

"Liar. Use your fingers. Show me how you do it when you get off."

She stilled for a moment and he worried the game was over. Too far? A second later her finger disappeared between her folds as her body arched and her head dropped back. Her lips parted as she breathed and that petite finger pumped in and out of her tight pink folds.

He strode to the chair, mesmerized. Standing beside her, he thickened under his own steady touch as she cupped her breasts, pinched her nipple, and continued to finger herself—graduating to the hottest girl he'd ever met.

Licking his dry lips, he touched her cheek and her eyes opened. She seemed to read the plea in his gaze and understand his need. Rolling to her knees, she bent over the back of the chair and parted her lips. He stepped forward and gradually fed himself deep into her hot mouth.

Those dark eyes widened as she moaned, long and needy, vibrating his flesh. He'd never seen a girl take so much pleasure from giving head. She sucked hard and he rose to his toes. "Don't stop touching yourself."

Her hand disappeared under her soft body.

She moaned as he thrust in and out, gradually increasing his speed. It was so much pleasure and still not enough. Faster, he pumped his hips.

Her gaze remained soft as he touched her hair, scented her arousal. His hands cupped the back of her neck and he slowed, his thumbs tracing over her delicate jaw, as he pressed deeper. She took it, hummed, and begged for more.

"So fucking sexy, Emma."

Her hand rubbed between her legs as her gaze appeared drunk with lust.

"Make yourself come. Are you a dirty girl? Or are you a good girl?" The more he spoke the more excited she got. "Keep going until you come, dirty girl."

Two seconds later her body quaked as her eyes closed. Releasing him, she cried out her self-induced orgasm. It was easily the hottest display he'd ever witnessed. So sexy, he had to pinch off his own release at the sound of her climax.

Enough.

Rounding the chair, he snatched up the condom and tore it open with his teeth, gliding it over his engorged flesh. He grabbed her by the waist and lifted her off the chair. As tempting as nailing that alluring ass from behind was, he wanted to look into those eyes some more.

He carried her back to her room and dropped her on the bed. Pulling both ankles, he centered her on the mattress and climbed over her. "Ready?"

"Ready," she rasped, face soft with sated lust and endless temptation.

He caught his weight on his palms and lined his body up with hers, drew in one last breath, and thrust. His eyes momentarily shut in intense bliss. There would be absolutely no going back now. He slid deep, not stopping until her pelvis kissed his.

She whimpered and his eyes quickly opened. "You okay?"

Blinking, she swallowed. "You're bigger than…what I'm used to."

His ego selfishly swelled. "Do you wanna stop?" *Please, God, no.*

The briefest shake of her head told him to hold tight. He should have eased back a little, but he couldn't. She fit him like a glove. He *liked* being fully inside of her.

The selfish prick that he was, he refused to budge, wanting her body to mold to his and erase the memory of anyone else. He gently touched her cheek as he offered a comforting kiss. "Just take a minute to adjust."

She nodded and caught her breath. It was intense. He needed a minute, too, if he was expected to last—

"Riley?"

"Yeah."

"You're inside of my bajingo right now."

His thoughts swung like a boomerang in the total opposite direction. Rolling his eyes he started to laugh. "And you think there's something wrong with me? We're having a moment,

Emma. It's not the time to use weird names for anatomy."

"Bunny muff," she said and snorted.

He shook his head.

"Pink mink," she chuckled and then fell into a full fit of giggles. "Wizard's sleeve!"

He withdrew and shoved forward. All humor left her expression. "It's impolite to laugh the first time a man puts it inside. You'll give him a complex."

"Sorry." She was still smirking, the wench.

He leaned over her, lowering to his elbows so they were intimately face-to-face. He brushed the hair away from her eyes and kissed her lips. As much as they could amuse each other, there was no ignoring the significance of the moment.

"Does it still hurt?" he whispered.

She shook her head. "No."

"Good." He sighed as he shifted his hips, his face sliding to that sensitive spot where her shoulder curved into her neck. He breathed her in. Just breathed.

There were countless ways to have sex, yet he couldn't remember a time more intimate than this one. He could have sat up for deeper penetration, or perhaps done some fancy hip work to increase the pleasure, but neither of them seemed to want to let the other go.

Belly to belly, chest to chest, they rocked slowly, holding each other close. Rising gently, he stared into her eyes as her pupils bloomed and dilated. The entire experience was incomparable to all others. He'd never taken the time to watch a woman the way he studied Emma, never *enjoyed* watching a woman that much.

Pleasure built like a slow and steady rainfall, washing away all that came before. The longer it lasted, the deeper he fell. They were damp to the tips of their hair and shivering under the intensity of their joining.

It was like a sexual reincarnation, because after sleeping with Emma all other experiences paled. She'd somehow redefined his standards, making them unattainable for all other women.

Her nails scraped over his shoulders as she trembled through another climax, this time triggering his. Pressing his face to the curve of her shoulder, he lost a piece of himself there, inside of her.

She was different. He wasn't sure what made her so, but being with Emma changed him in ways that could never be undone.

It was the first time, since becoming a man, he could recall having something to fear. As he lay there, trying to recover, one truth became perfectly clear. He could *not* lose this connection.

CHAPTER 7

Still adjusting to the circumstances of pet ownership, Emma awoke to the strange scratching and clatter of Marla racing into the loft from her early morning walk. Chairs squealed as they skidded across the floor and Riley cursed in a hushed hiss.

The sound of his voice twisted a secret smile onto her lips as she hid her blush against the pillow and hugged her belly where all the butterflies played. It actually took effort not to squeal like a thirteen-year-old girl.

Biting her lip, she sighed, remembering the way he touched her, looked at her, made her—for the first time—feel like a hot, red blooded woman.

Two sharp barks and the sound of glass breaking penetrated her dreamy fog. She should probably see if he needed help. Marla was usually a gentle and lazy giant, but once she got excited she was a force to be reckoned with.

"Damn it, Marla. Sit!" A quiet, sympathetic chuckle slipped out at the exasperated tone of his voice. He was the one that insisted they have a dog.

Emma rose and winced as her tender insides protested, reminding her to take it slow. Last night was insane. She never saw that side of herself.

Something about already being friends with Riley and knowing he'd seen her at her worst made her fearless. She took what she wanted without getting hung up on what he might think. There was no fear of consequence and it was liberating and exhilarating and easily the most erotic experience of her life.

The trick—now that the night was over—was surviving and snuffing out any awkwardness. She intended to keep Riley as her friend, which meant she had to keep it together and not freak him out by assuming one hookup meant more than it did.

Yes, he'd shown her what it meant to have mind-blowing sex and she'd never stop being grateful for the experience. He'd taught her more about herself in one night than Becket had taught her over their entire relationship. However, he'd warned her about the dangers of casual sex, many times voicing his concerns that she might not be able to handle such blasé terms.

She needed to handle it. Riley lived in a land of casual, so clearly that's what this was. She couldn't allow herself to assume anything more, because that would be the fastest way to destroy their friendship.

Riley never let himself get close to women. It was inevitable that he'd eventually be in someone else's bed—a thought that already pissed her off. She had to prepare for that, adapt a nonchalant attitude about the whole encounter—keep it light, no pressure. Anticipating his withdrawal from the get-go seemed the wisest move.

Tying her robe, she visited the bathroom then joined him in the kitchen. Marla greeted her first with an inappropriate sniff of her pushy snout. "Hey, boundaries!" Emma shoved the dog away from her crotch.

"She's wild today," Riley said and there was that acute pinch of awareness. *I saw your penis and you saw my boobies.* Annnnd she was regressing to a juvenile idiot.

All she could think was *he was all up in my bajingo last night.* She didn't know, exactly, what a bajingo was, but she liked using the term. It was fun to say. *Bajingo.*

Pasting on her big girl smile, she pretended to be a mature adult and greeted him. "Hi."

His gaze locked with hers and heat swirled in her belly. "Hi."

Mmmm, he had a great morning voice, all gravelly and deep. She'd never realized how intense his eyes were, but now…they were potent, capable of wrecking every defense she had. Those eyes, the way they smoldered and pinned her in place, they were lady kryptonite.

She glanced at the counter. "Did you get coffee?"

Taking advantage of the distraction, she uncapped one of the paper cups and tore open three packets of sugar. Of course he didn't know how she took her coffee. Why would he? They were only friends.

Her body stilled, pulling taut as he stepped behind her. His arms crossed over her ribs as his face pressed to the curve of her neck. "I didn't know how you took your coffee."

"Oh." She cleared her throat. "It's no big deal. Three sugars and a splash of cream. I—" All thoughts cut off as his hand slid under the lapel of her robe and cupped her breast. "Um."

"Mmm. You're so warm." His lips pressed into the sensitive spot behind her ear.

Ohmygod, ohmygod, ohmygod! She stepped out of his hold and faced him, quickly tightening her robe. "What are you doing, Riley?"

His head tilted in confusion. "What do you mean? I was saying good morning."

"No, you were copping a feel."

"Is that not allowed? I didn't get a copy of your rules, so I just assumed…"

She shook her head. "Riley, last night was a one time thing. If we make it a habit things will get messy and end badly. I like you. I like our living situation. I don't want to do anything to jeopardize that."

"But…we saw each other naked."

"So?"

He frowned. "Emma, I was inside of you five hours ago."

Oh, she remembered. The mere mention of it had her knees going weak.

I was inside of you...

What was it about the way he talked that made her so hot? His words were crude and unsophisticated, yet they turned her on. She loved the way he told it like it was. And when he called her a dirty girl… she really liked that.

Because you are dirty.

She cleared her throat and did her best impression of a mature woman. "Riley, I remember, but a one-night-stand is just that. One night."

He shook his head and frowned. "So that's it? That's all this was to you? A one night stand?"

"Was it more to you?" Maybe she'd misjudged him. The dirty girl in her head let out a giddy squeal at the possibility. If that were the case she'd be happy to reassess—

"No. Just sex. I'm glad you see it that way too."

And that pinch of disappointment after letting herself believe it could be more for only a split second was exactly why she couldn't go down that road. Tightness contracted inside her chest and her eyes closed. Shit, that feeling sucked. She cursed herself for permitting hope, when she specifically told herself that was against the rules.

Trying not to tremble or show her disappointment, she nodded. "Good. I'm glad we agree."

Sipping her coffee as a distraction, she

winced as it burned her lip. The awkward silence carried on for far too long. And now she was shaking. They hadn't been awkward all week, and now, since sleeping together, things were more uncomfortable than ever.

What if we're never the same again? What if he brings a woman to the loft tonight? What if she's prettier than me and I have to sit around acting unaffected while he flirts and touches her and makes her—

"We need to talk about it!" she blurted.

Riley stilled and set his coffee on the counter. "Okay."

Taking a deep breath, she settled onto a stool. "Okay. The way I see it, last night was fun for both of us."

"Agreed."

"I—Really?" She wasn't sure if she'd done everything right or on par with his previous experiences.

He laughed. "Really. I had a great time, Emma."

It was strange, revisiting the encounter and receiving feedback. More impersonal than she'd like, but still, feedback was good. "Good. Okay then. I think we should keep what happened only between us. There's no reason for anyone else to know and if Rarity found out—"

"Nobody tells Rarity," he agreed.

Relieved, she went on. "I think if she knew, it would just make things weird and we're not weird. I mean, I'm not weird. Are you weird? I'm not."

"Not weird."

"See, no one's weird." Her voice was getting really high pitched. "So, I'd like to go back to the way things were, but still be friends. You know, the way things were after Becket and I broke up, but before all the sex happened. Let's call that the friend zone. That's where I want to be. Right there in that zone." She enunciated by pointing to a sugar packet sitting like an island on the vacant counter.

Riley's fingers reached for the packet of sugar and trapped hers. "Friends."

Her breath hitched as he pinned her with that stare again. "Right. Friends." He might as well be touching her nipple. She pulled her hand away.

"So, if I wanted to toss you over that chair and fuck you from behind, that would be off limits? Outside of 'the zone'?" The air quotes weren't really necessary, were they?

She swallowed. "Well, friends don't really do that."

"They don't?"

"I don't think so." Friends didn't sleep together. *Come on, Emma!* Right, she knew that.

"You sound unsure."

She was sure, but maybe they could fool around one more time before Rarity got home. *No! That's how things get messy.*

He rounded the island until he was standing behind her stool. Refusing to look at him, she focused on the microwave. Without asking permission, his hands slid around her waist and unknotted the tie of her robe.

"Oh God," she breathed as he parted the lapels.

Cool air tickled her chest as her nipples pulled tight. He didn't just open her robe. He glided his fingers over her shoulders until the satin fell down her arms and draped over the stool. Hands dangling by her hips, she sat completely naked for his inspection—*like friends often do.*

His fingers traced down her back, tripping over every notch of her spine. Her shoulders rose as goose bumps chased down her arms and over her legs. No one had ever treated her body so carnally.

Stepping closer, he kissed her shoulder and twisted the stool until she swiveled enough to face him. He parted her knees, making room for his hips and brazenly reached for her nipples.

She watched in awe as his rough fingers pinched the tips, sending sensation shooting through her womb to her sex. She should cover herself. The way she was sitting, her belly was creasing and showing its softness. But Riley didn't seem to mind. As a matter of fact, he seemed so in tune with her in that moment she was oddly secure in all her feminine flaws.

"Maybe friends touch each other sometimes, Emma. I mean, I'm your friend and I'm clearly playing with your pretty tits right now. How can that be?"

Her lips were dry. So was her throat. The more he touched her the harder it was to think.

"I like seeing my hands on your body." He released her nipples and guided his palms around her hips. "Counter's gonna be cold."

She gasped as he lifted her and squeaked when he set her on the chilled granite. Unsure what he had planned, her breath quickened. *I'm sitting on the counter buck-naked!*

He went to the fridge and returned a moment later holding a jar of grape jelly. Keeping his eyes on her, he unscrewed the lid with a pop and dipped two fingers into the purple jam.

Holding a good clump of jam on his fingers, he placed the jar on the stool. She flinched the second cold jelly smeared over her belly. The chilled, sticky substance had her sucking in a deep breath and squirming as he painted her skin.

"Lie back." Carnal curiosity overrode logic and commonsense as she allowed him to ease her toward the counter, gradually laying her down.

Her body jerked and tensed as the chilled granite pressed into her heated shoulders and shocked her lower back. All objections about friends not touching each other disappeared.

She did exactly as he asked; even let him adjust her legs the way he wanted. Any protests silenced as he blew cool air *right* on her bajingo. Her modesty was gone, yet when he made her the center of his attention, she didn't really miss it.

"Maybe you're right, Emma," he said, again dipping his fingers in the jar of jam. "Maybe friends don't fuck." She gasped as he painted her breasts. "But I'm pretty sure they eat together. You make me very, very hungry, Emma."

The counter no longer felt cold as her body heated under his touch. Everything smelled of grapes and sugar as he dragged his sticky fingers over her belly, around her breasts, and down to her sex.

"Look at what a mess I've made," he whispered, tipping the jar over and showing her it was empty. Hoisting himself onto the counter, he braced his arms on either side of her, planting himself directly over her breasts. "Friends help friends when they have a mess on their hands, don't they?"

She nodded. No one had ever painted her with food before, or paint for that matter. She was sticky and slightly concerned about stains, but more than anything, she wanted him to continue this game.

He held up two purple fingers. "Will you clean them up for me?" He pressed the digits to her mouth and her lips closed around them. Sweet, sugary jam melted on her tongue as she sucked. "Mmm, I love your mouth on me."

Heat burned low in her belly as he watched her suck his fingers. Gradually, he probed her mouth, gliding those sweet fingers over her tongue. Just as her dirty girl started doing cartwheels he withdrew them with a pop.

In one quick move, he crossed his arms at his hips and stripped off his shirt. She couldn't see beyond his chest, but sensed him toeing off his shoes. They landed on the floor with two claps.

Her body was on fire as she waited for whatever came next. Lost, she stared at his chest, wondering why she'd never realized how sexy he was. His broad shoulders were smooth and perfectly proportioned for his strong arms. Her palm rested lightly against his cut waist. He might not have had a six-pack, but he was damn close.

Sitting up to undo his pants, she got a chance to admire the play of muscles in his arms. He crawled over her and smiled, that sweet, boyish grin she loved. "You're all...*dirty*."

She was. Five minutes ago she was having a logical discussion about why they should be friends, and now she was sprawled naked on the countertop covered in jam—and loving it. And she was pretty sure she was about to get fucked.

"Do you have anything to say for yourself?" he asked, brow arched playfully.

Her lips pursed as she tried to match his serious tone as she rasped, "I'm a dirty, dirty girl."

Growling, he sealed his lips to hers in a passionate kiss. Her mind reeled, shouting things like *Look away, children!* as he did deliciously erotic things to her mouth with his tongue. Spiraling into a frenzy of need, she gripped his shoulder, locked her legs around his hips, and took what she wanted—*him!*

His hands aggressively dragged over her sticky flesh. His mouth was forceful, his teeth nipping and biting as he licked up the sweet jelly. His hips dragged over her belly and she reached for him, wanting to touch as much as he did.

"Fuck, Emma. Where's a condom?"

"My purse. By the door."

He jumped off the counter and ran to the door. Snatching up her little bag, he fumbled with the zipper.

"The inside pocket."

Opening the purse, he dug around, cursing when he pulled out Midol, tampons, credit cards, keys, and everything but a condom. "Damn it." Turning the purse inside out, he shook as coins, receipts, and chapsticks went pinging and rolling across the floor.

"No!" She'd never find everything.

"Why do you have so much crap in here?" he snapped, still digging. "Hah!" Producing a condom, he tossed the purse aside.

"All my stuff," she pouted as he shucked his pants and climbed back on the counter. "My coupons and subway—"

He kissed her, scrambling her thoughts and bringing her back to the moment. "Shut up and kiss me."

All worries about disorganized purses fled as his mouth toyed with hers. "From now on," he said against her lips, biting and licking between words. "You keep your condoms in an easily accessible storage compartment."

She parted her legs, wanting him inside of her with an urgency she didn't understand. "I will."

"We should keep them in a bowl on the coffee table or in a basket by the napkins, maybe have a lanyard made so there's always one at the ready." He nudged her sex and her body opened.

"You're absolutely right."

He slid in to the hilt and she moaned, quickly adjusting to the delicious intrusion. God, it was fantastic how completely he filled her. His face tucked into the curve of her shoulder and he held her for a long moment.

There was something sacred about the action. Becket never did anything like that when they made love. It was never this intimate. With Riley, there was no hiding. She was as exposed as he was vulnerable.

Was he like this with all women? Something told her he wasn't. Her hand gradually lifted and rested on his hair, soothing him and drawing comfort from his closeness.

"Emma," he whispered.

Her heart stuttered as her name came like a quiet murmur of affection, whispered over his breath. That single word on his lips rocked her calm, making it almost impossible to adapt to the intrusive intimacy. There was nothing casual about this—about them.

He slowly drew back and pressed forward, bringing her body to attention, her mind racing to keep up with her heart. They silently watched each other for several minutes as their bodies connected. No hiding.

"You know," he whispered. "If you were on the pill we wouldn't have to think about condoms or how messy your pocketbook is."

"Old lady's carry pocketbooks. I have a purse." Her response was totally incongruent to the panic ripping through her sex-addled mind.

He thrust again. "I want to be able to have you whenever, Emma. I don't want to waste time digging around for condoms or making sure we go to the store." His hips rocked in a steady motion.

She couldn't concentrate. Her body stretched as her brain could hardly keep up.

"We could make love in the mornings, late at night, when we're passing in the hall."

As he spoke, his words penetrated the haze of lust clouding her mind.

"You'll never have to worry about douchebags at bars. I'll give you everything you need. Just tell me what you want and I'll do it. You're not ashamed to ask and I love that."

Her panting turned erratic, but not because of the sex. She couldn't breathe. What—what was he suggesting? That they be each other's booty call? No condoms? That was serious stuff —something even she and Becket hadn't discussed and they were going to be husband and wife.

His grip tightened and he pulled her into him, his intimate hold pushing past anything she'd ever known. Grabbing his shoulders in a panic, she stopped him and made him look at her. "Wait a minute. Riley, what are you saying?"

His lashes lowered as insecurity flashed in his eyes. "I don't want us to just be a one night stand. I like you, Emma. I like you a lot."

Her chest tightened. She couldn't breathe. Tapping his shoulder, she sucked in a breath, only half of it reaching her lungs. "Get up."

"What?" He frowned.

She pushed at his chest. "Get up. I need you to get off of me. I can't breathe."

He quickly sat up, withdrawing from her body, his face taut with concern. "Are you okay? Did I hurt you?"

Panting—not in a good way—she slid off the counter and glanced down at her body. She was a purple mess. She looked beaten to a pulp and smelled like a Blow Pop.

"Emma, what's wrong?" Riley asked, voice stern with frantic frustration.

Shaking her hands, no longer seeing the jelly as sexy, her self-esteem plummeted and she snapped, "Look at me!"

"I've been looking at you. I don't understand why you're freaking out."

She didn't either. "Because it isn't supposed to be like this. There's jelly *everywhere* and your sister could walk through that door any second! I told you we shouldn't let this happen again and we let it happen anyway."

"Are you blaming this on me?"

"No, it's both our faults. But, Riley, you *cannot* act like you're into me for more than sex. You're the one that said I was fragile and inexperienced —which I'm not—but making me believe you want more than sex is only going to lead me on and give me a farther fall back to reality. I'm not too fragile for honesty, but I am breakable damn it, so don't lead me on."

"What the hell are you talking about?"

"Us!" She flung out her hands then covered a purple smear drawing too much attention to her pudgy tummy. "Come on, Riley. Look at you and look at me. You're Mr. Popularity. You're easygoing and cool and hip with your vintage clothes and disregard for social class. I mean, your name should have been Omar or Shiloh or something. Then there's me. I'm awkward and dorky and I *never* know where to put my hands." Sliding her palms more over her belly, she angled her shoulders wishing she could hide her breasts. "You want me because I'm convenient. I'm the pathetic girl you don't have to try with. We live together so I'm easy access and—"

"That's enough!" He slid off the counter and stood, eyes hard.

She flinched and immediately silenced her rambling at his sharp tone. He scowled and she tried pinpointing what part of her tirade might have offended him, but everything she said was true.

He jerked his pants off the floor and stepped into them. "You just have everything figured out, don't you, Emma? You're the only one with insecurities." He laughed without humor. "You think you're easy? Newsflash, you're not. You're one of the most difficult women I've ever met. I fucking try!"

Crossing her arms over her chest, she strained to hide her nudity. "I'm sorry. I wasn't saying it to upset you," she whispered. But someone had to protect her heart and be honest for the both of them.

He stilled, seething in the silent kitchen. The energy shifted. He glared at her. Then, as if

something occurred to him, his expression softened. He stepped close and she tensed as the
pressure of building tears came out of nowhere.
It was their first fight.

His arms wrapped around her and he pulled
her close. "I'm sorry," he whispered.

She wasn't sure what was happening between
them.

"I shouldn't have yelled at you or said that."
His arms tightened around her as he kissed the
top of her head. "I didn't expect to care this
much. But I try with you, Emma. So when you
accuse me of not putting out any effort, it pisses
me off." He kissed her head again, holding his lips
to her temple. "I try."

She sniffled. "What are we doing, Riley? I
don't understand."

He sighed. "You're shivering. Let's get you
cleaned up."

Taking her hand, he led her to the bathroom
and started the shower. Once the water was
warm, he held the curtain as she stepped in. Confused, she took a startled step back as he followed, taking up more than half the space in the
tiny stall.

The spray ran over her skin, making pale vi-
olet puddles at the bottom of the tub. He held her
close, tucking her head under his chin as they
swayed in the rush of warm water.

"I care about you, Emma. I don't want it to be
just a night."

That didn't make sense. They had nothing in

common. "The longer we do this the more of a mess it'll be when it ends."

"It doesn't have to be a mess. You're my friend. I've known you all my life. I'd never do anything to deliberately hurt you."

But he didn't deny it would eventually end.

"What about Rarity?" If Rarity suspected they were more than friends it would freak her out. Rarity didn't believe in clean breaks and was a firm believer that friends didn't cross certain lines.

"It's none of Rarity's business. We won't tell her."

She didn't like keeping a secret from her best friend, but on the other hand, she didn't know what was going to happen between her and Riley. This morning was a perfect example of how far logic got them.

Kissing the side of her neck, he rubbed her breasts with a soapy cloth. The way he touched her, it seemed so natural, as if he'd always been entitled to caress her with such familiarity. Each stroke of his hand was a phenomenon, as if they'd shared this intimacy for years. It didn't make sense.

"I've never done anything like this before," she confessed.

"What do you mean?" His palm dragged the washcloth over her belly and gently massaged between her legs, keeping her on the sharp edge of arousal.

"Casual sex."

"Who says we're casual."

"Aren't we?" She was such a novice when it came to experience with men and reading people. She'd spent years with Becket, promised him her future, and that turned out to be a total misread.

"I guess it depends on your definition of casual. We live together. That's not casual."

She rolled her eyes. "We're roommates. It's not the same as a couple that lives together on their own."

"But think of all the ways I can wake you up when I get home from work." He thrust his hips forward making it clear that he was hard again.

Momentarily distracted, she tried to shift away, but he cajoled her back to him. "I'm trying to be serious, Riley."

Turning her around, he hunched low so he was looking in her eyes. "I want you, Emma. I don't want you hooking up with other guys. Is that serious enough for you?"

Her expression fell and she swallowed, foolish hope tempting again. None of what he was saying matched the impression she had of him. "What about you?"

"So long as we're doing this, I have no desire to even look at another woman. If that changes, I promise I'll be upfront with you. I'm not Becket. I won't hurt you."

She appreciated him making his position abundantly clear. "So not casual?"

"In terms of exclusivity, no. It's new territory for me, too, but the thought of you and other guys makes me nuts. We could talk about you and other women—"

She smacked him in the stomach. "No."

He laughed and turned her back around so he could continue washing the jelly from her skin.

It was such a big leap, but at the same time it was an easy fall. Natural and strangely right. Everything was changing so fast. She couldn't explain it, which meant she'd never be able to justify it to someone else.

Rarity would harp on all the reasons this was a bad idea, and Emma's instinct told her she was due to take some risks regardless of the consequences. She didn't want her friend to ruin what could be an amazing experience, reckless or not.

"We seriously can't let your sister know about us, Riley. She'll freak out."

"As much as you seem to think I like to include my sister in my sexual exploits, I promise, I don't. She's not going to find out."

That was true. It wasn't like Rarity and Riley talked about sex. Emma had seen them check out the same woman and have a laugh about it, but she'd never heard them discuss individual conquests.

"Did you really mean it when you said I should go on the pill?"

His hand, still massaging her, paused for a brief second. "That's up to you. I can wear condoms. I always have. It's just...with you it seems a little...I mean... I *know* you."

"And I know you. You've been with a lot of women, Riley."

"I'll admit I topped your three, but there aren't as many as you think. I'd say I'm somewhere between ten and fifteen."

"You don't know the exact number?"

"Don't sound so appalled. I could figure it out, but I'd have to think for a minute and I only want to think about us right now."

For a twenty-six year old man she supposed a rough dozen women wasn't a lot. "You wore a condom with all of them?"

"Every single one. And I had my blood work done last month. If you need the reassurance I can have it run again, but I haven't been with anyone since then. I'm clean as a whistle."

If it were any other guy she'd require more proof, but she trusted Riley and believed he wouldn't lie. "I'm due to see my OBGYN soon. I can have her run my blood work."

His brows drew together. "I thought you saw the lady doctor on Thursday."

She bit her lip and he turned her until she was facing him again.

"Em?"

Her cheeks heated. "I lied."

He frowned. "You lied? Where were you?"

"Walking around. I was…" She shrugged. "…avoiding you."

"Why?" He appeared genuinely hurt by this confession.

"You yelled at Becket and came to my rescue. It was having all sorts of weird effects on me."

"Like what?"

"You know… inappropriate feelings." She fidgeted, looking away until his laughter broke the awkward silence.

"It made you horny when I yelled at Becket?"

Her face turned scorching hot and she scowled at him. "I don't get horny." Guys got horny. Women become aroused.

Tossing his head back, he laughed. "Oh, yeah you do! Ha! Did it get you all hot and bothered? Mmmm. You like when I go all caveman, don't you?"

"Shut up."

The water was cooling. He grinned at her and kissed her nose. "I'll always defend you, Emma—from assholes like Grayson and the assholes you don't suspect. That's what friends do."

Her chest tightened. She pressed her lips to his and he pulled her close, deepening the kiss. "I want to be with you before my sister gets home."

Her heart fluttered as his unguarded confession struck a chord buried deep inside of her. "Okay."

He kissed her, slow and passionately. Reaching back, she shut off the water. They dried each other sharing the same towel and he carried her out of the bathroom to his bed.

Shivering, she pulled the covers over them. "Riley?"

"Yeah?"

"I'm already on the pill if you want to…"

The brown irises of his eyes darkened as his pupils dilated and his lips slowly parted. "Put me inside of you."

Biting her lip, she reached between their

bodies and found him warm and hard. Stroking him a few times, she glided his wide tip along the seam of her sex, opening her body. Their breath mingled as she braced her feet apart and lifted, accepting him.

He moaned and, again, pressed his face to her shoulder and cursed, his voice hoarse. "You feel incredible like this. It's so real."

She noticed the difference too.

As he gained his composure, he rocked against her. Long, deep strokes built and added to the sensual pressure churning inside. The longer they made love the more she spotted the tiny details of him she'd somehow overlooked.

Riley was a beautiful man. His full lashes gave his dark eyes dimension against his tanned skin. When his hair was wet, it curled tighter and darker than his usual chestnut waves. His skin had a unique scent she couldn't place, but now identified as his natural fragrance.

Beyond his unarguable handsomeness, was his kind and honest soul. He was refreshing and exceptional, because he was so genuine. That was his most attractive trait.

Every bit of him appealed to her and the more she opened herself to those charming qualities, the more she realized how much she'd been purposely overlooking them. Maybe she'd always found him attractive, but assumed he was out of her league and therefore convinced herself he wasn't anything special. But, oh, he was special.

His breath coasted over her throat as he

throbbed deep inside of her. "Are you ready?" She loved the way he asked.

"Yes."

With a final push, he filled her and they shivered as they caught their breath.

"Hello?"

Their twisted bodies tensed. "Shit," he hissed.

"Oh my God, it's Rarity." *Shit. Shit. Shit. Shit. Shit.*

She shoved him off of her with more strength than she intended. His legs tangled in the blankets. "Wait. No—don't push—let me—ah, fuck—" He went down like a stack of books and groaned a garbled curse.

She jumped off the bed and frantically paced. "I need clothes!" she hissed.

"Just grab anything." He hoisted himself off the floor and tossed her a flannel shirt.

She smiled and held it to her nose, breathing it in—

"Uh, hello? We have time to sniff the clothing later."

She blushed. "Sorry. Pants?"

He tossed her a pair of nondescript pajama bottoms. Stepping into them, she cinched the drawstring to keep them up. Sliding the shirt over her shoulders, she quickly fastened the buttons and stilled when she found him staring at her. "What?"

His head dipped to the side. "You look hot in my clothes."

"Riley?" Rarity called. "Hello? Em? Anyone home?"

"Your hair's wet," she whispered.

"So?"

"So we both can't go out there with wet hair. She'll know we showered together."

"I'm pretty sure we've had wet hair at the same time before and no one jumped to that conclusion."

"Just cover your head!"

He rolled his eyes. "Fine." Snatching a knit winter hat off his bedpost he shoved it on his head.

Emma stilled. It was a sock monkey face, complete with ears and button eyes and a tail sticking out the back of his head. He looked like one of Nurse Ratchet's patients, escaped from the cuckoo's nest. "*Where* did you get that?"

"You don't want to know."

"You're probably right. I'll go out first."

Cracking open his bedroom door, she spotted Rarity going through mail at the front table. Emma quickly slid into the hall. "Hey!"

"Hey, toots!" Rarity tossed the mail aside to hug her. "What the hell happened in here?"

Emma turned and snatched her robe off the stool, tossing it behind a chair. "What do you mean?"

"What's all over the counter? Is that jelly?"

"Jam," Riley corrected, walking out of his room, nonchalant expression on his face. "Welcome home."

"Thanks," Rarity said, a look of confusion on her face. "What the hell are you wearing and why is there jam everywhere?"

"This is my lucky sock hat, what?" he stated with absolute seriousness. "And there's jam everywhere because I made a bagel."

She frowned and shook her head. "Whatever. You're cleaning this up."

"How was the shoot?" Emma asked, drawing her attention away from the disaster they'd left in the kitchen. Her toe casually nudged her purse under the table as her eyes widened, her foot subtly covering the condom wrapper.

"The shoot was good. I got a lot of nice pictures and made some good connections. I'm exhausted. As fancy as that hotel was, I missed my bed. I think I'm going to unpack later. All I want to do is curl up on my own mattress and sleep for a few hours."

"That sounds like a nice plan. Maybe later we can grab dinner," Emma offered.

"Sure." Rarity studied her for a moment. "You look…*really* good, Em. I'm glad you're off the couch. I'm not real sure about this," she waved a finger at Emma's outfit, "but your eyes look happy."

"I am happy. Becket did me a favor."

"Yeah." She nodded. "Okay, I'm going to lie down. We'll talk about this more over a bottle of wine later."

"Okay. We'll keep it down so you can rest." They smiled as Rarity disappeared down the hall. "That wasn't so hard," Emma whispered.

A blood-curdling scream broke the silence followed by three hearty barks and the sound of

Marla charging down the hall. The frightened dog barreled into Riley and cowered at his feet.

Rarity stumbled into view, eyes bulging as she raised an accusing finger at the dog. "What the hell is that?"

"Oh, we got a dog," Riley explained. "Marla, this is Rarity. Rarity, meet Marla Hooch. She really likes your bed."

Shaking her head, she waved a finger. "Absolutely not. No dogs."

"Well, we voted and…"

Rarity looked at Emma. "You want this animal in our home?"

"She's really not that bad. All she does is sleep. She only gets excited when you talk to her or take her anywhere or bring out food or—"

Rarity threw up her hands. "Unbelievable." Shaking her head, she snickered. "I get it. You two are all *Harry met Sally* now and my opinion counts for nothing. Well, I don't want a dog. They're shaggy, they shed, they're noisy, and they smell bad."

Riley gasped. "Marla smells like a dream," he argued indignantly.

Rolling her eyes, Emma attempted to pacify her friend. "We'll try to keep her away from your stuff, Rarity."

She scowled at Riley. "This has your stank all over it. You couldn't have brought home a houseplant or a fish. No, you get a hundred pound beast."

"She was homeless," he hollered as she

marched away. "Where's your sense of compassion?"

"I don't have one." The door slammed.

Emma looked up at Riley. "Do you think she'll make us get rid of Marla?"

"No, but I think you should come back to bed with me while she's napping."

"Riley." She shook her head and yipped when he scooped her up and tossed her over his shoulder. "What about the mess?"

He swatted her bottom. "Shhh. She'll hear you. Keep quiet and no one'll get hurt."

She silently laughed as he lugged her back to his room, Marla watching with a curious look of confusion and longing as the door closed behind them.

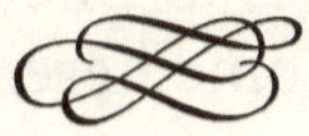

"It's like having a show horse," Riley decided as he brushed Marla's flank.

His sister rolled her eyes. "Someone should tell the village we found their idiot."

Emma kept quiet, but he caught her little smirk. She didn't think he was an idiot. Over the past several weeks of their double o'seven affair she made him feel more like a god than anything else—sex god, that was.

"I hate that dog," Rarity grumbled.

"For your information, Marla *loves* you, Rarity. It's cruel and hurtful for you not to reciprocate her affection."

"I still have pictures of that crotch sniffer online, so I wouldn't get too attached if I were you."

"Too late." Slipping Marla a treat, he petted her heavy head. If no one called about Marla by now, she was staying. "There's a pretty girl. Now go give Aunt Rarity some love. She likes when pretty girls lick her."

"Don't be jealous—Oh, yuck!" His sister groaned as Marla shoved her face in her lap, but Riley caught the tender way she stroked the dog's ears. She was full of crap. She liked Marla.

Lexi laughed. "Come here, Marla. You can lay with me."

The dog trotted over to Lexi and Rarity rolled her eyes. "You're as bad as them."

His focus shifted when he noticed Emma looking for her shoes. "Where are you going?"

She paused at the door. Today she wore a teal sundress with red ballet slipper type shoes to match her cardigan. She looked hot and he wanted to do stuff to her.

"What are you, her keeper?" Rarity asked.

Emma drew in a deep breath, but kept her expression neutral. "I was going to the market to get some groceries. We're almost out of bananas and I need shampoo."

"Can you get me some new razors?" Rarity asked.

"Yeah. Do you need anything, Riley?"

He needed her—needed her in a bad way. It had been almost four days since they'd last slept together due to womanly things and he'd grown quite used to their regular schedule. On top of that, Rarity had been monopolizing all of Emma's time and he was starting to get jealous. "Yeah. I…maybe I'll just go with you."

"Really?" Both Emma and Rarity asked at the same time.

"Yeah. I haven't been to the market in… six years." He nodded. "I'm due."

"Okay. Get your shoes."

Shoving out of the chair, his feet fit into his shoes as he patted his pockets. Phone. Wallet. Golden. He met Emma at the elevator, giddy to finally have some Emma time to himself.

"She's totally freaked out you're going with me."

"Why?" He pushed the button for down. "Lexi's there. Maybe I just wanted to give them some privacy."

"Because you *never* do the food shopping."

He shrugged. "Maybe I don't like the raisins you buy."

She shook her head and stepped inside, pressing the button for the bottom floor. The metal doors glided shut and the elevator moved. His finger stabbed the stop button and the cart jerked to a halt.

"Riley, what are you doing?"

Grabbing her arms, he pinned them above her head on the wall, eyes rolling back with anticipation as he breathed her in. "Elevator sex." His mouth crashed over hers and she moaned.

He unbuckled his belt and unzipped his pants. Hiking up her dress, he reached down the front of her panties and tested her arousal. She was soaked. He chuckled, and bit her lip. "Dirty girl."

"I've been dying to be alone with you," she breathed, pulling his hair and shoving his face to her breasts.

Elated to be reacquainted with her body, he

kissed her and mumbled, "Between my stupid sister and your stupid job I never get to be alone with you."

She bit his neck. "I'll quit and become a hobo. We can have all the sex you want, but you'll have to pay my phone bill and share of the rent."

He shoved her panties down her legs and she awkwardly stepped out of them. He pocketed the white cotton. "I'll pay whatever you want. God, I love your boobs."

He slipped a finger into her sex and she moaned. He chuckled, "Shhh…sound travels."

"I don't care," she hissed, shoving his shirt out of the way and reaching in his pants. He loved when she was aggressive. He sucked on the soft side of her breast as she stroked him. "Lift me up."

"So demanding," he teased. Holding her by the ribs, he lifted and she wrapped her legs around him. He aligned their bodies and thrust deep.

"Yes!"

"It's gonna be quick, Em."

"Just do it."

She rode him hard and fast, her nails digging into his shoulders through his shirt as she panted out his name. It had been six weeks since they'd started sneaking around and their flame had yet to flicker. She was as insatiable and adventurous as he was when it came to bedsport and he'd never been happier.

"Yes, yes, yes, yes, *yes!*" Her mouth latched onto his neck as her body contracted around him. Her orgasm milked his release as he pumped into her a few last times, trembling the way only she could make him tremble. Fuck. She was amazing.

He lowered her feet to the ground and caught his breath. "You okay?"

Gazing at him with half lidded eyes, she grinned. "Never better." She brushed the wrinkles from her dress and fluffed her hair. "Where are my panties?"

"In my pocket. I want them." When he was with her he was a pervert like that—but only with her.

"Let me see them."

Disappointed, he handed them over. She bunched up the fabric and used it to clean herself up. "Here you go." He grinned as she handed them back. She *so* got him.

Facing forward as if nothing happened, they hit the go button and the elevator jolted. They were so perfectly in sync they glanced at each other and snickered.

On key, once they were a few blocks away from the loft, she laced her fingers with his. He was never one to hold hands, but with Emma, he liked touching her any way he could.

"You know, one stiff breeze and everyone will see your bare bajingo."

She chuckled, chin high, seemingly unfazed by the possibility. Her confidence, this new level of coolness he'd never expected, filled him with an urge to take her all over again.

When they reached the store he was on an endorphin high. While she behaved like a respectable adult, he acted like a toddler. "Can we get some licorice?"

She rolled her eyes. "Put it in the cart."

As she selected limes he perused the options and paused, his mouth stretching into a juvenile smirk. "*What* is this?" He picked up the funny shaped orange.

Tying off her bag of limes she frowned. "Isn't it an orange?"

"Nope!" He laughed, reading the sign. "It's a kumquat." Why this was so hysterical to him he hadn't a clue.

"Did you want some?"

"Some kumquats? Who doesn't? Kumquats. Ha. That's the best fruit name I've ever heard."

She laughed and handed him a produce bag. "Here."

As they traveled the aisles, she never got annoyed with him, even when he couldn't stop using kumquat in sentences. It was amazing. Sometimes he watched her and couldn't figure out why anyone that sweet would want to waste time on him. She could have anyone. Grayson was a dick, but she could easily blend with those upper class yuppies and find herself a better blueblood to take her sailing.

Who was he, a bartender with an unfinished degree? He had no clue where he was going or what he was working toward. The farthest he thought into his future was ten days, max.

He didn't have a five-year plan or one for however many years people were planning these days. The fact that he was dating Emma could have been deemed the eighth natural wonder of the world. There was simply no rational explanation for such an improbable thing.

When she wasn't looking he slipped a bottle of lube into the cart next to the obscenely large cucumber he'd snagged in the produce section. This was the shit he needed to stop doing. Emma was a grownup. Sure, she was two years younger than him, but she wouldn't want to date some man child that got a kick out of oversize phallic produce and lube.

He reached in and she turned. "Do you like this cereal?"

Back stiff, hands innocently at his side, he nodded. He needed to get that crap out of the cart before she saw it. Panicking, he tried to distract her, but she kept piling food on top.

"Will you grab tissues? I think we're out."

Abandoning his search he nodded. "Sure. Tissues…" He grabbed three boxes and followed her to the last aisle.

"I think I'm going to make Mexican this week. You like tacos, right?"

"I like your taco." Fuck. Why did he keep saying dumb shit like that?

She shook her head.

"Sorry."

She frowned. "Sorry for what?"

"Calling your bajingo a taco."

She laughed. "Like you haven't called it a hundred other weird things. I'm used to it, Riley."

He paused. "Really?"

"Yeah. Why else would I let you name my boobs Starsky and Hutch?"

"They do have streetwise mannerisms and sometimes perky moods."

"Exactly. I get it."

Feeling relieved, he asked, "It doesn't get on your nerves?"

"What?"

"My…immaturity?"

"If you're immature, so am I. Look, stop freaking out about whatever you're stressing over. We're fine. You're happy. I'm happy. You've got my underwear in your pocket. I'm shopping for tortillas commando. Sounds like a recipe for bliss if I've ever heard one."

Coolest. Chick. Ever. Maybe she was right. Maybe he was freaking out over nothing.

They waited in line at the register and he fidgeted the moment the guy behind them started unloading his cart. Grocery stores made him claustrophobic. He continued to help her unpack their items on the belt while mentally telling the guy crowding his six to back off.

When she discovered the enormous cucumber she held it up and arched a brow. "Did you put this in here?"

"Uh…maybe."

She shook her head and tossed it on the belt then reached in the cart again, this time holding up the lube. "And this?"

His neck prickled as the guy behind him scrutinized their order. "I'm a sophomoric man child," he mumbled.

She glanced at the bottle and picked up the cucumber again. "We can try it, but I don't wanna hear you crying when you can't walk right the next day."

And there it was…he loved her.

She winked, tossing both items on the belt, careless of their proximity and what the clerk might assume. She was priceless, taking a practical joke and turning it back on him. A champion of sarcasm and wit, a master in the sack as well as the elevator, and sexy as sin with her Jessica Rabbit curves and tiny, deformed Frodo toes. In a word, she was perfect.

Several things became incredibly clear as he acknowledged his love for Emma. One, he couldn't let her go. Two, he needed to make sure he didn't ruin this. Three, he had to play it cool so she didn't freak out. And four, he wanted to hold her and smother her like a stage five clinger and do a million and one non-masculine things with her that definitely broke guy code.

The bottom line, this relationship was suddenly the most important thing in the world to him, but could run so much smoother without him there to jeopardize it with all his stupid tendencies. Tendencies she was slowly learning to tolerate. Could she really be immune to all his idiosyncrasies? Perhaps find them cute, or would it only be a matter of time before he screwed up the greatest relationship he'd ever had?

~

THE MOONLIGHT SLIPPED past the curtains and colored her skin a silver shade of blue. "How do you get your pillows to smell so good?"

She chuckled and curled into him. "I wash them."

"I wash mine too."

"I do it regularly."

He breathed in the soft scent of her hair, loving the fact that he'd smell her on his skin well past morning. "Em?"

"Yeah?"

He kissed her ear. "Are you happy?"

"Of course I'm happy."

"With me?"

She turned and faced him. "What's going on, Riley?"

He didn't like needing this much reassurance. "It's been almost two months since you and Becket broke up."

"So?"

The plan was for her to move out and marry the guy. How did she adjust from all that to this so smoothly? He was coming from the total opposite end of the spectrum and it was definitely surreal finding her in the middle. Yet she seemed to just accept what they'd created as if it were nothing out of the ordinary. But to Riley, it was extraordinary.

"You probably would've been apartment hunting by now."

She scowled at him. "But I'm not."

"Doesn't that bother you?" She had to feel

something in regard to how much her life wasn't moving in the direction she'd planned.

"Well, apartments are really expensive and we would've needed a big one—for me, Becket, and all the other women, so no, I'm not bothered. I'm relieved."

"Okay." But was she relieved because she'd dodged a bullet or because she found something better? He wanted to be better than that preppy little shit.

She brushed a hand over his hair. "What's bothering you, Riley?"

"I don't know." *I think I'm turning into a chick.* "I can't seem to get a handle on my feelings."

"What sort of feelings?" She sat up. "Are you freaking out? You promised to talk to me if you started having second thoughts about us. Oh my God, is that what this is? Are you having second thoughts?"

"No." He sat up too. "I'm not…I'm not having second thoughts. I'm…" He didn't know how to explain what was happening to him. "The other day I heard a Luther Vandross song and it made me emotional. I get home from work and I can't wait to climb in your bed just to watch you sleep. I worry about shit I never cared about, like should I have a 401K, and do you prefer the suburbs to the city? Then I panic, because I don't know the answer. Do you like one over the other? And what about children? Do you want children? Some women have a timeframe for that stuff, because their gynecological clock is ticking. Is yours? And if so, how many? Does it piss you off that I'm just a bartender? And what about the way I dress? You never rag on me for the way I dress—"

"Whoa. Whoa. Whoa. Riley, take a breath."

He did, big and slow. "Sorry. It's like everything started piling up on me at once." When he looked at her she was smiling.

"First of all, it's a *biological clock* and mine's not making a peep. I'm twenty-four and not even thinking about kids yet. Second of all, why would I care that you're a bartender? I spend my day picking up people's dry cleaning, making coffee, and getting lunch orders together. Third, I like the way you dress. Fourth, maybe we should both look into 401K's. I'm not really sure what they are. And lastly, I absolutely love the fact that you watch me when I sleep."

"Really? That's not creepy stalker boyfriend territory?"

She shrugged. "It might be to others, but I think it's sweet. If you were my ex and breaking into my place, then yeah, that would be creepy, but you're invited. I think it's romantic."

He grinned. "Sometimes you snore and get this little bit of drool—"

"Ruining it."

"Sorry."

She leaned forward and kissed him. "Why is all this suddenly bothering you?"

"I just…" Honesty? He took a deep breath. "I don't want you to be embarrassed by me."

Her brow crinkled. "Embarrassed by you? Why would I be?"

"Well, we've been seeing each other for almost two months and the holidays are right around the corner. What are we going to do for Christmas? I don't want to do separate things and pretend we're just friends. I want to share the holidays with you as my *girlfriend*. I don't know why we're still hiding our relationship, unless it's because you're ashamed of me or maybe it's just a fling thing to you. I want to introduce you to my friends, but I don't know if you want to meet them."

"I'd love to meet your friends, Riley. You should have said something."

"You would?"

"Yes. And this is *not* just a fling thing for me. I just didn't want Rarity knowing about us because we were new and I wasn't sure if you were using me, or what, and I didn't want her cramming reality down my throat. If we were making a mistake I wanted the freedom to make it."

Her words were reassuring until she said that last part. "Using you? Are you serious?" Insulted, he waited for her to explain.

"You know what I mean."

"No, I don't. Emma, I would never take advantage of you."

Flustered, she waved out her hand. "How was I supposed to know that?"

"Because you know *me* and the kind of person I am."

"Don't get mad, Riley. I'd just gotten over a five-year relationship that ended with me engaged to someone who regularly slept with another woman. I'm *still* working out some trust issues. I know nothing lasts forever, but I wanted you, even if it was for a blink of forever. Your sister never would've understood that, because it was the first time in my life I wanted something enough to not care about the risks."

She sighed and cupped his face. "Hey. It doesn't matter to me what anyone else thinks. As long as you get me and I get you, that's all we need."

He nodded, but needed her to really get him in that moment. "Some things last forever, Em."

She shook her head. "Nothing lasts forever, Riley."

Sadness for what Becket had done to her took hold of him. She should believe love could be unconditional and last forever, even if it was a crock of shit or not in their destiny, it was definitely something she should believe was possible. The truth was *she* made *him* believe in such things. She had her whole life ahead of her to become jaded.

"If nothing lasts forever, then I'm glad I was your risk. But I'd rather be your nothing and last forever." Kissing her he toppled her to the pillows. "Can I be your nothing?"

Her lips curved under his. "You're not nothing, Riley. You're everything."

"You're everything too." His body stretched alongside of hers as he nibbled her shoulder.

She sighed and looked into his eyes with such intimacy. "I don't care if we tell Rarity about us now."

He sat back on his heels. "Really?" Immeasurable relief derailed his progress to her panties.

She laughed. "Yeah. I trust what we have."

He jumped out of bed and grabbed his pants off the floor.

"Where are you going?"

"To tell Rarity about us."

Her eyes widened. "It's four in the morning!"

No time like the present. "It'll only take a minute." He didn't want her to change her mind. The secrecy was making him insane. Marching down the hall, he knocked on Rarity's door.

Marla barked from the bed as he entered. "Rarity?"

She jolted upright and gasped. "What? What is it? Is something wrong? Fire?" Lexi lay in a comatose heap by her side.

"No. I just wanted to tell you Emma and me are sleeping together. There's nothing you can do about it and we're done keeping our relationship a secret. I love her and that's that."

Her eyes made a slow transformation from startled relief to comprehending fury. "*What?*" his sister shouted, her voice waking her girlfriend.

"We'll talk about it in the morning, but I thought you should know. Goodnight." His sister gaped at him and he grinned, quickly shutting the door.

He returned to Emma's bed, grateful he wouldn't have to sneak out before dawn. His smile faltered as he noted the look of shock on her face. "What? You said I could tell her." Did he misunderstand?

She blinked, but didn't move. "You...*love* me?"

Fuck. Had he said that out loud? Sighing, he put all his cards on the table. "I think I've been in love with you since you farted over the goat." She didn't laugh, so he threw out a, "Hashtag baa farts" and stamped it with a finger pound sign.

Okay, this was bad. She swallowed and blinked again only now her eyes were glazed with tears. He rushed to the bed.

"Hey, wait. Don't cry. Shit. Emma, I'll take it back. I don't love you. Most days you make me crazy and I want to throw you off a skyscraper, but I'd race to the street and catch you before you hit the ground, because deep down I know I can't live without you, but that's not necessarily love. I mean, when good things happen and you're not around, sure, I wish you were there, but that's normal. And some days I look at you and think you're cuter than a pigmy marmoset, but that's just my dirty lust. Blah!"

A tear fell and he really panicked.

"It was an accident! I fell in love with you before I realized it. I don't even really like you. I can't stand the way you always pick an ani-mated film over a movie with actual people. And you have this strange fascination with bad 80's television. *Perfect Strangers* was not that funny! I can't stand when you get the remote first and I *hate* when you're quiet, because I don't know if you're mad at me for doing something stupid, which I probably did, and I get this horrible knot in my stomach. I never had these problems before you came along. It's really hard dating you, but I can't stop, because…"

Christ, he was sweating. "Fuck it. I fucking love you, Emma. I'm sorry if that makes you cry, but it's the truth and I swore I'd always be honest with you. I love you. I'd do anything for you. You're the syrup to my pancakes."

She was really crying now, the ugly cry she saved for movies like *E.T.* and *Steel Magnolias*. That was never a good cry. "Please say something."

She sprung and knocked him to his back, her mouth finding his as she kissed him deeply. "I love you too, you stupid, stupid man."

Heat exploded in his chest as all tension shifted to shock. "You do?"

"Yes. God, Riley, don't you get it? You saved me. I didn't realize how many days passed without a single smile until you made me laugh so much my cheeks hurt. I can't go back to the girl I was. She was so sad and insecure. The girl I am with you, that's the real me. That's who I want to be. I like her and I love you for introducing me to that side of myself."

"Wow." He wasn't sure how to respond to that. "That's a lot of credit, Emma."

She nestled into his shoulder. "It's the truth."

His pride was unfathomable. She loved him. "Say it again," he whispered.

The soft curl of her smile pressed into his chest. "I love you, Riley."

Content, the most content he'd ever been, he sighed with a new level of gratification and hugged her. "You're the mashed potatoes to my gravy."

She hummed and squeezed him tighter.

"The moose to my squirrel," he added, in his best Russian accent.

She tapped his chest. "I get it."

"The bees to my honey."

"Riley."

"The Abbott to my Costello."

"That's enough."

"Sorry." He held her as he stared happily at the ceiling, basking in their new found—"The Frodo to my Sam."

"That's it." She grabbed her pillow and stood.

"Hey, where are you going?"

"To sleep. I have work in a few hours."

He glanced out the window as the dark sky gave way to shades of plum and sapphire then followed her to the couch. "Let's go to the roof and make love as the sun rises."

Her grin was exquisite. "You have a romantic soul, Riley Lockhart."

He kissed her nose. "I can be charming." He took the pillow and laced his fingers with hers as he led them to the roof.

~

"She's fucking awesome, Rarity."

"I know. Why do you think I picked her to be my best friend?" His sister bit into her falafel and mumbled, "I should cut your dick off."

"Please don't. My dick's very happy at the moment."

She wiped her mouth. "Seriously, Riley, if you hurt her—"

"I won't."

"But if you do—"

"I swear on my balls, I'm not going to hurt her."

She lowered the sandwich and dropped all facades. "I love her, Riley. I mean, I really love her, like you're lucky she's not gay because I'd take her from you in a heartbeat."

"I love her too—and I'm very grateful she doesn't like girls. Trust me, we talked about it at length. There are no threesomes in my future."

"Don't make me puke."

He paused while Marla sniffed a mailbox. "Are you mad?"

"That you fuckers kept this a secret from me? Yes."

"Seriously, Rarity."

She sighed and tossed her napkin in the trash. "No. I'm hurt. Emma's my best friend and she fell in love with someone and I didn't know until two months after the fact. Not *like*. Love. I don't even think she loved Becket, Riley. This is a big deal."

"She was afraid," he explained, not wanting their relationship to cause problems. "It was new, she was in a delicate state, and she figured you'd warn her away from me."

"I would have."

"See?"

Rarity took Marla's leash and directed them to a bench. His sister's usually jovial eyes showed the strain of worry. "Am I that judgmental of a friend that she couldn't tell me?"

They hadn't kept their relationship a secret to hurt Rarity and it upset him that she felt slighted. "No." He nudged her with his shoulder. "She was fragile. We didn't plan it. I swear we were just friends for a minute there, but then… Nothing ever came as natural as loving her, Rare. It's the easiest and the hardest thing I've ever done."

"I guess." Her lips twisted as they sat on a bench. "I'm just sulking because I feel left out."

"Emma looks at it like she might've been making a huge mistake with me, but she wanted to make it anyway. If anyone should be sulking it's me. I was brought in as the *mistake*."

"I guess." She scrubbed the side of Marla's face with her fingers, putting the dog in a pleasure coma. "So, you two are *serious* serious?"

"Yes."

She laughed.

"What?"

Her mouth hooked into a half-grin. "I'm impressed. You don't typically have 'girlfriends'."

His chest tightened. "What can I say? She makes me want to be a grownup."

"Look Geppetto, I'm a real boy," she teased in her best Pinocchio voice.

They sat silently as people exited the glass doors of the law firm. He hated that Emma still worked with Grayson's father. She'd applied for a couple other jobs, but nothing had panned out yet.

"There she is." Rarity stood.

As Emma spotted them, her expression transformed with a smile. "Hey! Isn't this a nice surprise?" Marla nearly knocked her over with an enthusiastic greeting. "Hello, pretty girl."

He leaned in and kissed her. "Missed you."

She stilled, cheerful, but nervously glanced at Rarity. It was the first time they'd openly displayed affection since informing his sister of their relationship.

Rarity scrunched up her nose. "It's just weird. Come on, I think Marla has to poop again and I'm out of bags." She turned and gave them some space.

"Was that weird?" Emma whispered. "It felt a little weird."

"We'll adjust," he said, taking her hand.

When they reached the apartment, Emma changed into comfortable clothes like she usually did after work. He followed her into her room, enjoying that he could openly be with her whenever. "I wish I didn't have work tonight. You should come by the bar."

"I can't. I promised Rarity we'd have an *us* night. No you. No Lexi." He admired her ass as she slid off her stockings and jumped into a pair of sweats.

When she glanced over her shoulder he shook off his ass trance and rejoined the conversation. "What do you guys do?"

"Pillow fights, lingerie, practice kissing, the usual." She stuck out her tongue and winked.

"Not funny." In any other case it would be, but not with his sister.

She laughed. "We're going to order food, watch a movie, and drink cheap wine."

Jealous, he plopped on her bed and distracted himself with a throw pillow. "What movie?"

"*Mr. and Mrs. Smith*. A little Brad for me and a little Angelina for her."

"Oh." He pouted.

She stilled and faced him. "What's wrong, Riley? Rarity and I always do stuff like this."

He tossed the pillow aside. "What are your plans this weekend?"

"Brace yourself, but I have none."

Perfect. He sat up. "You do now. I'm taking you out. We're going on our first official date."

Her face split with a smile. "We are?"

He loved that smile. "Yes. Expect to be dazzled."

"Where are we going?"

He didn't have all the details figured out yet, but it was going to be badass. "It's a surprise."

Leaning over, she kissed him. "I can't wait."

When they returned to the kitchen Rarity was observing them from the couch. He had to leave for work in a few minutes so he was on Emma like white on rice.

Rarity made an obnoxious gagging sound. "All right, enough! I get that you two are all 'in love'—"

"I find the air quotes insulting," he quietly stated.

"—but I cannot share an apartment with Morticia and Gomez. We're going to have to set some ground rules. Anything beyond a casual cuddle is bedroom conduct. There will be no public displays of affection, no French anything, and abso-freaking-lutely no sex on any common area surfaces. Is that clear?"

He cleared his throat and pointed to the couch. "We did it there."

"Oh my God!" she jumped up.

"And there." He pointed to the windowsill. "And basically on every other horizontal surface in the loft. Some vertical ones too."

Emma smacked him on the arm.

Rarity wore a look of absolute revulsion. "We're bleaching everything."

He laughed as his sister stomped into her room and slammed the door.

"You're rotten," Emma said as she flipped through the takeout menus.

He grabbed her wrist and spun her into his arms. "*Cara mia*." He kissed a trail down her neck. "You are dearer to me than all the bats in all the caves in the world."

Her eyes creased with laughter. "You're going to be late for work, Gomez."

He kissed her. "I know. I really gotta go." He grabbed his jacket. "But hey, that windowsill… we should do that again soon. I think the neighb's appreciated the show. They thought you were cute too."

"We'll see. Have a good night."

Working opposite schedules sucked. Leaving was always a process, the internal battle to let her go never easily won. He wondered if time would make it easier, but hoped not. It was exciting being this addicted to another person. Their time apart made the return that much sweeter.

He kissed her one last time. "Good night. Don't have too much fun without me."

"Never. Have fun at work."

He chuckled. "Never."

Entering the hall, he pressed the elevator key. The distant hum of the lift grew as it approached. Anxiously tapping his hand on his thigh, he pivoted and raced back to the loft. Storming through the door, catching her by surprise, she jumped and gasped.

Pulling her into his arms, he dipped her back and kissed her deeply. "I love you," he whispered, taking one last breath of her soft skin.

Winded, her soft gaze met his as she whispered, "I love you too."

The elevator pinged and he walked backward to the door, not letting their fingers unlace until he absolutely had to. He'd take the image of that last smile with him all night, like a mental postcard.

CHAPTER 9

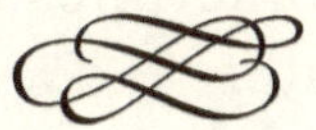

"**R**arity, can you come here for a sec?" Emma held up two pairs of shoes when the door opened. "The black ones or the silver?"

"Black," Rarity decided without waffling. She was better than a coin toss in matters of attire.

Tossing the silver heels into her closet, Emma hopped and inelegantly slid her foot into the strappy black ones. "How do I look?"

"Wow." Rarity stared at her for a long moment. "It kind of pisses me off that you're dating the penis version of me. I'm probably better in bed."

Flattered, she smirked and bashfully waved away her words. "You're just saying that. You love Lexi."

"I do. But you're smokin', toots. Really pretty."

"Thank you." She'd gone with a plum Coast Nadina dress that belted with a bow and cascaded in waterfall layers to the knee. "Is my makeup okay?"

"Yeah. Sexy."

"It's not too much?" She didn't usually wear dark shadow, but tonight she wanted dramatic.

"No. I like it." Sometimes it was really handy having Rarity around.

"I don't know why I'm so nervous." She transferred her ID and some other items into a small clutch that went with her outfit.

"Do you know where you're going?" Rarity asked, watching her get ready from the bed.

"No. I was hoping you got some information out of him while I was getting ready."

"He's not even here."

She stilled while trying to latch the clasp on her earring. "What?"

"He left like three hours ago."

She glanced at the clock. "We're supposed to leave in ten minutes. He said seven o'clock. Where is he?"

Rarity shrugged. "I'm sure he'll be here."

But didn't they have reservations? Wouldn't he have to get ready? Change?

Rarity laughed. "Relax, Emma. It's Riley. Why are you so nervous?"

"You're right." But she was nervous in an excited way. "This is new, that's all."

"Becket took you out all the time."

She snorted. "To his parents' functions and things we were invited to. He *never* made plans on his own and took the initiative like this. Probably not what you want to hear, but your brother's the most romantic guy I've ever met."

"The mind boggles." Rolling to her side, she made a sound of disgust. "Becket was a putz. You deserve romance. I'm glad Riley's making you happy."

Turning from the mirror, she grinned at Rarity. "You are?"

She shrugged. "Yeah. If he hurts you I'll kill him, but if he's making you happy…" she spread her fingers wide. "I'm accepting it."

"Thank you. I want you to be okay with us dating. It means a lot that you're accepting it." She checked her lip gloss and silently giggled. "It feels like prom."

"*Blah.* Sorry to hear that."

Tsking, she stashed her gloss in her clutch. "I *liked* prom, Rarity."

"Well, in keeping with tradition, I'm staying at Lexi's tonight so you can have loud, obnoxious sex in post-prom fashion. Just not near or around any of my things please."

She grinned. "That's very considerate of you."

They walked to the kitchen and again she stressed that Riley wasn't home yet. She didn't want to sit and get wrinkles.

There was a knock at the door. Rarity glanced through the peephole and laughed. "It's for you."

"Is it him?" He was knocking? Wasn't he cute, picking her up on time. She opened the door and her jaw dropped. *"Your hair!"* He went from chestnut Matthew McConaughey waves to cropped Jude Law curls. It was an immediate promotion.

The side of his mouth pulled in a self-conscious grin as he stood, hands hidden behind his back, dressed in clothes she was certain he hadn't owned yesterday, and looking like a prime cut of come to momma.

She swallowed, running a slow appraising eye over his impeccable choice of clothing. Gone were the jeans and faded T's. This Riley was all kinds of posh, Upper West Side, New York fine. Fitted onyx pants and jacket complemented his slate gray dress shirt and black leather shoes. He didn't wear a tie, which would have been too much. This was perfect. Hot.

"You look stunning," he said, producing a bouquet of purple calla lilies from behind his back. "These are for you."

She gasped. Flowers? He got her flowers! This was already the best date she'd ever had. "Thank you." She giggled and said something all women loved having the opportunity to say. "I'll put these in some water."

"May I come in?"

She laughed. "Of course, silly." Taking the flowers to the kitchen, she made a girlie smirk at Rarity who rolled her eyes.

"Your place is nice. Have you lived here long?" he asked as she produced a vase from below the sink.

"Oh, joy. Roleplaying," Rarity grumbled and Emma sent her a warning glare telling her to behave.

"Riley, this is my roommate, Rarity."

"Nope." Rarity held up her hands when Riley tried to introduce himself. "Too weird. I'm leaving. Have fun. I'll see you tomorrow." She grabbed her keys and left.

"Sorry," Emma apologized.

"That's okay."

She slid the flowers to the center of the island and grinned. Walking to him, she studied his hair, brushing her fingers through the trimmed ends as she approached. She kissed his lips and whispered, "I can't believe you cut your hair. It looks amazing." She pressed her front to his.

"Whoa." He caught her wrists and stepped back. "This is a little forward for a first date."

She frowned and giggled. "What?"

Gently, he turned her wrists and tucked her hands behind her back, arching her away from him and kissing her neck. He whispered, "I did my homework. I read an article in *Cosmo* about the perfect first date. The kissing doesn't come till the end, but don't worry, it will, because Starsky and Hutch are looking mighty fine in this dress."

Ohhh...now she understood. Wasn't he adorable? She could play that game. It added an element of suspense. She liked it.

"Okay, Mr. Lockhart. Where are you taking me?"

He held out her wrap and she stepped in as he lifted her hair and slid it over her arms. "Tonight we're going to a little place called Jean Georges."

She faced him, quite impressed. "I've always wanted to eat there!"

He drew her wrap together over her front. "Shall we?"

As they walked, Riley was an absolute gentleman, holding doors, blocking her from foot traffic, and slowing his pace to match her shorter strides. It occurred to her that these were things he'd always done, but tonight she noticed and really appreciated them.

When they reached the Trump Towers a sort of breathlessness came over her. Staring up at the looming building, she squeezed his hand. Stepping to the side, he looked at her in question.

"Riley, I just want you to know, this is already the most romantic night of my life. Thank you for doing this. I can't imagine how much planning it took to get reservations on such short notice. And your clothes and your hair—" He kissed her.

"Shh. Don't overthink it, cakes. I'm getting a shot at the prettiest girl in New York City tonight. She's worth a little planning and finagling."

The moment they entered the restaurant the staff fell into a choreographed rhythm that promised perfection and a one-of-a-kind dining experience. The white-gloved service began with her chair being withdrawn and a detailed description of the selection.

As the waiter walked away, she smirked at Riley. "This place is really fancy."

"That's why I got my fancy pants on."

The waiter returned and filled their glasses. When they were alone again, Riley held her hand under the table and looked at her the way he often did, as if they were making love with just their eyes. Their surroundings disappeared as they fell into intimate familiarity.

"So," he said softly once they'd sent their order to the chef. "In the Cosmo article, they claimed stimulating conversation was a must on a first date."

"They?"

"Yes, the romance experts."

She silently chuckled. "Okay."

"I've prepared a few topics. Would you like to go through them?"

She laughed. "Sure."

He nodded and sipped his wine. "Good. Topic one, Bill Murray versus Betty White, who would win?"

He stated the question so earnestly one would have thought he was discussing politics or religion, but no. She tried to curb her laughter out of respect for the other diners.

Smiling, she took a sip of wine and considered the question, answering with equal pomp. "Well, in a physical altercation, Bill Murray has youth on his side, but he's getting up there too."

"But Betty was a Golden Girl. That has to count for something," he countered.

"True. One took on Slimer. The other lived with Blanche. They're both courageous. And funny."

"I have to say, I think it's funnier when Betty

White mentions balls. Her age gives her a shock advantage."

She nodded. "I once saw a picture of her posing nude when she was young. She was pretty sexy."

Both his brows rose. "Emma, women like Betty White will *always* be sexy, because she's cool. Age doesn't play into it. What is she, ninety-four now? I'd totally put a poster of her in my room." And so it was settled, Betty was better than Bill.

After their first course, a delicious autumn pumpkin soup, they moved on to other stimulating topics.

"Do you worry about aging?" he asked.

"What kind of question is that?" she laughed, unsure if he was implying something.

He shrugged. "Your makeup looks pretty. You don't usually wear that much."

Self-conscious, she sipped her wine and considered visiting the ladies room. "Thanks?"

"You don't need it, is what I'm saying," he clarified. "Forget I said anything."

"It's okay."

He shook his head. "Sorry. I think you look really beautiful tonight. You're beautiful every night, with or without makeup. I'm just gonna stop talking."

"It's okay, Riley. Thank you."

He was quiet for a moment. "Sometimes I worry about aging. Guys can't hide stuff the way girls can. Like, what if in ten years my Adam's apple starts to sag and I look like I have chin balls?"

She snorted while taking a sip of wine and quickly grabbed a napkin. People glanced at them as she blotted up the dribble on her chin. "Jesus, Riley, chin balls? You're not a turkey."

"Would you still love me if I had a wattle?" he asked with the utmost gravity.

She smirked, sensing his fancy pants were getting a little tight. "Yes. I'd still love you."

The waiter brought out their second course, a spectacular crab ravioli that melted in her mouth. She didn't want to think about the price of their dinner. Everything was so lavish and delicious. She'd never tasted anything like it.

Once she'd spent Thanksgiving with the Lockharts. It was extravagant and formal, but mostly weird. Riley and Rarity were nothing like their parents. She wasn't sure what reminded her of that holiday, but now that she'd remembered how awkward that evening was she wanted to avoid a repeat episode.

"Would you like to come home with me for Thanksgiving?" she asked.

He stilled and slowly grinned. "Absolutely."

Sometimes, when she caught him off guard, she saw flashes of vulnerability behind the laughter. Inviting him to her home for the holidays did just that. Although he appeared unshakable, he harbored insecurities. It was endearing to be reminded that he was as human as she.

Sliding her hand into his, she squeezed. "I love you, Riley. Tonight's been amazing."

His smile faded as he leaned close and brushed his lips softly over hers. Chills chased over her arms as her chest lifted, pressing into him. She dragged the tip of her tongue over his full lower lip, not wanting to get too carried away in the fancy restaurant, but needing to taste him.

"Riley?"

"Hmmm," he hummed, nibbling.

Pressing her forehead to his, she whispered over his lips. "I know this is our first date and there were probably some rules in that article you read, but I'm pretty sure I'm going to let you have sex with me tonight."

"I'm pretty sure I'm gonna say yes."

She giggled as he kissed her once more, their desire mounting toward inappropriate.

A throat cleared. "Emma?"

Her entire body stiffened. Recognizing his voice, she took a moment to make eye contact with Riley. His expression hardened as she pulled back, took a galvanizing breath, and turned. But her gaze didn't go to Becket. It went to the long, artificially tanned legs leading into a very mini lace dress.

Goldie.

Her stomach dropped like a grand piano falling from a penthouse window, audibly forcing her breath out of her throat. The girl was a size negative two with double-D breasts and the whitest teeth she'd ever seen. Against her fake tan and platinum hair she looked as plastic and as flawless as Barbie herself.

"Grayson," Riley finally greeted, reminding Emma she was staring.

"Lockhart. I almost didn't recognize you."

Emma ripped her focus from the other woman. "What are you doing here, Becket?"

"We're meeting friends for dinner. How have you been?"

How had she been? A second ago she was fine. Now she wasn't sure how to describe her state.

"We're great," Riley answered for the both of them, sliding his arm over her shoulders.

"Where are my manners? Emma, this is Goldie Haslett. Goldie, this is Emma Sanders. We used to be an item."

Was he fucking kidding? They were supposed to get married. Didn't that tramp know who she was? Wasn't she aware that *she* was the other woman?

"It's nice to meet you," Goldie chirped and held out a hand, fingers down like she expected someone to kiss them. Emma stared at her airbrushed nails and swallowed back the taste of bile.

"Well, we won't keep you," Riley said.

Becket nodded. "Nice seeing you, Emma. Enjoy your evening." He took Malibu Barbie's arm and followed the patiently waiting hostess to their table.

"You okay?" Riley whispered the moment they were relatively alone again.

Slowly, she looked down at the table, feeling

like she'd fallen out of a dream and landed in a nightmare.

"Em?"

"Yeah," she rasped. "Sorry. I just… phew."

"Here, take a sip of wine." Her glass drifted into her line of vision.

She drank heavily until the goblet was empty. "She was, like, twelve." A sound of distaste formed in the back of her throat. "There wasn't one natural thing about her. I don't get it. How does someone go from me to that?"

"He downgraded, if you ask me," Riley joked, his quick laughter fading as she showed no sign of amusement.

"Where's the waiter? I need more wine."

"Here, have mine."

The weight of his glass filled her fingers. "I mean, I guess that's what guys want, big, perky breasts and a waist the size of my wrist. Her thighs didn't even touch in that handkerchief she was passing off as a dress. And did you see how high her shoes were?"

"I didn't look."

"Oh my God, he must think about me and my cheap clothes and laugh."

"Emma—"

"I mean what the hell? Her purse cost more than my entire outfit."

"So what?"

"What a joke I must be… *we used to be an item.* How about I was meant to be his fucking wife?"

"Shh…"

She reached for her purse, her hand notice-ably trembling. "I gotta get out of here."

Rising, she bumped the table, sloshing the water and causing silverware to clank. The humiliation just kept accumulating.

He caught her wrist, his eyes tight with concern as he studied her. "Emma, wait a second. Slow down."

If she didn't get out of there she'd start crying and really make a scene. Shaking off his grip, she whispered, "I can't. I'm sorry."

People turned to stare at her as she made a quick escape. There was nowhere to hide from their scrutiny.

Sliding around the table, she dodged a waiter and weaved through the dining room until she spotted the exit. Glancing back, she saw Riley reach for his wallet as a concerned waiter approached. Guilt swamped her as she fled. He'd created such a magical night, but Becket's sudden appearance brought every one of her flaws into the glaring light and spoiled everything.

How was it, in a city of eight million people and nearly twenty thousand restaurants, her ex picked this one on this night? Hurrying past the hostess desk, the doorman quickly held the doors as she rushed outside into the cool evening air.

"Emma!" Riley came after her.

Humiliated, she couldn't bring herself to face him. She didn't stop until she reached the curb and nearly walked right into traffic. He grabbed her arm and jerked her away from the street. "What are you doing?"

Shaking off his constricting hold, she scowled. "Don't grab me like that."

"Then get away from the street."

"I'm not a child, Riley! I know how to not get hit by a car."

"You went from totally okay to maniac in two seconds flat. Give me a moment to catch up."

Her mouth fell open and she shoved him. Didn't he get what just happened? "I'm not crazy!" Turning, she marched toward home.

"Damn it, Emma, wait!"

"Leave me alone. You don't get it."

He followed as she made her way through the oncoming pedestrians. "Leave you alone? Nice. We were having a perfectly good evening until they showed up. This isn't my fault, but you're sure acting like it is."

"That must be because I'm a maniac." She crossed the street.

"I meant you were *acting like one.* There's a difference."

He was right, but she couldn't get it together, not when all her imperfections were laid bare in the glaring light bouncing off Goldie's pearly teeth and frosted hair. Her chest tightened painfully. These shoes were not intended for fast getaways.

Her throat closed as she fought back the urge to cry. She *was* being a maniac and she didn't know why—well, she knew, but her excuse was shameful. No one liked insecure women. Riley didn't deserve this, but she was too far-gone to collect her dignity and act like nothing happened. She needed a few moments of privacy to fall apart in peace and then she could go back to acting like overly beautiful women didn't intimidate the crap out of her—even when they stole her life and were living it better than she ever had.

"Just leave me alone."

"God damn it, Emma. Do you want your wrap?"

"What?"

"Your shawl thing. We left without it."

"Great." She'd just bought that, but it's what she deserved for storming out of a four star restaurant like a jackass.

He sighed, his frustration clear. "I'll go back and get it."

"Forget it." She sniffled, the loss of her wrap being the straw that broke the fat ex-fiancée's back. "Please just leave me alone, Riley." She didn't want him to see her cry over stupid Becket. It was an unstoppable, pathetic female moment that was happening whether she permitted it or not. The less witnesses to her shame, the better.

He stopped following her and her tears fell faster. She expected too much from him. This wasn't Riley her roommate. It was Riley her boyfriend, and a breakdown over an ex-lover was the last thing he should have to witness, and the last thing she expected to happen—let alone tonight.

"I'm going back to get your shawl. I'll meet you at the loft."

She kept walking, needing the privacy to pull herself together. She'd ruined their night and that only made her more upset. The shock that Becket could still affect her in such a way was too much to process and the fact that it happened right in front of Riley was beyond humiliating.

When she finally entered the loft, she threw her purse at the couch and marched straight to her room. Yanking off her heels, she hurled them into the closet. The moment she caught her reflection in her vanity mirror, she broke and cried in earnest.

Lip gloss gone, her mouth was stained from merlot. Black makeup ran down her cheeks leaving her resembling a drunken raccoon. And under it all was her pale, unmanicured, frizzy haired, plump self. She yanked off her earrings and chucked them on the vanity.

The front door slammed and Marla let out a sleepy woof from the bed. "Emma?"

She really didn't want him to see her right now. Maybe if she were quiet he'd leave her alone.

The door creaked as he stood at the threshold to her bedroom, her wrap draped over his arm. "What are you doing?"

Wiping her eyes, she added another smudge of black to her cheeks. "Please go away, Riley."

"No." He walked into her room and tossed her wrap on the bed. She lowered her head as he paced behind her. Embarrassment constricted her breathing as she waited for him to yell at her for acting like a psycho and a shrew. He had every right to be angry. She was angry with herself.

"Why are we fighting over your ex?" he snapped.

"We're not fighting," she argued, her adrenaline fading to emotional exhaustion.

"The hell we aren't. You freaked out, left me in the middle of a restaurant, ran from Central Park West to here and freaking shoved me. What the hell, Emma?"

"You called me a maniac!" She lashed out, too overwhelmed to argue logically.

"You were acting like one! I was only trying to understand what was wrong and help you, but you jumped down my throat."

Disgusted with herself and her behavior, she wiped her nose. "I'm sorry."

He stopped pacing and shook his head. "Just…just tell me why you're so upset."

She laughed and started to cry again. "Weren't you there? Didn't you see her?"

"Who? Goldie? Yes, I saw her, but I didn't see anything special." He let out a frustrated breath. "Is it…Grayson? Are you jealous she has him?"

"No," she spat. "It's not that she has him, it's that he's with *her*."

She couldn't compete with that runway height or poise. There was an extreme difference between women like that and ordinary, dumpy women like her. Sooner or later there would be another *Goldie*, only this time she'd take Riley, which she couldn't stomach. Feeling threatened and small, she gave up, too much insecurity to explain in one evening.

"I don't understand why she matters, Emma. Please talk to me."

Wiping her nose with the back of her hand, she mumbled, "All this time I've been telling myself he downgraded." She laughed derisively. "What a joke. *Clearly*, I was wrong."

"Are you…" He laughed. "Are you out of your mind? Emma, that girl back there, nothing about her was real. She probably spends hours trying to imitate a quarter of the natural beauty you have. Girls like that are everywhere. It's a matter of buying the skank clothes and paying for a spray tan, some Botox, and whatever else the sugar daddy will provide. It's all fake."

"You don't understand. It's what guys like and *none of it* is me."

In a low voice, he said, "It's not what I like."

He crouched beside her vanity and cupped his hands on the side of her neck, urging her to face him. "You're beautiful, Emma. You don't need any of that fake crap. Girls like her wish they had what you have."

He handed her a tissue and she wiped her nose. "But *he* doesn't see it that way."

He looked down and she hated that her confession hurt him. "I see."

"I just wish he knew what he lost. I wish he saw me the way you do." *And I wish I had a guarantee that you'll always see me that way.*

"Why does it matter, Emma? There are some people in this world whose views and priorities are so screwed up we're never gonna impress them without sacrificing what really counts. They're judgmental and critical and overly concerned with superficial bullshit. Don't lower yourself to be something according to their standards, because their standards are garbage."

He shook his head, as if struggling to clearly explain his thoughts. "You're a unique brand others can't replicate, Em. Be okay with being you."

Even in her most illogical state, he was patient. When would she finally accept that he was *not* like other men? Her mouth tightened as she wiped her eyes. "I'm sorry I shoved you and spoke to you that way."

He kissed her nose. "I forgive you." He stood and pulled her to stand. "Come with me."

She followed him into the kitchen where he sat her on a stool. Unfolding a dishtowel, he ran warm water over it, and wrung it out. Tipping up her chin, he gently wiped at her eyes.

Concentration played on his face, as he focused on her cheeks and the soft skin beneath her lashes. She closed her eyes, trembling, trying to recall when anyone other than her mother took this much care or showed such concern for her.

"You don't need any of this," he whispered, swiping the wet cloth over her lids. "There."

Cool air teased her damp face as she opened her eyes and blinked at him. Her heart pinched so tight with unprecedented emotion, her voice strained to speak. "Where did you come from, Riley?"

He smirked and tossed the cloth in the sink. Taking her hand, he led her to the couch. Stripping off his jacket, he sat in the center, and pulled her to his lap so she was straddling him.

She was wrung out from crying. Tired. Pulling her into a hug, he pressed her cheek to his shoulder and rubbed her back. After a few minutes of simply holding her, he gently unzipped her dress and ran his fingers over her spine. His touch soothed her like nothing else could.

His mouth closed over the edge of her shoulder, gently kissed as the sleeve of her dress lowered. "These shoulders," he whispered, "they say a lot about you."

He caressed her throat and dragged his lips to her other collarbone. "When they're low, I know something's weighing on you. Do you know how beautifully you wear your courage? I love watching your shoulders rise in the face of a challenge. It's not the delicate slope that turns me on. It's the language they speak when you're silent. Your whole face lights up when you hold your shoulders high. It's like you're fearless."

His hands traced her calves, up to her knees then to her hips. As he gathered the skirt of her dress, she lifted, allowing him to pull it off. A slow chill crept over her exposed skin as he studied her.

"What you call flaws I call feminine, Emma. Your curves don't detract from your beauty. I like softness, boobs, hips, and all those things I don't have. Don't let some plastic reproduction make you ashamed of your natural form."

He dragged his hand over her lower belly and she instinctively sat up. "See this," he whispered. "Soft. I love your little tummy. I think it's ultra feminine, like your thighs. Those curves are lush, fruitful, something a healthy woman should have."

He unhooked her bra and pulled it away. Cupping her breasts, he leisurely massaged. "I don't care about the symmetry of your tits or the size. I just like to hold them, play with them, watch the blood rush to the tips as your nipples get hard and you get aroused. I think about your boobs all the time, Emma, and I *never* think a negative thought. I love them. I want to build a fort between them and suck them and blow motorboats on them because I'm a guy and that's the dumb shit we're into."

She laughed, her tears of sadness washed away by tears of relief. He was right—perfect even—and she hated that running into her ex had made her question their special connection.

"There's that beautiful smile." He grinned. "The day we went to the park, right after we got Marla, I told you that you were a great person and you turned and smiled at me. I was lost in that moment, Em. Between your smile and those sweet brown eyes, I'm a goner."

He nudged her hip. "Stand up."

She slid off of his lap and stood in front of him as he unbuttoned his shirt and tossed it aside. His belt loosened and he unclasped his slacks, noticeably hard.

When he rested his arms on the back of the couch, he took a long look at her. She tried not to fidget, but it wasn't easy.

"I think the most attractive thing about you, Em, is that you have no idea how beautiful you really are. Your laugh, your scent, they're all parts of your attractiveness, but everyone doesn't get the chance to make you laugh or smell your neck first thing in the morning. That mole you hate on your back? I'm obsessed with it. It makes me crazy when I catch a glimpse of it under your bra strap."

He leaned forward and carefully removed her panties. Her lashes lowered as excruciating awareness stole over her, making it difficult not to cover herself, but she remained still for him. His finger teased at the soft hair at her apex and she sighed. Her sex pulsed when she heard the clank of his belt hit the floor. Scooting forward, he kissed her stomach and cupped her ass, pulling her closer as he stroked himself.

His teeth nipped her hip as he pulled back and took her hands, guiding her to his lap again. Although they were running through every flaw she personally hated, he'd somehow managed to change her thinking, offering the slightest glimpse of her through his eyes. If he only knew how she saw him. But he never would, because there simply weren't words for how incredible he was to her.

Straddling him, she braced her hands on his

shoulders as he stretched, dragging his arousal between her thighs. Parting her sex, he released his flesh and cupped her hips, pressing her low.

She gasped as he slowly filled her. He thrust leisurely, dragging her body over his, creating delicious friction as she adjusted to his width. His hands fondled her breasts as he studied her.

"It doesn't matter how you dress or do your hair, Emma." He leaned close and kissed her shoulder. "The sexiest thing you can wear is a smile I gave you, the kind that goes all the way to your eyes."

Locking her fingers behind his neck, she lifted and deliberately came down, taking him deep. His words, more than his body, had her physically trembling.

Pulling his mouth to hers, she kissed him and whispered, "You're the most amazing man I've ever met. I love you for loving me the way you do."

"I love you so much. Never doubt that, Em."

She tightened her arms around his neck and found his mouth with hers. Making love had never been so raw or vulnerable, but she had no defense against him.

There was no hiding from Riley and there never would be, so long as he continued to look past the surface and see the real her he'd always have every bit of her soul, even the ugly pieces she struggled to disguise. But that was okay, because he apparently wanted them too.

CHAPTER 10

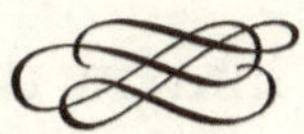

"Can you wash the strawberries?"

Riley carried the basket to the sink and adjusted the water. It was Thanksgiving and Emma was wearing the little apron with the pink polka dots, so he was on high alert. Whatever she was baking smelled awesome and he couldn't wait to eat it.

Lexi came out of Rarity's bedroom, her black hair in perfect order as she buttoned her jacket. "Something smells delicious. What are you making, Emma?"

"Strawberry short cake. It's my special recipe."

Rarity joined them, stealing a strawberry. She hugged Lexi and kissed her long cocoa neck. "I'll call you when I'm back."

Lexi sent her a sidelong glance, which he interpreted as disappointment.

"Sittin' out another holiday, Lex?" Riley

thought it was ridiculous that his sister still hid the fact that she was a lesbian from their parents.

"Not by choice," Lexi said, her frustration clear. Nabbing a berry for the road, she grinned and grabbed her purse. "I'll see you guys later. Happy Thanksgiving."

Rarity smacked him in the head and water splashed on his shirt. "Watch it! I'm handling the berries."

"Thanks, moron," she snapped, going after Lexi.

"You shouldn't have said that, Riley. You know how your parents are."

He shut off the faucet and carried the fruit to the counter. Maybe they were all hiding from his parents to some degree. "I know. I can be a jerk. I'll apologize when she comes back."

"Do you want to start slicing?"

"Sure." He grabbed a knife and began butchering a strawberry.

"No." Emma took the knife. "Like this."

Stepping behind her he rested his chin on her shoulder as she showed him how to properly chop a berry. Sighing, he slipped his arms around her waist, hugging her from behind. "I'm not gonna lie, you in the kitchen totally turns me on."

She giggled. "It does?"

"Mmm-hmm." He breathed in her scent, pressing his face to the curve of her neck.

"Riley, I'm using a knife."

He kissed her ear and she shivered, pressing her cheek to her shoulder and forcing him out.

"Let me feed you berries while you're wearing nothing but that apron."

"Okay," she agreed easily, immediately doubling his excitement. "But not today. We have too much to do."

He groaned. Holidays were so tedious. His family always managed to screw up the simplest meal with talk of disappointments and unreachable expectations. Maybe her family dinners would be different.

She handed him the knife and he carefully cut them as instructed. He really would've liked some morning sex before they started the busy day, but when he woke up she was already running around like a crazy person. The idea of meeting her parents had him mildly freaked out. Sex would've been a nice stress reliever.

Trying to keep his thoughts away from the boudoir, he focused on other things. "I think strawberries are one of the sexier fruits." He really had a one-dimensional mind.

"What?"

"Well, there's the banana, of course, but that's obvious."

"Are you telling me you find fruit erotic?" She used that weird wire tool to make the frosting he wasn't allowed to taste.

"Only the sexy ones. Kumquats should be sexy, but they're not. They're just a sad cross between a yellow tomato and an orange, but with a filthy name—kumquats." He loved pronouncing it in a slow Sean Connery voice.

She added sugar. "You've really thought about this."

"Doesn't everyone?"

"No."

"I bet they do. They just don't talk about it."

"I'm pretty sure they don't. When you're done slicing them put them in this bowl."

He scooped up a handful and tossed them in the dish. "Not only is the juice of a strawberry sexy, like, I want to smear it on your boobies sexy, but the seeds scream suggestive. I mean, they're wearing their fertility where everyone can see. It's more than sexy, really, they're a little slutty."

"That should be enough berries. Stick the rest back in the fridge." She took the bowl of cut berries and sprinkled sugar on top.

He frowned.

She glanced at him, smirked, and continued to toss the berries in her sexy apron. "What's the matter, Riley?"

"I'm all turned on from strawberries."

"Then go take a shower, because I still have to do my hair and make the cranberry sauce."

He pouted. "You're mean on Thanksgiving."

The elevator pinged in the hall. "And your sister's back."

"Damn it." He went to grab a towel.

～

THE CLOSER THEY got to Emma's parents' house the more he fidgeted. He'd never met a girl's parents before—not as the official boyfriend. He didn't know what to expect and kept thinking of his parents—the people expected to unconditionally love and accept him—but they didn't like him very much, so why would someone else's parents like him at all?

"Turn right at that stop sign."

He slowed and turned onto a street with small, two story homes that looked remarkably alike. Though they were in the suburbs, the houses were right on top of each other, providing minimal privacy between neighbors.

"It's that one there, with the blue door."

He parked in front of the mailbox since the driveway was full. The house was plain brick, but well kept. It wasn't until they were walking up the path that he realized it was a duplex. The moment they stepped on the porch claustrophobia set in.

Not giving him much time to prepare, Emma opened the door and walked in. "Mom? Dad? We're here."

The house smelled like other people's cooking and fake gingerbread. He was immediately homesick for the loft.

"Emma? Oh, you made it!"

Though he'd seen her parents in a sea of other parents years ago during school events, he never took the time to really look at them. Mrs. Sanders was Emma twenty years from now, but with straight hair and different laugh lines. She was younger than he expected.

"You must be Riley. I know we've met before,

but you were a boy the last time I saw you. My goodness you resemble your sister—in a handsome way of course." She hugged him and he wasn't sure where to put his hands.

"Nice to see you again, Mrs. Sanders."

She tsked. "Call me Sarah. Emma's dad's around here somewhere." She turned away from them. "Jim? Emma's here."

A man, wearing dark jeans and a US Navy T-shirt, came in from the back door. "Hey, Emmy!" He hugged her and Riley stepped back, his confidence falling off kilter as Emma's attention turned to her father.

This was the man he needed to impress. Strangely, his casual appearance made him more intimidating, like they were closer to equals and he'd easily sniff out any bullshit regarding his daughter.

"Dad, you know Riley. Riley, this is my dad."

"Hey there, Riley." The man had a casual but firm shake.

"How are you, sir?"

"Good. That your DeVille out there?"

God, he was sweating. "Yes, sir."

Mr. Sanders nodded and peeked out the front window. "What year's that?"

"Fifty-seven, sir. It was a gift from my grandfather."

"Nice. You want a beer?"

Emma smiled at him and his apprehension somewhat eased, the day sliding into a place he hadn't expected, yet her parents' personable attitudes adding to his paranoia in a strange way.

These people were *nothing* like the people who raised him—or paid nannies to do the job. These were just good old regular people, and he wasn't used to that where parents were concerned.

He smiled at Mr. Sanders. "A beer would be great."

The women went to the kitchen as he and Jim watched football in the living room. The furniture was dated and the décor was nothing his mother would approve or even sit on, but Riley absolutely loved it. He even adjusted to the gingerbread smell, which he discovered came from a plugin air freshener.

The food was awesome, deep fried turkey, boxed mac and cheese, stuffing that tasted incredible, yams with melted marshmallows on top, and Emma's sweet strawberry shortcake.

After dinner Sarah brewed a pot of coffee and placed it on a stained potholder right on the dining room table. None of their mugs matched.

Everything was so spectacularly different from what he'd known, he pitied Rarity for missing it. She was probably contemplating suicide as their mother passed around cordials.

"Did you hear anything on the job front, Emma?" Sarah asked.

"Nothing yet. I sent out four more resumes. For now I'm stuck at Phibbs & Grayson."

"I'd like to have an hour alone with that Grayson kid," her dad mumbled.

"You and me both," Riley agreed.

Jim eyed him for a moment and nodded. "I like you, Riley. I have a good feeling about you."

It was amazing how much weight he'd placed in her parents' approval. "Thank you, sir."

"You'll have to come visit again sometime," Sarah invited. "And bring this dog I keep hearing about."

"I think Marla's a little too wild to travel, Mom."

"Nonsense. I miss having a dog. I'd love to meet her."

He spoke before giving his words a second thought. "You guys are always welcome at the loft."

Sarah and Jim shared a mutual look of surprise. "Well, that's a first. We'd love to come for a visit, maybe see the Empire State Building or the Statue of Liberty."

He smiled, ignoring the look of panic Emma sent him. "It'll be great. We'll make a day of it, visit Central Park, have dinner at Peter Lugers. You'll love it."

"What does a New York cut of beef sell for at a place like that?" Jim asked.

"It would be my treat."

The energy at the table shifted. Shit. Had he insulted them? He was merely trying to be accommodating, polite. A New York steakhouse usually averaged a hundred dollars per person for dinner and he'd wanted to show them a nice time.

"There are other places we could eat in the city too," Emma chimed in. "Riley took me to this great food festival in Brooklyn and it was amazing."

"That sounds more our pace." Sarah smiled.

"I'm sorry. I didn't—"

"It's fine, hon," she interrupted, patting his hand.

"Well, we should get going. Marla's been alone all day and she's probably pacing by now."

They stood and Riley hated leaving things as they were. Everything had been going so smooth. He wasn't a pretentious prick and he didn't want them thinking he was.

Emma hugged her mom at the door and Jim faced him. "Good seeing you again, Riley."

He shook his hand. "Nice seeing you too, sir."

He held out his arms and hugged his daughter. "Be safe, Emmy."

"I will, Dad. Love you."

Fascinated, Riley watched as her eyes closed and she hugged her father close. He'd never hugged either of his parents like that. He'd once had a nanny that liked to tousle his hair, but that wasn't the same.

The drive home was passed in quiet reflection. Emma seemed sad to leave her parents, but anxious to get back to Marla. Meeting her parents as more than an acquaintance and getting a glimpse of where she came from filled in a lot of gaps in the Emma puzzle.

Although neither he nor Rarity was captivated by wealth, they'd grown up with a great deal of it and had an easy life by default. There were trusts and bonds they both had waiting, should they jump through the prerequisite hoops stipulated in their ancestor's wills. As it were, they hardly needed to work, but found it rewarding and refreshingly normal in comparison to what they grew up around.

Emma, on the other hand, absolutely needed to work. According to his sister, Emma's grandparents had sent her to private schools and left a supplemental income for books, boarding, and transportation, but that money was long gone, skipping right over her parents as a direct investment in their only child's future.

As well intentioned as it was, they hadn't planned nearly enough, because once Emma finished her first year of college that money was gone, which was how she'd ended up working at Grayson's dad's firm—something that really needed to end. After their date the other night, he didn't like the chance of her running into that guy again.

When they got home there was a note on the fridge from Rarity saying she was spending the night at Lexi's.

"I'm going to walk Marla," Emma announced as the dog wagged wildly at the door.

"Do you want me to come with you?"

"That's okay. I won't be long."

When she left he changed into lounge pants and grabbed his copy of *As the Great World Turns.* The peaceful apartment made an easy escape from the day left behind. Settling onto his bed, he opened the book.

Deep into the chapter, Marla greeted him, having returned from their walk then disappeared—probably to lie on Rarity's bed. He was just falling asleep when Emma cleared her throat.

Unhurriedly glancing to the door he—*sweet mother of sex.*

She was holding a bowl of strawberries, wearing nothing but the apron. He tossed the book to the floor and scooted back. "Come to poppa."

Her lips pursed in a flirty smile as she sauntered inside, bumping the door shut with her hip. God, he loved her and her sexy ass fruit.

"I have some berries I'd like you to taste."

He tugged her to his lap and she giggled. Biting her lips, he untied the neck of the apron and sung, "*Let me pull this down cause I'm going to... your strawberry fields.*" His mouth found hers, sweeter than any berry.

Dirty, dirty girl.

~

THE DOOR SLAMMED and he jolted awake. Emma tossed her coat on the floor by the pile of wrapped Christmas presents and kicked a box of ribbons. Shit. She didn't get the job.

Scrubbing his face with his hands he sat up. "How did the interview go?"

"Horrible. What a joke! By the time it was my turn they'd already given the job to the guy's niece. If people are going to practice nepotism they should at least own it and not waste everyone else's time making them think there's an actual shot!"

"I'm sorry, cakes."

She tugged the pins out of her hair and kicked off her shoes, growling as she untwisted her bun. "I'm going to be stuck at Phibbs & Grayson for the rest of my freaking life!"

"No, you're not. Eventually something will pan out."

She dropped on the bed and fisted her hands in her lap. "Becket starts his internship this spring. I cannot work there with him, Riley."

"So quit."

She laughed without humor. "Oh, okay." Shaking her head she sighed. "I never should've taken this stupid job."

Truthfully, he didn't want her working with her ex either. "If you could be anything in the world, what would it be?"

Her shoulders drooped. "Happy."

Was it wrong he found her pathetic pout adorable? "Aw, look at you. That's the cutest answer ever."

"Yeah, well I can't pay the rent with smiles, so I still need another goal."

He pulled her to the pillows. "Do you like being a personal assistant?"

She shrugged. "I don't know. It's a fun job in a way, different every day, fast paced. I like keeping things organized and planning events."

She really was organized. If not for her, the loft would be a dump. She always had handy ideas, like using the tabs from bread bags to label the cluster fuck of extension cords behind the television.

"Maybe you could be an independent organizer."

Her mouth twisted. "That's not a real job."

"Sure it is. There are always those people on those shows with the hoarders. There's the host, the carpenter, the designer, and the organizational chick. Sometimes it's a gay guy."

"That's on TV."

When she adopted a stubborn attitude he found it difficult to talk to her. "Fine. Go back to working with your ex in-laws." He pulled a pillow over his head and shut his eyes.

She was quiet for a few minutes. "Do you really think there's work out there for people like that?"

Without moving, he said, "I think we live in a city of millions where people want to maximize every expensive square inch they're paying top dollar for, so yes, I think there's a demand for organization."

"But would someone actually hire someone to do that for them?"

"Why not?" He removed the pillow from his face. "Alicia Keys said it's a concrete jungle dreams are made of. Listen to the woman."

She swatted him. "I'm being serious."

He grinned, seeing a bit of her tension slip away. "New York's a costly place to live, Emma. People have to work in order to stay here. People who have demanding jobs often contract out the maintenance stuff."

"Yeah, but that would require running a business. I don't know how to do that."

"You run everything for the CEO of a major law firm. I'm sure you could figure it out. You could build a webpage, have Rarity take some pictures, create a brand, and market your services toward Manhattan clientele. I bet you could make a killing. The thing about New York real estate is there's a fast turnover rate of residents. Once you get your name out there, who knows what could happen?"

Her eyes widened at the possibility. "Did you just think of all that?"

He shrugged. "Yeah."

"You're a genius, Riley. Thank you." She kissed his head. "I gotta go talk to Rarity." She jumped off the bed and raced out of the room.

"I also work for blowjobs," he yelled.

She peeked back into the room, a wide grin spread across her face. "Tonight." And she, again, disappeared.

"Anything for that smile," he mumbled and curled back into the pillows, happy to have helped.

~

"So I was thinking some dirty Disney sex tonight, hmm? Maybe some Little Mermaid post-fin fun? I could show you how to use those new legs and you could try to communicate using only your eyes and body." He was already getting a semi.

Without glancing away from the laptop, her

hand jotted down notes on a post-it as she asked, "What are you saying?"

He nudged her with his hip. "I wanna have sex."

She still didn't look at him. "I don't know where I put it."

He huffed. "You aren't even listening to me."

She made another note. "Sorry. I'm just trying to figure out these codes for this website host. Do you know what a widget is?"

"I think it's that little nub above your hoo-ha that makes you squeal and call my name."

She laughed and rolled her eyes. At least she heard him that time. "You know, if I make flyers and put them by the mailboxes of high rises, all I'd need is one client and then tenants would talk and my name would be passed around. I need all of this stuff to match. The cards, the flyers, the website. If I could just get this stupid widget coding figured out."

"Emma," he whined. "Come on, you've been staring at that computer for days. I wanna play with your widget! You're wearing your glasses and your hair's all sloppy. You know what that does to me! I need attention."

She sighed. "If you can be quiet for thirty minutes so I can figure this out I'll give you a blowjob."

He sat up. "Really?"

"Yes. Shh."

Buttoning his lips tight, he waited. How did he want to do this? Should he be standing or on his back? Maybe on his knees with her on her back? There were so many options and he was already hard. Twenty-nine minutes to go.

His toes twitched as he tried to pass the time. Steve Miller Band sung in his head. Emma didn't move. She just stared at the computer and clicked and made notes and did that adorable squish thing her nose did when she got frustrated.

Twenty-seven minutes.

He quietly whistled. She could at least work naked. Glasses on, panties off…

"You're the cutest thing I—"

"Shhh…"

Twenty-three minutes. *"Really love your peaches—"*

"Come on, Riley!"

He held out his hands in surrender. "Hey, I'm ready."

She slapped down her pen. "It hasn't even been ten minutes."

"You *know* I can't be silent. It's torture."

"I need to get this done. My business cards are coming in two days and I can't hand them out until the website's finished."

"I don't know why you insist on doing all this by yourself. There are people that can design that stuff for you."

"I can't afford a web designer at this stage. It's not in my budget plan."

"I'll get one for you. We'll pretend it's a Christmas present."

"Riley." That was her serious voice.

"Fine." Clearly there was no persuading her

away from that computer. She was really excited about this new venture and he was excited she'd soon be leaving her crappy job. "I'm going to find food."

He left her alone to finish her work and ended up getting wrapped up in some reality show with Rarity and passing out on the couch. When he finally made it to bed it was after four in the morning.

Grabbing a bottle of water, he staggered down the hall. Just about to fall into bed, he stopped when he found Emma still hunched over the computer. "You're still up?"

Her eyes were frantic and there were coffee cups all over the vanity, which was now her workstation. "Yeah. I just read this article about holding a virtual campaign. I don't have any of this done. I need a mailing list, a uniformed font to brand my company, a mission statement—"

He shut her laptop.

"Hey!"

"You need sleep." Picking her up, he carried her to the bed and pulled off her pants. Stripping, he climbed under the covers and pulled her close.

"I have so much to do if I want to open for business by the New Year."

He leaned over and shut off the lamp. "Go to sleep, Emma."

Wrapping his body around hers, he hugged her like a pillow and shut his eyes, already half-asleep. She'd be up, stressing, for at least another hour, but he wasn't letting her out of bed. Everything else could wait. It was his time now and she was putting herself under way too much stress. It would all be there in the morning.

∼

ALL SIGNALS WERE A GO.

Rarity was gone for the night. Emma hadn't touched her laptop all day. When he'd spotted her curled up on the couch with the boo-boo blanket he suspected he'd miscalculated her cycle, but after checking the bathroom cabinet he ascertained he was in the clear.

It was go time. Sex was happening.

Locking the door, he snatched a dog treat for Marla and threw it on his sister's bed. Marla happily chased after it and curled into Rarity's pillows. Door closed, one obstacle handled.

As he returned to the kitchen, he lowered the lights and lit the flowery scented candle Emma had picked up at Pier One. Ambiance—check! It was time to pounce.

His prey rests unsuspecting in her remote habitat commonly referred to as the couch. Drifting slowly in the shadows, he, the predator, breaches her sanctuary. Unaware, the female lay with her crown poised vulnerably on her raised knee as she perches in wait.

The female tolerates the dominant male in the den of iniquity, as he reveals his position. Settling beside her, he conspicuously unveils his desire with a glance, commonly recognized by the female of the species as the pre-mating smolder. Prepared to ravish the female, the predator eases in for the hunt and reaches for a teat.

Emma shouldered him away. "I'm not in the mood."

Crikey! Shot down again. And why was his inner monologue suddenly in an Australian accent?

He shook off her rejection and tried for a different approach. Casually rubbing her knee through the blanket, he smiled. "You feelin' okay?"

"I'm fine." She didn't take her gaze off the television.

"Everything going okay with your website?" Maybe she was overwhelmed.

"It's good enough."

This was not his little perfectionist. Something was wrong. "Emma, did I do something to upset you?"

"Jesus, Riley, not everything has to do with you!"

Drawing back, he scowled at her. "What's wrong with you?"

She turned, her eyes glassy with tears. "There automatically has to be something wrong with *me* because I don't feel like fucking you?"

"*Whoa!*" He held up his hands in surrender. "What crawled up your ass? I was just playing around. You know what?" He scoffed and stood. "Forget it. I'm going out. Have a fun night by yourself."

"Whatever." She stared back at the television no longer acknowledging his presence.

Whatever was right. Women and their fucking moods. He'd had enough.

CHAPTER 11

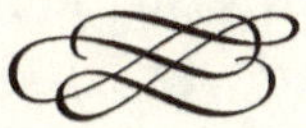

The moment Riley left Emma shut off the television. She'd been staring at it all day and not sure of a single thing she'd watched. Her entire body was tense and she was one tear away from shattering into a million pieces.

Locking the door and latching the chain, she went to the bathroom and tried to gather her courage. She'd waited all day for a moment alone, but now that it was here, she wished Riley or Rarity would come barging in. She couldn't do this.

Forcing the motions, not thinking about the purpose, she stripped. Staring at her reflection, seeing the woman before her as suddenly different, she studied herself. Her mind could only acknowledge bits and pieces of why she was staring at herself naked—not something she frequently did.

Her opinions were no longer harsh. On the

contrary, they were forgiving, remorseful. Those wrinkles by her eyes were too fine. Yesterday they marked her age, but today they marked her youth, tallied her smiles and she wanted more.

Her heart pounded beneath her breasts the lower her gaze dropped. Pale and translucent at parts, her breasts had yet to serve their true purpose. They were meant to nurse and that would leave stretch marks, scars she desperately wanted.

Her mouth tightened as her chin trembled and her throat went dry. Unshed tears blurred her vision. *No.* She was not going to cry like a little girl. She was going to power through and deal with whatever this was like a woman. *I'm a grown woman.*

Her eyes closed. *Then why do I still feel like a little kid?*

Her body was imperfect, but it was hers, her temple, her home, her only vessel in this world and it was possibly betraying her. Biting her lip, she opened her eyes and a wall of tears collapsed and fell unchecked.

Glancing at the door, she lifted her left arm over her head and breathed. She was an adult. She could face this. With the fingers of her right hand, she gently cupped her left breast and massaged. Using slow, circular motions she inspected the soft tissue, much like she had that morning while lying in bed, only this time she was alone.

Maybe this morning she'd made a mistake. Everything felt fine now. Nothing out of the—

"No," her voice croaked as if miles away.

Chin trembling, her fingers stilled over the hard mass in her left breast and the woman in the reflection broke. "No," she cried, stunned that something was there that hadn't been a week ago.

Her feet shifted as her posture twisted. No matter which way she turned it was there. Now that she'd located it her fingers couldn't seem to lose it. Tiny, hard, possibly just some fat or maybe an ingrown hair, but something was definitely there. It was real, not something she'd imagined.

Lowering her hand, forcing her inspecting fingers to still, she frowned at the irritated blotch now marking her soft flesh. No longer able to watch her reflection, she hugged her body and leaned into the tile wall. Her body shivered and she swore it was due to her lack of clothes, but her excuses fell short when the sudden urge to vomit hit.

Flashes of scalpels, needles, doctors' eyes peeking over medical masks collided in her mind's eye. Lowering her body to the floor, the strangest sensation took hold. It was as if she were a hostage in her own body, but nothing was familiar.

Her fingers pinched her thigh and she hissed. Very real. Not a dream. Tipping her head back, tears slowly rolled into her hair as she stared at the ceiling light until her vision bleached with white spots.

She wouldn't tell her mom. Maybe not even Riley. He'd freak out. She'd tell Rarity and make an appointment—hopefully before the holidays—shit. She'd probably have to wait until after Christmas. But once she had the appointment, she'd have the little cyst removed and then she'd tell Riley, proving there was nothing to worry about. He wouldn't be able to get mad she'd kept it from him, because it would be nothing. Nothing.

So much for concentrating on her business. She'd been unable to focus all day. If she didn't want him to suspect something was wrong, she'd have to be less transparent. He was already mad at her. She should call him and apologize.

The absolute ridiculousness of her inner debate jerked her back to reality. He was mad because she'd acted like a bitch. She acted like a bitch because she was terrified there might be a lump in her breast. She was now naked, crying on the bathroom floor because there was a lump. No maybe about it.

"Oh, God…" Her stomach twisted, but there was no nausea, not enough to induce vomiting. Still, everything inside of her wanted to throw up. Not only was vomiting impossible, her tears disappeared. Unable to properly cry, she sobbed and wailed a painful half cry unlike anything she'd ever experienced. The longer it went on the more furious she became that her body wasn't cooperating in *any* way. It was as if she no longer had control or a say in anything.

Unsure how long she sat there holding her body as she half cried, Emma considered all the fears she had yesterday and how small and silly they suddenly seemed.

She'd been so focused on starting her business and getting it off the ground by the New Year. What if this was her last year? She thought of her parents and Rarity and, hardest of all, Riley. As if an elephant were sitting on her chest, she gasped for air, unable to draw a full breath or shed one fucking tear.

All she could hear was absolute denial playing through her head as she rocked and whimpered. But the lump was there and no matter how she cried or twisted, she felt it every time.

It was too much. Her little world couldn't withstand this overwhelming fear, as everything she held dear seemed to be slipping away.

It took hours to form simple thoughts. She was supposed to be some guru of organization, yet she could barely recall her doctor's name, was utterly incapable of scheduling an appointment. She was in some state of shock, bordering on paralysis, and no one could help her. So she simply sat and stared.

The level of bravery needed to move was beyond her capabilities. This wasn't her life. It had to be a bad dream. Tomorrow she'd wake up and the lump would be gone, all of this a nightmare that seemed so real, but wasn't.

Too young. Too happy. Too personal. It was simply too much to be happening to her.

~

RILEY WAS MAD AT HER. She didn't blame him, but she also didn't have the energy to justify her cold attitude. Christmas was in less than a week and no one was taking appointments until well after the New Year.

Emma locked herself in her bedroom all day, claiming to wrap presents, unable to face her roommates, but she hadn't tied a single bow.

After only purchasing half the items on her list, she knew she wouldn't be shopping again. This was supposed to be a fun holiday with Riley. She had so many great gift ideas, yet only got him a few items and a shirt that said Save Ferris.

Around eight o'clock, she left her room, certain he'd gone to the inn for his shift and heartbroken all the more for the confusion her depression was causing him.

"It lives," Rarity teased as she walked down the hall.

Marla leapt from the bed and ran to greet her, but Emma wasn't in the mood. Locking herself in the bathroom, she stripped and took a long shower. The lump was the same, only now it hurt, which might have been from her incessant touching, but she wasn't sure.

After drying off, Emma wrapped the towel under her arms and brushed her wet hair. Her eyes looked terrible. She'd barely slept and almost every minute she'd been awake she'd cried. The tears she'd been waiting for now wouldn't stop. She couldn't go on like this.

Standing outside of Rarity's room, she quietly knocked on the door.

"Yesssss," Rarity called, being her usual quirky self.

Emma slid the door open and simply waited in her towel.

"What's wrong, toots?" Her friend's expression turned serious as she climbed off the bed.

"Can I talk to you?" Emma asked, trying her best not to fall apart.

"Of course." She pulled her into the room and they sat on the edge of the bed. She didn't know where to start. Eventually, Rarity asked, "Is this about Riley?"

She shook her head.

Rarity gripped her hands. "Did something happen at work?"

Swallowing, Emma rasped, "I found something."

"Where? What is it?"

"I found…a lump," she choked. "In my breast."

Rarity's hold tightened. Her lips parted as she blinked and whispered, "How long ago?"

"The other day, but it's real. It just showed up and now…" The pain in her chest expanded, engulfing her heart and she tensed.

Rarity pulled her into a hug. "Shhh…it's okay." Her reassurance seemed intended for both of them. Brushing a hand over her damp hair, she looked into her eyes and asked, "Can I see it?"

Emma nodded and sat back. Her hands trembled as she unknotted the towel. Her throat hurt from holding in her sobs. Lowering the damp terrycloth to her waist, she sat up and pointed to where the lump was. "It's right here."

Rarity squinted as she looked closely at the area. "It's red. Is it tender?"

"I keep touching it."

She nodded. "Can I feel it?"

Emma nodded and lifted her arm. Rarity scooted closer and delicately cupped the side of her breast. She massaged the tissue and Emma saw in her eyes the moment she felt the lump.

"I feel it. Right here. Does that hurt?"

"The skin's a little sore, but the lump doesn't really feel like anything."

Rarity lowered her hand. "Are there any more?"

"Not that I felt."

She exhaled roughly. "Does Riley know?"

Emma swallowed and dropped her face into her hands as she moaned through the incredible tension tying her inside in knots. The pressure in her chest was so extreme she could barely breathe. "I can't tell him. What if it's…" The word made her want to vomit. She couldn't say it out loud no matter how she tried. Her mind could barely think it. "…something bad?"

"What if it's nothing?"

"But what if it's something?"

Rarity hugged her and pulled the towel over her shoulders, carefully covering her up. "Emma, people have abnormalities all the time. You need to see a specialist before you assume anything. And I really think you need to tell my brother."

"I can't," she choked.

"Emma, how would you feel if Riley discovered an abnormality in his body and kept it from you? He loves you. You need to tell him."

"I don't want him to worry over nothing."

Rarity's shoulders slumped. "Toots, what do you think he's doing now? For two days you've done nothing but mope around like some zombie. You're not even speaking to each other. I know you're scared, but you're also scaring him. He thinks he did something wrong and it's killing him."

Her stomach twisted and her shoulders tightened as if she were going to be sick. It was the same nauseous reflex she'd been tolerating for days, but nothing ever came of it. It was just emotion and—

She quickly covered her mouth and forced herself to hold it together.

Rarity stood. "You okay? You need to go to the bathroom?"

She just needed a min—her shoulders locked again and Rarity flew into action, reaching for a wastepaper basket and quickly pulling her hair out of her face. Emma didn't have time to prepare as everything in her upset stomach rushed out.

The second it was over she started to sob. "I'm so sorry, Rarity."

"Shhh. It's fine. You're upset." She handed her a bottle of water and Emma drank. "Let's get you dressed and I'll make you some soup. We'll put on *Love Actually* and snuggle and talk. Sound good?"

Shaking, Emma nodded, unsure how this had

become her life when three days ago everything was perfect—she just hadn't realized that's what perfect looked like at the time.

~

IT HAD to be after two in the morning, but Emma wasn't tired. Confiding in Rarity was the best decision she'd made. Her stomach was somewhat settled and they were curled up on the couch watching reruns of SNL.

"What if I have to have a mastectomy?" she wondered aloud.

"Stop."

"I'm serious, Rarity. Don't act like that's an impossible outcome." No matter how much it seemed like an impossibility in her world, forcing herself to ask the question somehow braced her for the possibility.

"You're borrowing trouble, Emma."

"Then loan me some courage. Please. Because whether I discuss it or not, I can't stop the horrible thoughts from flinging around my head. I feel like I'm losing my mind and I have no idea how I'll survive myself over the next two weeks of waiting."

Her friend sighed. "Then you have a mastectomy, Emma. Saving you is more important than saving your breasts. Do you understand me?"

She nodded, needing to hear that. Rarity knew nothing more than she did on these matters, but somehow her no nonsense way was the balm Emma needed to get through the hysteria. Her mind was a scary place at the moment.

"It's just so hard. Once this is over, I may never be the same. Even if it turns out to be nothing, I've never been this scared in my life."

Rarity looked at her and rubbed her hand. "Honey, you're already different. This is daunting. It's so terrifying, the scare alone changes everything. This morning I was pissed off you used the rest of the cream cheese. Do you know how stupid that makes me feel now? You go ahead and use all the cheese you need. We'll get more."

She sniffled and squeezed her hand, drawing immeasurable comfort from her touch. "I love you, Rarity."

Studying her, Rarity slowly smiled and held out her arms. Emma slid into them and hugged her. "I love you too, toots." She kissed her head and squeezed, good and tight the way real hugs were meant to be.

The door opened and they froze. Emma turned in Rarity's arms and faced Riley. His eyes, taking in the moment, turned cold and distrustful. "What the fucks going on?"

"Riley—"

"I'm not talking to you, Rarity."

Emma frowned at him, disappointed he'd speak to his sister that way. "Riley, come inside and sit down."

Mouth tight, a mistrusting glint in his eyes, he dropped his keys in the bowl by the door and stepped into the living room.

Rarity stood and placed the blanket over Emma's legs. "I'll let you two talk. Goodnight, toots." She kissed her head. "Come on, Marla." The dog happily followed Rarity to what she now considered *her* bed.

As soon as the door shut, Riley spoke. "Feeling better?"

"Not really. Could you not be nasty right now?"

"Could you maybe tell me what the hell's been going on? You haven't said more than two words to me in over three days. Every time I try to touch even your hand you shove me away then I come home and you're curled up with my sister like long lost lovers."

She deserved that after not offering any explanation for her horrible mood of late. Drawing in a deep breath, she deliberately released it and looked at her lap. "Riley, I might be sick."

He stilled, his tense body shifting with jerky motions. "W—what?"

"I'm not sure yet, but I've called the doc—"

His entire demeanor changed and suddenly he was sitting beside her, pulling her close. "What kind of sick?"

He smelled so good. She pressed her face to his shirt and breathed. "I don't know anything yet. I haven't been to a doctor and no one can get me in until the second."

"I don't understand, Em. Are you throwing up? Do you have a fever? We can take you to an emergency clinic if you need to see someone."

She shook her head. "No. I need to see my

personal physician before I do anything. I'm gonna need a referral."

"Okay, but what's wrong?"

Sitting back, she took his hand and played with his fingers, drawing comfort from his nearness. Rarity was right, she had to tell him no matter how difficult it was. Taking a deep breath, she whispered, "I found a lump in my breast."

He stilled. "A lump? I've never felt it."

"I found it the other morning. It's like it showed up overnight."

"Are you sure it's that sort of lump? Maybe it's something else, an ingrown hair or a pimple or some sort of...of...fuck, Emma, are you positive?" His eyes, moved with utter panic, searched hers and she wished she could tell him it was a mistake.

She sniffled and nodded. "It could be anything. I tried looking online, but it freaked me out really bad. I'm seeing the doctor on January second and if it's still there they'll run some tests and I'll know more."

"January second? That's like two weeks from now. Can't they get you in sooner?"

"No. I explained everything to the receptionist, but that's the usual wait period. She said two weeks is actually a pretty short wait."

His eyes were creased with worry, his breathing erratic. His distress proved a distraction from her own.

She gently rubbed his shoulder. "Are you okay?"

He laughed without humor. "No. Are you?"

"No." Mouth tight, her vision blurred. "I'm sorry to put you through this, Riley."

His attention jerked to her. "Jesus, Emma, don't apologize. It's not like you chose this. I'm sorry *you* have to go through this, but I'm sure it's nothing. Either way, I'm here. I'm with you. Whatever it is…" He pulled her close and kissed her jaw, her lips, her eyes, her nose as he hugged her extremely tight, yet somehow held her gently. "We got this."

He held her, rocking, never letting her go. It wasn't the same as when she told Rarity. With Rarity there had been a sense of shared fear, a sort of solidarity that didn't come with telling Riley. Seeing his worry only scared her that much more, because it proved how much he truly loved her and that was something she'd never had before him—the one thing she feared losing should this end badly.

After a long while, he asked, "Can I see it?"

She nodded and eased back. Her fingers trembled as she unbuttoned her shirt. "It's this one."

"Starsky?" He sat up, gently cupped her breast, and stilled. "Fuck. I feel it." Breath expelled in a shocked wheeze. "Jesus. That wasn't there before."

"I'm sure it's nothing." It seemed instinctual to lie in order to curb his distress. If he lost it, she'd be a disaster. She couldn't carry his worry on top of her own. She simply didn't possess the strength.

His breathing turned uneven. She was teetering on a slightly stable, albeit false, sense of security for the first time in days and needed him to hold it together for the sake of her sanity. She was probably too exhausted to cry anymore, but seeing him worry really pushed her boundaries.

Bending low, he gently kissed her breast. It wasn't sexual. It was the way a mother kissed a boo-boo and magically made it all better. She wished in that moment that Riley's kisses were magic, but she doubted such things existed.

Sitting up, he touched her chin. "Emma, nothing can happen to you. You're... You're my best friend. Of all the people in this world, you're my favorite. Whatever needs to happen, whatever has to be done, we're doing it. You and me. Team Starsky."

A slip of laughter escaped in a snuffle. "Team Starsky," she agreed.

"Let's go to bed," he whispered, picking up what he called the 'boo-boo blanket'. She followed him to his room, not wanting to be in her bed at the moment.

They curled close under the covers and stared into each other's eyes. He kissed her nose. "This."

"This?" she asked.

He nodded. "This. This moment, you lying here, facing me, filling my arms. *This* is everything to me, Emma. This. Us."

She smiled. This was her everything too. "This."

It was everything she existed for, everything she was afraid of losing.

This.

CHAPTER 12

Outside of Riley's door the strings and celestial cymbals of *The Cure* could be heard. It was Christmas Eve and he was barely speaking. Emma took a deep breath and knocked.

Lyrics about the sky falling in on lovers kissing in the rain and the courage to let go swathed the dim room in poetic melancholy. *Pictures of You* was one of her favorite songs by The Cure.

She stepped inside, fearful of pushing him too hard. "Riley?"

Sitting on the floor with his back to the wall and his knees up, lucky sock monkey hat pulled low on his head, he grimaced as he stared at his phone, his thumb swiping over images every few seconds.

"What are you doing?" Deliberately stepping over a pile of books on the floor she tried to find a place to fit. His palm slid the hat lower on his brow, hiding his eyes. Was he crying?

Dressed for dinner at his parents', she gathered her emerald skirt, crossed her ankles, and sank to the carpet beside him. "This song reminds me of the day we sat on the roof," she whispered, trying to find a smile.

He sniffed and nodded. He wasn't dressed for dinner. It was nerve wracking reintroducing herself to his parents as more than Rarity's friend. But Riley, not being his usual upbeat self, was more concerning.

The Lockhart's had always made her nervous, the sort of people that naturally induced pressure on others. Today, she was oddly indifferent about such things, but she still hoped to make a good impression for Riley's benefit—if he cared. Maybe he didn't.

"Shouldn't you be getting dressed? We're supposed to be there in an hour."

He shrugged and crossed his arms over his knees, pulling them close and lowering his face into the hollowed space by his elbows. She smiled at the back of the ridiculous hat and gave the monkey tail a slow tug.

"Tomorrow's Christmas," she whispered, wishing some magical spell of merriment would fall upon them and they'd slide back into normal. They needed a reprieve from all the heaviness. "Santa's coming…"

He said nothing.

She reached for his hand and tilted his phone. "What are you looking at?"

Her lips parted as she saw the image. It was her, sleeping. "When did you take this?"

"In August."

That was when they'd first started dating. Had it only been four months? In comparison to every other relationship she'd had, theirs felt lifetimes long.

Did he look at this picture a lot? Maybe he did in the beginning, when they were hiding their relationship and they couldn't openly be together, sleeping under the same roof but walls apart. Bitter that she didn't have such a picture of him sleeping, she felt a pinch cheated. In the beginning there were plenty of nights she wanted to watch him sleep and couldn't.

She still liked staring at him, but now she could do so whenever the mood struck. How did people carry on when the one person they longed to look at wasn't there? She shoved the morbid question into a dark corner with the rest of her morose thoughts. But she was glad he had that picture.

Was it normal to be so obsessed with another person? To want to spend every waking second and every sleeping breath within his reach? Becket had never been that invested in her. Even in the end, when they were 'engaged', they worked on a 'by appointment only' arrangement. She laughed inwardly, understanding why that suited him.

There was nothing planned about her and Riley. Not in the beginning and not now. That wasn't how they operated. They flowed naturally, on a current of laughter and desire that formed a rhythm, like stars drawn across the universe into the other's orbit, drifting close until they collided. Never the same again.

The music ended, the room silent as the tape stopped with a sharp snap. "You and your cassettes."

He laughed, but the sound was clipped and hollow.

"Riley, you can't let this consume you. We don't even know anything yet. It could just be a cyst."

She'd been trapped where he was. The worry was enough to swallow a person whole. She wasn't strong enough to bear it, so she took it in doses. Right now she was coping by pretending the worry wasn't there, somehow convinced life was normal. But it wasn't.

"I looked on the internet," he quietly admitted.

Her eyes closed, as sympathy tightened her heart. She'd made the same mistake when she'd been curious and overwhelmed herself in a matter of minutes. She understood the temptation, but should have warned him there was no comfort to be found in such searches. Rarity made her promise to stay away from medical websites and patient forums. She should've made Riley promise the same.

"Did you find anything good?" None of it was good. People visited those sites begging for peace of mind, but signed off with nothing more than terrifying paranoia.

"There're so many cases. Thousands."

She nodded. *Daunting.* "I know. It's a little shocking that I'm the first person we know to go through something like this."

"You're so young, Emma. *We're* so young."

Her breathing turned jagged as she faced the wall, watching the items on his desk blur under a fresh gloss of tears. It was impossible to hide from the worry when he wanted to discuss it, but they needed to talk about this, she supposed.

She needed him to be able to handle this, because she couldn't handle it alone. Her biggest fear, maybe more than the C-word, was coping with something so life altering without Riley there to make her smile. If this turned into too much for him to handle... She couldn't even imagine what she'd do.

Her head rested on his shoulder. "I know I'm young, but that's a good thing, right? It's really rare at this age, so maybe it *is* nothing. Maybe, in a few weeks, we'll all be laughing about how dramatic we got and how we let one little pea sized cyst ruin Christmas." *Wouldn't that be nice?*

Resting his chin on his arms, he mumbled, "I read the survival rate's good with treatment for women your age."

Survival rate.

That wasn't really a phrase she needed to incorporate in her life, was it? Those sorts of words came after a diagnosis. Right now she just had a foreign hard spot in her body. That could be anything. But his words lingered in her mind.

Good news was a jagged pill to swallow when

it came with words like survival rate. Things got very real very fast. Her chest tightened and whatever comfortable cloud of distraction she'd been hiding behind dissolved.

Her breathing turned heavy, but she tried to hide her stress from him. Staring at the floor, she blinked and casually wiped away the start of tears. "It could be nothing," she rasped. *Broken record. Broken woman.*

Her wrist throbbed as she became hyper-focused on her health, the blood flowing through her veins, the cells mutating, and a world of science she didn't understand. As her fingers went numb, a tingling sensation traveled up her arms and over her shoulders. Pressure built in her chest and a small voice inside her head, very far away, started to scream.

Is this what a panic attack feels like? Amazingly, she remained perfectly still.

"I think you should have it removed, even if it's just a cyst," Riley said.

Her entire chest vibrated so acutely, yet her trembling was imperceptible. Her mind wove together images of her body, red with blood and floating cells as her imagination drifted from her brain stem, down her spine, through her chest, and into her breast, following those little ducts like roots of a tree. And there, at the end of it all, was a small little pea.

What color was it? It pissed her off that she couldn't decide on a color when imagining the lump, pissed her off she knew absolutely nothing about breast cancer and she was a woman. Her imagination took her on a tour of her anatomy with the precision one would garner from a cartoonist illustrating a skit about the human body on Sesame Street.

She could sense it, beneath her skin and tissue. A phantom presence that was actually quite solid. An abnormality she wanted gone. How could something so small be so powerful, so lethal? What if she had it removed and it came back? Did that happen? She didn't know how cancer worked, didn't know how a woman went from losing a pea-sized lump to losing both her breasts.

Something like one in every eight women faced the risk of breast cancer, so why wasn't she more educated on the subject? And of those diagnosed, only two of every three survived.

Suddenly furious and unspeakably petrified, she stood. "You should get dressed. We have to leave soon."

"I don't wanna go."

She paused. They needed to go, because if she stayed in the loft another minute she'd freak out. As unpleasant as his parents could be, she needed the distraction—desperately.

"Riley, it's Christmas Eve. They're expecting us. We have to go."

"Why? It won't be the first time my parents expected something from me and were disappointed."

Taking a slow breath, she pinched the bridge of her nose. "I want to go."

He frowned at her from the floor. "Why? They're assholes, Emma. We should stay here."

"And do what, sit on the floor and listen to The Cure?"

He looked away. "I don't wanna go."

"Riley," she pleaded. "I'm dressed. I did my hair and put on makeup and squeezed into these tights. We don't have to stay long—"

"You look pretty."

"Th—thank you." She sighed. "Rarity's going. We made her do Thanksgiving on her own. We can't abandon her for Christmas too."

"She can stay with us."

She was silent for a few minutes, running out of methods of persuasion. "Just an hour. You can do sixty minutes with them. I know you can."

Glancing up at her, his eyes narrowed. "Why do you want to go so badly?"

She shrugged. "I don't know. They're your parents."

She couldn't let him know how scared she was. He was dealing with his own trepidation, and fear was contagious. Their anxiety would feed off each other so for the moment she kept her worry to herself.

Shaking his head, he rolled his eyes. "They're gonna judge you."

"So? Let them."

"You say that now."

Sighing, she lowered herself to the floor again, this time kneeling before him so they were looking into each other's eyes. "Riley, I know you hate being around them and I know you're only trying to protect me, but I've known them since I was a child. I get that they don't really like me, but they don't like anyone, so I'm not taking it too personally. What they think can't hurt me."

He prepared to argue, but there was a fast rap on the door and Rarity came in. "Are you guys ready? We have to get a move on." She frowned. "Please tell me you're wearing that hat. It'll keep mom bitching all night and then I don't have to hear about how I'm wasting away my ovaries watching life go by through a camera lens."

"He's not going," Emma said, knowing Rarity wouldn't stand for that.

"The hell you aren't. I did Thanksgiving by myself. There's no way I'm doing Christmas. Get your ass off the floor and get dressed. I'm walking Marla and then we're leaving. Emma, get his suit out of the closet."

She stood and did as Rarity instructed, once again grateful for her best friend.

~

RILEY DROVE while Emma fidgeted beside him. Rarity texted Lexi from the backseat. Lexi would stay at the loft tonight so they could all be together for Christmas morning. There had been so much going on that week, so many surprises, all of their plans sort of fell apart, but being together, doing nothing, sounded just fine to Emma.

Originally, she intended to have a traditional brunch, but she'd forgotten her shopping list and been so distracted at the grocery store, she wasn't sure what they had in the pantry. Tomorrow's menu would be another surprise.

She smiled at Riley who scowled as he maneuvered through traffic toward Park Ave. The last time she'd been to the Lockhart's condo she was ten. Rarity and Riley spent most of their childhood living on the family estate, outside of the city. Her only memory of the condo was not being able to touch anything. There was a lot of white and almost everything was glass.

As they took the elevator, the three of them shifted with resigned apprehension. Rarity reached in her shirt and hoisted up her breasts while loosening a button. She also rolled her sleeves so the tattoos running up her forearms were on full display.

Emma drew pleasure from watching her friend flaunt her diversity. From her short hair, buzzed close on the sides, to her oxblood boots, Rarity was everything her name claimed.

Deposited into a private foyer with vaulted ceilings and a sparkling chandelier, the scent of wealth and conceit churned up prickly memories.

The door opened and an older gentleman dressed in gray greeted them. "Mr. Lockhart. Ms. Lockhart."

"Harold, you remember Emma," Rarity said.

"Of course." Tipping his head, he greeted. "Miss."

Right.

Although every exterior wall was made of

glass, displaying the gaping panorama of New York and a gazillion dollar view of Central Park, the condo was taciturn and unwelcoming. Monochromatic, eccentric, and ugly were the words that came to mind.

Marble walls complemented the pale zebra wood flooring and cold metal furniture. Art deco lines created an abundance of space, so much so it became a piece of art in itself, the pricey square footage so blatantly displayed it surpassed braggadocios.

Harold took their coats and they shuffled into what the Lockharts called the fore room where white leather chairs sat beside an étagère wall displaying glass pieces of objects d'art. She hated it.

"You made it." There she was, Sophia Morgan-Lockhart. "Most people send notice if they're delayed beyond an hour. I see you've brought a guest without advanced notification." She smiled tightly, as if she tasted something unsavory. "Emma, how nice to have you with us." There was nothing sincere in her greeting.

Rarity and Riley tolerated air kisses and a short debriefing of what their mother found tedious so far that day. Emma tried to keep to the shadows, but everything was freaking white and wide open. Fidgeting, she toyed with various poses and places to keep her hands. Rarity collapsed on a settee and Riley filled a leather chair.

Mr. Lockhart entered from a set of gray pocket doors she hadn't noticed.

"Oliver, the children are here and they've

brought a guest." Sophia gestured as if Emma were a stain they needed to address, her enormous canary diamond glinting in the high altitude sunlight.

"Riley." Mr. Lockhart shook his son's hand, but only nodded at Rarity. He barely acknowledged Emma. "Your hair's gotten shorter, Rarity. I sometimes wonder what happened to my little girl in Mary Jane's and lace."

"I killed her," Rarity announced dryly.

"Don't start," Mrs. Lockhart admonished. "Shall we have a toast? Harold, tell Lillian we'd like a cordial." Turning to her husband she mumbled, "Honestly, Oliver, what is she thinking? They've been here almost five minutes." She tsked.

It was clear Riley didn't want to be in his parents' presence, but they were there and he should make the best of it. They'd eat and leave and it would all be over soon.

A woman in black wheeled out a glass cart filled with fancy liqueurs and tiny stemmed glasses.

"I'll take a beer," Riley announced.

"We're having cordials, Riley."

"Bully for you. I'd like a beer."

"I'll take one too," Rarity said.

It clearly took an effort for Mrs. Lockhart to hold her tongue. Shooting Rarity a disapproving look, she said, "Lillian, please bring Riley a glass of whatever ale we have. Rarity, you may have one of the liqueurs if you'd like a cocktail before dinner."

The maid disappeared and returned with a tall pilsner of amber beer for Riley. She poured several small glasses as Mrs. Lockhart directed her every move down to how she carried the silver tray. Emma carefully took a small glass and sipped the citrus flavored alcohol. *Gross.*

"No thank you, Lillian," Rarity said as the tray came to her.

Riley took a long sip of his beer, eyed his mother, and passed the glass to Rarity who chugged the remainder.

"Your manners are abysmal." Mrs. Lockhart tsked again. "Lillian, we'll be moving to the dining room."

"Yes, ma'am."

The dining room resembled a tomb. Great windows on each wall overlooked the New York skyline. A slab of marble long enough to fit twenty men was coldly dressed with square, white dishes and multiple forks and stemware. Emma settled into an S chair between Rarity and Riley.

Placing her napkin on her lap, she took a moment to squeeze Riley's thigh under the table. He snatched her fingers so fast it surprised her. He'd been so distant and indifferent since they'd arrived, but as his grip tightened over her hand as if he were drawing strength, she understood how far being here was pushing him.

Here, he was just a boy and these people were, unfortunately, the parents that would never appreciate the incredible man he'd become. She squeezed his hand back. *I appreciate you.*

"I haven't seen you in some time, Riley. What have you been doing with yourself?"

"Same old, same old."

"I see. And I suppose it's too much to ask that we have lunch on occasion so you might enlighten me about this secret life you lead."

"I have no secrets, Mother."

"Of course not—Rarity, put that phone away. We're at the table, for the love of decency. I swear, your lack of couth and etiquette is dreadful."

Rarity finished typing a text and stuffed her phone in her pocket. The servants carried out the first course and Emma watched discreetly to see which fork to use.

"Mazie Sinclair's daughter is shopping for a place in Manhattan, Riley," Mrs. Lockhart announced and Emma stilled. "Perhaps you could give her a call and see if she needs anything."

"Because I'm suddenly a realtor? I think I maybe said ten words to the girl in my entire life."

"She's quite pretty." She glanced at Rarity. "Long dark hair, trim figure. Her new nose transforms her face."

"No thanks," he muttered.

Emma frowned. Was he purposely hiding the fact that they were dating? He'd wanted her here. It was part of his argument when he'd confessed wanting to stop hiding their relationship—spending holidays as a couple.

As they ate in silence, Mrs. Lockhart continued to passively berate her children and promote the beautiful New York transplant she wanted Riley to marry. Emma's appetite disappeared the longer Riley remained silent.

As horrid as his mother was, his neglect to introduce Emma, as his girlfriend was worse. If he'd just tell his mother they were involved she'd likely stop pimping her friend's daughter. Why wasn't he speaking up?

The first course was cleared and Mrs. Lockhart appeared perturbed—an ongoing state. "I don't understand why you won't consider it. She's a sweet young woman who—"

"Jesus Christ, Mom, he's dating Emma," Rarity snapped.

Riley's eyes jerked in his sister's direction and he scowled. Apparently he *hadn't* wanted to disclose that bit of information for some reason. "What the fuck, Rarity?"

"Watch your tongue," Mr. Lockhart muttered.

Mrs. Lockhart scoffed. "I beg your pardon?"

Rarity turned, sending a challenging glance past Emma to her brother. Emma folded her hands on her lap. *Dear God.*

"Is this true?" his mother asked, appalled.

"Tell them," Rarity demanded through gritted teeth.

His fork clattered to the table. "Yes."

Feeling devalued, Emma stared at her lap.

"Oliver, say something."

"Men often pass their time with various women before settling down. I see no cause for alarm."

Her breath choked out of her. *Stand up. Get your coat. And leave.* She couldn't move.

"That's not what this is," Riley said. Did anyone see her? "I'm not *passing time.* I love her."

Mrs. Lockhart laughed. "Love? I don't think so, dear."

"It's true—"

"Then that's unfortunate," his mother snapped. "You're a *Lockhart.* Act like one. I refuse to have some girl, who couldn't afford the inheritance tax of her family's sole legacy, sponging off my only son like some New Jersey parasite."

"That's it," Riley stated calmly and stood, pulling Emma up by her elbow. "Get your coat, Em. We're leaving."

"Sit down, Riley," his father directed.

Rarity stood. "Merry Christmas. Yay..." Rolling her eyes she took Emma's hand and walked her toward the door.

"Everyone sit down!" Mr. Lockhart snapped, rising from his chair.

Riley bunched up his napkin and tossed it on his plate. "This is fucking bullshit," he mumbled.

"Think about what you're doing, Riley. We're your parents." Then in a more severe tone, she threatened, "You need us."

He turned and hissed, "For what? What could I possibly need from you? Money? I have my own. You can hold whatever's left, but you can't touch what's legitimately mine. I'd freeze and starve before I'd ever ask for help from you."

Heart pounding, Emma stood at the entrance

to the dining room, stunned. Rarity returned with their coats, appearing unaffected.

His father shook his head. "You're behaving like a child, Riley. When will you finally become a man? We spoiled you, humored this ridiculous portrayal of some low class, provincial nobody, but enough is enough. Where's your motivation to do better? Your drive? We gave two children every opportunity to be something great and they're both living like hippies, surviving on wasted potential and their grandparents' hard-earned money. It's a disgrace!"

"I have drive," Riley growled. "Every day, every single fucking day, I wake up and do my best not to become you."

Emma's jaw unhinged as she caught the perverse glint in his mother's overdone eyes. It was as if she were taking pleasure in this disgraceful spectacle.

His father's voice pitched low and harsh. "Take your friend and leave."

Trembling, Emma stared as he turned and took her hand.

"Rarity," their mother called.

She groaned and turned. "What?"

"We still expect to see you tomorrow evening."

Rarity glanced at Emma and slowly smiled. "Sorry. I have plans. I'll be spending Christmas with family—the ones that are there for me and love me no matter what." She looked at her parents and held out her hands, shrugging. "I can't keep coming here, pretending to be someone I'm not."

Together, the three of them turned and left.

❧

"OPEN IT, open it, open it, open it!" Riley bounced on the floor next to their horribly decorated Christmas tree. Whatever tinsel still clung to the tree was not earning any points in holiday glamour.

Rarity laughed from the couch where she and Lexi lounged together under the boo-boo blanket. Emma peeled back the paper of the large gift. The box was bright with a young girl on the front. *"Nerf Rebelle Agent Bow,"* she read and gave a nervous laugh. "It's a toy bow and arrow."

"It's a crossbow!" he said excitedly. "It shoots up to eighty-five feet! We can use it for zombie apocalypse practice!"

"Thanks." She smiled and kissed him.

Despite the unfortunate turn of events last night, the moment they returned to the comfort of their home, Riley's mood returned to his usual upbeat, hyper self. She wasn't sure if he simply loved Christmas that much or if he was overcompensating for fear that the ominous atmosphere of the previous days would return. Though he usually had more energy than the rest of them combined, today he acted like an excitable squirrel battling an attention deficit disorder in a room full of shiny objects—on speed. Still, it was better than seeing him sad. As far as defense mechanisms went, his was a harmless one.

"You want more coffee, baby?" Lexi asked as she stood. Her long, dark legs stepping around the piles of paper as Emma made room by gathering the shredded trash and crumpling it into a ball.

"Can you grab me a trash bag, Lexi?"

"Sure, Em."

"Now, open this one," Riley insisted.

He'd bought her so many gifts. The vintage shaving kit she got him no longer seemed like the great present she thought it would be. "Okay."

Pulling back the wrapping, she discovered an old hat box. There was obviously something fairly large inside, heavier than a hat. Unlacing the string, she lifted the lid and smirked, amused. "A Polaroid camera?"

"Now we can actually print and hold our pictures instead of posting them on social files for a bunch of people we hardly know to critique and judge. That whole box over there is filled with film. Enough to take a picture every day for a year."

She smiled, unprepared for the tickle of sadness that seeped in. What would her pictures look like in a year?

"Do you like it?"

She lifted the pink camera and opened the flash. A strange hum started as the camera turned on. "I love it."

He kissed her. "Come on." Pulling her to the floor on a pile of crumpled paper, he held the camera over them. "Vintage Christmas selfie—hashtag old school. Everyone say sex please."

She laughed. "Sex please!"

The flash went off, bright and loud. As the bulb whistled the camera processed the picture, sluggishly purging it from the slit. He took the picture and fanned it in the air.

"Vintage and hashtag don't belong in the same sentence," Rarity commented as Emma blinked, momentarily blinded.

"Fine. I'll say pound sign," Riley argued. "Rarity's annoying—pound sign: brat."

As Emma's vision restored, Rarity gave her brother the finger.

"Look," Riley said, holding the picture out for her. A poor resolution image of the two of them landed in her hand.

He kissed her ear and whispered in a voice too low for anyone else to hear, "Pound sign: beautiful." She shut her eyes, thinking the exact same thing. He was beautiful.

Taking the picture, she studied it as it came into focus. If she'd taken it on a digital camera she would've fussed with her hair and edited it twenty times. There was no such thing as candid photos anymore. But what she saw, that expression of total happiness and love in his eyes, that was real.

Her gaze was turned toward him, as her mouth opened in a crooked smile. Lying back the way they were, she had a double chin. But she looked so happy. Real.

Turning, she kissed his cheek. "I love it. We should take a picture every day."

"For a year?" he grinned, staring close into her eyes.

"Forever." That way, they'd always be together, even when they couldn't sleep side by side.

He nodded. "I like it."

Marla, sniffing out affection, barged between them and nuzzled Riley's neck. Rarity and Lexi bundled up and took the dog for a walk while Emma cleaned up and started breakfast. Based on their supplies, they would be having eggless pancakes and orange juice, since she'd forgotten everything else at the market.

As she mixed the batter Riley slipped his arms around her waist and pressed his face to her neck, hugging her from behind. "I love all my presents."

She grinned. "I planned on getting you more, but…"

He grunted. "You're my favorite gift."

She rested her cheek against the top of his head. It had been over a week since they'd slept together and she missed him. It was a strange place to be mentally, totally attracted to him, yet stuck in a body that seemed—at the moment—broken. He'd been really patient with her, but she didn't want to add another strain to their relationship.

"I miss you," she whispered.

He hummed and kissed her shoulder.

"Maybe tonight we can…"

"But…what about Starsky?"

Did it gross him out? "Does it bother you?"

"God, no, Emma. I just don't want to hurt you."

"You won't hurt me. Just…pretend it's not there."

Mastectomy.

She winced, as the word unexpectedly flung into her head.

She just wanted a few minutes without fear, but that seemed impossible. Her check up couldn't come fast enough. Would he still love her if she lost her breast? The breath knocked out of her lungs and she gripped the counter.

"What's the matter?"

"Nothing," she lied, a million times more fragile than she'd been a moment ago.

"Does something hurt?"

Only my heart.

She shook her head. "I'm okay." Reaching for the bowl, she continued to mix the batter. Just breathe. Keep moving.

She couldn't make assumptions until they spoke to the right people. Everything took time. Time…the one thing she'd never have enough of and the only commodity as precious as air. How did people deal with this sort of thing? Her mind couldn't fathom the worst-case scenarios, though it tried often enough without her permission. How did people deal with tragic news, being told they only had a limited time to finish living?

Stop thinking like that. You're fine.

All she could do was put one foot in front of

the other, walk until she reached the end—or the next hurdle if that's what would come. When she got to the hurdle, she'd run, but she couldn't take that leap without getting there first, so there was no sense in rushing forward.

When Lexi and Rarity returned, breakfast was ready. They sat at the island and laughed over Emma's terrible pancakes while sipping coffee and reminiscing. Marla was in heaven, having been thoroughly spoiled by her owners. Even Lexi gifted the dog with a special holiday bone.

Riley, too hyper to sit with the grownups, wandered around and took pictures of random objects with the Polaroid. It wasn't quite the Christmas she'd imagined, but she loved it all the same. Judy Garland crooned about Christmas, promising their troubles would be far away by next year, and even that seemed a little too far away to count on, so she simply savored the now.

Emma committed that moment to memory, the way Lexi smiled at Rarity as she brushed a loving hand over her leg and laughed at some private joke. Riley drifting around the loft, shirtless in his pajama pants with her pink crossbow strapped to his back and that ridiculous monkey hat on his head. Marla, sound asleep in a puddle of drool on Rarity's shoe surrounded by untouched dog treats.

It was the 'this' she and Riley had come to love. It was her everything, the quiet chaos, the dependable presence of friends, the easy expectations for shitty pancakes and quality coffee. *This* was her life. And though she had a long road of unknown hurdles ahead, she felt incredibly lucky to know 'this' right now.

As long as she had 'this' she could face anything. One step at a time, conquering one hurdle before thinking about the next.

Riley jumped into the kitchen, landing hard with both legs braced wide, startling the crap out of them. The pink crossbow aimed to the ceiling as his lucky sock monkey hat slid low on his head, and he shouted, *"I am Katniss Everdeen!"*

He let out a battle cry, releasing one foam arrow after another, and ran into the living room, jumping from the coffee table to the couch until he slipped and fell with a boom, taking down the lamp and rocking the whole tree. "Oh shit…"

The three women collectively gasped as the tree tipped, landing on top of him with a crunch of branches as he grunted, "Mockingjay down."

Rarity and Lexi, eyes wide, looked back at her. Emma simply smiled. "I love this."

PART II

...tied up with bows...

**There's always a beginning and there's always
an end.
Love is the beautiful chaos in between.**

CHAPTER 13

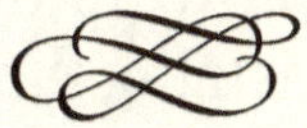

"In *The Color Purple* there's a line about God getting pissed off because people don't appreciate how pretty purple is. Maybe that's what God's doing now, reminding us to stop and appreciate life before it's gone."

Riley forced a smile. "Maybe."

Emma had been having a lot of those enlightened moments lately. She often expressed them, but he wasn't sure if she was sharing them because she wanted him to hypothesize with her or because she wanted to reassure God she received the warning loud and clear, and would cease taking life for granted.

At the moment, as he drove her to her appointment, he didn't give a lavender tinted fuck about the color purple. He wanted to punch God in the face and demand guarantees that his girlfriend was going to be all right.

"It's up there on the left."

"I know."

Her energy had been high since that morning. He wasn't sure how she was functioning, because neither of them slept the night before. This was another example of how optimistic and good she was, thereby emphasizing how screwed up life could be, putting someone as undeserving as Emma through this.

I take that back. No one deserves this. Maybe they were both making deals with a god they didn't completely trust.

His head was a mess. He was angry and scared, overly emotional, and in some sort of bidding war with a Santa Zeus God he wasn't sure existed. This might be happening to her, but it seemed like a way to punish him. For what, he wasn't sure, but he was convinced it was his fault.

"There's a spot."

How was she so calm? He pulled the car into the parking space and shut off the engine. "You ready?"

"I waited the longest two weeks of my life for this. *Yes*, I'm ready. I want to get this over with and get back to normal."

Terrified, he faced her and attempted a smile. They might never see normal again. "Then let's do this." They opened the doors and climbed out.

"Wait," she called, rushing over to his side of the car.

She held up the Polaroid, angling the camera so the doctor's office was in the background. "I want to remember this. When I look back from whatever happens next it'll remind me to always appreciate life, even the rainy days."

The bulb flashed and he blinked. He hadn't had a chance to smile. She tossed the camera on the front seat and waved the picture. As it came into view she giggled. "Look at your face."

He glanced at the photograph, ignoring his staggered expression. It didn't matter. She was there, always smiling. "Look how lovely you are."

It wasn't her clothing or her makeup and that claw thing in her hair. It was her. She was just a lovely person, so silly and easygoing—most days. Sure she had quirks and got overly sensitive when he didn't hang the dishcloth on the hook, but most of the time she was perfect.

She hummed, but her smile faded. "My looks might change, Riley. Getting this thing out might leave a scar."

If that was all it left he'd consider it a win. "I'm not talking about your looks, Emma." It was her spirit, right there, bolder than life, captured in a picture that he worried might be in jeopardy.

Once they stepped through those doors, everything could change, but he wasn't worried about superficial blemishes. If it were up to him, he'd accept a thousand scars to know the threat was gone. But if this was something serious, he feared it would change the person she was on the inside a hundred times more than it could touch the person on the outside. He didn't want her to lose that part of her, because those were the parts he loved most.

Everyone had a breaking point. What if this

was hers? Whatever changes came, he hoped they were the kind she could handle.

Please don't break her...

Her mood sobered as they entered the quiet facility and she started to fill out the multiple forms. There weren't enough cheery paintings in the world to blot out the dread smothering that waiting room. *Fuck this place.*

A lump formed in his throat as he watched her hand shake when she struggled to write their address. "Want me to do it?"

"That's okay." Letting out a frustrated breath, she shook her hand and continued writing.

He read her response to each question, finding it reassuring that no one in her immediate family had cancer. She never smoked and seldom drank. In his opinion, she was a healthy woman.

The longer the waiting lasted the more fragile she seemed. She fidgeted and fussed, trying to provide simple details like her age and the date of her last period. Finally, he took the clipboard and finished filling out the form for her. She breathed out a staggering sigh of relief and stared blankly as he returned the clipboard to the desk.

When he sat back down, she folded her hand around his and squeezed. She was scared.

"Emma?" a nurse called from the entrance to the exam rooms.

They stood and he considered vomiting in the fake ficus by the corner. They followed the nurse to a scale and Emma laughed. "I'm not that shameless. Turn around, Riley."

He stared at an advertisement for some sort of prescription drug as the nurse took her height and weight.

"Good. Right this way," the nurse said and they were moving again.

They entered a room and the woman instructed Emma to sit on the exam table. He sat in a chair in the corner while the nurse asked questions and strapped Emma to the cuff of a sphygmomanometer—totally shocked he knew the name of such a thing.

"So what brings you in?"

"I…uh…think I found a lump in my breast." She spoke like she was unsure. There absolutely was a lump. They were there to find out what that lump meant.

"Have you ever felt a mass before?"

"No."

"A lot of times a lump can be nothing more than fatty tissue, but it's good you came in and great that you're checking your breasts at home."

She unstrapped her from the blood pressure cuff. "Pressure's a little high." She reached in a drawer and produced a smock wrapped in plastic. "Put this on, open in the front, and the doctor will be in shortly."

They were silent when the nurse left.

Emma deliberately removed her shirt and bra and peeled open the smock. Her shoulders hunched as she slid her arms through the sleeves as if she were physically shrinking from fear.

He swallowed, the tiny room not holding enough air for both of them to catch their breath.

"It's probably just tissue," he asserted, repeating what the nurse said.

But something in his gut warned him that wasn't the case. He'd felt it, again and again. There was definitely something solid there. He didn't think tissue could feel like that.

The doctor came in, throwing everything into fast-forward with her cheery mood as if this was just another Wednesday. Her blasé attitude immediately pissed him off, like maybe they could wrap this up quick and go grab some frozen yogurt.

Once she breezed through Emma's family history, confirming she ranked low risk according to statistics, she instructed Emma to lie back. The blood immediately drained from Emma's face as she eased onto the table and he could tell the doctor was moving too fast for her as well.

The doctor stared at the wall as she examined Emma's right breast. "This one feels fine." She shifted to examine the left. Her brow wrinkled as her touch focused on the area where the lump was.

"Do you feel it?" Emma asked, voice strained.

"I feel something, but it's most likely a cyst." All too abrupt, the doctor stepped back and instructed Emma to sit up. "I'm going to write a referral for a diagnostic mammogram and a follow up ultrasound. Once your results are in we'll go from there. But I wouldn't worry. Like I said, at your age and with your family's history, it's probably a small cyst."

Oh, she wouldn't worry... Five minutes ago it was just tissue.

Emma smiled. "Thank you. That's a relief."

He frowned. A relief? They learned *nothing*! What the hell was the point of coming here? Now they had to wait for another appointment and then another one before they knew anything conclusive. Why did she look so relieved?

"Go ahead and get dressed. I'll leave your referral at the front desk."

The doctor left and Emma turned and beamed at him. "Did you hear that? It's probably nothing. Just a cyst."

He tried to smile and failed. "That's great." He needed a drink.

When they returned to the car he tried to calm down. He didn't want to overreact and he seriously hoped it *was* nothing, but he wanted something a little more concrete than one drive-by opinion of a woman in a lab coat. He wanted someone to verify she was healthy!

Emma buckled her seatbelt and hummed. "I should text Rarity."

"Maybe you should call and set up the appointment for the ultrasound and stuff. Who knows how long we'll have to wait for that."

"I will." She texted Rarity.

When they got home he had to go to work. "Em, the office probably closes soon. Are you gonna call?"

"I will, Riley. I said I would."

Biting his lips, he nodded. It wasn't like her to procrastinate. "Okay. I have to go." He leaned in and kissed her as she stared at the television. "I love you."

"I love you, too."

Sighing, he left.

~

"You promised you'd call." Fuming, he paced to the kitchen and opened the fridge, but what he was searching for wasn't there.

"I said I would call and I will. It's been two days, Riley. Relax!"

He slammed the fridge. "Exactly, Emma, two fucking days. You have something inside of you and no clue if it's spreading or harmless. What the hell are you waiting for?"

Her jaw twitched as she stared at him, her eyes hardening and glazing with unshed tears. Fuck.

"I just want to know what's going on, Emma. Don't you?"

"I just…" She shook her head and pressed her lips tight. "I just wanted a moment to breathe."

"Then let's deal with this so we can," he argued in a calmer voice.

"You don't get it," she barked. "The moment those real tests start there's no slowing down. I'm not ready for this. I'm scared, Riley."

Jesus, how did people do this? He was losing his fucking mind waiting. Sitting beside her on the couch, he exhaled. "I know, cakes. I'm scared too. That's why I want us to deal with this. We have to be aggressive so it doesn't get ahead of us."

Her eyes narrowed as she stared at the table. "Don't you get it? There *is* no us. This is happening to *me*. It's *my* body. *My* decision. And I'll make the appointment when *I'm* emotionally ready to do so."

It was happening. She was changing, pulling away from him. Her words stabbed into him, sharp and careless, cutting him to pieces as he bled with worry. The stress this was putting on their relationship was wearing their patience thin.

Something had to give. Fighting back the chronic nausea brought on by fear, he shook his head. "How do you turn it off?" he whispered, truly curious.

"Turn what off?"

His heart raced. They were losing ground. They needed to stay on the same foundation if they expected to get through this. "The worry. The love."

Turning from the window, her jaw trembled and her scowl softened as her head lowered. "I don't," she whispered almost shamefully.

The pressure in his chest was nearly crippling. "Then how can you say this is only happening to you?"

A tear fell to her jeans leaving a dark spot. "Honestly, I'm terrified, Riley. I think the doctor was wrong. I feel it, in my gut. I *know* something isn't right. Tissue shouldn't feel like that and even if it is just a cyst, it doesn't belong there and that freaks me out. I know my body. But it felt so good believing her for a split second. I just wanted to hold on to that feeling a little bit longer."

Understanding the temptation of false security, he felt like the worst villain stealing it from her, but just because someone fed her an optimistic assumption didn't mean she was safe. He wouldn't be able to breathe right until he was absolutely certain she was in the clear.

"You can't hide from this, Emma. I'm scared too, but it's real and it's happening whether you acknowledge it or not. If you want a fighting chance, you have to get in the ring."

Sniffling, she wiped her nose. "I'm not tough. What if it knocks me down and I can't pull myself back up?"

"You *are* tough." He tucked a curl behind her ear. "And if it knocks you down, I'll help you up every time you fall. I promise. I'll catch you."

Her lips tightened with tension. "What if it beats me up? I could walk away from this scarred and ugly."

The damage was already taking its toll whether she realized it or not. This experience had its claws so deep in her it was leaving marks on her soul. Gripping her hands, he stared into her eyes and fiercely vowed, "You could never be ugly, Emma. Scars don't matter. *You* do. Please, just make the appointments."

She wiped her eyes. Seeing her so worn down

ripped at his gut. He'd take a thousand other horrible punishments if he could just spare her this.

Her shoulders lowered and she nodded.

He kissed her nose and made her look at him. "This may be your body, but I'm in love with the woman inside. Anything that happens to her, happens to me. This is happening to *us*, Emma." His voice ceased as his greatest fears choked him. "Don't push me away. I don't like it and I won't let you."

She pressed her forehead to his. "Thank you," she whispered. "I needed to hear you say that more than you'll ever know."

"I love you. I'll never stop reminding you." Pulling back, he reached into his pocket and handed her the phone. "It's time to get into the ring."

~

RILEY FIDGETED in the ultra feminine waiting room, grateful the receptionist was the only one playing witness to his sketchy behavior. His fingers drummed rapidly over the veneer armrest and the woman glanced over the desk.

"Sorry," he mumbled.

Emma had been gone for nearly twenty minutes. He wasn't sure how long a mammogram took, but once he'd had his wisdom teeth x-rayed and that only took a few seconds. The door opened and his heart jolted as he spotted Emma and stood. *Thank God.*

Her mouth formed a polite smile, but he read the stress in her eyes. The sooner they got the hell out of there the better. Taking her hand, he led her to the exit, anxious to get somewhere they could talk.

Holding the door, he squinted at the sun and whispered, "How was it?"

"Uncomfortable, but not too painful." Her voice was trancelike, different from her usual upbeat tone.

He wasn't allowed in the examination room for safety reasons, which was probably for the best. Seeing her in any sort of pain made him crazy and he heard mammograms weren't pleasant. "Were they able to tell you anything?"

"No. I didn't even see the images. They go somewhere else. I won't hear anything for a week or so." The knot in his intestines tightened. His stomach couldn't handle much more suspense.

Once he started the car his head pressed against the seat and he let out a frustrated breath. She did the same. They sat in the parked car for several minutes not saying a word.

Silence.

Too many chaotic thoughts raced through his head, yet the world around them continued at its peaceful rhythm. Forcing out a calming breath, he tried to get a hold of his bearings, but nothing seemed capable of silencing the pandemonium in his mind.

Emma twisted, her hair dragging against the leather of the seat as their gazes met. He had no doubt she was struggling with the same inner turmoil. "You know what we should do?"

"What?" Fraught, he prayed she had a solution. He needed to escape the pressure, even if only for a moment.

Her lips curled in a slow, mischievous grin. He arched a brow, intrigued. Oh yeah, she had a plan. Good thing, because he was going out of his skull overthinking everything and desperately needed a distraction.

"Do you trust me?"

He smiled. "With everything I've got."

"Good. Let's go home."

~

THE ENTIRE LOFT stunk of skunk weed. Emma fell over Rarity as she giggled hysterically, Lexi's legs draped haphazardly over her lap. Riley continued to look around the kitchen, checking every drawer, but momentarily unsure what he was searching for.

He paused and pulled at the tag on his shirt, really enjoying the swishy sound it made. Tags were the same material as satin bows, weren't they? Bows…

David Bowie is highly underappreciated. I should eat a banana. Where's my monkey hat? Emma has the best laugh. Marla's a good dog. Brown is such a weird word. Brown. Berrrrwown.

Abandoning the kitchen he shuffled to his bedroom, swishing his tag along the way.

Stuffing his head in his sock monkey hat, he grabbed a box of cassettes, and returned to the couch, wedging himself between his sister and Lexi.

"Hey," Lexi complained, poking his ribs with her big toe. "I was cozy."

"Sit with me, Riley."

Emma. He stared at her for a moment wondering if she was speaking low or if his ears were moving too fast. Wait. Ears didn't move, but it would be funny if they did. The image of Dumbo's mom popped in his head and he snorted. The pot had definitely hit him.

His face suffered a sort of grin paralysis, but every muscle in his body was at ease. As he sifted through the tapes he continued to mumble, because the girls were laughing about something else and he wasn't sure what he'd missed. "Brown. Br-br-br-br-brown clown." He found what he wanted. "Put this on," he yelled, handing his sister the *Ziggy Stardust* album.

"Why are you yelling?" Lexi shouted and they all started cracking up.

"I feel so good right now," Emma sighed. "The only thing that could make me feel better is ice cream. I really want some ice cream."

Rarity shoved him off the couch and he crawled over to Emma's chair. Falling onto the cushion beside her, he pulled on her curls. His eyes were getting heavy. "You're cute, cakes."

Her cheeks tinged with pink. Damn, she was sexy. "So are you, syrup."

"You guys have the weirdest pet names,"

Rarity said, her voice strained as she bent to reach the tape player behind the couch.

Emma abruptly sat up. "Hey! You know what we should do?" The table jolted as she inelegantly stumbled and caught her balance.

"Oh no!" A cup of coffee teetered and spilled.

"Grab the pot!" Rarity shouted and Emma started cracking up.

Unable to take her adorableness, he tackled her to the floor and buried his face in her neck. His body molded to hers as she sighed and combed her fingers through his hair. "I love you," he mumbled, smashing his lips to her shoulder.

She turned and grinned, her eyes little slices of color. "I fell over."

He snorted. "Yeah, you did." He kissed her little ear.

Lexi cleaned up the table, making more of a mess as she kept knocking other things to the ground and laughing.

Emma hummed and melted into him. His body swelled as her limbs molded to his. Her small, squinty eyes smiled at him as she pulled his mouth to hers and closed his hands over her ass.

Something hit him in the side of the head and he jerked back. Rarity stood like Braveheart with the crossbow aimed at them. "Knock it off!"

He tossed the foam dart at her. "Cock blocker."

"You know what we should do?" Emma repeated, laughing.

"What?" The three of them burst into laughter as they went in circles.

Rarity plopped onto the couch, pulling Lexi down with her. Emma shoved him as she struggled to sit up. "We should make a bucket list."

His mouth twitched, loving her more than he had a minute ago. "Like to climb Mount Everest?"

"No, nothing that hard. All fun stuff."

"Like what?" Rarity asked, shoving Lexi's feet out of the way as she reclaimed her seat.

Emma smiled as if about to share the secret to life. "Like, go ice skating in Rockefeller Center."

Rarity snorted. "I've done that a hundred times."

Emma pouted. "I haven't. I've never even been in the Empire State Building. Riley calls me the worst New Yorker ever."

"True story," he added.

"You've never been in the Empire State Building?" Lexi barked, now sitting up with her feet on the ground. "You live here!"

"I know! That's why I need a bucket list. I should be doing all these things."

Rarity reached in the drawer and produced a notepad and pen. "Em-ma's Buck-et List," she said as she wrote across the top of the page. They waited as she jotted down the first two items—skating and the Empire State Building. "Okay, what else?"

"She's never been inside the Statue of Liberty either," he told his sister.

"Jesus, you *are* the worst New Yorker ever."

Emma threw her hands up and guffawed. "I know! This is what I'm saying."

Rarity tapped the pen on the notepad. "Okay, what else?"

"Pay for a perfect stranger's dinner."

He stilled, entranced. The soft ivory of her cheeks tinged with pink as a little cockeyed curl clung to the tip of her lashes. Her shirt didn't match her pants and she was only wearing one sock, but in that moment, she was the most put together, logical, and stunning woman in the world.

She shrugged. "What? I think that would be cool. Mysterious. Plus, it would make me feel good and spread good karma."

He was going to maul her the moment they got to bed. His gaze dropped to her sockless foot and he smirked at her curled hobbit toe. Oh yeah, she was gonna get it.

"Okay," Rarity jotted a few words on the paper. "Pay for a stranger's meal."

Their world suddenly seemed so contained, unintentionally limited when there was an entire universe to experience outside of their little bubble. The desire to pull her away from this place and explore life's secrets consumed him. Driven to show her the world and witness its splendor through her laughter and smiles, his focus shifted to commitments that would take longer than a day. "Swim with the dolphins."

"Oh, good one," Lexi agreed. "Rare and I did that last summer. Totally awesome."

"There are no dolphins in New York."

"It's called traveling, Em." He'd take her wherever she wanted to go. Having something to anticipate was way better than having something to dread.

"How about sex in an elevator," Rarity suggested.

"Did it," he and Emma said at the same time and laughed, their eyes meeting in shared nostalgia.

Falling back into the cushions of the chair, Emma sighed dreamily. "Dance in the rain."

His head tilted, mesmerized with the fanciful look in her eyes, so weightless as if she didn't have a care in the world. "Why?"

She shrugged. "It's romantic." Her eyes, though small at the moment, glinted with enchantment. "Imagine how in love a couple must be to dance in the freezing rain, where nothing matters beyond being in each other's arms."

He wished it were raining right now, because he wanted that too. He vowed to make sure her wish eventually came true, because he loved her that much and she was right, it was incredibly romantic and he wanted to be the only guy that danced with her and did romantic things for her —ever. Him.

They continued listing various objectives, but Emma never suggested anything that cost more than a hundred dollars. It pissed him off that she dreamed on a budget, because life should be limitless, a gross indulgence from beginning to end.

Cold cut through his haze, bringing about a

sense of urgency he could barely combat sober and refused to face stoned. She had so much to accomplish, so much to experience, but an unquestionable amount of time. They all did, but hers seemed to be spiraling faster.

He needed her to be there with him. He wanted to watch her face change every time she saw something new. No matter how pretty the site, the awe in her eyes would always win.

"See the Northern Lights," he suggested. She gave him a look he couldn't decipher, but she also didn't object when Rarity wrote it down. "Go to the top of the Eiffel Tower," he added, thinking of every possible place that might leave her as breathless as she left him.

"Cliché," Rarity commented, but wrote it down anyway. "Oh, see the Fairy Pools on the Isle of Skye."

Lexi pointed, taking a sip of her drink. "Good one."

"What are the Fairy Pools?" Emma asked.

Rarity gazed at her and hummed, her eyes lighting as though she were seeing the pools now. "A place in Scotland. It's beautiful, like heaven on earth. I want to photograph them one day."

"Then you should go," Emma said. "Put it on the list! This will be *our* bucket list and we'll make sure each one of us does everything we hoped to do before it's too late."

He stared at her, enthralled, or maybe perplexed. Perhaps it was fear. Perhaps it was the ganja. He didn't care what the cause. He never wanted to stop dreaming with her, never wanted it to be too late.

Wanting things he never thought about seemed to be the norm since falling in love with Emma—*she* made certain things worth wanting. Staring at her, the words slipped out, but no regret followed. "Get married."

Both Emma and Rarity pivoted and gawked at him, eyes wide, mouths opened like a couple of trout.

He shrugged. "It's on my list."

Rarity turned, observing Emma who was still staring at him.

"Riley…" Emma rasped, her chest lifting with each breath.

He swallowed. Maybe he shouldn't have said anything. No one said she'd want to spend the rest of her life with him. His sister actually blushed, clearly embarrassed for him.

Lexi took the notebook and pen from her and jotted it on the list. "That's on my list too." She gave his sister a meaningful smile.

Emma looked down, a strange expression on her face he'd never seen before. She smirked, but her eyes were so incredibly sad.

No sadness!

He stood and cranked up the stereo, doing his best Bowie impression and belting out the chorus of *Suffragette City*. He didn't stop dancing until the sadness in her eyes was gone.

~

THEY HEARD BACK from the doctor sooner than expected. Emma's ultrasound was scheduled immediately, throwing them all in a state of alarm. Very little talking happened over the following two days as they prepared for whatever information might come.

The doctor told Emma that while there was a small abnormality in the mammogram results, they needed an ultrasound to determine if the mass was made of fluid, like a cyst, or if it was solid, like a tumor. It seemed words like tumor took up so much space in his mind there wasn't room for much else.

Sitting beside her on the couch, he tried to follow the punch lines of the sitcom, but couldn't tell if they were watching *Friends* or *Big Bang*. His head was so fucked up. A tumor? A *tumor*? People their age didn't worry about things like tumors.

Fighting back the queasiness that persisted since she got her results, he laced his fingers in hers and squeezed. It was just a mass, some foreign abnormality that would get taken out and everything would go back to normal. But as the day carried on the memory of normal blurred. Borrowing trouble seemed an unavoidable habit he couldn't break and soon, as if she could sense his worry, she withdrew, sitting too far for him to touch.

The deprivation of contact ate at him, gnawing at his already chewed up gut. Rarity cleaned like a possessed woman as Emma sat unmoving and he existed in a brutal state of turmoil. Desperation, to say *anything* beat at him, but no one wanted to talk. What was there to say?

She sat on the far end of the couch with Marla, hugging the boo-boo blanket like a depressed Linus. He hated when the girls got quiet. The second they started acting stranger than usual, withdrawing, the world tipped on end.

He had no control over the balance of his life, which was fine until he found something he wanted to control, to keep. Now his world rested in the balance of another person's happiness and it was torture not knowing what was going through her head. Maybe she wasn't thinking about it at all.

Why did they get all the control, their moods affecting the ecosystem of an otherwise passive moment? The news was terrifying enough, but the shrouding weight that came with their silence made his apprehension that much more problematic—horrifyingly so. They were like witches, with their cycles all connected to the moon and shit. It was supernatural sorcery he didn't trust and that only convinced him more bad news was coming and they —the witch women—somehow already knew.

Ready to scream, he scrubbed his hands down his face and groaned. "Let's get out of the apartment for a while."

Emma didn't lift her gaze from the television. "I don't feel like it." Her voice gave no clue to her mood. Maybe she was just tired. Maybe she was actually watching the show. If she was going as crazy as he was wouldn't she want a distraction?

Unable to sit any longer in a guessing game of *if she was sulking or fine*, he grabbed his coat and left. No one seemed to mind.

Shoving his hands in his pockets, he aimlessly drifted into the gaggles of pedestrians, weaving in and out of the foot traffic. But no matter how far he walked he couldn't escape his thoughts.

Of course the mammogram identified something. They all felt it. If the results had come back inconclusive they wouldn't have found peace of mind, because they all knew *something* was there. The ultrasound was inevitable, so why had the act of scheduling it plunged the loft's residents into an impending sense of doom? Where was the hope? This was just the next step toward getting the lump out, not a death sentence.

He swallowed, wooziness once again making his mouth water. It was *not* a death sentence. The ultrasound would identify the mass, she'd have a few more tests, and they'd get it the hell out. Then life would return to normal and this bad dream would end.

He roamed the city, unsure where he was heading until he was knocking on his friend Jake's door. Unclear what he was doing there or what his friend had been up to for the past five months, he considered leaving, but the door opened.

Jake did a double take. "Riley? Holy shit. What are you doing here?"

"Freezing," he said, hunching into his coat. "You busy? Wanna grab a beer?" He needed to piss and find a place to warm up—someplace other than home.

"Yeah. Come in. Let me get my shoes and fleece."

He followed Jake inside and waited as he searched for his boots. "Mind if I use your john?"

"You know where it is."

When he came out of the bathroom Jake was ready. "So where have you been? I haven't see you since Jillian's Fourth of July thing."

"I, uh, actually started dating someone."

He stilled and cocked a brow. "Really? Like… serious dating?"

"Yeah, it's pretty serious. You know my roommate, Emma?"

Jake's mouth turned up with a slow smile. "Rarity's friend?"

He nodded. "Yeah." Laughing at how ridiculous he must sound, he admitted, "I'm totally gone for her. It's crazy."

"No freaking way." He zipped up his fleece. "Let's go to McFadden's. First round's on me."

As they briskly walked to the pub, Riley explained how different Emma was from every other girl. He couldn't stop going on about her. Even when they had their first drink finished, he continued rambling about how great she was.

It was unheard of, the irony that he had become *that guy.* He could've written a hundred sonnets about just one of her eyelashes. But there was no mocking or ball breaking coming from Jake, nor was there any shame in Riley's affection. She was awesome and he knew how lucky he was to finally realize that.

"You really are a goner," Jake said. "Does she have any friends?"

He chuckled. "Only lesbians and men."

Jake laughed and sat back with his beer. "I'm really happy for you, Ri. It sounds like you found *The One*. You gonna marry her, take roomie to groomie?"

His smile faded, recalling how sad her eyes got the last time he brought up the subject. "I don't know. It's too soon for that, but… I kind of feel like it's a now or never thing."

"Why now or never? There's nothing wrong with waiting."

Maybe he was just freaking out. "She's having some tests done. Shit's been a little stressful lately."

His friend frowned. "What kind of tests?"

Flagging down the bartender, he ordered another drink. "She found a cyst in her breast. Tomorrow we find out if it's cancerous or not." It was the first time any of them had spoken the word out loud.

Jake's face froze. "Holy fuck, are you serious?"

"Yeah." He laughed nervously and rubbed the heel of his palms over his forehead. "I'm freaking out."

His friend glanced at the bar, only bringing his gaze halfway back to him. "I wish I knew what to say." He shook his head. "She's young for that, right?"

Riley waved away the whole injustice of her

age. It had been a repetitive complaint in his mind since the start of this and getting infuriated over the unfairness of the situation didn't make life any more bearable. "It's not unheard of."

"I'm sorry, man." And that was it. No *it'll be all right.* No *I'm sure the tests will come back negative.* Cancer was fucking scary and people avoided even breathing the word into conversation for fear they might tempt its hideousness into their lives.

The bartender delivered his beer as the companionable conversation waned into utter silence. He knew what he was thinking, could almost scent his discomfort. The statistics were broadcasted in every ribbon, parade, and donation bin they passed on a daily basis.

Riley stared at his bottle, his friend's apology ringing in his ears. It was a sincere attempt to comfort, but his situation was so personal, so isolated, there could be no empathy when the reality was simply unimaginable. Jake couldn't possibly understand what he was going through or grasp the fear rushing through his mind. The terror he couldn't curb by even one degree until this nightmare ended.

He appreciated his attempted sympathy, but it was more manners and an ingrained response than anything else. When you heard someone might have cancer, you showed the proper amount of concern, pinned a ribbon on your clothes, and forgot as quickly as you heard—out of sight out of mind. It wasn't fair, it wasn't enough, but it was the reality.

Living it was a different actuality. It was raw, inescapable, and so much more than a blip of unfortunate circumstances that might pass. The worry, the wavering prediction of how much time this would steal, the taxing amount of stress it put on every aching brain cell from over-thinking every possible fucking outcome. In the blink of an eye that blip blotted out his entire view, and nothing he did could make him see things the same again.

He didn't need his friends to understand the fear, but he wanted them to appreciate how important Emma was, how different she was from every other girl. But they never would because all the laughter, all the secret moments of trust, they were private and not meant for others, which was exactly why it was so meaningful that she shared them with him.

No one would ever understand how much she meant to him. She was his everything. What would he do without her? Who would he lean on? He'd be so alone if anything happened to her, alone with unbearable grief no one else could comprehend.

Realizing this, made it imperative that he somehow remain stoic for her. Emma could never know the severity of his fear. Days like today when he wanted to get it out and talk it through, he'd have to swallow his feelings whole, because saying them out loud would only transfer his worry to her and he couldn't let that happen. He couldn't let his grief destroy him. He had to be a man, her rock to lean on when she was ready. But who would be his?

Daunted by the unavoidable role he'd have to fill over the next few weeks or however long it took to straighten this shit out, he stuffed down his fear. No amount of hoping would change what was. All he could do was be there for her until the experts figured everything out.

"I'm an idiot," he mumbled and Jake took his eyes off the bar television that had been acting as a buffer since Riley dropped a bomb on their conversation.

"Why?"

Time suddenly appeared fleeting and precious. "I should be home. She didn't want to go out and I just left her there." It didn't matter that she hadn't asked him to stay. Since when did girls use anything other than subliminal communication to get what they needed?

Abruptly, he stood and slapped some money on the bar. "I gotta go. Thanks for listening to me."

"You okay?"

"Yeah. I needed to clear my head and you helped me do that." He edged toward the door. "Once everything calms down and we know where things stand, we'll get together. I want you to meet her." He nodded and grinned, his fear stuffed down, deep enough that he could envision a positive outcome. Pointing a finger gun at his friend, he clicked his tongue in his cheek, the end target in view. "My future wife."

Jake lifted his beer and laughed. "To your future wife."

Riley ran out of the bar, his legs pumping as the cold January wind cut through his clothes. She was sad and he thought he couldn't handle it. He'd run away, but now he'd found steady ground and needed to get back. He'd be there for her, stoic, solid, a rock. So long as he didn't forget his duty, she shouldn't question whether he could handle her darkest fears. He'd bear whatever ugly thoughts she had, give her a place to spew her worry so she didn't have to hold it inside. But for her to trust that he could handle it, he had to be present—always by her side and steadily grounded.

He didn't stop running until he entered the loft. "Emma!"

"She's sleeping," Rarity hissed from the chair.

Emma lay curled up on the couch where he'd left her. Carefully, he slid his arms under her body and lifted her to his chest.

She roused, eyes heavy and brow wrinkled. "Riley?"

"Shh... I'm taking you to bed."

Her arms tightened around his neck as he carried her to her room. "Where were you?"

Gently placing her on the bed, he drew the covers over her. "I went for a walk. I needed to clear my head. Emma..." He quickly gathered his thoughts. "I need you to understand how much I love you. It's... the biggest feeling I've ever had." Bigger than any fear or any complication. Bigger than… He was done thinking that word. "*Nothing* can make me stop loving you."

She smiled and cupped a hand to his jaw. "It's the biggest feeling I've ever had too."

He kissed her. "It's bigger than *this*," he said, delicately cupping her breast. "I want you to know, the girl I love, she's here." He tapped her forehead. "I don't care if she gets old or gains weight or…anything else. As long as she lets me hold her from time to time and accepts that I'll love her no matter what shape she's in, I'm a happy man."

Her eyes closed as she drew in a slow breath, her mouth curling into her first smile that day. Her lashes spiked with moisture. "I love you, Riley. These past few weeks have just…" She exhaled. "…shattered parts of me to the point that I hardly recognize my own thinking. Every day I think I can't feel anymore, but I do. Sometimes I can't handle it. There are just so many feelings."

"I know. That's what I mean. This is scary and fear changes people. Don't change without me. You have to let me come with you, Emma. Let me be your rock, because you're my rock too. We're a team and we're gonna kick this thing in the balls."

She laughed, her eyes tired. "I'm in the ring."

"Damn right." He rolled to his side and pulled her with him. Together they could beat this.

Lost in thought, they were silent for several minutes as if experiencing the same epiphanies at the same time—or at least he hoped. Life was too short to postpone living. They'd get through this however they had to and then they'd get through the next big hurdle and the next, because life was a journey and he'd be by her side so she didn't have to go through it alone.

"If it's nothing, which I hope it is, let's not go backwards, Em. I don't want to waste any more time on things that don't matter. I wanna live. I want you to start your business and I want...*you*. I don't care if it's fast or people think it's too soon. Life's fast and I wanna milk it for everything while I'm still...milking."

She let out a huge sigh, relief sparking in her eyes as she faced him. "I totally agree. I've been so consumed by this, worrying what my life will be a week from now."

"We can't waste any more time on the crap. It's all unnecessary stress. Life's too short."

"Yes! I hate this emotional paralysis. But I get it now, all the stress we were wasting on meaningless worries. I don't want to forget how horrible it feels to think it'll all be over soon, but I also don't want to live like there's no end. I'm not making any sense."

She was making total sense. "But I get it too. All these rules we live by—other people's rules, when it's our life."

"Exactly. This has been the scare of a lifetime and I can barely remember the girl I was three weeks ago, but in a way I like this girl more. It's like everything became complicated and simplified at the same time."

He understood completely. This scare had

prioritized life. "I want to live with abandon, but only if you're with me."

She stared into his eyes and whispered, "For better or for worse, tomorrow's the first day of the rest of my life. I might not always be able to choose where this life takes me."

"Me neither, but wherever it takes you, I intend to follow." He caught her tear on his thumb and gently wiped it away. "Our life. We got this, cakes. We got this."

CHAPTER 14

At the base of every person is an animal. And deep down, inside that animal, exists a beast. Emma finally understood how mothers found the strength of twenty men in life or death situations, how bears went grizzly to defend their cubs. Because the moment she saw the *three* gray masses in her ultrasound, it was game on, survival of the fittest, and she was prepared to do whatever it took to protect her body from the threat inside.

"Notice how this spot is black," the tech pointed to her results. "That's liquid. The gray shows the mass is solid like a tumor."

Three. There were three. Were they growing overnight? "I don't understand how I missed the other ones. Did they just appear?"

"Sometimes a mass can live inside of you for ten years undetected. It's good that you practice home exams," the tech said, and Emma felt a surge of gratitude because she'd caught this when she had. "Early detection really does save lives, so now that we know what we're dealing with we can treat it aggressively."

Aggressively. She clung to the word, its meaning defining salvation itself.

Totally focused on every word the doctor said, Emma paid absolute attention, trusting these people to save her precious life. She didn't look at Riley, because she feared the emotion on his face would trigger her feelings, which were oddly absent.

She was a soldier on the frontlines of an endless battle. There would be time for feelings when she was…

Maybe she was in shock. Or maybe she'd known all along something wasn't right and she'd subconsciously prepared for this moment. It didn't matter. This was now and this was everything they were up against. There was no time to look back.

The enduring suspense of waiting for a diagnosis was hell and it was far from over. Only a biopsy would tell what sort of tumor they were up against. It was a coin toss, but they were now one step closer, and it was time to take action.

The doctor came in and studied the results. She immediately jumped into explanations, preparing her for the next step. "We're going to send you for a biopsy. That's where we collect a sample of tissue and get more information. Eighty percent of the time, biopsies come back benign, so try not to get ahead of yourself. It's a minimally invasive procedure done with a needle."

Emma fought the urge to squirm. She'd never been good with medical things, but chances were, in the next few weeks she'd be getting over any hang-ups. Nothing was definite. They seemed optimistic these little intruders could be benign.

No fear. Focus on necessity. "Do I need a referral?"

"Our nurses will handle that for you."

She nodded, knowing her best bet was to trust these people—they were her only hope, the only weapon she really had in this battle. She couldn't look at it any other way. Her life was literally in their hands.

At the front desk, a nurse handed her a pamphlet explaining what happened during a biopsy. Once the procedure was scheduled for Friday, they walked out of the facility in a trance. One steady breath after another, left foot then right, she got through. She'd jumped the first hurdle and landed on her feet—for the most part.

As they approached the car she finally looked at Riley, who had been uncharacteristically quiet through everything. She touched his arm. "You okay? Oh—"

She grunted as he nearly tackled her, wrapping his arms tight around her body and hugging her hard. She laughed nervously as his face pressed into her neck and he breathed.

Voice muffled, he hissed, "Love you."

There was so much weight in those two

words, her body sank a bit closer to the earth, closer to him, bearing such crushing implications she accepted that this wasn't just happening to her.

Her hand trembled as it settled on his back. "I love you too."

His arms remained snug around her waist, holding her immobile as people walked by. Shutting her eyes, she let his affection wash over her.

~

FRIDAY MORNING she was back in a hospital gown. Riley was in the waiting room and she was waiting for the doctors to come in. It had been a crazy week.

Her boss was beginning to suspect something was up with all the time she'd requested off. As a personal assistant, there were certain responsibilities a temp couldn't handle. Luckily, the firm had a woman pretty familiar with each partners' idiosyncrasies. But Mr. Phibbs' patience was wearing thin.

She had planned to apply for government healthcare when she left her job and started her own business, something she still planned to do. But at the moment, that sort of career change didn't seem wise, so she put her dreams aside and did the logical thing.

She needed her benefits and the company had a program that allowed her to collect a supplemental income, should she take a leave of absence. There was a fifty-fifty chance she'd be filing that paperwork soon, but nothing was certain yet.

The door opened and the technician returned. "Okay, Emma, are you ready?"

She nodded and took a shaky breath. Who was ever ready for this sort of thing?

The tech helped her onto the exam table. "Guide your left breast into the opening and find a relaxed position. You'll have to remain still when we take the sample, so we want you to be comfortable."

She settled on the table and curled up much like she did in bed, only here her breast was hanging through a hole. Imagining a cow preparing to milk on a commercialized dairy farm, she shoved away the degrading impression of being so exposed.

They do this every day. You're only shocking yourself.

The table elevated putting her breast at the technician's eye level. She wished she knew a joke about people staring at women's breasts.

"We're going to take a few x-rays to pinpoint the location of the tissue."

Doing her best not to move, she shut her eyes, and imagined a field of wild flowers. She was the wind passing through the reeds, the bees lazing in the pollen. She pretended to be anything but herself in that moment so she didn't have to acknowledge where she was.

When she was a young girl she had a fanciful imagination. Her father had a hammock in the backyard and she'd pretend it was a cobweb.

With her mother's quilt gripped in her hands she was the beautiful butterfly set to escape the trap. As she got older, her fantasies turned to those of women. High heels and fancy pearls, there was nothing better than dancing around in her grandmother's pretty things, watching them dazzle and catch in the sunlight.

Why her mind was recalling her favorite childhood pastimes she didn't know. Perhaps it was the recollection of her love for all things girlie, her brain paying homage to what once was and accepting that the most feminine part of her might be lost.

"Okay, you can relax, but try to keep your position."

Releasing a breath, she opened her eyes—back to reality. The images displayed on a computer screen at the desk made her wonder if she'd ever look at her boobs the same again. These slides of webbed anatomy were not at all what she used to imagine when she pictured breasts, but they were all she thought of now, whenever she imagined her own.

The door opened and a male doctor entered. It took great restraint not to hide her body from his view, but he seemed impervious to any breach of propriety she suffered.

"Emma," he greeted with a welcoming grin. "I'm Dr. Lindsay. How are you feeling today?"

She gave a shaky smile. "I'm okay." *Just hanging with my boob dangling through a table.*

"Good. Let's see what we found." He went to the

computer and keyed in some information. "We're marking the precise location on these stereo images to guide the biopsy device to its target. Try and remain still so we can hit our target on the first try. If you shift too much the reading won't be accurate."

She was barely breathing.

The nurse uncapped something at the counter, but stood outside of her peripheral. As she stepped close, she said, "Just my hands." And applied something cool to her breast. "I'm cleaning the incision zone so we can numb the area."

Everything was so unexpected she became a silent passenger on a journey that belonged to someone else. She'd gone from horrible, endless waiting to racing full speed ahead. There was no time to panic, because weird things kept forcing her to move forward, which was good. If she couldn't think about what was happening she couldn't freak out.

She sucked in a breath as a needle pressed into her skin then the sensation was gone and the nurse stepped back to the counter, tossing something in the biohazard bin on the wall.

"Stay very still," the doctor reminded, his eyes on the screen. "I'm going to trigger the instrument. You'll hear a click and feel pressure."

No time to worry. *Click*.

A strange sensation traveled through her breast and her brow tightened. It wasn't excruciating, but it was unrelenting. The computer showed exactly where the needle was embedded, bringing about a sudden wooziness. She shut her eyes. *Too much reality.*

"Okay, we're all lined up. We're going to take four samples and it'll be over in a minute. Hold perfectly still."

Squeezing her eyes tight, she waited. Discomfort was as much mental as it was physical. Trying to lose herself without crying, she focused only on things that made her happy.

My parents. Marla. Rarity laughing at some sarcastic comment she made. Rarity smiling at Lexi.

Riley...

The discomfort subsided as he overshadowed all else in her world. She kept with that train of thought, losing herself in all things Riley.

Riley grinning at me. The day he first kissed me. Making love as the sun came up the morning he said I love you. Riley biting my hobbit toes. Trying to watch television as he shoved his finger up my nose because he needs constant attention. Making love. Riley staring into my eyes... I wish I knew what he saw there.

"All done."

Blinking, she realized the table had lowered and the procedure was over. The doctor helped her sit up and taped a small piece of gauze to the incision.

"I'd like you to keep pressure on that for ten minutes and then you can go. You'll have a tiny nick that'll take a few days to heal. There might be some mild discomfort, but you should feel well enough to return to your normal routine right away. Nothing too rough, though." He smiled. "We should have the results by Tuesday."

More waiting. The weekend was going to be hell. "Thank you."

Another hurdle jumped. An unknown amount left to go. She had to be getting closer to the end. Every step was progress.

~

IT SEEMED an unspoken pact to get through the weekend with no talk of appointments, boobs, or medical anything. Friday night, Riley took her to a pub and she'd had too much to drink. She recalled talking a big game of sex, but remembered nothing past walking home. Apparently she had a debt to pay.

As they watched a season one marathon of *Sex in the City*, selected to keep the content light, Rarity stood. "I gotta get moving. Lexi's meeting me in twenty minutes. God, this show sucks you in."

"Why don't you tell Lexi to come here?" Emma suggested, head resting on Riley's shoulder.

"Can't. She wants to go out and I promised."

Rarity disappeared in her room and they went back to watching their marathon. Riley mumbled, "At least some women keep their promises…"

Emma snickered, but continued playing an unending game in her head of which character was her favorite. "You'll get yours," she promised —not that her word carried much weight today.

Riley shifted and pulled the blanket covering her legs over his lap. His hand slipped underneath the covers, gently massaging her knee. Rarity came back out wearing a different outfit and searched the chair, flipping up cushions and moving pillows.

"What are you looking for?" Emma asked.

"My phone."

"Isn't that it on the counter?"

She turned and sighed in relief. Rarity moved around the apartment, oblivious to their presence as she gathered her personal belongings. Riley's hand slid higher on her thigh and Emma sent him a sidelong glance. "What are you doing?" she whispered from the corner of her mouth.

He arched a brow, sliding his hand higher. He appeared engrossed in the show, but that sneaky hand proved his attention was elsewhere.

"Riley," she hissed, as his hand dipped behind the waistband of her pants. "Your sister's here."

"She's leaving." His fingers slid into her panties as he eyed her. "Just be cool."

Paranoid, she pulled the blanket up to her chest so his hand was less noticeable. His fingers brushed her sex and she sucked in a breath as he lowered his hand and slid his touch between her folds.

Rarity came back out of her room and disappeared in the bathroom. Emma's face burned as his finger slid inside of her. She stared wide-eyed at the TV, her mind totally focused on his touch and their roommate's whereabouts.

Glancing to her right, she smirked. He appeared totally captivated by Carrie Bradshaw's drama. Rarity returned and shifted a bag over her shoulder. "I'm outta here. Behave, children."

"See ya."

"Bye." Neither of them took their eyes off the television.

The door closed and she exhaled, slouching into the couch. He turned and kissed her, a mischievous grin on his lips. "Dirty girl, letting me finger you with others in the room." He rolled on top of her, his touch sinking deeper.

"The *other* was your sister, pervert. I can't believe you did that."

His unabashed smile widened. "She'd do the same thing in my shoes. Besides, you promised a whole bunch of goodness last night then passed out on me—snoring with your mouth open, I might add. Totally not the picture you painted at the bar."

The blanket fell to the floor and she giggled. "Sorry."

Removing his hand, he pulled her pants and panties down her hips and shifted to his knees. "I'm collecting."

"Oh, are you?" she teased.

"Yup." He nudged her knees apart and placed a kiss low on her belly.

As his mouth traveled lower she eased back and sighed. "Is this what I promised?" It seemed like a win for her.

He didn't answer, too distracted with what he was doing so she shut her eyes and let him go—not one to leave an outstanding debt unpaid. He was so attentive to her every response, touching her in all the right places until she was cresting a wave of pure ecstasy and gripping his hair between her thighs.

Her eyes closed on a wash of color, blanking her mind of anything beyond the pleasure. Free. She was so free in those fleeting moments, yet he was right there with her.

Her chest rose and fell with each labored breath as he rested his cheek on her thigh. His nearness didn't faze her and there was no call to cover her bare parts. With Riley she never felt so much exposed, as she did unveiled. He loved looking at her and she loved that no shyness separated them when it came to intimacy. Their lovemaking was so open, shameless, and unlike any past reference.

As she came down, he dragged his fingers over her thigh, allowing her time to savor each aftershock. She sighed. "If I'd known that was what I promised I would have paid up this morning."

He chuckled and lifted his head, hair mussed from her fingers and a self-satisfied smirk on his lips. "You're not off the hook yet. I want you."

"I'm yours." She rolled to her stomach and he stripped in record time.

Rising behind her, his palm swatted her ass. "Love your little bubble butt," he teased, the crinkly hair on his thighs brushing the backs of her legs. His palms slid over her hips as their bodies aligned. His grip flexed as he hummed in pleasure, sliding into her.

Her inhalation faded to a moan as he filled her in one sure stroke. His fingers dug into her flesh as he thrust. Gasps broke the silence, a gentle pulse of noise that filled her with pure delight.

It was an escape they both needed, a connection she'd craved that mended parts of her soul she couldn't patch on her own. Despite his pace, there was an intrinsic sense of closeness, something hidden in his touch. The way the pads of his fingers glided over her skin, how the backs of his nails delicately traced the line of her spine almost reverently. He was always so careful with her, yet reckless in a calculated way. That was Riley, carefully careless and singularly adding up to everything she wanted in a man.

As he came, his hold flexed, sliding up her body and pulling her down to rest in his embrace as he shivered. Those were her favorite moments of making love, the little flashes of trust when he vulnerably fell into his own pleasure and snuggled her close as if the sex was just the prelude and the real bonding came in all that followed.

He kissed her ear and hummed a satisfied male groan. "I love being inside you as we come down."

As if he'd read her mind, she curled into him, their bodies still connected. "I love it too."

"Can you reach the blanket?"

Stretching her arm, she pulled it onto the

couch and he adjusted it over their legs as he snuggled into her back, sandwiching himself between her body and the couch cushions.

A sense of peace held them, suspended in time. She didn't want to think about the future. She only wanted to enjoy the now—the *this.*

Her lashes lowered as his fingers ghosted over her arm, drawing patterns and putting her in a dreamlike state. Nothing encroached on the moment. It was solely theirs, and she reveled in the beauty of how two people, so different, could complement each other so exactly.

~

ENTERING THE LOFT, Emma unhooked Marla's leash and the dog bolted to Riley, knocking him over as he searched the couch for something. Affectionately tousling the dog's ears, he got in her face. "What did you do with my shoe, Marla? I have to go to work."

Marla slobbered a kiss over his chin and panted, unfazed by his dilemma. Riley returned to his search as Emma kicked off her shoes and unbuttoned her coat.

Like a stormy sky overpowering the light of dawn, the most ordinary day suddenly turned into something inconceivable. Her phone rang and they both stilled, staring at her purse ringing on the counter. Without identifying the caller, she knew it was the doctor.

Skin racing from cool to clammy, her stomach dropped to the soles of her feet as her gaze found his and their illusion of peace was shattered. Riley stood and dropped his shoe. Even Marla seemed to settle. Reality had returned.

"Do you want me to get it?" he offered, voice devoid of emotion.

Shaking her head, she forced her feet to move. Stepping to the counter, she lifted her phone out of her purse, the tiny vibrations of each ring shaking her to the core. Swallowing tightly, she brought the phone to her ear. "Hello?"

"Hi. Is this Emma?"

"Yes." Her voice was hollow, much like her stomach.

"Emma, this is Dr. Lindsay. Is this a good time?"

She sent Riley a stiff nod as she shifted closer to a chair, no longer trusting her legs to hold her. "Mmm-hmm."

"Well, we have the results of your biopsy and the tumors tested positive…"

Her gaze locked with Riley's and his brow lowered, his mouth tightening as comprehension registered in his eyes. Her vision blurred. Horrible knots tightened in her chest as the doctor went on using unfamiliar words. Her hand trembled as she choked back a sob.

"Do you have a surgeon chosen yet?"

Her brain, trapped in a web of confusion, processed his question in slow motion. She swallowed again. "I have a referral."

"Good. Have you considered the likelihood of

chemotherapy prior to the various options of lumpectomies?"

From the start, she'd told every doctor that if the lump proved cancerous she wanted to have it removed. But that was before it was real. This was suddenly *so* real.

Goose bumps traveled up her legs, chilling even the breath in her lungs. Her bravery shifted into cold fear. She couldn't handle this. Why had she thought she could?

Words like chemotherapy didn't belong in her vocabulary, yet here she was, being asked if she'd considered such treatment before having the lumps in her breast removed. No, she hadn't considered it. Despite all her thinking and the long weeks of waiting passed in deep reflection, she never truly considered she'd be on the losing side of the statistics.

Breath uneven, she forced herself to talk. "What exactly are the options for getting it removed?" *Just get them out of me. Oh God...*

"When you have your consultation with the surgeon he'll go over everything in more detail, but a mastectomy removes the entire breast while a lumpectomy conserves the breast and only removes the tumors and the tissue surrounding them."

She couldn't breathe. "Do I have to decide that now?"

"Of course not, but you'll want to move quickly and schedule the surgery as soon as possible, whichever you decide."

Her heart beat erratically in her chest. It hurt

—her poor damaged chest hurt. "Is one more effective?" Chills traveled to her arms as her entire body trembled.

"It all depends on the patient. A lumpectomy followed by radiation can be as effective as a mastectomy, however, there's always a threat of the cancer returning."

Cancer. The word exploded in her head, reverberating with a physical sting that left her weak.

"Radiation may still be necessary after surgery, but that depends on how the cancer reacts to the chemotherapy and procedure. Our first step is preventing the cancer from traveling."

So chemo was unavoidable. As was surgery, be it a simple procedure or a major augmentation. This wasn't happening.

"For some women it offers peace of mind to remove the breast all together. There have been incredible advances in reconstructive surgery…"

She couldn't listen anymore. She had questions, but lacked the courage to ask them. So. Many. Questions. At the top of the list…*Why?*

Dr. Lindsay continued, but she could no longer make sense of his words. She'd been so strong, so patient at all her appointments thus far, certain she could handle whatever this was. It was just a series of hurdles to jump. But now, she wasn't in an office or surrounded by a bunch of strangers in a waiting room. She was home and she was freaking out.

Words like lymph nodes and pathology reports and other things she didn't want to hear made it hard not to cover her ears and scream. Her entire body shook uncontrollably as the tightness inside of her twisted, constricting her lungs, locking her muscles, and making it impossible to do more than barely breathe.

No!

Was this because she hadn't appreciated her body? Thought it flawed and ugly in spots? Was that why it was betraying her? Regret swamped her in the wake of countless apologies to herself. She didn't want to die.

Bile rose in her throat. *Am I going to die? How much time do I have left?*

The doctor made his goodbye and she somehow thanked him. *Thanked him.*

Her arm lowered, the weight of the phone slipping away. Her mouth opened as the muscles in her face collapsed and she wailed so hard, from a place so deep inside of her, the cry didn't make a sound.

Riley's arms grabbed hold of her and squeezed, catching her before she collapsed to the floor, holding her together, but even he wasn't strong enough. She was broken—possibly dying—and nothing could make it stop.

Lowering their bodies to the ground, he squeezed her tight and rocked. Her voice came, wrenched from the depths of her soul, bellowing out of her in nonsense. The worst of her agony was her regret, her life possibly cut down before she'd had the chance to truly live. There were no words for such realizations, only pain that came rushing out in the form of tears. Every diluted idea of control was stripped away as she shattered into a million pieces.

Riley caught her hand as she clawed at her skin, lost in hysteria. This wasn't happening to her. How had her body betrayed her so? Everything she knew felt foreign and she was trapped inside, yet suffering from the outside looking in. It was too much for her mind to bear and in a silent breath the world went quiet, the last of her defenses kicking in and shutting all the fear and hurt away.

He lifted her off the floor, his voice a distant whisper but he never stopped reassuring that somehow they'd get through this. He placed her someplace soft, but she wasn't sure where. Didn't care. He couldn't take her out of this body.

Trapped.

"Shh…shh…shh…" The tears in his voice gutted her.

He rocked her, holding her so tight, as if the movement could stop her from falling apart. But everything was slipping away.

Her throat burned as she sucked in breath after breath. Not enough. Pulling her hair, her pretty hair that would likely fall out, she silently wept. Why? Why was this happening to her? Why did such a horrible thing exist?

His hands brushed over her head as if she were a child. Out of nowhere, her entire world lost its balance and fell down a rabbit hole, spiraling through infinite darkness. She had no idea how much longer she'd have to fall before she reached the end. Up was down and solid ground was a thing of the past. Nothing could save her from this fall.

Dear God, the thought of telling her parents...

Heaving sob after forceful sob, she cried harder than she'd ever cried before. It was a brutal and painful exorcism she never saw coming. Every weakness she'd kept hidden behind her stoic façade was now exposed in glaring light. She was petrified and lacked the strength to pretend to be anything else.

This was her first scar. Plenty would follow, but like beauty and grace, all things physical would fade. But not this. This moment of raw agony would always stay raised a little bit higher than the rest of her soul. Her first scar, borne of a diagnosis delivered over the fucking phone!

Silence came in doses. Her shivers interrupted his whispered words she sensed but couldn't hear. She blinked, unclear of the time, uncaring of anything happening outside of that moment. Her turbulent thoughts were too chaotic. There was nothing beyond the fear of the unknown and the absolute terror of the little knowledge she had. Cancer.

Down, down, down she fell, losing sight of everything that came before and unclear of what lay ahead. The world never seemed as dark as it did in those fleeting moments that somehow wouldn't end.

Reality blurred, blending objects of their home with visions of an unpredictable future.

Her mind, forced to go where her traitorous body led, pitched into a terrifying place she didn't know.

She wanted it to be over before it began, but what if the conclusion was truly the end? And with the last of her hope, she wept a bit more, knowing her world was forever changed…the day she earned her first scar.

~

WHEN SHE WAS a little girl her mother always made sick days nice. She'd spread the boo-boo blanket on the couch and bring down the pillows from her bedroom. Using one of the tables kept in the corner, she'd set out cough drops, tissues, a glass of orange juice, and the remote. Emma would sleep in between episodes of bad 80's sitcoms.

She'd always milked that sort of care to the last drop, claiming she was sick a day longer than she actually was. Emma never minded being sick. Staying home from school was a vacation, a coddled escape from childhood responsibility that made her feel special and loved.

Cancer was different.

It didn't matter that she was still in shock or had yet to accept reality. Cancer moved at its own pace. It didn't respect age or race or social status. It didn't care that she had a life or hobbies or a job. It was single-mindedly the most evil enemy she'd ever faced. Being that there was no rest for the wicked, she couldn't rest until she beat it, knowing full well if she didn't kill the cancer it would surely kill her.

Plain and simple, she wanted to live.

In a blur she moved from one doctor appointment to the next, having more tests done than she'd ever imagined possible. PET scans, MRIs, Echocardiograms, uncountable screenings of blood work, her body was given to science the moment she consented to putting her fate in her doctors' hands. A pincushion for those who knew what came next, she was poked, prodded, prepped, and placed in one strange machine after another.

There was no evading the necessity of the attention cancer demanded. Even at home, her phone steadily rang with news and reminders of upcoming appointments.

Everything was urgent. Everything needed her absolute attention. And everything took an incredible amount of time. She wanted to live, but her existence was suddenly a revolving door of exams and procedures, not resembling her previous life at all. This was life with cancer.

As Emma watched the days go by like an outsider looking in, her world was colored in pink. So many shades, so many versions, so many untied dreams wrapped up in a silly little bow.

Why the color sometimes irritated her, she hadn't a clue. Perhaps it bothered her because pink was merely the offspring of red and she still wanted to be bold. Or maybe she hated the association because pink had always been her favorite color and it now represented the ugliest time of her life.

Blush over a bruise, her life was no longer a story, but a picture book others viewed as pages and pages painted in rose. It was as though everything she'd ever done, every trait she'd ever owned, was washed away by something as delicate as pink. She resented how easily her life fit into a color coded category, how neatly her world became tied up in bows.

She didn't want to be a soft pastel memory people wore in a race, no longer blonde, no longer a thirty-six C, nothing more than a pale color in a sea of ribbons racing toward a cure that was too late to save her. She wasn't ready to fade into pink. But the more that delicate color spilled into her world the less the old Emma seemed to exist.

Perhaps she was still in denial.

Her trips to the oncology office were never pleasant. Rather than look around the waiting room at the various women in the process of losing their hair, she buried her nose in a magazine. She could empathize, but it broke a bit of her every time she came face to face with a woman a few steps ahead in her treatment.

Riley was adapting faster than her, but he wasn't the one suffering every prick and poke either. She couldn't fault him though. He'd been incredible, adjusting his schedule to drive her to appointments and helping her with the ungodly amount of paperwork. Knowing he was coming off of night shift and surviving on only a few hours sleep, she insisted he rest when he could and they soon developed a reputation for hogging the corners of waiting rooms.

Once she signed in at the desk of her oncologist's office, she reached into her bag for her latest copy of *Rolling Stone*, finding pop culture a comfortable bridge between her surreal existence and the reality she used to know.

"You sure you're okay?" Riley asked as he structured a temporary cot out of two chairs.

"I'll be fine. Take a nap." The word *fine* had been renovated, its new definition quite different from its old meaning.

As he hunkered down, shifting to find the most comfortable position in an obviously uncomfortable place, she paged through her magazine. Life was all about little compromises, they were coming to learn.

As patients drifted into the back new ones arrived. Sometimes the amount of patients being treated for such a hideous disease was startling, which was another reason she chose not to watch the waiting rooms too closely.

"You waiting?"

Pulling her attention from the article she read, Emma faced a woman who came from the double doors, unsure if she was a nurse or a patient. "I'm sorry?"

"You've been here a while. I was wondering if you were waiting for someone or waiting to be seen."

"Oh. Waiting to be seen," she explained,

hating the pinch that still stung every time she voiced that truth.

The woman smiled. "Mind if I sit?"

Emma waved her to the open seat.

The woman settled in the seat beside her, posture at ease. "What are you in for?"

Dog-earing her page, she tucked her magazine away. "More tests."

Lips pressed tight, the woman smiled and nodded as if she could relate. Maybe she was here with someone. Maybe she was someone's Riley.

"It's a lot," the woman said. "How are you handling everything so far?"

Though the woman was a stranger, Emma found herself pressed to answer honestly, divulge things she didn't often say in front of those she loved. "Honestly? I'm terrified."

She nodded. "It is that—terrifying."

Emma scrutinized the woman. Her hair was cut in a short, trendy style that took more confidence then attractiveness to pull off. Her calming presence lent an uncategorized beauty to her otherwise ordinary features. And her understated clothing and lack of jewelry didn't help her discern if she was an employee, a supportive friend or a patient. *Just ask.* "Are you a patient?"

"No. I'm just a helper."

Like an angel? There was definitely something soothing in her proximity.

"I used to be a patient though." She smiled, her expression proud but a little sad, falling short of reaching her eyes. There was something else in her eyes though—a story. "I've been cancer free for ten years."

Goose bumps lifted on Emma's skin, perhaps pushed into place by a surge of envy. "That's wonderful." Would she ever have the chance to make such a statement?

Her gaze dropped to her shirt. She couldn't tell what was under the loose material. Some women just had smaller frames, though this woman was tall.

"I'm Anna, by the way." She held out her hand.

"Emma." Her soft fingers held hers a second longer than most handshakes lasted.

"It's nice to meet you, Emma. So…does that belong to you?" She tipped her chin at Riley, who was conked out on the chair in the corner.

Her cheeks heated. "Yeah. He works nights and my appointments are always early."

"Sweet of him to still come to keep you company, even if he's unconscious."

She smiled. "Yeah. He's sort of wonderful like that."

After a few moments of silence, Anna cut to the chase. "So… How did you get here?"

Startled by her bluntness, which somehow remained in the realms of polite chitchat, Emma snorted and said the first response that came to mind. "I have no idea."

Anna giggled. "Me neither. But here I am, happy, healthy, and whole—for the most part. Others might debate my sanity. Some say I'm lacking a screw or two."

"I'd question anyone who went through this and came out totally sane."

"Right?" She laughed. "It's not a bad version of crazy though. Cancer definitely has a way of making you see the beauty in things. Makes you ditch all the nonsense in between. It sort of gives you an *I don't give a fuck* attitude. And no one's going to criticize you to your face, because you have *cancer,*" she whispered the last word.

"I'm still not able to say it out loud," she confessed.

Anna's smile gentled as sympathy filled her eyes. "I'm not making light of it, sweetie. I joke, because laughter blunts the pain. Good medicine and all that."

Emma nodded. "I'll take any medicine I can at this point. I just want to get well."

They chatted a while longer as more patients came and others were called back behind the double doors. Anna never seemed in a rush to be anywhere else and the longer they talked, the more Emma found herself confessing what were unspeakable fears only minutes ago.

Anna listened and sympathized, sharing anecdotes from her own experiences. They weren't necessarily reassuring, but somehow put her at ease, prepared her in a way nothing else had. There was simply something special about this woman that she found attractive, almost magnetic.

When the nurse called Emma's name, she found herself reluctant to leave Anna's side. Riley woke and gave her a questioning look, not expecting her to make friends when she'd been working so hard to be invisible.

As she stood, Anna surprised her with a hug. "You take care of yourself, Emma. We'll chat again soon."

She didn't know if their paths would ever cross again, but it was a comforting thought, one that made the fear of visiting the oncology office a little less intimidating.

At her next appointment, Emma suffered a pinch of disappointment when Anna wasn't in the waiting room, which made her sudden appearance all the more pleasant. "Anna," she greeted as the woman came out, holding a bag of popcorn.

"I thought I heard the nurses say you were here. Popcorn?" She tipped the bag as she took a seat.

Riley grinned, knowing she'd hoped to see her friend again, and shut his eyes, catching his usual nap in the corner. And so a new routine was born. She'd arrive and Anna would soon surprise her with some sort of snack or drink and plenty of good conversation.

She was so lovely and feminine, so unmistakably female, and funny too. In truth, she wasn't traditionally beautiful at all. Her smile was crooked and there wasn't anything physically striking about her features, but she remained one of the prettiest people Emma knew. Every time she thought of Anna, her chest warmed as if filling with a cozy blush. Anna made her feel…pink.

It took Emma a solid month to realize this radiant woman no longer had breasts, and that was only when Riley brought it to her attention.

"She has boobs, Riley," she argued on their way to the grocery store.

"Emma, she does not."

"And how would you know? Did you see her topless?"

"No, I asked her."

Her steps faltered and he paused, facing her as she stepped out of the way of the surrounding pedestrians. "You *asked* her? How? When?"

"During one of your appointments."

She wasn't sure what shocked her more, that he'd had the balls to ask something like that or that he'd actually conversed with Anna. "I didn't know you two talked."

"We talk all the time. Awesome person. Terrible at Crazy Eights, but other than that I think she's great."

"You played cards with her?"

"Emma, you're usually back there for over an hour. Am I not allowed to talk to her?"

"No..." Why was she being so weird about this? "Do you talk about me?"

"Yes, but it's not like I have anything bad to say. You know she was married before she got diagnosed?"

"I know." But her husband left her shortly after she went into remission. Was it because of the stress or perhaps due to all the physical changes her body had undergone? "You guys talked about that?"

He shrugged. "A little. I don't know the details or anything, but she's always telling me how supportive I am." He shrugged again, minimizing. "It's not like I'd let you go through this alone."

On the verge of tears, she grabbed his hand and squeezed. That's what was so special about him. He did all these great things and didn't even realize how great they were. "She's right. You're the most supportive person in my life. I love that you come to all my appointments, even if it's just to sleep."

He waved a finger. "I also play cards. It's not all for you. I've been mopping the floor with your peers."

But it was for her. There were a million things he could do with his days, but he put that all aside to be by her side, knowing she was too afraid to go at this alone. "I love you." It was all she could say, yet those three words didn't seem to be enough to truly express everything he made her feel.

Leaning close, he kissed her nose. "Come on. I want to get food and get back before Rarity leaves. If we nag her enough we can probably get her to cook dinner." That night they enjoyed a huge pasta dinner in a delicious pesto sauce, compliments of Chef Rarity.

Emma's life had become totally unrecognizable from what it once was. Based on all her test results and numerous consultations, they decided the best treatment for her unique case. A lumpectomy was in her future, but first, the doctors wanted to treat the tumors with chemo-therapy to kill off any rapidly growing cells.

"That's a pretty common approach," Anna told her after Emma shared the news. "The un-fortunate thing about chemo is that while it kills the bad cells, it also kills good ones. My advice is eat while you can and don't get hung up on van-ity. Cancer's ugly and when it's inside of us, it isn't pretty."

She appreciated her sage advice, being that it was firsthand. Emma understood more than she did a month ago, but still felt half as informed as everyone else. The doctors had explained that chemo affected the lining of the stomach, which was why people often got sick during treatment. She understood the risks and saw the side effects as a distant outsider, right here in the waiting room.

"I never expected this," she confessed, a broken record even to her own ears.

Anna's hand pressed into her knee, but she remained facing forward. "No one does."

Once the first round of chemo was scheduled, Emma requested an official leave of absence from work and they prepared as much as one could for the unexpected. Riley moved into her bedroom and converted his room into a guest room since her mother and father would prob-ably be staying with them from time to time. Her mother was steadily freezing meals and sending them over. Between her parents and roommates, they were unstoppable and it humbled her in indescribable ways to be so looked after with so much tenderness.

Rarity had become obsessed with nutrition. She believed supplements and eating a plant based diet were key in defeating cancer. Their kitchen was filled with various cookbooks based on veganism and macrobiotics. All processed foods were donated to the local pantry and re-placed with organic grains and unprocessed goods.

Though her doctors were strictly supervising any supplements, Rarity insisted she eventually start taking things like black cumin seed, turmeric, and the list continued to grow. Every-thing they ate was cooked with ginger or garlic or whatever herb claimed to be the miracle plant of the minute.

It was obvious how much her friends derailed their own lives in order to help sustain hers. She'd tried to help as often as she could, but the stress and endless appointments were already ex-hausting. She couldn't imagine how rundown she'd be once chemo started.

The plan was to administer chemo in two-week increments. There would be short breaks in between so that her body could recover and they could reassess the cell growth, but as soon as she started feeling better the treatment would start again. This would go on intermittently until the threat was gone or she was, whichever came first.

No one acted like the chemo would finish the job. According to her doctors and what they knew of her strand of cancer, she was constantly reminded that somewhere in the midst of all this the tumors would be surgically removed, but her mind couldn't handle that yet.

Every time she looked at her schedule and tried to plan ahead, she got physically, emotionally, and mentally overwhelmed. What if there was no ahead?

As the days ticked down, she found it impossible to hide her fear. Not only was she worried about her own mortality and afraid of the pain that would inevitably come with the treatment, she worried about those around her. They tirelessly worked to make sure she had everything she needed.

Their ceaseless openhandedness often brought her to tears and she intended to pay back their kindness tenfold, once this was all over—she just needed the chance.

CHAPTER 15

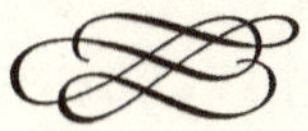

Riley placed *The Cure* album in the bag on top of the boo-boo blanket. Glancing around the loft, he wondered if there was anything else he was forgetting. The front door quietly opened and Rarity walked in with Marla. He gave the dog a bone so she would settle quickly.

"Do you want some coffee?" he whispered to his sister as he poured a second cup.

"Yeah. She up yet?" She washed her hands, something they were getting in the habit of doing routinely since Emma's immune system was now at risk and a common cold suddenly ranked as life threatening.

He slid Rarity the Rosie the Riveter mug. "No. I figured I'd let her sleep until the last minute. She was up late."

His sister nodded. "Will they let you in with her?"

"No. The nurses are all suited up with gloves and goggles. It's not safe."

"It's amazing that stuff's meant to heal."

He glanced at the supply of disinfectant products stashed on the counter next to the trashcan liners. How had this become his life? He resented having to take such precautions with her, but her medications could not only be harmful to others, it was imperative they all stay healthy. If they got sick, who would take care of her? They had to be vigilant about containing anything that came in contact with the chemo while avoiding anything contaminated with outside germs.

"I can't believe this is happening," Rarity said, a dazed look in her eyes as she held her untouched coffee.

It was something he'd try to comprehend for the rest of his life. With a flurry of appointments and staggering results, it had been an ongoing process of elimination, jumping from A to B back to A until they finally landed at C. Cancer.

That word, that horrible fucking word. It was a life sentence people could barely whisper and he heard it every hour of every day. He had no choice but to go against everything he knew and declare, no, it was *not* a death sentence.

His heart demanded he reorder his thinking and now every thought was geared toward what mattered most. Survival. She would survive. She would beat this. She had to, because he couldn't imagine life without her.

The speed the doctors were moving was horrifying, her treatment had immediately consumed everyone in her immediate circle. What if this obsessive treatment was the last part of her life? She was missing her chance to live because it took so much damn effort to survive.

He shut his eyes. There was just so much resentment.

The prevalent ache in his chest tightened as he once again struggled to come to terms with his despair, hiding it away before Emma could see how badly this was crushing him. The chronic weight he bore was indescribable and beyond anything he anticipated carrying on his shoulders in this lifetime. But what choice did he have? All he wanted was her, safe and alive. It was an eye-opening crush that kept him awake at night, and a daunting responsibility during the day. But he desperately wanted to be her rock.

She wanted to do the chemotherapy to try to save her breast. He respected her choice, but worried it was because she feared losing her breast would steal her beauty. That was bullshit. Take both of them, but spare her life. That was all that mattered. *She* was all that mattered. Still, it was her choice and she'd chosen to shrink the tumors and proceed with a lumpectomy if possible.

And so, today it would begin. Poison poised against poison. He'd done everything he could think of to ensure the process went as comfortably as possible, but nothing removed his hope that this would all suddenly disappear. It was a fantasy, but it crossed his mind every day all the same.

At one point in his life he was foolish enough

to believe he had control. There was no control, no guarantee. Now, he was handing over the little control he had and placing everything he loved in the care of strangers. It wasn't easy and though he'd been gearing himself up for this very moment, he never felt more unprepared in his life.

It would start with an injection, killing tiny, little mutated cells and some innocent ones along the way. Then they'd remove the three pea-sized lumps that started everything. But would it stop there? What if the chemo didn't move fast enough and the cancer spread? How much would she pay to have her life back? And what quality of life would there be when this was finally over? These were the resounding worries that filled every waking moment of his days.

Despite his outward calm, every smile, every encouraging word was carefully pulled from the chaos in his mind. Inside, he hid his fears in the blackest corners of his mind, crevices he was too ashamed to admit his worries dwelled, worries even his sister couldn't know existed. It was imperative they only give voice to the positive, but the pessimism existed all the same. It was his, a burden he bore alone, speaking not even a whisper of doubt for the others to hear.

The toilet flushed and he turned. Emma shuffled from the hall, her hair standing on end, sheet prints pressed into her face. "Morning."

His breath sucked in as he committed the image to memory, classifying it in his mind as *before*. God, she was magnificent.

Strolling to her, he didn't stop until they were hugging, his face pressing into her neck as he breathed in her scent. "Morning, beautiful."

She sighed. "You guys ready for today?"

Amused that she'd worry if *they* were ready, he brought her attention to everything he'd packed. "I packed you a bag." Rarity dumped her coffee and his, sensitive to the fact that Emma was fasting.

Emma peeked in the bag. "My boo-boo blanket." She smiled at him. "I love you for being so sweet and thoughtful."

"I also packed you a Walkman with fresh batteries. The Cure's all cued up. Side One."

"When will you invest in an iPod?" His sister grumbled.

"Cassettes are where it's at," he argued.

"You're an idiot. Vinyl, at least, has some lure. Cassettes are stupid. The sound quality's shit, they break easily and you have to crank them with a pencil, and no one feels like waiting for rewind anymore."

He frowned at his sister and mumbled, "Your sound quality's shit." So what if they took a little longer to fix than digital music? They were classic and he'd put time into his collection. He wasn't going to throw them away just because there were more efficient ways to hear the music he liked.

"Don't fight, guys," Emma said. She pressed a hand to his chest. "You're wearing your Save Ferris shirt. Is that for me?"

"Oh, well, you're *very* popular," he quoted.

"Everyone adores you, geeks, sluts, dickheads, dweebies…" He loved that movie.

She laughed and glanced at his sister. "Rarity, I need you to help me with something before we go."

"Whatever you need, toots."

"I can help," he offered, not wanting to be left out.

She smiled. "Okay. I'm going to take a shower first. We have time, right?"

He glanced at the clock. "We don't have to leave for at least an hour."

"Good."

While Emma showered they grabbed something quick to eat. He made their bed and stashed unopened bottles of water in every room. When he finished, she was dressed in comfortable clothes and had her hair braided to the side.

"Here." She handed Rarity a pair of scissors.

Riley stilled. He didn't care about her hair, but this was a big deal. This was her way of taking a bit of control while the ball was still in her court and deciding—on her terms—it was time for kickoff.

Rarity carefully took the scissors. "Are you sure, toots?"

She took a steadying breath. "Yeah. My hairdresser's connected with Locks of Love. I want to donate it while I can." She glanced at him and laughed, but the hollow sound was far from happy. "It's just gonna fall out anyway, right?"

As always, her fear fed his, but so did her courage. He moved into the kitchen. "I'll do it."

Emma's eyes glazed, as her lips pursed in a tight smile. Before anyone could comment about what a monumental moment this was, she tipped her head back and broke eye contact, her braid falling down her back.

"Hand me the scissors, Rare." He took the shears and stroked her damp braid, another moment committed to memory. "One," he counted.

"Two," Rarity whispered.

"Three." Emma rasped and he carved the scissors through the thick braid as quickly as possible.

Once the ponytail was free, he handed it to Rarity who zipped it in a sandwich bag. Emma exhaled and tousled her hair; sending short curls spiraling around her face. She turned to them and drew in a deep breath.

Her cheeks glowed with a fearless smile, as if she'd somehow relieved a burden she didn't have the strength to carry. "Let's do this."

~

THE GIRL HE KISSED GOODBYE, outside of the chemotherapy room, was not the girl that came back to him. Emma walked sluggishly through the double doors, a nurse by her side and he immediately stood.

"Are you Riley?" The nurse asked handing him her bag. "Emma told me all about you."

He caught Emma's arm and helped her walk. "How was it?"

She groaned. "I did it."

Leave it to her not to mention how awful he could only imagine it was. "This is normal?" He looked at the nurse.

"Oh, yeah. She'll be weak for the next few days. Plenty of rest so her body can heal and the chemo can do its job."

Jesus. Her eyes were so puffy and red. "Were you crying?"

"No. My head feels really weird right now though. I wanna go home."

Grateful they took care of all the paperwork ahead of time, he walked her to the car. The most minor things seemed to be a struggle. He fastened her seatbelt, mindful of the small catheter port in her chest. He laid the boo-boo blanket over her lap and she slept the entire way home.

When they reached the loft he texted Rarity and gently woke Emma. "We're here, cakes."

Her mouth clicked as she dryly swallowed. "Thirsty."

He uncapped a bottle of water and handed it to her. Rarity came down and, for the first time in a very long time, he saw fear in his sister's eyes. Forcing back all the warnings he wanted to say, he simply nodded, and exited the car as she climbed behind the wheel.

She pressed a hand to Emma's shoulder, their smiles reflecting the same tragic happiness that the hard part of the morning was over. "You made it, toots."

"I made it," Emma agreed, sluggishly.

"The couch is all set up and so is your bed. I'll

be back as soon as I park Riley's car. *Love Actually's* cued up and waiting."

She chuckled, but he could tell it cost her. "You're the best."

"Let's get you inside," he said, taking her arm and guiding her to the door.

If she had a preference between her bed and the couch she didn't voice it. The second she stepped through the door she went straight to the couch and curled into a ball.

Marla watched her, a curious look in her chocolate eyes as though she sensed something wasn't right. Slowly, she padded over to the sofa, sniffed Emma, and curled on the floor beside her, which was where she stayed.

Emma was asleep before Rarity returned from parking the car. The waiting game had begun again as Emma slept and continued to sleep as they tried to prepare for whatever came next.

Hours passed in silence as they simply watched her, unspeakable things running through their terrified minds. It was the realest experience of his life. Nothing compared and he never wanted to experience anything this real again. But he would. This was only the beginning and there was a long road ahead. Knowing that, made living this all the more distressing.

❧

SOMETHING WAS WRONG. His eyes opened as a small moan echoed in the dark loft. Bolting upright he sprung into action as Emma hunched over the couch and groaned into the trash bin. Falling to his knees, he crawled to her and brushed the hair away from her face.

"Don't," she whined, but he ignored her.

She heaved, but very little came out. Her skin was soaked in sweat and her motor skills were noticeably off as she weakly trembled at the edge of the couch.

"What can I do?"

She retched again and groaned. "God, this sucks."

He uncapped a bottle of water, waiting for her to finish. She eased back, fatigued and moaning. Handing her the water, he rushed to the kitchen, wet a cloth and returned to her side, pressing the cool compress to her head. He wanted to know what it felt like, what might make her more comfortable, but he already knew the answer. Awful and nothing.

The chemo was doing what it was designed to do—rip her apart. If she was experiencing the effects already that had to mean the tumors were being affected too. He told himself so, over and over again, because it was the only justification for anyone to volunteer for this sort of torture.

He pressed the cool cloth to the back of her neck. "It'll pass, cakes. Just breathe."

The following day they returned to the oncologist so Emma could get a shot that would stimulate cell growth in her bone marrow. The nurse, when Emma wasn't present, described it as excruciating, but Emma never complained. Still, he saw the agony in her eyes.

The moment they returned home she had a small snack, curled up on the couch, and fell asleep. Marla climbed off of Rarity's bed and lay beside Emma on the floor, her silent guardian.

As the days passed, hushed and curious, Emma was too exhausted to do more than sit quietly. Her breathing became the steady melody he built his world around. When they watched television, her head rested on his shoulder and their hands held each other, the soft in and out of her breath was the most reassuring sound to his ears. His heart seemed to adjust to the rhythm, as it became the sole focus of his existence.

It was all he needed in that moment, for her to breathe. Just breathe.

He wondered how parents dealt with the agony of love, assuming most parents held an unconditional affection for their children the way his did not. Scraped knees and bloody noses, so many boo-boos through the years. He wasn't sure he'd ever be strong enough to love more than one person that deeply, because loving Emma unconditionally ripped his heart to shreds every time she suffered.

Perhaps he loved her too much, but there was never any middle with him. It was all or nothing. The only thing worse than the pain of loving her so hard was the absolute, insufferable agony of imagining a world without that love. There wasn't a choice. He needed to love her and so he did. He loved her with every ounce of his being.

When the second round of chemo started, Emma lacked the verve she possessed in the beginning. Although she'd survived round one, the aftermath had devastated her sense of optimism, given them all a startling glimpse of the horrific side effects that came with modern treatments.

Perhaps, knowing what to expect and being weakened by the enemy she still had to face, made it all the more terrifying. He finally understood what people meant when they said the cure was worse than the disease.

Cancer, that tiny little cell that started all this, was silent and painless. Chemotherapy, on the other hand, the venom strong enough to kill said cancer, made so much noise it silenced life itself, the painful aftermath all that echoed in their home.

As Emma clung to the toilet, refusing to get off the bathroom floor, he waited for the sickness to pass. But there was never any warning when it would strike, and chances were as soon as he helped her back to bed she'd puke again. After twenty minutes of nothing but moans leaving her mouth, he lifted her off the floor and carried her to bed.

"I'm sorry," she apologized, but he ignored her apology like he did every time. This wasn't her fault.

"Try drinking some water." He uncapped the bottle and held it to her lips. Her eyes closed and she turned away after only a few sips. "Good?"

"Mmm."

He covered her and returned to the bathroom. He wasn't sure what time it was, but he didn't want to fall asleep again until he was certain she was in the clear. Pulling out the disinfectant, he wiped down the toilet and vanity, tossing away uncountable strands of Emma's hair.

"That shit is killing her," Rarity whispered, startling him.

His sister was steadily increasing the long list of strange foods in their diet. It was impossible to talk to her sometimes. Everything she read argued chemo came with more risks than guarantees.

"It'll pass." He sprayed the toilet and placed a clean stack of towels by the tub.

"They say the third round's the worst."

He ignored her, incapable of imagining anything worse than what they'd already witnessed.

"Doesn't it bother you that she has to sign papers saying she understands this treatment might cause other cancers down the road?"

Having heard enough, he threw the toilet brush against the wall and snapped, *"What do you want me to do, Rarity?* This is the only option we have! People survive this way! They beat it! I can't gamble her life on herbs and supplements!"

"She's gotten sicker since it started!" she hissed. "How much worse can it get? When does it end?"

Gripping the vanity he looked away. He didn't have the fucking answers. "It ends when it starts to make her better."

"And then what? We wait some more. She has surgery? More waiting. And it either starts all over again or they burn the shit out of her with radiation. They'll kill her before the cancer does!"

Breathing hard, he bit his lip. He was so damn tired. "This is *her* choice. It's her life. What do you want from me?"

"What if it's the wrong choice?"

"What if it's not?"

"But what if it is?"

"Jesus, Rarity, I can't do this right now! Do you see what I'm dealing with? She's weak. She's sick. And she's suffering. Don't you think if there was any fucking way I could take some of that pain from her I would? If you think it isn't killing me watching her go through this, you're a fucking idiot!" He shoved past her and went to clean up the living room.

The swish of her slippers followed him. "I'm sorry."

He ignored her.

"Riley...please, don't be mad at me. I'm just so afraid she isn't going to make it through this."

His jaw tightened. "Shut. Up." The words barely fit through his clenched teeth.

She sniffled. "What'll we do without her?"

"God damn it, Rarity, shut up!"

She grabbed his arms and he tried to shove her away, but she refused to let him go. Yanking him to her, she hugged him, and the tightness in his chest exploded. Fear burned his throat as he gripped her tight.

He choked as his eyes flooded with tears. "I can't lose her." He clung to her shoulders as his lips tightened and his eyes squeezed shut against the pain. "I can't."

"I know," Rarity whispered. Her hand cupped the back of his head. "I know."

It was the first time he cried since finding out it was cancer and he was certain it wouldn't be the last. They sat in the dark for several hours, hardly talking, yet having one of the most earth-shattering conversations of his life.

He couldn't be mad at Rarity for loving Emma. He understood. Loving someone with cancer meant carrying a love greater than any hate. Because he absolutely despised what this disease was doing to her, but he stuck around because he loved her a thousand times more.

~

IT WAS TIME. Riley stuffed his lucky monkey hat on his head and nodded at his sister. "Let's do this."

Emma stood at the counter eating a bowl of granola cereal as he and Rarity tiptoed into the kitchen. She grinned nervously and wiped a dribble of almond milk off her chin. "Whhhhat are you guys doing?"

"Nothin'," Rarity sung, folding her hands innocently behind her back and rocking on her heels. She wore overalls and a blue knit hat with mustache trim.

Emma put down her spoon and arched a brow in his direction. "And you? You're definitely up to something. I can always tell."

Still in his pajamas, he beamed. It wasn't unusual for him to wander around in his monkey hat. "How do you feel today?"

"Better."

"Good. We have a surprise for you."

She smiled. "I like surprises—the good kind at least."

He looked at Rarity. "Ready?" She nodded and he counted off. "One."

"Two," Rarity chanted.

They turned to Emma and smiled expectantly. Her eyes moved from side to side. "Three?"

Together, they pulled off their hats and she gasped. "You're bald!"

He gave her his most cheeky grin and winked. "Pound sign no hair don't care."

"Hair is so passé," Rarity said. "Bald's the new beard."

Emma's expression was priceless. He hadn't seen her smile like that in weeks. Reaching behind her ear, she touched a thinning patch of her hair. "Will you do mine?"

Rarity hugged her and placed a smacking kiss on her cheek. "Come on. I left the clippers out."

In the end, she looked totally different, but her beauty somehow became even more pronounced. Those fascinating eyes shined, because she was—for that moment—happy, and that was all he could ask for.

For now, that was enough.

CHAPTER 16

When it was time for round three Emma appeared optimistic once again. Prepared and acting like somewhat of an old pro, she had a stronger attitude than ever.

"Let's get'er done," she said, bouncing by the front door, dressed in her sweats, his Save Ferris shirt, and his lucky monkey hat. She was fucking hot in his clothes and he wanted to do stuff to her.

"Come here," he ordered as he sat on the couch.

She giggled and skipped over to him, her clumsy little hop the most motion he saw from her in weeks. He patted his lap and she straddled his legs on the sofa. Cupping both hands at the side of her neck, he drew her in for a kiss.

"Mmm," she hummed.

"We have some time," he whispered, pressing his hips into her.

She pulled back slowly and looked at his lap as if considering his offer. They hadn't had sex since she'd started chemo. Biting her lip, she blushed, and whispered, "I feel funny."

"I feel horny."

Pushing his chest, she laughed. "No, I mean… I feel weird."

His smile bent with concern. "Why?"

She shrugged. "It's been a while."

He tsked. "So? Don't feel weird. It's just us. I think we'll remember how it goes." Arching a brow, trying to dispel any worry, he joked, "I'm quite the expert on all things bajingo."

"I know you are, but I'm…" She glanced at the bandage covering the port on her chest. "I'm gross."

His humor disappeared. "You are *not* gross, Emma. I don't care about any of that. I don't even see it. If it bothers you, leave your shirt on, but don't stay dressed on my account. I love you no matter what your body looks like."

Her eyes closed and he tried not to be mad at her for thinking such things. She wasn't gross, or anything close to it. She was Emma. His Emma.

"Hey." He brushed a thumb over her cheek and she lifted her lashes. "I *love* you. Don't hide yourself from me. I don't want you to."

She swallowed and deliberately stood. Disappointment tightened his chest, but then his breath held as she eased down her sweats. There was no hair, something he should have expected, but didn't. His body reacted to her, regardless of the physical changes he noted. Leaning forward, he kissed her hip and leisurely slid his hands to cup her behind.

Sliding off of the couch and onto the floor, he parted her thighs and kissed her warm skin. Lingering kisses trailed over her tender flesh and she gasped.

He'd missed her taste. Longed for the heat of her body against his. After today's treatment she'd be under the weather for a while so he wanted to make it count, wanted to remind her how beautiful she was.

He nudged her back to the couch and turned so he could face her. She was nervous, but that was ridiculous. This was them. There was no reason to feel funny around him.

He kissed her slowly, reminding her how wonderful they could make each other feel, and lost himself in her familiar body. She'd been through so much, he wanted to give her pure pleasure, make it all about her and remove any doubts she might have about his feelings. Nothing could detract from the attraction he had for this woman.

Taking his time, he paid homage to every dip and curve he crossed, bringing her swiftly to a state of desire and need. Her release was quick and sharp. And once he had her at ease, her inhibitions blessedly disappeared.

She pulled him to the couch, unlatched his belt and climbed on top of him. Something inside of him gave pause as he caught her hips at the last moment. "Wait."

"For what? I'm ready."

"We need a condom." With everything else she'd been prescribed, they'd decided birth control would only complicate matters. Also, its effectiveness was questionable with all her other meds. However, while she was undergoing treatment, they couldn't risk pregnancy.

"Damn it! Do we have any?"

He thought for a moment, hardly remembering the last time he'd bought some. "Don't you?"

"No!"

"Maybe Rarity has some—"

"What the hell would your sister be doing with condoms, Riley?"

"Good point. Damn it!" He scooted out from under her and placed her on the couch. "Wait here."

She lounged against the cushions, in her Save Ferris T-shirt and monkey hat. No panties and one sock on her left foot. Seriously, the hottest chick he'd ever seen. He better have a freaking condom somewhere.

Racing to the bedroom, he ripped open one drawer after another, making an absolute mess as he scrounged for a rubber.

"Check my vanity!" she yelled.

His pants slipped down his hips so he jacked them back up, but didn't bother fastening the belt. "Vanity, vanity, vanity..." he mumbled, turning in circles until he spotted the vanity—same place it had always been since Emma moved into the loft. *"Vanity!"*

He rummaged through each dainty drawer

finding everything *but* a condom. "I'm not finding one!" His eyes burned as sweat collected at his brow.

"What about the nightstand?"

"Nightstand." He ran to the small end table and dug through the drawer. "Nothing!"

"Oh! What about that weird wooden box you won't let anyone look in?"

He stilled. His memory box? No. "Stop trying to get in my secret box!"

"Well, if you ever want to get in mine you better find something!"

"Shit," he hissed. "Gotta get in her box. Gotta get in her box." Scanning the room he spotted a small bag hanging in the closet and recognized it from when they first started dating. "Come to poppa."

He rushed to the bag and turned it inside out, fishing in every pocket he could find. Certain the purse was empty, he threw it and cursed. Just then, a small purple foil slid onto the carpet. Skies opened, angels sung, doves released from the heavens, and trumpets played. Diving to the ground, he snatched up the condom. *"I got one!"*

"Yes!"

Running out of the room, he raced down the hall and tripped as his pants fell to his ankles. "I'm okay!" He bounded to his feet.

A smile spread across her face as she eased back and clapped. "Thank God." She parted her thighs.

He tore open the condom, fitted it to his erection, and the front door suddenly opened as a shrill scream rent the air. He pivoted, clapping his hands over his dick. *"Get out, Rarity!"*

"Oh my, God!" His sister turned and came face to face with Emma's bajingo. "What the fuck!" Her hands lifted in distress, covering her eyes. "I'm blind! My retinas! Why are you sitting like that?"

Emma screamed, clamping her legs shut.

"Stop looking at my girlfriend's prizes!" he shouted over his shoulder as his sister barreled full speed into the wall, missing the door by a foot.

Marla barked, not sure what the hell was happening. Rarity screamed again.

"Get! Out!" he shouted and she turned, crashed into the door, opened it, and raced into the hall. The door slammed and he faced Emma. "Unbelievable."

She was hysterical. Her head fell back as she straight up cackled and hooted.

"Oh, you're gonna get it." Adjusting the condom, he dove on top of her. "I thought we talked about laughing during sex."

"I'm sorry," she cracked up.

"That's it." Lifting her leg, he slid into her. Her laughter silenced abruptly as her eyes softened and her gaze found his.

"I missed this," she whispered, catching her breath.

He leaned in and brushed his lips to hers, thrusting gently. Sweet heaven, he missed this too. "I missed *you.*"

Wrapping her arms around his neck, she

rubbed a hand over his bald head. Pushing her hat away, he did the same. Pressing their foreheads together, they stared into one another's eyes. It was nice to have *this* again.

~

IT WAS BAD, worse than ever before. None of the other times hit her this hard and all Riley could do was sit back and pray for it to end. She was so beaten down, so tense with discomfort, he could barely touch her without adding to her agony.

"Do you want more ice chips?" he whispered, sitting on the floor beside the couch where she trembled, silently tolerating the poison ripping her apart from the inside out. She wasn't eating on account of how badly the heartburn had gotten.

"No," she rasped.

Staring at the rain pelting the window, wishing there was something he could do, he bottled up the rage inside of him. So much anger borne of utter fear. It was like she had the flu but a thousand times worse. She liked the cool damp cloth on her head so he continued to hold it there.

"Riley," she whispered, her eyes barely open.

He wished she had the strength to look at him. He always felt safe when her eyes were on him. "Yeah, cakes?"

"Do you think I'm going to die?"

His throat closed, every muscle in his body

locking. "No," he rasped. "Don't say stuff like that, Emma."

She twitched and shivered. "My heart's beating so fast."

"Try not to think about anything. Just breathe."

"Tell me a story," she whispered, voice weak. There wasn't much color in her lips and her nostrils were raw and pink from too many nosebleeds. "Tell me where the monkey hat came from."

His jaw tightened. It seemed a major process to unearth his voice and get it past the lump in his throat. "I stole it."

"What?" Her eyes showed as little slits, but then closed. It was enough to make him go on with the story.

"I was in Central Park one day and there was a street festival going on. People were selling all sorts of junk. This little kid went up to a lady selling sock monkeys and hats."

She shivered again and he covered her with the blanket, but then she feebly pushed it off as if she were hot, so he lowered it and she sighed.

He swallowed and shut his eyes, trying to remember the day clear enough to tell the story as vividly as possible, hopefully enough to distract her from the pain.

"The kid tried on a hat and the lady flipped out, told him he had to buy it. He had no money and got upset when the lady just kept yelling at him, like she could get blood from a stone."

He dragged the damp cloth under her nose as

he noticed a fresh trickle of blood. "I was so pissed off at the way she talked to the little boy, when she wheeled her cart away I snatched a hat from the back."

The corner of her mouth twitched with the start of a smile she wasn't strong enough to finish. "Did she see you?"

His shoulders vibrated as the first breath of a laugh slipped past his lips. "Yeah. She threatened to call the constable over, so I bought the whole bag of hats and she shut up. Once I paid, I told her exactly what I thought about her manners."

He lost sight of his surroundings for a few seconds as he thought back to that day. "I'm so fucked up from my parents. People forget how impressionable kids can be. She didn't want to hear that though. Some people are just mean and there isn't enough time to figure out why."

Though she was lying very still, a slight smile curved her lips. Keeping her eyes closed, she whispered, "You gave that boy a hat, didn't you?"

"I gave all the kids hats that day. Central Park was infested with sock monkeys. I thought they were cool so I kept one for myself."

"You…" She went completely motionless.

"Emma?" he touched her forehead, her fever was climbing and if it didn't drop soon he was taking her to the ER.

She moaned, her arms sliding over her stomach as she breathed through the pain. Once she got a handle on it, she slurred, "I… love you, Riley… because you… gave that boy a hat."

His molars locked as he scrutinized her, unsure if he should have let her convince him to leave her on the couch when everything in him demanded he take her to the hospital. "I love you too," he whispered, kissing her cool lips. "Rest."

She was silent for a long time and he assumed she'd fallen asleep. The pattering of rain against the windows was the only sound, but then she whispered, "There's so much…"

He leaned close, barely hearing her words. "What, cakes?"

Her chest lifted, the effort to speak taking her breath away. "Our list…" She licked her lips, her eyes still closed. "We have… so much to do." Her hand opened and he gently touched her palm. "I'm not ready to die, Riley."

Moisture filled his eyes as his lips tightened. "You're not gonna die, Em. Goonies never say die. We'll get to the list."

But he wasn't sure if that was true. So far, all they'd accomplished was taking a picture every day. Emma was big on documenting this year. Turning out of earshot he sniffled and wiped his tears on his shoulder without letting go of her fingers.

"I want… to do all those things, Riley."

"Me too."

"Promise… we'll do them."

He blinked as his vision blurred and his throat contracted. What if he couldn't? There were so many things she had yet to do, but in her state they seemed impossible. "I promise," he rasped.

"Don't wait too long."

He wouldn't. The moment her strength returned he'd take her to the Empire State Building. And as soon as she felt well enough, they'd go skating in Rockefeller Center. He'd make all her wishes come true, the first chance he got—

His attention returned to the window, a sudden thought coming to mind. Forcing the fear back, he stood on shaky legs. "Come with me," he whispered, gently lifting her to his chest.

Gathering the boo-boo blanket around her and making sure she was covered, he carefully maneuvered his way to the door. She moaned and he adjusted his hold. "I got you."

Her breathing leveled out as he left the loft. "You okay?"

Her eyes remained closed. "Mm-hm."

Climbing the stairs, he held her close and pulled the blanket to her neck as he pushed through the door leading to the roof. He tucked her hat around her ears as the rain pelted his back.

She sucked in a breath, but didn't open her eyes. "It's raining."

"Shh. Just rest."

Humming, he swayed, pressing his lips to her eyes. Voice shaking, he shivered in the chill, as he tried to think of any song. The warmth of her body burned through his clothes. It wasn't The Cure or any other album from his collection that came to mind. Rather, it was the classic *Stand By Me*.

He hummed the lyrics he couldn't remember. His tears mixed with the rain, his voice cracking with each verse, especially the ones vowing he would not be afraid. He rocked, dancing slow enough not to wake her, but steady enough for it to count. It wasn't the romantic dance in the rain either of them pictured when they made their list, but it was something. And right now, every bit of living counted.

Her hand weakly curled into his shirt and he stilled, studying her face. The corners of her mouth turned up and he leaned close, afraid he'd miss her words under the steady tempo of raindrops hitting the roof.

Her lips parted and she breathed, "You remembered."

Blinking hard, he tightened his arms. He'd never forget.

CHAPTER 17

$\mathcal{E}$mma lowered herself to the couch and caught her breath. Winded, blurry eyed, and incredibly dizzy—all for a bottle of water. That sickeningly sweet smell was back and her saliva burned like acid. So thirsty, but by the time she made it back to the couch she was too exhausted to twist the damn cap off the bottle of water. So she lay there.

The toilet flushed. "Emma? Honey, are you all right?" her mom asked, seeing she'd moved. Her voice sounded so muffled, like she was talking under water, but it wasn't her mom's voice, just Emma's ears.

Waiting for the dizziness to slow, she calmed her breathing so the nausea would ease. Her hands and feet tingled and she was burning cold, somehow sweating yet shivering. Perhaps she was freezing hot.

When they explained chemotherapy to her,

she blended that information with everything she'd seen on television. That pretty anchor-woman that beat breast cancer made it look so classy, so achievable. It was hard to imagine her ever feeling this terrible, but Emma was sure the woman had her own moments of despair too. Right now, Emma doubted she'd ever find grace or class again.

Life seemed to be rotting within her, which was exactly why she hadn't been outside of her home or the hospital in weeks. She wanted to die with dignity, not where others could watch the inexplicable horror of what she'd become. Again, she wondered why this disease was painted pink —her once favorite color.

Deep ruby stains marked the tissue in her fist as her nose ran. Red, not pink. Red because when she bled it was real, not some delicate act of femininity. She didn't feel very pretty right now and she certainly didn't feel like pretending.

I'm going to die like this.

There was nothing soft and rosy about her thoughts. Cancer was so deep and so personal, the actuality was murky, no way to explain such ugliness, but never would she define it as pink.

Bubblegum and taffy shades of punch wrapped around billboards and people. From pink ballet slippers to magenta wigs, it just seemed too bright for the last forty-eight hours. It was a brilliant distraction, but one that made her sad, because putting on pink in a show of solidarity wasn't enough to save her. It was only a color and she needed a cure.

That party happening around the world with marches, runs, and parades…it was something Emma felt painfully excluded from. Disconnected, an outsider looking in from the ugly side of a pretty picture. She could barely walk, let alone dance or run. The pink had become so commonplace and so powerful it distracted people from the reality. She wanted the distraction too.

Sometimes she hated not being able to smile through the fear. Her inability to put on a happy face and act as though everything would come up roses left her with a sense of inadequacy on top of everything else she was trying not to feel.

I don't want to smile anyway. I'm dying. I want to be fucking sad.

The anger was getting to her today.

Word was getting around that she was sick. She didn't care. She wasn't ashamed to have cancer. The text messages—yes, *text* messages—were very sympathetic—at first.

"This is terrible."

"I'm so sorry to hear…"

But after a while, they stopped, not even a cricket chirp from her phone. And then, they gradually started again, people calling, feeling terrible they waited so long. It was all very considerate and overwhelming, but she didn't want their apologies. She just wanted her life back.

She hadn't known so many people cared about her. However, the longer her health remained unpredictable, the more people's condolences changed. There became an almost universal tone to every call she received. She was the patient so, *clearly*, she'd done something wrong, knew a little less than everyone else who still had their health and therefore thought they possessed a magic cure.

"I have this book..."

"Blueberries! Blueberries! And more blueberries!"

"Pray."

"Try not to worry. Stress makes a breeding ground for cancer." That one was a fucking joke. Like she could just turn off her emotions. Sure. Her life wasn't anything to fret over.

They were very kind suggestions, however, she was too exhausted to hold a book and lacked the vision to read. The thought of food, even the almighty blueberry, turned her stomach. And pray? She laughed. Every thought she had was a prayer. Didn't they know that?

All she had the strength to do was think, and even that she did inadequately, her mind sloshing around in a steady stew of confusion. But when she laid still, her loved ones moving quietly around her so she could rest, her mind always returned to the question that started everything. Why? What caused this to happen to her?

She'd never done so little and known so much. Every waking second, there were thoughts, feelings, emotions, and fears about heavy things like life, relationships, and, above all, death. Maybe it was just her time.

But what about Riley? Who would look out for him? And what about her parents and Rarity? It was infuriating, knowing she might die and her death did nothing to bring them closer to any answers. Tomorrow it could be them. Why did this happen to people? Maybe they didn't need a cure as much as they needed to understand the cause.

She didn't blame people for not knowing how to act or what to say. She didn't know either. Cancer overhauled lives, the lives of the patients and those closest to them. Most people didn't want to spend an abundance of time worrying or being reminded how meaningless their new sunglasses were. It didn't make them bad. It made them human. If Emma had a place to run and hide, she'd go.

I wish, for just one day, the word cancer didn't exist.

Maybe the pink ribbons were all some people could manage. She glanced at her mother, working tediously to fold and pin the pastel bows as her basket gradually filled.

Making ribbons had become her mother's latest hobby. She sold them at work and sent a check in Emma's name each month to a cancer research center. And while her dad didn't visit often, every time she saw him he wore his pink proudly. So perhaps the ribbons were healing in a different way—healing those trying to cope with cancer by proxy.

When she saw a stranger wearing a ribbon a slow awareness took hold…*hey, that's for me.* And then her mind would travel the same path of questions. *Do they know someone with cancer? Did she have it? Is she a survivor? Did the person they know live?*

The ribbons were the softest edge of awareness, but maybe the pin itself was the better symbol. It didn't matter. None of it mattered. Perhaps she was just looking for something to blame, a place to direct her anger while she waited to see if she'd live or die.

There was no room to hide—even on the days she wanted nothing more. She'd surrendered her strength, her vanity, and a great deal of dignity in order to accept that she actually *needed* help, needed all the pink because this was what her life had become. Once she let go of her ego and let others in, the battle became a bit more manageable.

Damn she was thirsty. Tired of waiting for her strength to return, she, again, let out a frustrated breath. "Mom?"

"Yes, sweetie?"

She nudged the bottle of water. "Can you please open this?"

"Of course."

Her thirst, for the moment, was quenched. A small but notable win.

~

SHE SAT on the plastic bench Riley had put in the shower. How pathetic was it that she didn't even have the strength to take a five-minute shower, which actually turned out to take over twenty-five minutes?

This would be the highlight of her day. After waking less than an hour ago, she'd gone and exhausted herself already.

As she deliberately dried her body she stared at the girl in the mirror, no longer recognizing the woman as herself. She'd lost so much weight. Her cheeks were so gaunt her eyes looked enormous, making the purple circles all the more prominent against her sharp, protruding bones. How had that happened so fast?

No hair, no eyelashes left to wish on. It was a new naked.

The trouble with not recognizing her physical self was that she'd also lost sight of her inner self. The thoughts filling her head were no longer her own. What happened to Emma? Where did she go? Would she ever be back? She was too tired to miss her, but eventually she might—if she made it that far.

It had been seven weeks and she could barely remember the woman she was, the girl she'd always been. Vaguely, she recalled a girl that was careless and free, but also burdened by stupid worries, like if the cabinets were organized or if last year's jeans were still in style. How strange to concern oneself with such trivial nonsense.

She looked again at the reflection in the mirror. If that wasn't her and the thoughts in her head didn't seem her own did she even exist anymore? Was she dead? Dying?

Maybe she was being reborn.

The longer this went on the more she was certain she knew nothing at all.

~

CANCER WAS STEALTH, sneaking in like a phantom breeze, setting down roots like a weed, and rapidly overtaking what was once a beautiful place of life. Chemo was a gamble. They were poisoning the weed, but it was so strong it became a guessing game if they'd kill the weed without taking the flowers or destroying the garden.

Her breast hurt. Maybe it wasn't working. Maybe it was spreading. So many unanswered questions.

Shoving such unknowns away, she reminded herself of the facts. She *trusted* her doctors—*literally* with her life. If they could cure her they would. She respected their advice and truly believed the chemo would do its job and kill the cancer cells.

Those were the promises she repeated every day, because every day she lost her faith and had to find it again. They'd kill the cancer cells. They would. She just hoped the process didn't kill her too.

"Cakes, you didn't take your pills."

She glanced at Riley. "What? Oh." She was so grateful he and Rarity were always there to remind her when to do things like take her medicine. The doctors were constantly prescribing new medications and she'd given up trying to keep track.

Struggling to sit up, she accepted the water he

handed her and swallowed the pills he'd slid into her palm. "Thank you."

He settled onto the couch and she nestled into his side. Happiness.

She'd been cooped up in the loft for weeks, only leaving when she had an appointment and then coming right back. It was cold outside and flu season, so everyone was adamant that she remained in a warm, clean environment.

Her mother hadn't been by in over a week because her dad was sick and she was afraid she was a carrier of whatever bug he had. But she called several times a day. It was like living in a petri dish where every microscopic variable counted and needed to be analyzed.

"When's the last time you ate?" Riley asked.

She tried to recall her last meal. It had been a while, but she didn't have an appetite. He needed to get out of the house. "You should go out with Jake for a while, Riley."

"Knock it off. When did you eat?"

She sighed, wishing her life hadn't derailed his. He loved her too much. She worried what he'd have left to love after she was gone. "Not too long ago."

"Emma," he warned.

"I had half a banana this morning."

"I saw the banana. That wasn't half. You took a bite and left it on the counter."

"I wasn't finished," she teased, but he didn't laugh. They used to laugh all the time.

"How about soup?"

Her belly revolted. "No, thank you."

"Rarity made fruit pops. Want one of them?"

That would make her mouth feel better for a while, but she didn't want that either.

"How about a smoothie?" he offered.

That was where they usually came to an agreement. Riley would leave her be about eating for a while if she drank one of his magic smoothies. "Okay."

Food no longer had much taste, so she didn't mind. He stuffed them full of leafy greens and all kinds of healing fruits and vegetables. She wasn't sure what they did for her, but they gave him peace of mind, so she always said yes.

He stood and went to the kitchen. This new routine, already familiar and old, was all they ever did. As she watched him something came over her, a moment of insight, a dark, reoccurring epiphany that could knock her down if she weren't already sitting. *I have cancer.*

Staggering.

Nauseating awareness pinched a nerve, yet she remained calm. Every few days when the epiphany came it had the same unpleasant effect. It didn't matter that every thought had to do with cancer. There was no preparing for those chilling moments of awareness when *cancer* was actually happening to her.

But she didn't cry. Maybe this uncharacteristic, unruffled acceptance was a new side of her. She was getting stronger, unshakable. She was still terrified, but there was a new layer of peace blanketing the ongoing shock. Was this numb surrender a good thing or a bad thing? All things to think about—and think she did.

The blender brashly buzzed then silenced. Riley returned with a dark green shake disguised in a pink cup. "Here you go."

She took the drink like a good little soldier and sipped it so he'd relax. He was so good—good to her, good to his sister, good to her parents, good to Marla. She'd never believed such an incredible man could exist.

It seemed a shame to waste all that goodness. Hopefully by winters end this nightmare would be over, but that seemed unlikely. Losing a winter to play nursemaid was fine, but he couldn't sacrifice more than that, not when he was perfectly healthy and capable of doing all the things she was not.

He was too good to waste another second on this disease. And what if there weren't any more winters? What if this one was it? He was too invested, losing himself in her decline. He couldn't forget who he was like she'd forgotten who she used to be. He had to live, because he still had the privilege. Placing her hand in his, he turned and smiled.

"Don't wait too long, Riley."

His mouth curved down and he scowled. "What?"

"If I go, don't wait too long to fall in love again. You're too good at it to put it aside for grief. Promise me you won't wait too long."

His eyes scorched with dark rage. He'd never looked at her with such anger. "Shut. Up."

She couldn't shut up. This was important. Who knew if the treatment was working or how much time they actually had left? "I want you to know I'd be okay if you found someone else—"

"Knock it off!" Ripping his hand from hers, he stood. Snatching up the empty cup, he marched it to the kitchen where he angrily threw it in the sink.

She flinched, but waited for him to collect himself, knowing this was a difficult but inevitable conversation. The water shut off and he braced his hands on the lip of the counter, his back toward her.

"I have cancer, Riley."

He turned, a look of confusion on his face. Maybe it was more obvious to him. He'd been watching it happen. She, on the other hand, had been riding along, staring perplexedly at the stranger now controlling her body. She was that stranger and she'd never felt more detached from herself.

"Why are you saying shit like that?"

Her head lowered. Didn't he understand? She loved him too. Not only was this disease killing her, it was killing parts of him. He didn't deserve to suffer. She was the abnormal part to his once normal life. And when an abnormality was found, it was removed, wasn't that right?

His face softened and he returned to her side, taking up the empty space on the couch. "Em?"

Lifting her wrist, she noted how thin it had become. "How do you love this, Riley?"

"Don't start this, Emma."

"I mean it. How do you do it? How do you continue to watch me wither away and make me smoothies and love me the way you do?"

"I just do." He shook his head, a baffled look in his eyes. "I didn't fall in love with your wrists or your breasts or your hair. It's *you* I love."

"I know you do." His love was the best medicine. It healed her in a way modern medicine couldn't. His reassurance was essential in this scary state of mind, but not enough to relieve her turmoil. As much as his love saved her on her worst days, it could kill him if he never let it go.

She selfishly wanted his love, knowing every drop was a part of him he'd never get back, but she couldn't let him lose himself to a memory. "All your love…it won't reach my grave, Riley. Don't waste everything you have to offer on a ghost. I love *you* too much to let that happen."

"Stop it. We aren't having this conversation."

She caught his arm, stilling him from getting away. She didn't have the strength to chase or argue. "But I need to have it." Something major had occurred to her, something life altering. She needed to get it out. "You're an incredible man. Whatever happens, don't rob the world of that. You have so much love in your heart. Give it to someone who's living."

His jaw shifted. "Damn it, Emma. Stop."

But she couldn't. "The idea that I might have to do chemo again scares the hell out of me, Riley. Every day I don't think I can get any weaker, but I do."

Breathing roughly, he sat and cupped her face

in his palms, his intense eyes staring into hers. "You're strong, Emma. The second you start planning for death you get weak. Don't get weak when you've fought so hard this far."

She sighed. She was already weaker than he realized. "I'm scared."

"You're not going to die."

"It's not death that scares me. I think what it all comes down to is my fear of being alone. Cancer's lonely."

"I'm here," he argued. "Rarity and your parents are here. You're not alone."

She blinked, her eyes burning more than usual. "But if I die, I can't take any of you with me." Her voice cracked. "That's what makes this so terrifying. No matter how much support I have here and now, the connection will get severed at some point."

"I want you to stop talking like that, Emma. I'm serious."

No matter how much the words hurt to say, they didn't penetrate her calm. For weeks she'd done little more than think. Somewhere in the process of all that thinking, she started accepting her fate. "We're all dying, Riley. Some a little faster than others, but it's the only guarantee in this world. We will all eventually die. I'm not afraid to say it, because death doesn't matter—it's a given. The privilege is life, and I so *desperately* want another chance at living."

"You'll get one."

"If I don't, you have to promise you'll live for me. Do everything you can, Riley, and *live*. Don't waste a single minute thinking about death. A broken heart won't bring me back and I don't want to think of you broken if I have to go. When I leave, I know you'll be the last worry I hold in my heart, because you'll always be my first concern."

His face tightened and he glanced away, shoulders jerking as he gave an admirable effort to keep his composure. He sniffled, wiped his nose, and cleared his throat. "Emma, I *swear* to you, I'm living. I know I don't have to be here, but this is where I want to be and it's where I'll stay until this is over and *we* have our regular lives back. I don't want to love someone else. I'd give you anything in the world, but I can't give you that."

"Riley, you have to be—"

"No!" His hand slashed in the air. In a calmer voice, he repeated, "No."

Facing her again, he blinked, the whites of his eyes a soft shade of pink. "You're the syrup to my pancakes, Em. I don't want it without you. I know we're all going to eventually die, but you're early. It's not your time yet and I'm not letting go until I'm sure I've pulled you back."

Her fingers curled around his hand as the tears broke free. Damn him. The sight of his distress ripped her apart. His tears could save her and slay her at the same time.

"Riley, I'm fighting so hard, because you make me want to live. I don't ever want to be so far away I can't feel your love anymore. But I'm tired and I'm scared."

Gently, he lifted her fingers to his lips and kissed them. "I'll always love you, cakes. I'm sorry, but you can't tell me not to. And I'm never gonna stop so you're just gonna have to suck it up."

"And that's why I'm too afraid to let go. I could let it all go. But not you. I don't want to ever let you go."

"Then don't ask it of me." He kissed her between the eyes. "I'm glad you can't, because none of this compares to the sort of suffering I'd face living without you."

In that moment, her fear subsided, making room for a smidge of selfish hope. Maybe Riley's love was so powerful it could sustain her life. Maybe it could at least reach her in heaven. Then she wouldn't have to worry about being so alone.

~

Emma's chest had been killing her for a solid week, so she braved the shower and examined her breasts only to find something amazing had happened. The tumors were…gone. She couldn't feel a single lump. It was going to be a good day.

"Riley!" she screamed and he burst into the bathroom, panic etched across his face.

"What's wrong?"

She held out her hand, not meaning to traumatize him. "Nothing. I'm okay—"

"Then why'd you yell like that?"

Taking his hand, she brought it to her breast. "Feel."

His brow lowered in concentration as his fingers tenderly inspected her breast. "What am I looking for? Did you find something?"

"No. There's nothing there." He didn't seem as impressed by this miracle as she was. Her confidence trembled. Maybe she was wrong. "Do you feel anything?"

His touch was so clinical. The longer he held her boob so raptly fixated on it like he was dismantling a bomb or trying to crack a safe, she started to giggle.

"Shh."

She shook her head. "*So* serious. Do you feel them?"

He stepped back, folded his arms, and frowned at her chest. "No."

A deep breath siphoned in her lungs, lifting her breast as she smiled. "I knew it! They're gone!"

His eyes jumped to hers, pleading. "You don't know that, Emma. They were there long before you felt them."

Her face hardened as he stuck a pin in her positive mood. She had enough doubt and cynicism. She didn't want that right now. "Why aren't you happy?"

"I…I *am* happy, but I don't want you to get false hope."

"There's no such thing as *false* hope, Riley. There's hope or there's nothing. Period." Pushing past him, she wrapped herself in a towel.

"Then I don't want you to get your hopes up—"

She growled and walked away. "I need to get dressed."

"Emma—"

"Just leave me alone." Blinking back tears she marched to her room and shut the door before he could follow her. Then she cried. Her short-lived excitement dashed before she had the chance to fully embrace it.

Later that night, he came to bed and apologized. "This past month's put me on the frontlines of what's real, Em. I have a hard time believing what's not."

"Do you believe the chemo's working?" she asked, needing to hear him say he did.

"I have to believe that, otherwise there's no justification for the hell you've been through."

"Well, I believe it's working, Riley. Not because it's the only choice I have, but because deep down I truly trust it. I suddenly believe I *will* survive after weeks of preparing for death. I can't float in between like you do."

"I *never* said anything about death. I said we need to see for sure, meaning without an ultrasound and blood work we know nothing."

"The tumors were there and now they're not, Riley. It's the first tangible proof I have that tells me this was worth it. I know they might still be in there, but they shrunk or moved or something. It changed. *I* did something and changed *cancer*. I pushed back. It pushed me and I pushed back."

She couldn't explain it any other way. Maybe

she wouldn't win, but he'd told her in the very beginning to get in the ring and she did. She'd fought harder than she ever thought she was capable of fighting. It wasn't over yet. Most days she felt beaten and outmatched, but today…today felt like she landed a punch and *that* was a game changer.

His head lowered. "I get it. I'm sorry I shit on your parade. I didn't mean to. You're right. We should've celebrated today."

She smiled, believing his second apology to be more genuine than the first. Brushing a hand down his cheek, she grinned. "Day's not over yet. We could still celebrate."

His lashes slowly lifted as his gaze melded with hers. "What do you mean?"

She laughed. "What do you think I mean?"

"Sex? You mean sex?"

His shock was comical, but then she sort of shocked herself. Did she want to have sex? "I don't know."

He tried to hide his disappointment, but there was no disguising the way his smile left his eyes. "We don't have to."

"No," she quickly reassured him. "I mean…we can."

He frowned. "Do you want to?"

She wasn't sure. She shrugged. The words just sort of fell out, lost little clouds floating through stormy skies, so reminiscent of the girl she used to be. Those familiar pieces were so comforting. She wanted nothing more than for them to be true, but as she considered her exhaustion and the effort it would take, disappointment crushed her.

Reading her, he settled on his back, compensating by holding her hand. "Let's get some sleep," he whispered.

She nodded as he reached for the lamp, setting the room to darkness. Turning away from him, she silently cried. What if they never had sex again? As much as the instinct felt right the motion felt wrong. What if this was what their relationship would always be, him worrying about her delicate state and her being too fragile to prove to *anyone* that she could be strong again.

She huffed and he turned. "It's fine, Emma."

"It's not fine. Everything is not always fine."

"I'm not going to sit here and fight with you."

"We're not fighting, Riley, but I'm allowed to get frustrated. The fact that you're acting like this is okay is only frustrating me more."

He sat up. "What do you want me to do, demand sex? You're being irrational."

"No. I just… I just want to be normal again."

Sliding back under the covers he took her hand, lacing her fingers with his. "We'll get there."

As much as she envied his confidence, she didn't always share the same beliefs. But in moments like this all she could do was hope he was right.

~

THE FOLLOWING WEEK, as they waited for Dr. Lindsay in his office, anxious curiosity made it impossible to stay calm. This was the big one, the moment they found out how the cancer responded to the chemotherapy.

She didn't want to face another round of chemo, but if that was what she needed to do, she would. Hearing more chemo would be better than hearing the cancer progressed and the treatment failed. Every day she felt around and still couldn't find the tumors, so she was hopeful.

When the door opened Riley noticeably tensed and she stopped breathing. Her body surged on the verge of passing out as Riley grabbed her hand, squeezing tightly.

Dr. Lindsay sat down at his desk. "Emma. Riley. How are you feeling today?"

"Nervous," she answered honestly. God, she was so tense.

"Understandable. Well, I have some good news."

Good!

Her mind latched on to the word *good,* but then panicked at the term *some.* "Okay." She breathed and squeezed Riley's hand a little harder.

"Your test results show a partial response to the chemotherapy." *Partial.* "What that means is, while the cancer didn't totally disappear," *It's not gone...* "There's been a notable reduction in the size of the tumors. In other words, it's working."

She exhaled and panted for a few seconds,

possibly smiling. Her face was totally numb. "It worked?"

"But the tumors are still there?" Riley asked.

"Yes, the tumors are still present, but the markers have fallen. You're not out of the woods yet, but this is great progress and definitely a reason to be happy."

She was happy, so happy there should be a bigger word for the emotion. Elated. Jubilant. Nothing was enough. "What happens now?"

"Well, you have a few options. The chemo can continue, but I'm going to advise against that based on your personal response to the therapy for the time being. The next option is to remove the remainder of the tumors in a partial mastectomy—a lumpectomy."

She'd definitely been smiling, because she was very aware of her expression falling. "But... they're shrinking." She, of course wanted them gone, so a lumpectomy was always on her radar, but having that foreshadowed thought shoved into the present managed to shock her all the same.

"They are—a great sign. But, based on your recent tests, I think it's best we pull back while your body's at it's strongest."

Strongest? She was weaker than a baby calf. "You don't think my body could handle more chemo?"

"Not without significant damage. Keep in mind, we're looking at your entire system, not just your breast tissue. The progress you've made is notable and enough that I'm confident we've reached the time to discuss surgery. This option will conserve a portion of the breast and hopefully some breast sensitivity."

Riley leaned forward. "Is it possible for the cancer to return after that? Could she still need chemo? I mean, if you think she shouldn't have anymore, what are the chances she won't have to if she has the tumors removed?"

Dr. Lindsay offered a sympathetic smile. "Unfortunately, until we know more about the cause of breast cancer, there will always be a threat to women with Emma's diagnosis. Breast cancer isn't something contracted. It's a mutation of cells and researchers are still trying to identify the trigger. By removing the tumors and a fair amount of healthy tissue surrounding the masses, we diminish the chances of the damage spreading. The surgery's often followed by radiation and in some cases, additional surgeries."

The end—she wanted to get to the end so her life could begin. "What's the other option?"

"The other option is an MRM, Modified Radical Mastectomy." The gravity of option B dramatically altered the energy of the room.

"Losing my breast?" The words were possibly the most painful words she'd ever spoken, heavy and clunky, jagged and crude against her tongue.

Dr. Lindsay nodded. "Yes, removing the affected breast." He folded his hands and adjusted his posture. "I want you to understand the advances that have been made, Emma. This isn't the same procedure practiced twenty years ago. This sort of surgery no longer removes the pectoral muscles, only the breast and the affected lymph nodes. Cosmetically, there are countless reconstructive options. You might be a good candidate for nipple sparing as well, meaning the incisions are fairly hidden and the nipple is conserved."

"Is the MRM more effective than the partial mastectomy?" Riley asked, taking the next question from her mind.

She was so grateful he was there. She'd never be able to handle all this on her own.

"The chance of reoccurrence is slightly higher with a lumpectomy, but still considerably low; that's why radiation's used, thereby making both procedures equally effective. The decision comes down to the patient and peace of mind."

She supposed it was like weeding a garden. They could remove the weeds, bit by bit, but if they missed any seeds the weeds would return, and they'd treat the area with more poison. Or, they could remove the garden forever. But there would always be the chance one of those pesky seeds might get left behind and form in the surrounding areas where the beds once were.

"Does keeping the nipple raise the chance of reoccurrence?"

"Unfortunately, yes, but the risk is very low."

Pressure. Ungodly pressure built in her shoulders and tugged at her belly as if his words physically pushed her down. Riley stood and dispensed a glass of water from the cooler in the corner and handed it to her. "Have some water."

"Thank you." She sipped and looked back at

the doctor. Exhaling harshly, she shook off the fear and sat a little straighter. "Sorry. Go on."

"I want you to understand, one operation does not guarantee survival anymore than the other, Emma."

Bleak. Every time she leaned on the slightest reassurance someone shook her, reminding her there were no assurances. "I understand."

"Neither does either surgery guarantee a future free of chemotherapy or radiation, and because this is an invasive kind of cancer, patients often need additional therapies."

He steepled his fingers. "I want to be perfectly clear on that matter, because I don't want you to make your decision and then get blindsided if things don't turn out the way you expected. Every patient's different. We can only go by what we know. You're very young and the strand of breast cancer you're dealing with is aggressive and requires equally aggressive treatment, but we've reached a point where *you* get to decide which angle of approach we take."

Her hands trembled so she lowered them to her lap, wrapping her numb fingers around the empty cup. "What about my other breast?"

"If you opt for the MRM?" He nodded as though expecting the question. "There are prosthetics available, but each woman's different. Some women opt for a prophylactic mastectomy —or double mastectomy—in this case for multiple reasons. It might be a desire for reconstructive symmetry or a method to put their mind at ease."

She glanced at her chest, oddly recalling a time she'd wanted boobs so badly she stuffed an entire box of tissues in her bra. "What would you tell your wife if she was in my shoes?"

He slid her a pamphlet. "I'd tell her this isn't an easy decision and there are always going to be benefits and risks. It's natural for a woman to want to maintain her breasts, but we also live in a time when augmentation isn't unheard of. I'd support her decision either way, because it's a very *personal* decision. But at the end of the day, it would be hers."

Doctors were experts of evasion. She was glad she wasn't married to one. Blowing out a slow breath she sat back. An unexpected sense of empowerment washed over her. She just had to decide and then they'd move to round two. If she made the right decision, it could possibly be the last round of this tiring war.

It was *her* decision. She smiled, her expression a bit shaky. "I appreciate having a choice at all."

She hadn't decided anything in quite some time. The last choice she made was to fight and from then on she'd fought without rest. Now things had calmed and she was given a choice again. She blew out a breath. "It's a lot to consider."

"I advise my patients to write down the pros and cons, really take your time considering how each approach will put you at risk or be beneficial, and which is going to affect you most on a personal level. Every woman's different as is each case of breast cancer. You don't have to decide what's right for womankind. You only need to choose what the best solution is for you."

"Thank you." Yes, she said thank you—as far as messengers went, he was a decent one and didn't deserve to be shot.

As they left the office she reconsidered this new information, simplifying the facts as much as possible. Somehow that made the news more manageable.

Was her cancer gone? Not at all.

Did her tumors disappear from chemo? Nope.

Would she keep her breasts? Maybe. Maybe one, maybe half of one, maybe none. It was mind boggling that this still felt like good news.

This disease might very well be the fastest overhaul a person could experience in terms of the way they viewed the world. Had she gotten this news two months ago, she would've been in an inconsolable puddle on the floor. Having gone through hell and back, things looked different. In her opinion, she was handling everything quite well.

Riley was silent as he started the car. She'd been so lost in her own thoughts she'd barely noticed he hadn't spoken a word since leaving the office. Once they were driving she turned to him. "Are you going to say anything?"

He kept his eyes on the road. "I don't want to influence you either way."

"So you have an opinion."

"I have lots of opinions, but I don't know if any of them are right."

She chuckled. "Human."

She had opinions too. First, chemotherapy sucked, hardcore—a thousand times worse than anything she'd ever expected. Yet, she'd do it again if she had to. Strange that fact never changed. Her instinct to survive always outweighed the temptation to give up. But if there were ways to reduce her chances of suffering chemo again, she'd do them first.

Being diagnosed with cancer was the tip of the iceberg. Cancer was quiet. It silently crept into an unsuspecting life and secretly destroyed one cell at a time. Fighting cancer on the other hand was war. It was brutal and volatile. Cells—friends and foes—were massacred. It was a struggle that pushed a person as close to death as possible and then fought to bring them back, leaving all the bad behind.

She didn't want to spend her life fighting that war. There was no quality of life when submerged in such an endless battle. She wanted to live. It was that simple.

Somewhere in the midst of ignoring the pain that stole her breath, the agony radiating in her bones, the absolute conviction that she would die before morning, somewhere in the middle of all that, the superficial worries were stripped away.

She never expected to think of herself as too skinny. And her hair, which she'd fussed over, singed, flattened, and tried to cook the curl right out of…she didn't care about that anymore either. She was so busy competing to survive, her instinct to compete with others disappeared.

There was no room for distractions like envy or hate, no time for strife or vanity. These months had taught her no one really had control. They only had an unpredictable amount of time, so she better make every second count.

It was a peaceful epiphany and, as she accepted this lesson into her heart, she found it ironic such accord could be borne of despair. Above all, she wanted to be whole again, spiritually *and* emotionally. The physical didn't so much matter anymore.

For the first time in a long time, she was confident enough to truly—*truly*—hope, and all the anger she'd lugged this far was swiftly put down and left behind. Her courage was borrowed, bullied out of her—by her—for those that longed to see her recover. She certainly wasn't going to let one boob get in the way of all that, not after everything they'd done to help her this far. If there was a way to end this, she wanted it over.

"Tell me your opinions," she said, concerned he might oppose her.

"I think this conversation deserves more attention and respect than us chatting it out on a car ride home from the oncologist's office, Emma."

"Then pull over and look at me, Riley. I want to know what you think. It matters to me. You're one of the few people in this world whose opinions mean something to me."

He bit his lip and maneuvered through traffic. Yanking the wheel, he pulled into an open spot on the shoulder and faced her. He was angry and she didn't understand why.

"Fine. If you died—" His words were harsh, dousing her with more reality. "—do I get to keep your boob?" He huffed out a breath, his knuckles white as his fingers gripped the wheel. "Do you hear how ridiculous that sounds? It's a tit, Emma. I don't care about it. I care about *you*. I care about having a life with *you,* by my side. I think letting something as meaningless as a boob get in the way of that happiness is insane."

Who knew how a normal girl would react to such a statement from her boyfriend? She stopped trying for normal a long time ago. What she did know was that she loved him. She loved him for getting angry, for caring enough that he could barely speak of her demise without crying. She loved him because he never lied to her and when he said her breasts didn't matter, she knew without a doubt, he was telling the truth. Honesty. Trust.

Her hand touched his. "I want the mastectomy."

As he exhaled a harsh breath, his shoulders drooped forward and his head rested on the steering wheel. "Are you sure?"

His face tightened and she silently counted the worry lines around his eyes that weren't there two months ago. He'd walk away from this scarred as well.

She rubbed her palm over his cheek until he faced her. Then she nodded. "It's just a tit."

His seatbelt unlatched and his arms wrapped

around her, his face burrowing deep inside her scarf until his warm lips found her neck and he sighed. "I love you."

"I love you too," she said, holding him tight. He really was the most incredible man she'd ever known.

~

SHE WAS SUPPOSED to be shockproof by now, but she wasn't. Once they'd told Dr. Lindsay her decision to have the mastectomy everything moved at jet speed and before she knew it, it was the eve of her surgery.

After endless research and exhausting deliberation, she opted for the bilateral mastectomy, removing the unhealthy breast as well as the unaffected one. It really was a personal decision; one she struggled to justify. The more she explained her choice the more frustrated and certain she became. Thankfully, Riley was open minded and shared many of her views.

Yes, there were risks to a double mastectomy and yes, the recovery would be longer and more difficult, but this decision felt right to her. No one knew what caused breast cancer. Was it plastic? Microwaves? Estrogen? The chemicals added to their foods? Stress? She was now mindful of all those things and her breasts were her greatest source of anxiety.

She once loved her boobs, long before they betrayed her. Her entire body battled against them and they no longer felt like a part of her whole. Detached.

The idea of removing her breasts brought an utter sense of comfort she didn't expect others to understand, but she was eager to be rid of the stress.

She'd be lying if she claimed to be above vanity. She wasn't. Symmetry had always appealed to her and she worried the asymmetrical shape of a unilateral mastectomy would break the remainder of her self-esteem. Right or wrong, she was human and she didn't want to break, not after sacrificing so much already.

She might be two-thirds the weight she was when this started and she might be balder than a baby boy, but she was still a woman and once she got her strength back she was putting on a sundress—breasts or no breasts.

Rolling to her back, she cupped her breasts through her nightshirt. "I can't believe I'm losing my boobs tomorrow." No matter how many times she said it, whatever she assumed to be a normal reaction, it didn't come. Shouldn't there be some sort of angst or doubt? There wasn't.

More reassurance you're making the right choice.

It was *real*; there was no denying that. Tomorrow, at nine-thirty, they were taking her breasts. How was she okay with this? Strange.

Certain hurdles couldn't be jumped. The stakes were just too high. Nor could they be maneuvered around without risk. Sometimes, the best option to get through something difficult was to just get through it. Tomorrow she'd be on the other side. All she had to do was get there.

She didn't want to dwell on the magnitude of the situation, because her mind was made up. It was happening. She wanted to keep it light. "Poor Starsky," she sighed.

Luckily, Riley was the perfect guy for that. Crawling under the covers, he covered her right hand and kissed her cheek. "He always was a trouble maker, but Hutch would never let him take the fall alone. And eventually, there's a remake."

She grinned. "Will we call the new guys Starsky and Hutch too?"

He shrugged. "Maybe Stiller and Wilson."

She laughed, resting her cheek on his chest, staring at the shadows of snow falling by the window. "Stiller and Wilson."

His arm wrapped around her and squeezed. "Try to get some sleep. Big day tomorrow, cakes." He kissed her smooth head. "Love you."

She wasn't tired. The snow was simply too beautiful not to watch. Too many days had passed resting. She was grateful for this quiet moment. It had been a while since she experienced *this.*

Caressing his hand affectionately, she stared at the majestic winter scene outside her window and whispered. "Goodnight, syrup."

CHAPTER 18

$\mathcal{R}$iley lifted the camera to his eyes, finding Emma's beautiful face through the lens. "Smile." His finger pressed the lever and the flash snapped.

As the photo ejected the air tinged with the scent of processing fluid. Removing the picture, he fanned it and handed it to her.

She studied the image and snorted. "Look at my eye," she laughed. "What is that face I'm making?" A hardier giggle. "This one goes in my favorites."

Digging in her bag, he unearthed the scrapbook where they put all the pictures. Those photographs told quite a story. Sometimes that story was a nightmare, sometimes it was a gift, but the record was there, proving they made it this far.

Tucking the image onto the page, he uncapped a marker. "Caption?" Minimizing his fear with meaningless tasks was necessary at the moment. It was surgery day and he was petrified.

She thought for a moment, her nose scrunching in that adorable way. "A farewell to Starsky and Hutch?"

He wrote the caption and dated the picture.

Her smile turned a bit dopey as the IV pumped her full of meds. Forcing his hands to remain steady, he returned the book to the bag. "Are you nervous?"

"No, just anxious to be done."

During the surgery they would take a biopsy of her auxiliary lymph nodes to see if the cancer had spread. In order to do this, they had to inject her with blue radioactive dye. It boggled his mind the toxic line healers toed in order to make people well.

Not once through this entire experience, had he come to terms with this being the best method of treatment. They were literally curing cancer by poisoning her.

His sister remained the resounding voice in their home, supervising everything that went into their bodies and constantly preaching about the healing powers of foods. He was beginning to think she was right, and that their diet could have deterred this as much as it directed it, but he wasn't a doctor.

Emma trusted the doctors, but most days he wondered if they were as clueless as they were twenty years ago. Where did all those pink dollars go? What exactly were they researching?

Stronger poisons? All that awareness didn't seem to leave women any less amputated in the end.

He didn't care about the scars or the physical changes. He cared about the enormous decision she had no choice but to rush into. She'd been so positive since making up her mind and he was one hundred percent onboard with her decision, but it still infuriated him that this is what it came down to. This was the best option available.

So long as cancer was playing offense and they were on the defense, there was no cure—it was all a race in avoidance. But without knowing the cause they had no idea what to avoid. Too many pink soldiers fighting this godforsaken war, battle scars worn like badges of honor, as they marched for a cure, but where did all the countless parades lead? The purpose was convoluted with marketing and praise for concern, when so many women needed so much more.

They needed progress, they needed knowledge about the possible causes so they would know what to avoid. It was as though people just accepted this as an unfortunate occurrence and nothing could be done, but he didn't believe that. He didn't believe the only option was reaction. There had to be proactive measures, but even now, in the trenches of the chaos, he wasn't sure what those proactive measures were.

He'd gladly walk in pink for her—with her. But he wanted to actually make a difference. Just because she was removing the source didn't mean they were out of the woods. Who knew how long this would carry on, how far it would go?

So much research went to stronger chemicals and better procedures. Maybe if they started with fewer chemicals, like the ones being added in their foods, there'd be fewer procedures. The same pharmaceutical companies making her medication also made the pesticides that contaminated their food. Agriculturists and pharmaceutical companies tangled in a steady tug of war, and nothing was natural anymore, everything aside from the small selection of organic goods was treated with toxic chemicals. What if people were getting sick from the food they thought would make them healthy?

He couldn't be the only person questioning such things, wondering if those hired to administer safe foods and drugs were somehow profiting off the country's illnesses. If the food was the cause and the drugs were the cure, the cycle was definitely making someone rich.

It infuriated him that someone—*many someones*—were making money off Emma's suffering, marking up the cost of one pill to more than two weeks of her average salary when she had an illness that prevented her from working. It was an unethical evil that kept him up at night.

There was so much to be angry about. So many lies and betrayals from the names and brands he trusted. He'd gone through the loft and thrown away any products that contained questionable ingredients, many outlawed in other countries, but not the United States. The moment of absolute disgust came when he read the cancer-warning label on one of Emma's lotion bottles—a bottle that also boasted a pink breast cancer ribbon. What sort of hypocrisy was that?

The weeks following Emma's diagnosis he'd bought every pink beribboned piece of merchandise he passed, thinking it could somehow save her. So naïve. Exactly which charity did that street vender donate to after his shirts were made of cotton soaked in cancer causing chemicals? So much of the "activism" was just pink noise and pretty chaos, marketing off of other's grief and despair. They needed action. The more he realized the lies they'd been told the louder the voice inside of him grew, begging for change.

Her fingers rubbed over his hand. "You're awfully quiet." Her eyes were soft from the medicine in her IV.

He kissed her head. "Just thinking."

"About what?"

"How horrible the cafeteria food probably is," he lied, shoving away his anger to be present where he was needed most, which in all honesty, was exactly where he wanted to be.

She softly laughed and her beauty grabbed hold of him, squeezing tight. This was exactly where he wanted to be, maybe not under these circumstances, but he, without a doubt, wanted to be by her side. Nothing had ever been clearer. "Emma?"

She glanced at him, her dopey eyes answering his plea.

He drew in a deep breath and let it out slowly. "I wanna marry you."

Her smile somehow turned more charming as her eyes shimmered and she whispered, "I want to marry you too."

"I'm serious. I don't want to wait. I know you probably want a big fancy party with basketball shaped flower things, and eighteen types of linen all in different shades of the same color, and those weird little action figures for the cake—and we can do all that if you want—but I just wanna marry you as soon as possible."

She bit her lip and smirked. "I don't care about any of that stuff, Riley. I just want forever with you. That's all I need."

Emotion stumbled out of him as he jaggedly exhaled. Propelling forward, his hand slid behind her neck, drawing her in for a kiss to seal the deal. "I love you so much."

"I love you too. You're the syrup to my pancakes."

"I promise I'll be a good husband."

She shook her head and whispered, "I have no doubt you'll be the absolute best."

"And I promise I'll take care of everything. I'll make it nice. If there's something you want, I'll get it, just tell me and it's yours."

"I'd like my parents there so my dad can give me away and I want Rarity there. As long as we have them and each other, I'll have everything I need."

He pressed his bald head to hers, his chest filling with a sense of serenity sweeter than anything he'd ever known. "My beautiful Emma."

~

SIX HOURS LASTED A LONG TIME. Those hours, waiting for Emma to come out of surgery, were passed in reflection, something he never did three months ago. Three months. It had been three tiny months that translated to the longest era of his life.

Three months ago they lost something they never had—the assumption of control. That imaginary security blanket they hid under when they wanted to pretend they were in charge was gone.

There had been denial, him arrogantly insisting that this couldn't possibly be life threatening. They were supposed to die like dignified old people, rocking in white wooden chairs, sipping sweet tea against a Georgian colonial backdrop. That Norman Rockwell fantasy must have been commissioned the same day his Santa God was.

Every time they received bad news a wall went up. But those reflexive defense mechanisms had to come tumbling down so they could face the enemy head on. And the slow lesson set in that some things were simply unfixable.

No control. None.

No choice but to surrender her survival to the hands of experts. But they weren't experts on *her*. They didn't love all of her the way he did. They didn't know what her tears tasted like or the scent of her neck first thing in the morning. They only knew the enemy, but maybe that was how wars were won. Maybe.

Ideals like karma and destiny became foul words and misunderstood, cruel tricks. His blame was endless. Someone or something had to be at fault.

He would beg, bargain, and sell his soul to secure her future. The 'what ifs' and 'whys' became a sickening torture that would not silence, even now, as he waited for her to safely wake. The challenging enigma of life was no more understood today than it was yesterday.

He'd bid farewell to the unnecessary bullshit. So many things he assumed he couldn't live without were cast away, worthless. It became abundantly clear what he truly needed was her.

Her hugs, her smiles, her laughter, her everlasting faith in him, it all equated to the air he breathed. *She* was what he lived for and if he couldn't have her, nothing else mattered.

He no longer thought in terms of *'me'*. It wasn't about *him* or what was happening *to* him. It wasn't even about her. It was about *life*. Human life.

They never had control nor would they ever. *This* was what he had, and they needed to make *this* count for all it was worth.

"Riley Lockhart?"

He turned, all thoughts scattering as he stood. "That's me." His heart kicked into overdrive as adrenaline raced through his veins and he quickly walked over to the nurse.

"The procedure went well. They're moving Emma to recovery now. If you follow me I'll take you to her."

Overwrought and unprepared, he quickly gathered her bag and personal items. The nurse grinned and held the door as nervous energy hummed inside of him. The never-ending maze of corridors eventually landed him in an inpatient room where Emma slept on an upright bed.

"She'll be groggy for a while. The doctor has her on pain meds, so she shouldn't experience much discomfort at this point."

Relief exploded in his chest as the monitors chirped steadily beside her bed. She did it. "Thank you."

He placed the bag on the counter and gently lowered himself into a chair. When the nurse left, he gently brushed a finger over her hand. There was a device clasped to her index finger tracking her pulse. "Hey."

She inhaled and slowly opened her eyes. "Hey." She smiled groggily. "It's over?"

I hope. Brushing a finger against her cheek he nodded. "You did it."

Her eyes were bleary, but her smile was priceless despite its subtlety. "Poor Starsky and Hutch." She glanced at her chest, but the motion seemed too difficult just yet.

"Are the expanders in?" The nurse hadn't told him much, or maybe she did. He'd been so concerned with seeing Emma, he might have missed something.

"I think so," she mumbled. "The plastic surgeon was here." Her eyes closed. "My throat hurts."

"That's from the anesthesia. Want me to get you something to drink?"

She shook her head. "Just stay with me for a bit." Her hand tightened around his and there was a moment that seemed to tremble through time, quaking the balance of the world around them.

"Em?"

Shutting her eyes, she sniffled as two tears chased down her cheek.

"Hey. Talk to me." He scooted closer and kissed her fingers. He didn't want to crowd her and inadvertently bump her.

"I don't have any boobs," she meekly whispered, her face tight as she struggled to hold in whatever was fighting to come out of her.

His heart broke, his own tears falling to her fingers. "Shh…I know, baby. I know, but you're here and as soon as the doctor comes in we'll know where we stand with everything else. You're still you and you're still beautiful."

The pressure in his chest, pressure he'd been living with for uncountable weeks seemed to pulse and explode, shaking him to the core. They were here. They made it this far, when even that was never promised. He choked and gasped, his emotions getting the better of him.

Clearing his throat, he rasped, "I'm so proud of you, cakes." Holding her fingers in his, he used them to wipe his eyes. "You're so damn strong."

His lips pressed into her knuckles as he

chafed her fingers. Sometimes, there were moments that just required tears, when words weren't enough, because the emotions were too complex and wide.

They cried for several minutes, perhaps even an hour. He simply held her any way he could, kissed her eyes and nose and told her any words that might make this easier. He wasn't sure if his comments helped her come to terms with her decision or not. Deep down, he believed she had no regrets, but he'd never know for sure.

"Are you sorry?" he asked, when she got quiet.

"No," she whispered, a sad smile curving her lips. "I'm proud." Her eyes opened, her pupils small from the meds. "I feel…beautifully brave. But I'm sad."

Again his vision blurred. He didn't want her to be sad. "Why are you sad?"

"Because strangers won't see this shade of beauty—they won't know that I fought for this choice and it was mine."

"They'll see you, Emma, and those of us that love you, we'll never overlook your courage." Rising, he kissed her lips, his hands gently cradling her face. "You're so beautifully brave."

Tears continued to trickle from her eyes, but her lips curved into a smile under his. "You make me strong, Riley. Thank you for that."

He'd promised himself, back when this all started, that he'd be her rock. And while her strength outweighed his, he believed he'd done a pretty decent job at keeping that promise.

"Knock, knock." He eased back as the doctor entered the room.

Emma grinned and Riley fought the urge to hug the man. There was still the question of her lymph nodes and the blue dye test, so he held off on celebrating.

Dr. Lindsay jumped right in to checking Emma's machines and comfort. "How do you feel, Emma?"

"Emotional, but good."

"Both very natural reactions. We have the pathology report from your sentinel nodes and you're in the clear. The biopsy came back negative—"

"*No* cancer?" he gasped, afraid to accept the surreal diagnosis.

The doctor smiled. "No cancer."

"Oh, my God." Emma gasped as he dropped into the chair.

No cancer.

As they digested this incredible news, the doctor advised about soreness and aftercare. It was all just noise. *No cancer. Remission.*

Once alone again, they stared at each other, an inexplicable emotion volleying between their smiles. *No cancer. It was gone.*

All the things he'd ever been grateful for paled in comparison to this. She was whole. She was healthy. She was alive. She was cancer free.

~

RARITY FOUND him in the food court and he immediately panicked. "Why aren't you with Emma?"

"Relax," his sister said, taking up the seat across from him. "Her parents are here. I gave them some time alone."

He settled back into his seat. Rarity raised an eyebrow and jutted her chin toward his phone. "What'chya doin'?"

His face heated as he swiped the image on the screen away. "Nothing."

Her mouth hooked into a half grin. "Liar. You have a *I got caught looking at porn* face. What are you looking at?"

He swallowed. Maybe he should tell her. "I was looking up mastectomy scars, but not for any perverted reasons. It just occurred to me that eventually Emma's going to remove her bandages and I'm probably going to be there. More than her scars, she's going to see my reaction and I want to be prepared."

His sister smiled and, in a strangely affectionate manner, brushed a hand down his arm. "You really are an amazing guy, Riley." She scooted her chair close to his. "Well, let me see so I know what to expect too. I don't want to give her any complexes either."

They thumbed through numerous images, each one different from the one before. Some pictures were dated and the advancements were evident. There were so many variations, unilateral, bilateral, reconstruction, tattoos, nipple sparing, MRM, and more.

His sister made an unexpected sound and he stilled. "Rare?"

"Sorry," she quickly apologized and wiped her eyes.

He frowned. "Are you crying?" Rarity didn't cry.

"No." She continued to wipe away her obvious tears. "God, I'm so stupid. I shouldn't be crying. I should be celebrating that my best friend's alive and in remission. Don't look at me. I'm an asshole."

He put down his phone and grabbed her shoulders. "Hey, you are not an asshole. We cry. It's fucking sad. There'd be something seriously wrong with a person if they made it through all this and didn't cry."

Her mouth tightened as she dragged in a deep breath. "How is she doing this, Riley? When did sweet little Emma become the bravest person I know?"

He smiled, tears gathering in the corners of his eyes, but they were tears of happiness, tears of pride. "I think she was secretly saving up her strength."

Rarity let out a watery laugh and rested her head on his shoulder. "She's my hero."

Drawing in a deep breath, he admitted, "Mine too."

～

RILEY EXITED the elevators and dug out his keys. It was time to take his cupcake home.

"Riley." He jerked to a stop and turned as Emma's father came out of the adjacent elevator. "Just a minute," he called and jogged after him.

A sense of doom filled him as if it had been waiting on standby since he'd been working to accept she was okay. "Is everything all right?"

"Yeah… I… uh…" He twisted and seemed to count nearby chairs. "Let's sit down for a second."

"Okay," Riley apprehensively agreed, following him to an open cubicle of seating. He waited several minutes for him to say whatever was on his mind.

Mr. Sanders let out a long breath. "I… I want to say thank you."

"You're welcome," he immediately replied, but the man waved off his response.

"Give me a minute." He rubbed his head.

"Take all the time you need, sir."

"What you did, for my Emmy…" His work-roughened hands curled into fists. "You're a good man, Riley."

"You don't have to thank me, sir. I love your daughter very much."

He laughed, but the sound was sad. "I love her too." He shook his head. "There's a moment, I expect you'll know it soon enough, when you hold your child in your arms and promise to never let anything bad happen to them. Feels like yesterday I held Emmy like that."

It was quite a struggle for him to get his words out without shedding a tear, but Riley patiently let him finish.

"When we heard what was happening, I didn't get it. Then I saw what it looked like, each week, my baby girl getting ripped to shreds by probably the most underestimated evil in the world. I... I couldn't do it. She had to, but I couldn't. I hate that some days I was too weak to face what she was up against. I broke that promise I made when she was born."

"No one can keep a promise like that, sir."

"I see that now," he agreed. "But you, son, you promised to stay by her side and you did, no matter how horrible it got. You're a good man, Riley and I know you're gonna be a good husband to my daughter."

Understanding dawned. "Ah...about that, I was gonna ask—"

"No need. Sarah and I want you to know we'd be honored to have you as our son-in-law." A flush colored the leathered skin at his neck, creased by age and time. "We can't offer much, but if there's anything you need that we can—"

"Walk her down the aisle," he quickly said. "That's all she wants, her dad to walk her down the aisle."

Grinning with relief, he nodded. "Done."

PART III

Tiny pearls, pinned in a row…

With enough patience,
A speck of grit can become a pearl,
exquisitely changed by tears and time. Life is dirty.
Live hard and count your scars as pearls.

CHAPTER 19

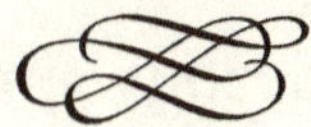

$\mathcal{E}$mma breathed through her nose, tightness, having nothing to do with her procedure, constricting her chest. Riley jotted down the measurement as she kept her eyes locked tight. It was her body and she couldn't even look. "Done?"

"Almost." He was so stoic, always following the doctors' orders and keeping a precise record for her next appointment. The satchel she'd been wearing for days zipped closed. "Done."

She let out a harsh breath. "I don't know how you do that."

He shrugged, carrying some things to the kitchen sink where he washed his hands. "I can't believe—after everything else you've gone through—that this is the part you can't handle."

"The drains make me queasy."

His teasing didn't bother her. She liked that

they were handling her recovery in a light, joking manner.

"After throwing up so much in the last few months, I hate anything that makes me nauseated. I'd be the happiest girl in the world if I never vomited again."

"The meds probably aren't making your stomach any better."

She gagged and rolled her eyes. She was so sick of feeling sick. But hey, she was alive. "I can't wait for the general wooziness to go away."

"Well, your numbers are going down so they might actually remove the drains tomorrow."

She hoped so. "I feel like I have a bomb strapped to me and I could detonate at any second."

He chuckled. "Here, take these."

Mmm... more medicine.

She accepted the pills and water, wincing as her arms struggled to lift the bottle. She was still quite weak.

"How about I help you in the shower and we get you cleaned up?"

Her stomach locked as everything inside of her protested. The idea of warm water rejuvenating her skin and cleaning her body was tempting, but the experience was tainted. Despite the awkwardness of sitting on a chair lacking the strength to wash her own body, there was the dominating fear of seeing her body uncovered.

It wasn't hers.

Still, she needed to bathe and she needed to

accept that this was what she had. Swallowing, she nodded. After days of sleeping awkwardly on the couch, accidentally dribbling soup on her pajamas, sweating, and all sorts of other stuff that made her want to shower, she put her dignity aside and braced herself.

Riley carefully helped her rise and held her elbow as she shuffled to the bathroom at a crippled turtle's pace.

"Come on, slow poke," she joked and he laughed. "Meep! Meep! I'm like the roadrunner." They continued shuffling down the hall.

"A snail knocks on a door," he said, providing entertainment for their long ten-foot journey. "A guy opens it, sees the snail, and yells *get out of here* as he kicks the snail to the other side of the fence." He paused as they turned into the bathroom. "A year later the snail knocks again and says, *what was that about?*"

She snorted and giggled at his corny joke as he carefully lowered her to the toilet seat so she could catch her breath. She was absolutely exhausted. "I'm just gonna nap here while you get the water going."

Shutting her eyes, she clung to the light mood, knowing the moment her shirt came off she'd be devastated all over again. Deep breaths still hurt, even with the pain meds, and getting upset would do her no favors.

The pipes hissed as water sprayed into the shower. Riley disappeared for a second as the bathroom slowly clouded with steam. He returned a moment later in a pair of shorts.

"Okay, let's get this shirt off." He was so incredible, so helpful. She watched as he carefully unbuttoned her shirt, gentle and mindful of all the tubes.

"Up you go." She carefully stood and he removed her pants and panties, sliding a towel on the toilet seat before she lowered her body again, sitting in only her compression bra.

Now for the hardest part.

The Velcro peeled apart like a scrape of pride ripping away. Her eyes closed as she braced herself once more. Each time it got a little easier, but at the same time her body remained so alien the process of viewing the changes ranked as excruciating.

The straps unhooked over the shoulder and the tight bra fell away. There was absolutely no sensation where the breast tissue had been removed.

"These look good I think," he whispered, gently peeling back one of the butterfly bandages. For all his gentle care, she couldn't feel his touch—a disarming realization every time.

She told herself not to look and though her head remained straight, her eyes wandered. Slowly, her chin tilted and there was her chest, vacant and battered. She saw a bit of her incisions through the bandages, but not much.

Her head turned away. Still not ready.

Riley slipped a lanyard over her neck and hooked it to her tubes for support. He did everything she needed done in order to bathe. Once she was sitting in her trusty plastic chair, he climbed in behind her and helped her get clean.

This is what normal couples do, right?

She suddenly laughed and laughed some more.

I have no hair, no breasts, no eyelashes, no nipples...

The laughter twisted sharply in her chest and escaped as a silent sob. Fuck. She didn't want to cry.

"You okay?"

She nodded, keeping her head down and eyes shut tight.

Rinsing off the remaining suds, he shut off the water. A towel draped over her shoulders. Either he didn't realize she was crying or he respected that sometimes she just needed to cry.

How was he dealing with this? She knew he loved her. She loved him too, and if he were sick she'd figure out a way to manage her limits in order to help him. But how was he doing everything so well and not obliterating whatever attraction was still left? She was mangled, yet every chance he got he told her she was beautiful. How?

Her hair would eventually grow back and the scars would fade. The expanders in her chest would gradually get filled with saline and eventually be replaced with implants. She wouldn't look like this forever, but how much of her raw self would have to be exposed before all the allure was gone?

Riley wasn't a superficial person, but he was

human. It was unnatural for a man to deal with all of this. She couldn't remember the last time they had sex and at present the idea of sex was debilitating. What if they never had sex again?

Her chest ached as she breathed deeply. All the pretty promises in the world couldn't prepare a woman for this level of acceptance. She was still a woman, but she'd been defeminized to an unrecognizable point and she wasn't sure she'd ever feel pretty again—no matter how many times he told her otherwise.

Her tears fell in silence as he dried and dressed her like a broken doll. She frowned when he massaged something slimy into her arms. "What is that?"

"Coconut oil."

She sniffled. Didn't he know she was on the verge of mental collapse? "Are you making me into a daiquiri?"

Wagging his brows, he shot her a cocky grin. "I could drink you up, but you're not ready for my parasol yet."

She giggled and the pain in her heart eased. "Why am I getting a coconut rub down?"

"It's good for your skin. I threw all your lotions away."

She frowned. "Why?"

"They're all filled with bullshit like sodium laurel sulfate, parabens, formaldehyde, and crap that's bad for you."

"Ew, formaldehyde? Like, what they use to embalm dead people?"

"Yup." He pushed up her pajama pants and rubbed down her leg.

"That's disgusting."

He gave a dry laugh. "The one with the most crap in it had a pink ribbon on the label. *That's* disgusting."

She continued to frown as he greased her up like a Thanksgiving turkey. When had he become so educated on this stuff? She didn't even know what a laurel sulf-whatever was. She supposed he had a lot of free time watching her sleep over the past one hundred days. He might have skimmed an article or two.

The more she thought about the lotion with the pink ribbon—she knew exactly which one he was talking about, because she picked it up right before she found the lump—the more pissed off she became. "That should be illegal."

"Yeah, it should." He dried his hands on a towel. "Good as new."

Hardly. She smiled. "Thank you. I smell like the beach."

Pampered and clean, he helped her lurch back to the couch where he freshened the pillows and blankets and they settled in for a movie marathon. She didn't make it through the opening credits.

~

"I can't believe this weather," Emma announced, breathing in the sunshine as it warmed her shoulders through her sweatshirt.

Reclined in a beach chair on the roof, she worked on upping her vitamin D.

Rarity grinned as she mixed together a bin of horseshit, which was infringing on the fresh air. "I'm so glad to see this winter end."

The breeze tickled her nose as the unpleasant aroma wafted over to her. "Now, tell me again, why are you playing in poo?"

"Not just poo. Good, certified organic poo I had shipped from a farm in Pennsylvania. I'm going to mix it with compost and use it to start our garden. Next year we'll use our own compost. I'm collecting it over there in that bin."

Again, the gaps in Emma's memory were brought to her attention. "You're going to grow food in the poo and garbage?"

"It's the best fertilizer there is. Would you rather buy food that was treated with carcinogenic pesticides and herbicides? This stuff's as clean as it gets."

Emma laughed. "Poop?"

"Organic poop," Rarity corrected. "What good's a vegetable if it's been treated with chemicals that make us sick. Everything we grow will be clean and one hundred percent natural."

"What are you talking about?" Vegetables were good. They regenerated cells. Doody was dirty.

"Trust me. I've read up on it. The things they're putting on our produce is the same shit the government uses in chemical warfare. It's disgusting and I refuse to give up my veggies, so

I'm growing our own. Then we don't have to worry."

"That can't be true." The FDA would never let farmers get away with such a thing. And why wasn't it on the news if their food was being poisoned?

Rarity snorted. "Don't underestimate the power of greed. GMOs are making farmers tons of money. No one cares that they're messing with the natural cycle of nature and possibly costing people their lives."

Two months ago she'd never thought twice about a GMO. To be honest, she wasn't sure if they were something she *should* be buying or *shouldn't*. They lived in a world where technology was good, so genetically modifying an organism just sounded like a great advance in science.

"So GMOs are bad?"

"Depends who you talk to, but in my personal opinion, there's nothing good about chemical agriculture."

"What was wrong with regular vegetables? They didn't always put stuff like that on them."

"The chemicals keep the bugs away. More crops equal more money," Rarity hissed, a look of disgust clear on her face. "Forget that they're stripping the minerals out of our food, minerals our bodies need to survive. The term *cide* as in pesti*cide*, literally means *kill*. If it's under our kitchen sink you wouldn't drink it, right? Well, we've been ingesting those lethal toxins for years, toxins that have been linked to birth defects, nerve damage, and cancer, all by eating supposedly *healthy* foods."

"Who's letting them do that?"

"Most people don't realize it's being done. They think organic living is just some hay brained hippie thing, but it's the only way to guarantee food hasn't been tainted."

Emma frowned as anger filled her. Not only was she among the ignorant population that wasn't aware of this, she might have actually been affected by it. "All non-organic produce is chemically treated?" That couldn't be right.

"Not all, but until they change the laws and make farmers label their produce with warnings, it's anyone's guess. Food's supposed to be medicine, but they've turned it into poison. It's sick —*literally*—which is why I'm growing our own."

"I find that hard to believe. Wouldn't the Food and Drug Administration be all over that?"

Rarity shrugged, sifting her gloved hands through the basin of soil and churning the muck. "I suppose it depends on where their interests lie. So long as the US government doesn't require GMO treated foods to be labeled, we'll never know which ones are safe and which are tainted. Plenty of other countries have laws in place."

"So we have to buy organic?"

"Organic's good—so long as it's certified. *Natural* doesn't mean shit."

What if the broccoli at dinner last night was poisoned? *Seconds anyone?*

While her roommates had a grip on this troubling information, it was news to Emma.

Somehow she felt responsible for their new attitudes toward proactive health, yet left out of the action. "I wanna help," she announced from her chair.

"Sorry. You're still too fragile to play in the mud."

She scrunched her nose. "I don't wanna play in the mud. Give me something else to do."

Rarity stood and brushed her gloves down her overalls. "Okay, grab that box filled with toilet paper rolls. I'll show you how to cut and fold them so we can plant seeds in them. They're biodegradable."

For the next hour they sat on the roof in the warm pre-spring sun and worked. Emma folded hundreds of toilet paper rolls into mini cups and Rarity hammered and sawed planks of cedar into raised vegetable beds. It was incredibly cathartic.

"Emma?"

She turned and grinned as Riley stepped onto the roof. "Good morning, sleepyhead."

He bent and kissed her. "Morning." Squinting at his sister he chuckled. "You're filthy."

Rarity shrugged and continued sawing. She looked so beautiful in her dusty overalls with a bandana wrapped around her head. "You're so pretty, Rare."

Her friend stilled and smiled at her. "Not half as pretty as you, toots."

She wished that were true.

Riley held out a hand to her. "I'm going to take Marla for a walk. Come with me. The exercise will do you good."

They thought they were slick, sneaking in little regimented walks here and there in between her coconut rub downs and organic shakes. Smirking at his head silhouetted against the sun, warmth filled her. His hair was growing back. "I love you."

"Love you too. Come on. Marla's pacing."

Though she still wasn't herself, she was feeling better than she had in months. Her tubes were gone and the incisions were healing nicely according to her surgeon.

She'd gotten her first injection in her expanders and other than random bouts of weakness that struck out of nowhere, she felt wonderful. Still, the minor set backs were buried by an overwhelming gratitude to be alive—something she hoped never faded.

"The sun will be setting soon, so I put your coat in the bag."

So thoughtful. She carefully laced her sneakers and covered her head—which got cold—with her monkey hat. Yes, it was now hers.

"Marla!" The dog came bounding out of Rarity's bedroom the second she called and she gave her a bumpy cuddle.

"Watch she doesn't get too rough," Riley warned and she tried not to get frustrated with his concern. He was right. She was still recovering. He took the leash and tossed the bag over his shoulder. "Ready?"

"Yeah." This felt semi-normal, like the things they used to do.

They walked for a long time and her legs

were getting tired, but the beautiful day was easing into such a lovely dusk she didn't want to go home just yet. As twilight approached, Riley stopped and handed her his jacket, which she gratefully accepted. It wasn't spring just yet.

"Look," he said, pointing as a young woman leisurely strummed a guitar over an empty case on the sidewalk. They walked closer as she crooned and played.

"I know this song," Emma said, grinning as a trumpeter joined from several paces away, startling her.

"La Vie en Rose," he said, as the girl hummed with the trumpet. He grinned. "Dance with me?"

She laughed and looked down at Marla, who was getting a good sniff of the woman's guitar case. "What about Marla?"

He looked around and held up a finger. Walking to a nearby bench he said something to an older woman sitting alone and pointed back at Emma. Her face heated as the woman waved and took Marla's leash. Riley returned. "We have a dog sitter."

His hand caught hers and he pulled her close, his arm wrapping around her back as they swayed on the corner of Fifth Ave. Her heart leapt as the girl sung of angels and love songs bringing magic to ordinary life.

What a beautiful song. She'd always enjoyed the French version, but this was the first time she'd ever heard the lyrics in English. They fit. A love story in a world of pink. La Vie en Rose.

The song ended too soon and Emma wished

the moment could have lasted forever. Riley nodded and dropped several dollars in the musician's case. Then thanked her for playing and went to collect Marla.

The woman holding the leash smiled, her teeth white against her dark skin. "A rose for your love?" she passed him a long stem pink rose.

"For you," he said, presenting her with the gift.

Like the song said, it was a magic spell he'd cast. Her cheeks stretched with a smile as she sniffed the rose. "Thank you."

"Look." He pointed, just beyond her shoulder and she turned.

The Empire State Building. "We still need to visit that. It's on my list."

"Let's go now."

She drew back. "We can't. We have Marla."

He waved away her words. "If anyone asks we'll say she's a service dog. She might as well be. Trust me, we'll be fine. You're wearing a monkey hat for crying out loud. No one's going to stop us."

He seemed determined so she followed, but knew in five minutes they were going to get thrown out of the Empire State Building. She tsked. And on her first visit.

As they entered the complex her eyes went wide. Glittering gold polished tile climbed the walls in an art deco masterpiece. It was like traveling back in time. Some people were dressed in jeans and some in suits. None were wearing monkey hats.

As Marla's nails ticked along the shiny floor she became self-conscious. "Maybe we should leave," she whispered.

"Relax." He approached a counter and passed the man his credit card. "Two passes for the main deck. We have a service dog with us today."

"Yes, sir." The man swiped the card and passed two tickets to Riley. "Enjoy."

He grinned and nudged her toward the bay of elevators where an usher waited. "Told ya."

Even the elevators were luxurious, though crowded. When the doors closed she giggled and he glanced at her. "What?"

She smirked and whispered, "I wanna push all the buttons like Buddy the Elf."

He chuckled as a man to her right gave a panicked look. "Please don't."

"Fine." She sighed.

Marla paced uneasily in the cramped space. "She's nervous."

He patted the dog's side and she settled. "Her ears probably feel the elevation. Do you feel it?"

"Sort of."

"It's gonna be a lot colder up here. You should button up."

Good idea. She tightened her coat and returned her attention to the climbing numbers. "Takes a while to go up eighty-six floors."

"It'll be worth it. Almost there."

They watched the numbers rise as the cart climbed. Finally it slowed and the doors opened. The passengers shuffled out and Marla seemed relieved to be out of the stuffy, traveling box.

Emma nodded politely at the suited man positioned at the entrance of the observation deck.

"My ears feel the altitude now."

"What?" he yelled and laughed. "Just kidding."

She hadn't expected it to be this crowded. Multiple people shuffled their way toward the elevators, but just as quickly more people arrived. She held onto his arm as they carefully maneuvered through the mob. "I feel like Meg Ryan."

"Really? I was thinking King-Kong."

She laughed as the wind cut through her clothing.

"There's an opening." He pointed to a corner where a couple stepped away from the glass and strolled on. She followed him and the closer they got to the edge the more sensitive her feet got.

Her breath caught in her throat as she looked over the edge. "Wow."

Riley stepped behind her, his front pressing to her back, his chin resting on her shoulder as he hunched around her. "Amazing, right?"

It was indescribable. "Definitely."

His lips curled into a smile against her neck. "So you can check two things off your bucket list tonight."

"Two?"

"Mmm-hmm." His arms released her, taking Marla's leash and he whispered, "Turn around."

Slowly, she pivoted and gasped when she spotted her mom and dad and then Rarity. She really needed to start paying more attention. "What are you guys doing here?"

Riley passed his sister Marla's leash and dropped to his knee.

Oh, my God.

He smiled and produced a small velvet box. "I figured we'd go traditional. Will you make an honest man out of me, Em? I'm a soiled dove and you're my only hope. I love you. Wear my ring and say you'll marry me."

"You jerk," she laughed as tears sprung to her eyes. "I thought we were just going for a walk."

"Is that a yes?"

Was he an idiot? "Of course that's a yes!"

Strangers smiled and clapped, as did her family.

He stood, his arms wrapping tight around her as he kissed her deeply, his hand cupping the back of her neck and pulling her hat clean off her head. They hadn't kissed like that in ages. The return of his lips to hers broke and healed so many parts at once.

She held his face and kissed him with all the passion she possessed. "I love you so much, Riley Morgan Lockhart."

"I love you too, Emma Ma'gotes Hobbit toes Sanders gonna be Lockhart." His forehead pressed to hers pulling her hand into his. "Lem'me put a ring on it."

Cool metal slid over her finger and she looked down, her jaw unhinging as the diamond glinted brightly in the evening lights. "Oh, Riley…it's beautiful."

They turned and their family cheered again, rushing at them in a group hug and attracting the attention of more strangers sharing the deck. People pointed and awed and she wanted so desperately to see what they saw—the beautiful man asking the bald, breastless woman to be his wife. *Love*.

"Smile," Rarity called and the Polaroid flashed. That one was getting its own page in the album for sure.

The incredible night concluded with dinner. Rarity returned Marla home and met them at the restaurant with Lexi. Emma had her first drink in months and everything played out like a majestic dream—until the cab ride home.

The closer they came to the loft the harder her heart beat. Her gaze returned to the beautiful ring on her finger and her happy fiancé by her side. All signs pointed to perfect—until she looked down.

Rarity went home with Lexi so the loft was empty. They were officially engaged. What couple got engaged and didn't celebrate with sex? The more she considered the norm, the more pressure she felt and her joy shifted into extreme anxiety.

Her heart wanted to make love to her future husband. She wanted to touch him and look into his eyes and feel his arms around her the way she used to, but now... her body was so detached. Should she do it anyway—for him? For both of them? Maybe just dive in? But what if it hurt— not physically, but emotionally? Too many changes at once. Why hadn't she had more wine with dinner?

"You okay?"

His question startled her. "Yeah. Fine."

His fingers laced with hers and squeezed.

She'd keep her shirt on. There. One decision made. There would be plenty of chances to take the shirt off, but for now it was staying on. And the lights were going to have to be off. Darkness was safer. But what if he inadvertently bumped her? They'd been so careful as her fragile body healed. Not only had he been treating her like glass, she still felt breakable.

God, this is just too much pressure. Who can think about sex with all this other crap to worry about?

The cab arrived at the loft and they took the elevator in silence. Marla greeted them when they entered the dark apartment and Riley grabbed her leash. "I'm going to take her down for a minute. I'll be right back."

"Take your time." Her voice was remarkably calm compared to what was going on inside her head.

He left and she rotated in a slow circle. Glancing down she shut her eyes and groaned. "I can't do this."

She walked to her bedroom, and rummaged through her lingerie drawer. Everything was too big and too sexy for her scraggy, flat chested figure. Hate and anger built into such frustration. She'd promised not to do this to herself.

Throwing the lingerie back in the drawer, she slammed it tight and grumbled, "You're alive. Who cares about this stuff?" But nothing penetrated the pain and sense of absolute inadequacy suffocating her. Opening the drawer again, she removed her smallest teddy, but couldn't bring herself to look at it.

Dropping to the mattress, she curled on her side and quietly wept. What if she never felt sexy again?

"Em?"

Startled, she brushed at her eyes, not expecting him home so quickly. Maybe if she were quiet he'd think she fell asl—

"What are you doing?"

Shaking her head, she sat up. "Nothing."

"Hey." He walked to the bed. Marla followed, giving her a wet snuffle, but she wasn't in the mood. "I thought we'd watch a movie."

She laughed, the sound hollow. Of course he'd think that. He probably didn't want to have sex with her anyway. "Okay."

He sat beside her. "Are you upset?"

"No." She was the worst liar.

Slowly, he extricated the crumpled piece of lace from her fist. "What are you doing with this?"

"Using it as a tissue." That was the truth. Might as well throw all those things away.

He frowned. "Are—are we having sex?"

Shutting her eyes, she shook her head. "I tried, but I can't."

"Hey, we don't have to rush into anything. Cakes, you're still getting back on your feet. Don't work yourself up like this. I'm fine. I promise."

She wiped her nose and stared at him

through bleary eyes. "It's so frustrating. I want to be with you, but I hate my body."

"Hey, no judging until it's fully healed. That's the rule, remember? You have a ways to go still."

She flopped back on the bed. "I don't feel my breasts, Riley. They're numb, because there's nothing real there."

He gently lay beside her, his face only a few inches from hers. His hand slowly came to rest high on her chest where her muscle retained some sensitivity. "But your heart's here. Do you feel that?"

She sniffled and he took her hand, pressing it into his shirt, over his heart. "When we kiss, my heart races. Feel."

His lips traced hers and her stomach tightened. The vacant sense of nothingness where her breasts used to be overwhelmed her, and she was about to pull away. But his heart pounded under her palm and she smiled, a breathless laugh falling from her lips to his.

His hand slid to her neck. "Being with you was more than boobs, Em. It's closeness. The feel of my body against yours. The weight of your fingers on my skin. The look in your eyes. The kiss of your lips. The tightness of your touch. The scent of your skin. The sound of your voice. It's so much more than just sex."

Her breath shook. "I wish I was prettier for you."

His head shook as disappointment flashed in his eyes. "Listen to me, Emma. You are the prettiest, most beautiful woman I've ever met. You're so afraid I'm going to see you and get grossed out. Well, I've seen you. I've seen you puking your guts out. I've seen you covered in bald patches. I've seen you go to the bathroom. But when we make love that's not what I see."

She wiped her eyes, the reminder of all those undignified moments stabbing deep. "But that's all I can see."

His eyes studied her for a long moment and he stood. He shut the door and removed her robe from the back. The sash slowly pulled through the loops as he rehung the robe. "Let's try something."

Her stomach knotted with excuses, but she kept them inside as her world went dark and the sash covered her eyes.

"Can you see?"

"No."

"Good. Try to relax. Just feel, Emma. If you want me to stop say stop and I will. This is just an experiment."

Protests rang in her head, but she humored him, truly wanting to get over this metaphorical hump. Blowing out a breath, she nodded. "Okay."

"Good."

His fingers trailed over her face and she grinned. Like soft flower petals they traced her nose and the raised shape of her lips. His feather light touch skated along her chin, around her ear, and down her throat. She sighed as the tension in her jaw gradually released beneath his tickling touch.

His mouth pressed to hers and she sucked in a

breath. He merely rested his lips over hers. The firm pressure was nice. His nose nestled with hers as he shifted. Her shoulder tensed and she winced as she braced for his weight, but it never came.

"I won't hurt you."

Fabric rasped and his hand gradually lifted hers. Warm lips pressed to the backs of her fingers, the soft side of her wrist. His lips brushed the skin over her pulse and her toes curled, her insides pulling at the sensual kiss.

He'd never kissed her wrist like that before. The delicate patch of skin was incredibly vulnerable and soft. She really liked his mouth there. He lifted her other hand and did the same as the knot in her belly loosened and tightened in a different way.

Her heart, as he said it would, raced. Gradually, her free hand glided up his arm and, as if drawn there by some unforeseen force, her fingers traced their way to his nipple. Recognition and safe familiarity blanketed her as the tip of her finger deliberately treaded over the tiny nub. Strangely, touching his nipples awakened something inside of her—a sort of mirror play she couldn't explain.

Rolling her baggy sleeve back, his mouth kissed up the tender inside of her arm on all the soft places she'd never noticed, her throat, her inner elbow, the curve of her shoulder. It was all so sensual.

His hand rubbed back and forth over her thighs, a caress that would bring pleasure to any person. Why had she underestimated the joys of touching? Everywhere he caressed, even through her clothing, felt magnificent.

But her body didn't react the way it was supposed to. As much as he was stimulating her flesh and awakening her desire, the parts she needed to do this were not cooperating. The doctors warned this might happen, as her hormones were being manipulated by multiple treatments.

"You're tensing. Stop overthinking, Emma. Just enjoy what's happening. Am I hurting you?"

"No," she said, trying to regroup and concentrate on his touch.

"I want to feel you," he whispered as his hands leisurely slid behind her waistband. "Let's take off our pants."

Curious if more would kick her reflexes into action, she nodded. He stripped away her sweats. The rough denim of his jeans slipped away and the wiry hair of his legs pressed to hers as their legs brushed together. His hands cupped her ass and she pressed her weight into the caress.

Cupping. He could cup her there.

His mouth kissed along her throat as he lay on his side, petting and gently groping any curve he could find. The heat of his body burned into hers. Lowering her hand, she followed the contour of his hip until her fingers closed around his heated flesh as he sighed.

"Yes…"

This was unchanged. She could touch him the same as she always had and deliver pleasure equivalent to any other time. His breath became labored, his body seeming to bulk in size, as he trembled under her caress.

Her wrist twisted as she pulled at his flesh. His legs rubbed against hers, as his hips deliberately pressed forward. "Jesus, Emma…"

Every time he whispered her name, or any sort of praise, her need to please him doubled. "I want to see you," she whispered, pushing the blindfold away.

He eased to his back and she rolled onto her side, stroking him firmly. The muscles of his stomach rippled as his pelvis lifted. His chest expanded the closer he came to his release. Just as she sensed his finish, his fingers laced with her free hand and he squeezed.

His flat belly tensed as his hips flexed and his knees bent. His eyes closed and his lips compressed in ecstasy as she gently finished him. The tension in his body left in a huff of air, as his head collapsed to the pillows and he caught his breath.

"Wow." He laughed. "I really thought we were just going to watch a movie and go to bed."

She smiled, a sense of unexpected accomplishment blanketing her. "I'm glad we did this."

Reaching to the nightstand he snatched a few tissues and quickly cleaned himself up then turned to his side. "Are you…if you want to try, we can…"

"No." Her body wasn't reacting properly at the moment and she didn't want to ruin what actually turned out to be something beautiful. "This was enough for me."

"Are you sure? I can take care of you. We don't have to have sex."

"I'm okay. I think I want to wait a little longer." She hoped it didn't take too long.

He kissed her. "I love you, Em. I know this is frustrating for you, but I'm not in any rush. We have the rest of our lives together. Never forget that. I'm not going anywhere."

"Thank you for being so patient." She let out a gusty breath. "I could use a hug."

He grinned and held out his arms. "Soft or hard? I got everything you need right here on tap."

"I'll take the Riley special," she said, sliding into his arms as they closed firmly around her. His face tucked into her shoulder, his five o'clock shadow scuffing her throat. She breathed him in and shut her eyes.

～

"Okay, direct eye contact for two minutes, no laughing. Winner gets the last cookie."

She hunkered down and stared at Riley, her mouth already twitching with the urge to smile. "Go."

"I can't believe you're letting her eat that shit," Rarity commented from the living room chair and Riley momentarily lost his focus.

His brow wrinkled. "I'm only going to let her eat it if she makes me laugh first."

"Whatever. You know what I'm talking about," Rarity grumbled.

Now Emma frowned. "If I want the cookie I'll eat the cookie, Rarity."

"It's your funeral."

The room chilled and Riley's eyes hardened like ice. "What the fuck did you just say?"

Rarity kept her eyes on the television as they both stared at her, waiting for an explanation. She shrugged. "You know what that shit does. Sugar shuts down the immune system—"

"I don't give a fuck about your theories on nutrition," Riley snapped. "Don't say shit like that!"

"Well do you give a fuck about her? You two destroyed that entire box."

"Whoa!" He jumped off the couch and got in his sister's face. "Don't hold back now, Rarity. Any other ways you want to make me feel guilty?"

What the hell was going on? Emma stood, forgetting about the cookies for a moment. "Guys, stop it."

"No, this is good," he argued. "Give me some more criticism, Rare. Tell me how else I'm screwing up—how I'm hurting her. We had beef the other day. You wanna yell at me for that too?"

Rarity rolled her eyes. "You think it's funny—"

"Yeah, I think it's fucking hilarious. Later on we're gonna go tour a chemical plant and cook on Styrofoam."

"Riley—"

"Don't defend her, Emma."

"Don't yell at me," she snapped. This was

ridiculous. They were fighting over cookies! "Both of you knock it off."

"You take her recovery for granted. Every day you get more and more lax!"

"And every day you get more and more rigid."

"It's called concern," Rarity snapped, raising her voice.

"It's called being a bitch!"

"Riley!" Emma gasped, but he ignored her.

Scowling at his sister, who scowled right back, he barked, "You're turning into a fanatic!"

"Well, you're a hypocrite!" She threw the remote into the chair and stood. "You say you're cutting out all the dangerous stuff but then you bring home junk!"

"It's my home! I'll bring whatever I want!"

They continued to snarl at each other, their voices rising as they screamed in each other's face. Finally, she couldn't take anymore and screamed, *"Shut up!"*

Grabbing the cookie off the table, she shoved it in her mouth. "There." Crumbs sputtered out of her mouth. "If it kills me you can say you were right and I'll be the one to blame." With that she marched to her room and slammed the door.

Idiots.

She scowled and chewed up the stupid cookie. Folding her arms, she sat on the chair at her vanity, wishing she had something to throw. She appreciated everything they were doing for her health, but their home was turning into a communist kitchen. There were too many rules —over a goddamn cookie!

There was a knock at the door. "Toots?"

Busying her hands, she straightened papers without reading what they were. "Go away, Rarity."

"I'm sorry. I shouldn't have said that."

Yeah, she shouldn't have. "I'm over it."

"I didn't mean it. Can I please come in?"

She couldn't stay in her room all day, but she wasn't going back out there if they continued to snap at each other. Blocking the entrance, she opened the door and huffed. "What do you want?"

Her eyes were apologetic. "I'm sorry. Please forgive me."

"Fine. But for the record, stress is just as harmful as sugar. I hate when you two fight and I refuse to be the cause of it."

"I know. But we're siblings. Sometimes siblings fight."

"Not an excuse."

"You're right. I'm sorry, Em. I was really wrong to say that. Please don't shut me out."

With a sigh, she stepped back and let her in. "Rarity, you have to accept that I'm going to eat cookies and cakes and ice cream still. I drink Riley's shakes, I take your supplements, and we only buy good organic food most of the time. I can't give up much more after I already sacrificed so much."

"I know." She sat on the bed, head lowered. "I just get scared. I read all these articles about free radicals and cell mutation and I'm a paranoid mess now. I don't want anything else to happen to you, Em."

Emma sat beside her. "I know you're scared, but we live really clean, Rare. We exercise every day to detoxify our bodies, we clean with home-made mixtures, and Riley won't even let me paint my nails without reading the label first. I can't handle much more than that. Sometimes I just… want the fucking cookie."

She laughed then her shoulders lowered. "You're right. I'm making everyone crazy around here—including myself. I don't know why I'm so obsessed with this."

"It's okay to be scared, Rarity."

"I don't like it. It all happened way too fast. I mean, we're so lucky you're in remission, but it was like one day you found a lump and a few months later this is where we are. What if it is all the junk we put in and on our bodies?"

"You can't live in a bubble."

"I know that, but I…" She huffed and growled, clearly frustrated by her uncharacteristic emo-tions. "If you want cookies, I'll bake them for you. I love you, Emma. I'm not ready to watch you take risks yet."

Emma snickered. "And what a dangerous life I lead, when eating a cookie is enough to qualify as risky behavior."

"See? I'm crazy. Gah, I'm sorry. I don't want to be this way!"

Emma plopped a hand on top of her head and pulled her close until their skulls were touching. "Yes, but we know it's out of love. I appreciate everything you're doing, so does Riley. I'll tell you what, if you keep that cookie jar filled I'll only eat what's in there. But I'd really appreciate something in the chocolate family. I am a woman after all."

She nodded. "Deal. I'm sorry."

"Hug?"

"Hug."

Emma wrapped her arms around her, and whispered, "Right now, I'm not going anywhere, Rare. So let's try to get past being afraid, at least for a little while."

Her arms tightened. "I love you."

"I love you too."

∽

IT TOOK three months for the chemo to officially be out of Emma's system. Her expanders were slowly doing their job and, in a few months, she'd be back under the knife getting implants. Her tests were all showing wonderful progress and, aside from the random bout of exhaustion that struck every couple of weeks, she was relishing life.

Late May, as they were on their way back from the musical *Wicked*, the subway raced toward home and she remembered the first time they'd ridden the train together and how Riley flirted with her to make the other girls jealous.

The train wasn't as full as it had been that day, but several women looked at her, when before she'd felt invisible. Now she was just aiming for normal—whatever that was.

Her hair was gradually filling in and her expanders gave her chest a bit of dimension. She could almost pass as an ordinary flat chested girl with a pixie cut.

She grinned at the one woman staring, not bothered by her curiosity. The woman nodded and casually lowered the collar of her shirt, exposing her shoulder where a pink ribbon was tattooed.

Emma's grin fell as chills raced up her legs. "What time is it?" she whispered to Riley, not taking her eyes off the other woman.

"Six-thirty."

Her smile returned. Six-thirty and she was just then having her first thought of cancer that day. It was incredible. How had the word that troubled every second of every day, slipped her mind for the past twelve hours? She hadn't thought of it once. Amazing.

The woman stood as the train stopped, sharing one last glance over her shoulder. A sense of camaraderie took hold of Emma in a way she never expected, as if she finally could understand the sisterhood that existed behind the pink. The solidarity she'd felt so apart from months ago, now engulfed her. She'd made it to the other side.

When she was in the thick of it, every attempt to pretty up her suffering with pink, grated. The expectation to *be* pink distorted the typical emotions she wanted to feel, like anger. It was cancer. There was nothing pretty about it. But today was not a day for anger.

Today was a day to celebrate, a day to embrace the slow return to normalcy. Today she actually felt a little pink—a little pretty. Maybe she'd get a tattoo. She wondered, if she hadn't seen that woman, how much more time might have passed before she thought about that atrocious C-word. Six months ago she never thought of it at all.

Resting her head on Riley's shoulder, she decided she'd like to live somewhere in between educated awareness and aggressive activism. That neighborhood seemed much nicer than responsive panic and unpreparedness.

Maybe she'd misunderstood the color all along. Perhaps it wasn't the color of breast cancer, but the pretty glow of survival, the blush returning to her cheeks. The shift in her eyes when she cried, because she was so happy to simply be alive. Sometimes pink wasn't a bad color at all.

Riley kissed her head. "You okay?"

"I'm better than okay. I'm really happy." She'd never wasted so much time thinking about a color until her life was washed in a million and one shades of pink, but the delicate shade fit her mood today.

He smiled at her. Life, when it was good, was indeed pink. *La vie en rose.*

CHAPTER 20

*R*iley glanced at the door as Rarity came inside. Emma rested on his lap, casually flipping through channels. His sister freed Marla from the leash and the dog shuffled over to greet them. As his sister sorted through the mail she paused and silently held up another bill.

Put it in the drawer, he mouthed and she nodded, sliding the medical bill next to the others. They were going to need bigger drawers.

Emma had insurance, but it was minimal. So much of her treatments and procedures came with out of pocket deductibles and, because she had a hundred different doctors, they billed her separately for each and every one.

They'd gone to great lengths to avoid unnecessary stress, agreeing that stress created an acidic environment in the body, and cancer just loved acidity. However, life had some stresses that couldn't be avoided.

Tension knotted in his shoulders, a special sort of worry he wasn't used to bearing. Maybe what he was going through wasn't special at all. Maybe this unannounced sense of heaviness was something every guy experienced. Perhaps it was because Emma now wore his ring. Or maybe he was simply coming down from all they'd been through at a different pace than everyone else and returning to normal suddenly felt wrong, like outgrowing jeans he'd worn his entire life. Or maybe it was just money.

He had money, a notable savings, plus the portion of his inheritance he couldn't access yet, but it seemed wrong to touch that—felt even worse to see how fast his savings was dwindling after something as costly as cancer. The days of banking his measly paychecks after deducting the cost of supporting only himself were over. Yeah, money was definitely stressing him out.

Finding the trigger to his anxiety did nothing to relieve the very real fact that he now shouldered some financial burdens a single man didn't have to worry about. He'd pay her bills like he'd been doing since December. Sometimes one got through the mail to her, but most days either he or Rarity intercepted. Emma assumed her co-pay was the end of her responsibility—which in all honesty was how insurance *should* work.

He wasn't complaining. Honestly he'd lost count after the first twenty-thousand dollars. She was alive, and that was all that counted. But he was concerned about their future and the sort of life he could provide on his annual salary once his savings ran out—which would eventually happen.

Everything cost so much money. How did people living on a budget afford sickness? The wealth he'd once taken for granted, now made him immeasurably grateful, but it was only a matter of time before that comfort was gone.

The rest of his inheritance was there, but he couldn't touch that money without an investment plan, according to his grandparents' will and his pretentious parents' impossible standards. It was sitting there, in untouched accounts racking up interest. He'd intended to leave this world never touching that money, but now he wasn't so sure. That money could make a life for them, a future, something great enough to sustain their family for generations. But it was earmarked for investments and he was the farthest thing from a businessman.

Emma had lost all sources of income. She had until August to return to her job, but they were no longer compensating her for missed work. If he hadn't been secretly paying for all her expenses, she'd be homeless and starving, debt collectors harassing her non-stop.

It was another reason why this disease needed to be stopped. People simply couldn't afford cancer.

If he had access to his money he'd talk to a lawyer about creating a fund in Emma's name, one that sponsored families with a member undergoing treatment. He could provide groceries or pay their utilities. The idea—though not necessarily a business plan—filled him with passion. His money could do things like that, but again… he couldn't touch it.

But people needed help. There was someone out there suffering, and someone else probably loved that person the way he loved Emma.

For weeks the idea had been kicking around in his head and he was tired of thinking about it, because so long as he didn't have a plan that promised capital gain he didn't have the funding for those sorts of dreams.

"What did you get at the store, Rare?" Emma asked as she stood and moved toward the bathroom.

"Goodies. Wanna play in the kitchen with me?"

"Sure. Let me use the bathroom first." Emma smiled, which she'd been doing a lot lately, and that made him happy. He wanted to make other people happy.

"You wanna help, too, Ri?"

He tossed the remote aside. "Sure. What are we making?" He hoped it was food because he was hungry.

"Deodorant."

"Oh."

Emma returned and washed her hands as his sister set up a bunch of ingredients. Rarity opened a bag of something called arrowroot and dumped a measurement of the powder into three bowls. She slid one in front of each of them and cracked open a jar of coconut oil.

Riley dug a spatula into the semi-solid oil. "Is this what we're mixing with it?"

"Yup," his sister said. "Get a glob and mush it with the arrowroot until it makes one big lump."

He took some and passed the oil to Emma. The three of them blended and poked, each working with their own concoction.

"I'm adding essential oils to mine," Rarity said. "I'm thinking lavender."

Emma frowned. "Mine's not working."

"Just keep mushing."

Today they were making deodorant. Yesterday they made laundry soap and tomorrow they were scheduled to make a new batch of kitchen disinfectant. Each product was derived from completely organic materials and one hundred percent toxin free.

"Now it's starting to gel together," Emma said as she squished the ingredients around in her bowl.

Rarity, the orchestrator of all this, had her solidified clump and was already fitting it into a jar. "Do you realize it costs less than a dollar to make deodorant for all three of us? The stuff I was using cost almost five bucks a stick."

Last week she made chapstick, they were stocked for the next decade. "How much do you think the chapsticks cost per stick?" They had to be a little more costly, since she'd purchased the lip balm tubes.

"Roughly? Maybe ten cents a tube?"

"Ten cents?" Emma remarked, seemingly impressed. "The ones I usually buy sell for around four dollars."

"That's the cost of mass production and marketing. I'm giving you a tube of balm. No labels or fancy artwork. My stuff's naked."

"*Au naturel!*" Emma laughed.

She showed him her progress, smiling proudly, and he slid her an empty jar. "You should sell this stuff, Rare. I bet a lot of people want to use cleaner products, but they don't have the time to make them."

His hand stilled. Sell green products?

His sister paused as well, her eyes going wide at the possibility. "Could you imagine?"

He could. He could very easily imagine selling stuff like this. His heartbeat went from a slow trot to a thundering gallop. "How would you market it? Online?"

Emma shrugged. "Why not a store? Oooh, it could be like an old apothecary! I'd shop there."

While Emma was simply fantasizing, he was strategizing. "Rare, what else have you made?"

"Well, I made shaving cream, which was awesome—Lexi's addicted to it. Hair gel, moisturizer, body wash, plenty of cleaning products, and next week I want to try shampoo."

His mind rapidly put together a rough inventory list. "Where are you getting the recipes?"

She shrugged. "I read up on a lot of stuff and once I've learned what uses something has, I play around with different mixtures and oils. There are plenty of ideas online that can be adapted. Why? Do you really think I could sell this stuff?"

"I do," Emma said, capping off her deodorant and frowning. "I'm definitely not the person to help you with presentation though. Why does mine look like a four year old mixed it?"

Riley laughed. "What did you do?"

"I just mixed the ingredients Rarity gave me."

Rarity shoved Emma's sad jar away. "Don't worry about that now. Let's go back to what we were saying. Do you think I could incorporate produce if I had a little stand?"

His mind took flight. Why stop there? Why not grow an inventory? No additives. No toxins. No worries. "If you're going organic you'd have to be certified and *everything* would have to be labeled."

"Definitely. How cool would that be, a totally home grown operation with everything people need to live, made fresh like the good old days? But we'd have a website."

"You could photograph your inventory for an online store," Emma added. "You could even teach people about your products, make it like a little school and host events like jarring nights for people like me who need help."

"Aw, cakes, I like your sad deodorant."

She sulked. "It is sad."

Rarity's smile bloomed. "And when they're too busy, they could place an order, personalized down to what scents they prefer and we'd jar it and label it like Chanel no. 5, but it would be Lexi no. 2 or Emma no. 1."

His stomach flipped. Would it really be that

complicated? "We should write down all our ideas."

Emma stopped pouting over her jar and looked at them. "Are you guys seriously considering opening a business?" Her expression seemed slightly withdrawn.

He frowned. "Don't you think it's a good idea?"

She shrugged. "Sure."

Rarity tipped her head, obviously noting Emma's averseness too. "What's wrong, toots?"

"Well, you guys are going to have this really cool thing and I'm going to be doing what exactly? Working as a clerk?"

"No," Riley objected. "You'd be a partner. It would be ours."

"I don't have any money to contribute to that," she argued.

"Do you think we do?" Rarity asked and snorted. "We'd have to start small with what's in our savings."

But his savings was all he had left and he couldn't tie it up in some half-baked business venture without calculating the risks. What if they needed that money? What if Emma needed more treatment? "I can't touch my savings, but we have the money."

His sister stilled. "Riley—"

"If the proposal was right—"

"No," his sister objected. "No one said it has to be that big. I'd be happy with a produce stand."

"You can't live off that."

"Who says I need to?"

"Think about it," he argued. "If we did this right, it could be our livelihood. We'd be doing something great that helped others. We're always talking about how we need to get back to basics and get rid of all the chemicals. We can't be the only people thinking that way. We could afford this, Rarity."

"I can't," she snapped. "I don't have the start up costs for something that big, neither does Emma, and for the record, neither do you."

She was wrong. If they presented it right, they could make the proposal and possibly have everything they needed. And he wouldn't have to worry about their future, because this would be an investment in it. "But we do have the money."

"Riley," she warned, shaking her head.

"Rarity, it's *our* money."

Emma's gaze bounced between them. "Are you talking about asking your parents for help?"

"*No.*"

"Yes," he spoke over his sister.

Rarity stood. "I'm not doing that, Riley. I'm not playing their games. Forget it."

"You won't have to play their games. They have to follow the rules as much as we do. The money's ours and if we meet the criteria, they can't deny us. This would fall under part of the requirements."

"Your trust is different than mine!" She snapped. "Mine requires I marry *a man.*"

He waved away her anxiety. "We wouldn't even have to touch your money."

Emma's shoulders lowered. "How much money do you guys have?"

"A lot," they both answered.

He looked at his sister. "Come on, Rare. Think about how cool that would be. Think of all the people we'd be helping. You *love* all this holistic stuff. You could go to school for it and actually do something that makes a difference. Emma could organize the business and design a brand for the company and I could run the financial end, I'd be your investor and allocate the funds for start up, because there'd be a return." He laughed. "See, I can talk like a businessman."

"You can't even match your clothes."

He winked at Emma. "I'll have a wife to dress me. Please. We'd all be partners. Emma will keep us organized, you've got the know-how and I—hopefully—will have the funding. Say yes."

He held his breath, waiting as he pleaded with his eyes. "Please." Maybe this was the fresh start they all needed.

She sighed. "Fine, but everything has to be affordable. I'm not into extortion. I want to sell *good* things that ordinary people can afford. If our deodorant costs less than a dollar we sell it for less than a dollar."

He held out his hand. "Deal!"

~

RILEY PLACED his keys by the door and quietly entered the loft. Marla lifted her head from Rarity's empty bed as he walked down the hall, but even she knew it was too late to play. Grabbing a towel, he went to the bathroom and showered.

When he made it to their room, Emma was curled up in bed on her back. Soft blonde curls pressed to her ears as she slept soundly. She'd gotten in the habit of sleeping in panties and a strip of stretched lace over her chest, claiming it made her feel sexy. She was always sexy.

Draping his towel over the chair, he climbed into bed and crawled over her. His nose nestled into her throat and he breathed. Emma.

Kissing down her shoulders to her elbows, he explored. She shifted, and hummed sleepily, from that tranquil place between sleep and awake. His body hardened as he dragged his tongue over her belly and leisurely peeled away her panties.

Sex was different now. It had taken some time to adjust. Mostly, he wanted Emma to be comfortable. It was an ongoing battle, getting her to realize her beauty had changed, but not faded. If anything, her strength made her more attractive. But he'd gladly remind her how incredible she was every day for the rest of their lives if that's what it took.

His mouth dragged over the gentle slope of her thighs, playfully biting and nibbling her tender spots as he scooted lower and parted her knees.

"You're boisterous tonight," she whispered. The moment she awoke was always his favorite part of coming home.

"I fantasized about this all night. I couldn't wait to get home and in between your legs."

She giggled and stretched, presenting him with an incredible view. "I'm happy to oblige."

His palms caressed up her inner thighs as he lowered to his elbows, scattering slow kisses over every inch of her delicate skin. Sex had definitely evolved. He preferred thinking in terms of evolution rather than change, because change implied something might be lacking, but, to Riley's thinking, they'd never been closer.

It had taken a great deal of trying to get to the comfortable point they now enjoyed, and he was certain there would be momentary setbacks still to come. But talking about it helped.

He liked sex. For him, it had always been a release. With Emma, they enjoyed silly banter, spontaneity, dirty talk, and fun. He didn't see why boobs were necessary for that to continue.

Initially, he'd been patient because she was healing. Abstinence was expected to a point. He understood her avoidance of sex, but it never occurred to him that her confidence would be so shaken after the mastectomy that she'd completely avoid intimacy.

Sex he could go without. Intimacy he could not. But after her surgery the mere possibility of sex seemed to tie her in anxious knots, creating a void so wide she'd dodge his hand when it reached for hers. His heart broke the day she avoided sitting on the couch with him and started sitting on the chair across the room, simply unreachable.

After everything they'd gone through, her nearness was something he depended on and he couldn't understand why she would take that away when they'd already lost enough. It all became clear one afternoon while watching a movie. There was a love scene playing and the man was kissing the woman's breasts. Emma stood and left the room.

When he found her, she said it gave her a visceral ache in her chest, because she'd never feel such a thing again. He had no response.

It wasn't helping matters that her treatment interfered with her body's natural responses. Emma was a sexual person and he knew she experienced arousal deep in her heart, but her body wasn't cooperating the way she wanted it to and that destroyed her.

When he finally insisted they talk about it, she cried, *"I'm twenty-four years old and I feel like I'm never going to have normal sex again. That isn't fair, not when I just found you and realized how wonderful sex can be."*

"It can still be like that, cakes." He'd kiss every square inch of her body if she'd just let him.

"But it doesn't feel the same. I want it to feel like it used to, but nothing's the same! My chest is numb, but I sense my nipples where they used to be. I'm aroused but I'm not wet—everything's broken!"

It was in that moment that he understood the depth of the issue. This was more than insecurities, more than a fear that he might find her undesirable. This was about... lubrication. It was totally inappropriate, but he laughed.

"Are you laughing at me?"

"I'm sorry. I know we have rules about laughing

and sex...but sweetheart, this is not the end of the world. You need to talk to your doctor. There are non-hormonal moisturizers, lube, and all kinds of other stuff to make you more comfortable. We can work around that. It's silly to let something that irrelevant stop you from getting everything you want."

They made an appointment that day and within a week she was back in control. He noted the transformation in her openness immediately. Flirtatious glances turned to sweet affectionate caresses and he was confident they'd find their way back to each other.

Once they opened Pandora's box a sense of security blanketed them. They mutually wanted to restore the sexual side of their relationship. It was important to both of them. The more they experimented, the more comfortable they became, which led to a brand new awakening.

When a person faced the terror of losing the one person they loved above all else, gratitude became a spice that intensified every element of living. The grass was greener, the sky was bluer, and the fucking was ridiculous.

Not only were he and Emma having sex regularly, they were having it obsessively. In the shower, on the couch, over breakfast, on top of the washing machine, in the backseat of his car—if the mood struck they were crack-a-lacking.

Their connection was stronger *because* of their desire to salvage the intimate parts of their relationship. Touching her, like he did now, had a way of spilling over into their day and seasoning all the small acts of love with a sense of chemistry. She was still his Emma and though their flame had flickered, there was no extinguishing the fire that burned in his blood for her.

"God, you're hot." Her eyes found his and he groaned, never growing tired of the way she looked at him when he pleasured her. He drove his fingers into her, pressing firmly as she arched and came. Beautiful.

Sliding up her body, she opened to him and he was home. She hummed as he kissed her. His body swelled as she pulled him close, her nearness blanketing him. Yes, this was an essential part of who they were, because nothing felt better than her arms holding him tight.

~

THE FROSTED glass doors opened and the receptionist returned. "Mr. Lockhart will see you now."

Riley nodded, wiped his clammy palms down the front of his pants, and stood. His father's professional preferences differed drastically from the style his parents kept at the condo. Here, everything was blue with gaudy gold accents and dripping crystal to complement the rich, over-polished wood furniture.

Last time he was in this office he was about nine. It hadn't changed.

Muttering a thank you to the secretary who left him at the door, he stepped into his father's office.

His dad stood. "Riley."

"Dad."

"Your sister's all right?"

"Rarity's fine."

He nodded and waved out a hand for him to enter. "Have a seat. I'm interested to hear what this visit's about."

He cleared his throat and continued to do so as some sort of nervous tic. As he settled on the blue chair he focused on not clearing his throat again, so he licked his lips and incessantly swallowed instead.

"How are things?" his father asked, most likely in an attempt to be polite and pretend they shared a normal interest in each other's lives.

"Good." This should be the moment he announced he was engaged, but he stowed that information for now. "I came to talk to you about the incentive trust."

His father tipped his head, giving no impression that this surprised him. "I suspected. You're familiar with your grandparents' expectations. Are you still tending bar?"

"Yes, but that's going to change."

"Something's inspired you. I'm curious to hear what it is."

"Rarity and I are starting a new company." There was no point in asking. They were doing it with or without his support, because once he'd laid out the plans on paper, it seemed stupid not to follow through. But without the trust, he'd have to downsize a lot of their ideals.

"And what sort of company do you have in

mind? Is Rarity struggling with her photography hobby?"

It pissed him off they never gave his sister the credit she deserved regarding her talent behind a lens. Her work had been featured in *Time,* but never garnered the slightest acknowledgement from their parents. But he wasn't here to have the same old arguments.

"It'll be green based and located in New York. A little seed money would help. We'd rather own than rent and our startup costs are substantial for the products we'll be producing."

"Define green."

"We want to produce holistic, organic merchandise for home, health, and hygiene."

His father nodded, keeping his expression blank. "A cosmetics store."

"No. This won't be anything like that. Our products are non-toxic, lacking all the unpronounceable ingredients. We'll be selling peace of mind."

"And you think there's a market for this?"

"I know there is. We have the means to make it affordable without selling our morals. People want to clean their homes with products that aren't harmful to their families, but they've lost sight of how easy that is because we're accustomed to buying products ready-made. Mass production's polluted ordinary products with chemicals and preservatives. We aren't interested in preserving our products. It's about freshness. Everything we sell will be made raw, organic, and specific to each customer's need. Nothing processed *in* a plant, but *from* plants. Over time, we'd like to incorporate produce as well, but that depends on our budget."

His father eased back in his chair and faced the window. His head shook and Riley recognized a flash of disenchantment in his eyes. "What the hell happened to this generation? When I was a boy, we drank out of garden hoses and only washed our hands when our mothers made us. I've never seen such a group of whiny, paranoid doves."

Riley stiffened. "You can thank yourself for that. All the urgency your generation demanded, meals in a minute, genetically modified seeds that bugs won't eat but people are expected to, hormone treated cattle that will never know what it is to graze a pasture, your greed came with a price and we're the ones picking up the bill. This is the first generation that isn't expected to outlive its parents. All this rushing to get ahead and mass-produce, there's no quality anymore, no security. The science your generation used to speed up nature's natural course is literally killing us."

He pointed to his father's coffee. "I'm betting the ingredients to your creamer look more like plasma than anything from a cow, and if you saw those chemicals in their raw form the last thing you'd do is swallow them. But they pretty it up with a label, inject some thickening serum and flavor in it, and no one's the wiser. You got your quick cup of Joe. All this instant satisfaction is costing us. We're racing to a faster death and somehow we've been convinced that's living."

He chuckled. "You're a kid, Riley. One little pink packet isn't going to kill us. People don't give a shit if a few whales die. They want the perfume the hottest pop star made."

"They care. People care, they just don't know how bad it's gotten."

His father laughed. "Like I said, delicate little doves. In my day men thought about wars and made products out of steel."

His shoulders drooped. They'd never see eye-to-eye.

"However," his father continued, "it is a generation of shadow fearing, riskless, crybabies out there and you may be on to something." He sighed. "I suppose it comes down to how many people think like you and how many think like me. I intend to keep my coffee the way I've been drinking it for the past forty years."

He didn't waste his breath trying to educate someone as bullheaded and ignorant as his father. Should he ever get sick, he'd justify it with some remote genetic strain traced back to his great uncle. Men like Oliver Lockhart didn't believe in powerlessness. Admitting there was something greater than him out there would be a gross show of vulnerability.

Tapping into his father's business sense, he said, "The market's there. You can take my word on it or send one of your drones to do the research for you."

He reached into his pocket and withdrew a

short printout of their expected product list, esti-mated overhead, and other relevant details he knew his father would be interested in. "If you read the fine print of the trust, you'll see your opinion doesn't play into the equation. Every-thing's outlined here. You have my number once you've thought it over." He stood.

"Riley. Why didn't your sister come with you?"

"The scent of the financial carrot only reaches so far, Dad. You can wave it in front of her all your life. She'll never bite. My advice is to stop trying to decide who Rarity should be and take a good look at the woman she is. She's awesome, and you're missing it."

With nothing more to say, he showed himself out.

~

Joey Vanguard owned an interesting enterprise and the moment Emma discovered him in a magazine, Riley agreed his services were abso-lutely in their best interests. He found the man, gave him money, and hoped to avoid as many discussions about linens as possible—which led them to their current expedition, the Gapstow Bridge in Central Park.

"Notice the lush green ivy here," Joey pointed out, as Emma dutifully followed with a notepad in hand. "In autumn it changes to a fiery red. I know we discussed September as a possible date for the wedding, but the season change is something to keep in mind when you're selecting your color scheme."

The wedding was definitely going to be in Central Park. It made perfect sense to him, being that the park was where he first wanted to kiss his future wife. It was a shame Marla was being left out, since she sort of orchestrated that fated day. "Can we train Marla to carry the rings?"

"No," both Emma and Joey answered at once.

He stroked the dog's ear. "Sorry, girl. I tried."

"Now, most couples say their vows here at the end, but I've done smaller weddings at the center of the bridge."

She glanced at him and he scurried over, sensing he was in the wrong place and should be paying attention.

"Where do you think, Riley?"

He scanned the bridge. "I like the middle."

"The middle," she told the planner.

"You guys are so easy." He made a note in his binder.

"When do we leave for the cake tasting?" Riley asked, cutting to the important issues.

"First we have to discuss color schemes. Let's find a bench."

He followed them to a bench and situated Marla with a treat. By the time he sat multiple decisions were already made. The wedding would be at night under the stars. Trees would be draped with twinkle lights and the bridge would be lined with luminaries to guide their way. He wasn't exactly sure what a luminary was, but he imagined a light saber.

"What do you envision for the reception?" Joey asked, taking rapid notes.

"The reception's going to be simple, small, just our immediate family and closest friends."

"Might I suggest your first dance be here, then? We could coordinate with the ceremony musicians and do something spectacularly wonderful like set off eco-friendly paper lanterns."

Emma's smile was precious, as her eyes turned dreamy, imagining everything the wedding planner described. Riley nodded and pointed at his tablet. "Yes, put us down for that."

Emma selected dark amethyst for the accent color, which he learned was a fancy word for purple. When they reached the bakery—heaven in the shape of a store—Riley sampled every single concoction offered.

"Did you know about grooms' cakes?" he asked, as they walked home.

"Yeah."

"I didn't know," he said, still processing the incredible news. "Do I have to share it?"

She laughed. "They're traditionally rich. I doubt you'd be able to eat the whole thing on your own."

"Well, not in one sitting, but I'd bring a doggy bag. I'm the groom. I shouldn't have to share."

"Fine. You can have the groom's cake all to yourself."

They took the elevator up and continued discussing the details. "I have to see if that date's okay with my parents. What are you going to do about your mom and dad?" she asked.

He shrugged. "I haven't decided."

"Well, the wedding's in three months, Riley. Invitations have to be ordered."

"Cakes, we're inviting a few friends and your parents. I think we can afford a spare invite if I decide to ask them at the last minute."

"True." She changed the subject. "Rarity will be happy there's no pink in the color scheme."

He laughed. "She's still going to fight you about making her wear a dress."

"No, she won't. I'm letting her wear a tux." She grinned over her shoulder and snatched a bag of corn chips from the cabinet.

"You are?"

"Yeah. I want my best friend there as my best friend. Why should she have to be someone she's not for the day? Besides, it's not like I'm going to be a runway bride. I'm working with minimal bumpage and Will Ferrell's hairdo. Besides, she's your best-*wo*-man too. It seems appropriate she wear a tux."

He pulled her to his side and kissed her temple. "You're my best woman. And I love your Will Ferrell curls. You're going to be a stunning bride."

"As long as I end up your wife, I'm good with whatever."

"We could wait until after the reconstruction if that's what you want?" he offered again. The last thing he wanted was for her to regret rushing things.

"I told you I don't want to do that. I'd have to

wait until I completely healed to even get sized for a dress. I don't wanna wait that long."

Leaning close, he whispered, "It's called a *gown*."

She smirked. "Smartass."

The door opened and Marla barked. "Get a room," Rarity called catching them mid-kiss.

"Hey, how was the shoot?" Emma asked.

"Good." She sifted through the mail. "Riley…" He glanced at his sister and stilled as she held up an envelope. "You have mail from the corporate branch of Lockhart." She frowned. "Did you talk to Dad?"

He'd been meaning to tell them about that, but then he didn't want them getting upset if his objective turned out to be an epic fail. "Uhh…"

She tossed the letter to him. "Open it."

"You don't have to open it now," Emma said.

"Yes, he does. Did you ask him about the trust?"

"Yeah."

Rarity shook her head. "If this is going to be a partnership, you have to tell us when you do stuff like that." She had an awful lot to say for someone who refused to face the benefactor of their finances. He tore open the letter.

RILEY,

After much deliberation, I have determined the best way to proceed. Despite your opposition to every bit of advice I ever bestowed, you, my son, have demonstrated efficaciousness and arrogance only a Lockhart can own.

You surprised me last week, something not easily done. Something has transformed you into a man, a competent one at that. Your proposal showed initiative and, despite our different outlooks, I'm proud of you. The money is yours. I wish you much success in your professional ventures.

Sincerely,
Oliver Lockhart

THE THICK LETTERHEAD trembled in his hand as he stared blankly. "Holy shit."

"What did it say?" Rarity demanded.

He shook his head. "He gave it to me." He laughed, never expecting to actually get through to the man. "He freaking gave it to me."

"You guys can open the store now!" Emma cheered. "This is wonderful! Maybe, after this, you and your parents can work things out."

"Doubtful," Rarity answered. He silently agreed.

"Holy shit," he muttered, still in shock. Looking at Emma he chuckled. She had no concept of how much money they were actually talking about. It was beyond what even he could comprehend, but she loved him with or without that money and that made her awesome.

The options for investments and charities were endless. They could make countless differences with this sort of wealth, hire and fund their own team of researchers. His palms moistened with sweat. This was a lot of responsibility and he could easily screw it up. Severely.

"Okay, first, we're going to invest it somewhere that will accumulate interest, but nothing high risk." People with money used words like high risk so that sounded good. "Then, we're going to look into charities. I want to do something worthwhile. We can't go giving it away willy-nilly."

He pointed at the future missus. "Emma, I want you to ask around and find out where we can get a list that details which cancer organizations dedicate the most money to researching the cause. I don't want to waste time on nonprofits with an overhead because the CEO makes millions a year. We have to know where every dollar goes. Maybe we should hire a financial advisor and our own environmentalists. We're definitely going to need an accountant we trust. I cheated my entire way through twelfth grade calculus, so I'm out."

"All right, settle down, Zuckerberg," Rarity interceded. "That money's going to your head so fast your eyes are turning green."

"Maybe you should give it back," Emma mumbled, bringing him back down to earth.

Rarity nearly choked. "Give it back? Are you nuts?"

His brow creased, never expecting her to be unhappy about this. "Why?"

Emma shrugged. "It just seems like an awful lot of money. That's a big responsibility. Money changes people."

"But it belongs to him," Rarity pointed out. "Our parents shouldn't have held it this long to begin with. I'll probably never see my half."

It was insane that his portion was only half. He took Emma's hand and chafed her fingers. "Cakes, I don't want to change who we are. I mean, yes, we'll buy a home and get you a car and maybe help out your parents if they accept our offer, but… I like how we live. I don't want to turn into some guy behind a tickertape machine, smoking cigars, and answering ten phones on his desk—"

"You're not a cartoon from the 1950's," Rarity muttered, rolling her eyes.

"I just want to make a difference." He sat back and took a deep breath. "We almost lost you. There needs to be more than races down the streets of Washington, DC."

Everyone's mood seemed to sober. "I know this is a lot of money, and I get that we aren't those people, but when do our people get this sort of opportunity? This isn't just about being green or wearing pink. It's about every cancer out there that could've possibly been avoided if people were better informed about what's being permitted into their homes, bodies and their environment."

"It's a good thing," Emma said, her smile sad. "But I don't want the rest of my life to revolve around cancer."

He squeezed her hand. "Maybe if there was less toxins in our day to day life, it wouldn't have to—for you or for anyone."

Rarity lowered herself into a chair. "He's right. What we're planning would take a great deal of the worry away."

Holding her hands in his, he met her gaze. "I swear to you, Emma, the only reason I want this money, is because all the pink in the world will never have the power of green. The ribbons aren't cutting it and I'm tired of accepting that this is the best we can do. I love you. You're my world, not a statistic. For months I couldn't protect you, but this…" He waved the letter. "This money could defend countless people from the shit out there making everyone sick."

She stared at him, her lips tight and trembling. "Okay, Riley." She took a shaky breath and nodded. "You take that money and make a difference, but don't let it change the man you are, because honestly, the world needs more people like you than they need money."

Drawing in a deep breath, he exhaled. "Thank you for believing in me."

CHAPTER 21

*I*t was early. The city seemed quieter for some reason, peaceful. Emma stared at the blushing metal of the building across the way as the sun climbed tall and proud into the radiant sky. *So pretty.*

Riley slept beside her, wrapped like a baby marsupial around her legs and she grinned. Life. Everything around her was alive.

Her neck stretched as the heat of the day trespassed through the screen, warm and invigorating. She had things to do, but this seemed more important, so she rested a while longer and took the time to appreciate the splendor of being alive.

Her mind randomly skipped from thought to thought. Riley. Her parents. Rarity. Lexi. Marla. Anna. Her wedding. She wondered if somewhere in the world at that very same moment someone else was thinking of all those things, or perhaps just one. There had to be someone appreciating this beautiful dawn. Then she randomly thought about snowflakes. In the June heat it was tricky to imagine a sky full of white.

Her hand pressed gently to her chest. Nothing. The subtle trace of her fingertips over the remaining muscle faintly tingled, but where her breasts once were… it was numb. It wasn't so shocking anymore.

Her mind sketched over her journey. It was the longest and shortest six months of her life. Everything changed and she was now unrecognizable compared to the person she once was. Oddly, the most drastic changes happened inside —not to her cells or her blood, but to her soul. How strange to prefer the person she'd become over the person she once was. What a misplaced but gratifying end to suffering.

Her life was like an avalanche, one tiny speck, smaller than a snowflake, and everything she'd depended on had come tumbling down. It almost killed her, but here she was, lazing in bed on a Sunday morning, staring at the sunshine.

She sighed. *I'm alive.*

A door slammed and she jumped. Riley grumbled in his sleep as a stampede sounded from the kitchen and Marla barked like a maniac.

"Carrots!" Rarity's voice echoed through the hall. "We have carrots!" The door to her bedroom flew open and Rarity beamed like the proudest Peter Pan. "We. Have. Carrots!"

Emma laughed. "That's wonderful!"

"Yeah, it is! I'm like a witch. I made food from dirt, eggshells, and seeds." She did a very uncoordinated victory dance while grunting and wiggling her butt.

"Get out," Riley groaned.

Rarity stilled. "I'm going to go see what else is sprouting." With that, she raced out of the loft and back to the roof. Emma giggled.

"We need to move," Riley groaned into his pillow.

"Stop. You love living here."

She wasn't ready to give up their loft. Eventually, they'd do the grown up thing and settle down—possibly in a house—but right now she liked their living situation. Even if it was chaotic at times.

He flopped to his back. "I'm awake now."

It was her turn to curl into him. She hummed and ran her palm gently over his warm skin. "Oh no…whatever will we do?"

He twisted and pinned her, his hands pressing into her wrists as his arousal prodded her belly. Smirking, his eyes darkened with desire. "Good morning, cakes."

"Good morning, my love."

His mouth dropped to her shoulder, nibbling and kissing a trail to her throat. "This is my favorite spot," he mumbled, voice muffled against her skin.

They rolled around under the covers, giggling and teasing until they were eventually panting and writhing. Despite all her personal hang-ups, she'd found her way back to a place of acceptance where closeness was concerned.

As their bodies stretched together, her nails

dug into his shoulders. Breathing through those climactic moments was once again like walking through the rain, soft, peaceful, invigorating, like being reborn.

Once they climbed out of bed and showered, they dedicated the day to online browsing. Rarity was compiling a list of suppliers while Riley was perusing real estate. Emma didn't have the focus they had so she spent most of her morning perusing shoes, not that she'd be buying any, but it was fun to look.

Her obsession with footwear developed during the early stages of her recovery. Shoes were sexy and her feet sometimes seemed her most feminine asset, despite her hobbit toes, which she still argued were shaped perfectly normal.

Spotting a pop up ad, she gave up her shoe search—like she'd ever wear heels that high anyway—and clicked on the banner sporting a pink ribbon. It was a race, right there in New York. She scanned the details and a fire built in her belly. How cool would it be to be a part of that?

"I want to do this," Emma said, turning her laptop so Rarity and Riley could see.

Riley looked up from his iPad and squinted at the picture on the screen of her laptop. "A walk?"

"That's a lot of pink," Rarity commented.

"It's a 5K for breast cancer and I want to do it. I think I can."

Riley reached forward and scrolled down the

page. "What do the proceeds go toward? What sort of research and what percentage—"

"Stop." She pulled the laptop out of his reach and took a breath. "I'm telling you, I *want* to do this. I don't care if one percent goes to researching what shade of pink looks best on a miter saw. I'm doing it."

"There are other races—"

She turned her laptop away from them and navigated her way to the sign up page. She understood some charities donated more than others, but every penny earned was money that wasn't there yesterday.

"Emma, no one's telling you not to walk—"

"Yes, you are, Riley." She kept her eyes on the computer, already typing in her information. "You think if it isn't distributing funds exactly where you believe they should go then it's pointless. It's not. Every cent, even the pennies, counts."

"I think we're just frustrated with the exploitation of pink and the lack of advancement," Rarity defended.

Emma shut her laptop and scowled at them. "I'm pink."

She wasn't sure when her opinion of the color changed or why, but she now took offense to outsiders putting down the pink as much as she took offense to corporations abusing the color. What she once criticized she now understood. Despite all the exploitation, there was something intangible behind the pink, a sense of connected-

ness, and she wanted to embrace that camaraderie.

"You don't get it," she explained. "A few months ago I was incapable of walking to the bathroom without help. Today I'm considering miles." Her eyes moistened and she was taken aback by the passionate satisfaction surging through her battered but strong body.

She smiled. "I want to do this walk because I can. I want to do it for all the people that can't and I will gladly pay my dues and wear my colors and support the cause because support doesn't just come in dollars and cents. It comes from here." Her hand rested on her breast. "I'm proud of the distance I've come and all the care my doctors gave me, and I'm thankful for all of you that got me through hell and back when all I wanted to do was stop fighting. I want to celebrate the empowering truth of survival with other survivors and they're going to be *at that race*."

Her head lowered. "I know the system has flaws. I know the treatment isn't perfect. But something's working, because I'm here. You can't improve anything from the outside looking in. So, like I said, I'm going to do *this* race."

No one said anything as her words resonated in the silent room. She wasn't poetic or any sort of brave activist. She was just a girl, but that didn't mean she couldn't contribute in some way.

"Sign me up," Riley quietly said.

"Me too." Rarity nodded.

Emma smiled. Sometimes it wasn't about politics or percentages. Sometimes it was just about people. "Thanks, guys."

~

THE MORNING of the race was sweltering. The three of them rummaged around the kitchen for granola and coffee foraging like sleepy little squirrels. By the time they made it out the door they were only placidly awake.

Emma's excitement churned at the first pink cone they passed. Streets were marked off and tents were erected. "It's so cool how they close down roads for this."

The closer they walked to the registration area the higher her energy climbed. A vibe pulsed with excitement, making her jittery and alert. Ditching the last of her coffee, she scanned the area, wanting to take in the entire experience.

Clusters and pairings of people bedecked in pink clogged the walkways as a ruckus of voices filled the air and microphones squeaked. The first strand of music came from an enormous speaker in the distance, as the recognizably upbeat tune by the band Rusted Root played.

Infused with vitality, she grinned at her friends and bounced to the familiar tune. Rarity rolled her eyes, but couldn't hide her smirk. The flutes sang as percussions tapped and strangers bounced to the music of *Send Me On My Way*.

Riley sauntered beside her, bopping his head to the music. He reached for her hand and she stretched for Rarity's as the three of them, and Marla, found their place in line.

More upbeat music continued to play as the crowd thickened. It was amazing how many people had gathered all for one purpose. Her throat tightened as she had the urge to hug and thank every single person there. There were hundreds, maybe thousands. They just kept coming.

"Emma?"

She turned at the familiar voice and her chest filled with warmth. "Anna?"

"How are you?" her friend asked, taking her into an affectionate hug.

"I'm…great. I didn't expect to see you here."

She waved off her surprise with a typical Anna grin. "This is my shtick. These are my peeps. See that handsome fellow over there?"

Emma craned her neck, spotting a tattooed hottie waiting in line behind Riley. "Yeah."

Anna winked. "He's mine."

Thrilled for her friend she beamed. "You're dating!"

"Yes, ma'am. Turns out I'm good at it too. We're coming up on our two month anniversary."

"That's fabulous! We should go out, the four of us."

Anna tapped her hand. "I see you've upgraded."

Glancing at her engagement ring, another rush of warmth hit her chest. "Yes." She smiled.

"The wedding's in September. I'd love for you to be there—and your boyfriend."

"I wouldn't miss it for the world. Riley's one of the great ones."

She glanced at him as he paid for their passes and her heart did a little jig. "He is."

"Well, I have to get back to my people before I get yelled at for taking off. I have a habit of floating wherever the wind blows. I'll see you at the finish?"

"Definitely." She hugged her friend tight.

"Tell Riley I said hi and nice work on the ring. You're going to be a stunning bride."

"I will."

Rarity returned from her search for a porta-potty. "Who was that?"

"That's my Anna. I love her."

"The one from the oncologist's office?"

Emma nodded. "The one and only."

Riley approached, handing them each a pink shirt. "We're in. Was that Anna?"

"Yeah, I invited her to the wedding."

"Awesome. I miss seeing her." He handed his sister her pink shirt.

Rarity grimaced at the fuchsia T and took a deep breath. "The things I do for you…"

Riley stuffed his arms into the shirt and shoved it over his head. "Oh, shut up and be a girl for once. I don't know about you, but I look fabulous in pink."

Rarity grudgingly put on her pink T and Emma—prepared and waiting—snapped a picture. "That's going online."

"I hate you," Rarity grumbled, but smiled as she rolled her eyes. "Let's do this."

On their journey to the starting line they were treated to incredible hospitality. People fed them, hydrated them, gave them high fives, colored their hair, and pinned and painted them with pink flair. Even Marla got a pink bandana.

"I look like the Easter Bunny threw up on me," Rarity laughed.

Emma shook her head. "Admit it. It's not that bad."

"It's not. I think I'm tapping into some deep-seated girl part of me I've been repressing since I started playing with Riley's GI Joe figures."

"There's a lady over there giving away oatmeal cookies the size of my face," Riley interrupted. "We need to get one before they're all gone."

Emma glanced at the crowd moving toward the main tent. "But people are lining up."

"I really need that cookie, Emma!"

She laughed. "Okay. Rarity, we'll meet you down there," she called as he dragged her toward the big cookie. He was so happy once he had it in his hands and the jerk only gave her a teeny, tiny bite.

The race started with a flood of bodies moving through the streets of Manhattan like the bulls moving through Spain. Thankfully, the pace was much slower.

Men, women, seniors, pets, and children all walked and chatted. By the end of the first mile Emma had shared bits of her story with a few new friends and heard parts of their stories as well.

Organizers cheered them on and music played throughout. The mood never lulled. Rest stops were positioned at various intervals and water was distributed frequently.

As the sun beamed overhead her skin slicked with sweat. Rarity and Riley didn't seem quite as winded as her, but she was proud to be keeping pace with the others. The humidity was so thick, she had one of those strange moments she appreciated being just past bald, because her old hair would have been a gigantic frizz ball in this weather.

During the second mile, the gods must have taken pity on them. The sun continued to beam overhead, but with the heat came cooling drops of rain. The drizzle didn't cease until they crossed the third mile. Her clothing was saturated and hanging sloppily from her frame. All the face paint had dribbled into smears, tinting the collars of their shirts.

"We're almost there," Riley yelled over the pumping music.

She glanced at Rarity who was wearing an expression of determination and pride, her sprayed pink hair washing down her neck in a trail of sweat and rain. Emma's heart pinched.

For all of her stubbornness and indifference, Rarity was just as fragile as the rest of them. To Rarity's way of thinking, she was never very good at being a girl, but that didn't excuse her from the perils. When it came to this, they were all on the same team.

As the finish came into view, something came over Emma, and she did something she hadn't done in a year. She ran. Her legs ached and her sneakers squished with every step, but she crossed that line no matter how much she wanted to collapse.

She did it. She made it to the other side.

They were each given medals of achievement. Even Marla got a pin for her collar. As she turned and stared back at the people still finishing, the entire event suddenly took her breath away. Not because she was winded or tired, but because it was absolutely beautiful.

Her throat tightened as she rubbed a hand over her short curls and laughed to herself. Every person that passed—and not a single one frowning—overwhelmed her.

She didn't care about the blister on her foot anymore than the spectators on the sidelines cared about the rain. The devotion and love was palpable. Her chin trembled as she worked to process such a remarkable sight. So many strangers united to embrace hope. It was simply awesome to be a part of such solidarity after going through something as isolating as cancer.

"I got you a water," Riley said as he jogged over. "Hey, you okay?"

She nodded and wiped her eyes. "I'm fabulous." And she was.

Looking at the bottle, she laughed as her fingers easily untwisted the cap, recalling a day when she lacked the strength. That plastic lid was her undoing as she held the suddenly significant cap out to him and smiled through her tears. "I did it."

"Yeah, you did." He grinned and pulled her in for a top of the line Riley hug. "You did great, cakes."

Did he understand? Did he know that a few months ago her mouth had burned like acid and she had to work up the strength to merely ask her mother to open her water bottle? She believed he did. She believed he truly got how monumental this day was for her.

If anyone understood cancer, it was those who loved its victims. Maybe they understood it more than the people suffering. Riley had memories she couldn't recall, moments when she was too lost to the pain and medication to view reality with lucid accuracy. But he was there through all of it, always by her side.

Her arms tightened around him. "You're my rock, Riley," she whispered.

He stilled as if her words triggered something monumental then he tipped his head, his gaze skating to the ground as a smile pulled at his lips. He looked at her, such genuine happiness in his eyes. "I love you, Emma."

She wasn't sure why, but it was a significant moment, a moment of clarity and understanding. It was too much to process surrounded by so many people. Clearing her throat, she pulled at her damp curls. "I must look scary."

"You look beautiful."

She laughed and wrung out her shirt. His un-wavering reassurance was as dependable as rain. No matter what, it would always come. "Where's your sister?"

He pointed. "She's making friends."

Rarity gathered with a group of young women all decked out in pink. Someone gave her a long fuchsia wig as they posed for pictures. She had a feeling her friend would be back the next time a walk came around, pink laces tied in little bows.

"Emma?"

She turned and stepped back as her system took a shock, the muscles in her face going instantly numb. "Becket?" Wow, she hadn't thought of him in ages. Her gaze drifted to the buildings surrounding them. They'd finished just outside of his complex.

"Your hair…" he glanced at all the people as if just noticing an event was taking place.

She laughed and nervously brushed a hand over her head. "Yeah." Feeling a bit exposed, she said, "I went short last January."

"I heard…you were sick."

"I was, but I'm doing great today." The longer she looked at him the sillier it seemed to be self-conscious. Who was Becket? He was no more special than anyone else there. "How are you?"

He seemed thrown off by her high spirit. "I'm…the same. Good."

"Good. How's Goldie?" The question didn't hurt like it might have a few months ago.

His attention dropped to her chest and darted

back to her face. "Um, Goldie's good. We're actually getting married next year."

She smiled, understanding this other woman was a better match for him than she'd ever been. Besides, she found her perfect match. "I'm glad you're happy, Becket."

He looked at her left hand. "You're engaged."

"Yup. We say 'I do' in two months."

"Wow." He stared at her like a puzzle he couldn't solve. Had he always viewed her that way?

"You seem so happy," he observed.

"I am. I'm happier than I've ever been."

"Becket." They turned as Goldie, with her familiar tinted tan and platinum blonde hair, approached. She was indeed pretty. Emma could admire her beauty without deducting points from her own esteem now.

"I don't believe we've been officially introduced. I'm Emma. This is my fiancé, Riley."

"Nice to meet you, Emma. I'm Goldie."

"Well, we should probably be going," Becket said, appearing uncomfortable in the presence of both his future wife and ex-fiancée.

"It was nice meeting you," Goldie smiled, her teeth perfect and white as snow.

"You too. Congrats on the engagement." Once they disappeared in the crowd she faced Riley. "Wow. I didn't feel *anything* when I saw them. I mean *nothing*. Not anger, jealousy, insecurity. I just…feel happy."

"That's awesome, cakes."

Rarity skipped over and slung her arm over

her brother's shoulders. "Hey, did I just see Becket and Barbie?"

"Yeah."

"Man," Rarity shook her head. "I am so glad you dodged that bullet. Let's go eat. I'm starved."

They went to lunch at a local pub and overheard the bartender talking about a building in his neighborhood that would likely be torn down because the buyer backed out at the last minute. Riley glommed onto the conversation and asked questions beyond the bartender's knowledge, so the man made some calls and got Riley the realtor's phone number.

On the cab ride home, they took a detour past the property. It was in a nice location, but the building was in need of some love and care. As they lay in bed that night, Riley seemed unable to sleep.

"The price was lowered again last week. I don't think we'll have an issue getting the sale so long as we want it."

She nestled into his side. "Did you plan on buying a place that would need that many renovations?"

He shrugged and bit his thumbnail, something he only did when nervous. "I didn't know what we'd find. I figured wherever we opened we'd have to paint and stuff, but this is a lot more than anything the three of us can do on our own."

"You could hire a contractor." He had the money.

"I know. I just want to be smart about our spending."

"It's *your* money, Riley."

Realizing he was biting his nail, he tucked it under the covers and faced her. "It's ours. This money's for us, Em, our future, our family."

They'd promised not to discuss children until she was past the three-year mark. A lot could happen to survivors during those first couple years of remission. "I think if you want this place you should buy it. This is your dream and I want to see it come true."

He let out a big breath. "I'm nervous. I don't know if I can handle all this on my own. I mean, I'm excited for the opportunity, but this is big. Like, after this, I might have to buy a suit for meetings and stuff. I don't know if I can be that guy."

Her fingers laced with his. "You just have to be you. You've always had a gift for drawing people in, Riley. You're charismatic and have a talent for putting people at ease. You don't need to change the way you dress to impress people. Just let them see the real you and they'll be impressed enough."

His hand tightened around hers. "Will you come with me tomorrow?"

"Of course. We're partners."

He nodded and smiled. "Syrup and pancakes."

The following day they went to visit what might be their future headquarters. It was exciting and scary.

Riley showed a side of himself she never saw

before. Perhaps his business sense came from some funky rich people gene. Every time he asked an important question she'd never think to ask, he impressed her. Aptitude was a very sexy thing.

When they returned home, no one seemed willing to speak first. Lexi was waiting at the loft, anxious to hear how it went. "So… How was it?"

Rarity's lips pursed around a poorly hidden smirk as she glanced at Emma. Unsure why no one was talking, she looked to Riley, who paced in the kitchen, head down in deep thought. Emma shrugged. "I thought it was great. The building definitely has potential."

Rarity exhaled. "I totally agree. I loved the exposed ceilings. There's enough room to make a second floor, like a loft. And there's an awesome back wing to store overhead."

They looked at Riley, who paused in his pacing and blinked at them. "What?"

Emma laughed. "Did you like it?"

He bit his thumb. Finally he said, "I think it's perfect." They all cheered, fumbling together in an inelegant hug tackle.

"Does that mean we're buying it?" Rarity asked.

"All that's missing is the name. I'm going to email the realtor in a few minutes."

The loft overflowed with exciting energy and they celebrated. Lexi and Rarity prepared a delicious meal and they toasted to their future venture while brainstorming on the perfect name for their operation. Though they were all a bit nervous, it was a magnificent feeling to have a sense of purpose. It was the first time in a long time that Emma allowed herself to look beyond a few months into the future.

Over the passing weeks, Rarity stayed busy gathering information about food and safety laws while looking into various education programs for herself. Emma's department was the branding and marketing. It was all overwhelming and surreal, but incredibly rewarding each time a decision was made.

One of the hardest decisions was coming up with the perfect name. It had been an ongoing debate, trying to find the perfect title that would encompass all they planned to do.

"Pure Foods," Riley suggested.

"Too generic and people might not get that we have more than food," Rarity argued, vetoing another choice.

"Earth to table?" Emma proposed.

"That's nice, but not perfect."

They continued brainstorming. "Customers should know it's more than food and all natural," Rarity reminded. "We really need to get the point across that everything we sell is for the body and not bad for it. Back to basics, you know? I feel like we're complicating it and we just need something simple so they know it's pure."

"Naked Goods," Emma said. "Au naturel. No additives."

They turned to her and both smiled, resembling each other in one of those strange moments she was reminded they were siblings. "That's great, toots. What do you think, Ri?"

"Who doesn't love naked?"

Rarity jotted down the name. "Naked Goods. Well, I never thought we'd use sex appeal to sell our products, but it works."

"Make it good with Naked Goods," Riley said, pitching his voice like a little jingle. "Labeled to be understood."

And so it was decided. Their company would be called Naked Goods. The most bizarre moment came on July thirteenth, when they signed the deed for the future Naked Goods.

The place desperately needed work. Everything needed to be removed, replaced, and reborn if they ever wanted customers to venture through their doors—especially if they were in the industry of selling products related to clean living. Riley hired a construction crew and Emma collaborated with an architect that specialized in up-cycling unwanted natural materials. Rarity busied herself with multiple lists of potential suppliers.

It was imperative that their products be completely trustworthy and non-toxic, so there were a lot of back and forth calls and queries. If a company didn't certify their products organic or GMO free—be it food, cotton, or cosmetic—Naked Goods wasn't interested.

Things were happening so fast. Her parents often came to sit with Marla so the three of them could road trip out to see nearby farms and get a better understanding for the organic process.

As contracts were signed her nerves jingled with implied responsibility. There was so much to consider, but with every decision came great satisfaction. They were doing something no one else in their local area was doing.

There, of course, were organic aisles and overlooked sections hidden away in most super-markets. And deep in the hipster sections of the city existed holistic healers and stores special-izing in oils and supplements that were other-wise hard to come by. But no one had done what they were doing to the degree they were doing it, all in one place.

They met other people like them and earned incredible support. While corporate companies and pharmaceuticals competed with each other, the people in their circle were more than happy to share ideas and knowledge.

Riley believed if enough people came to-gether there might someday be more stores like theirs. They didn't care about the competition. It was about the movement, the return to resources they could trust. Emma agreed with him. Expo-sure and a little knowledge was a very powerful thing.

Naked Goods was green from the solar panels that lit their displays down to the flooring they chose. They carried unprocessed grains, unre-fined oils, organic produce, supplements, house-hold supplies, clean cosmetics and personal hygiene products all made from safe and healthy ingredients. The second floor offered an eat-in, green café and sprout bar that doubled as a classroom for Rarity to host events. Emma planned on reasserting her deodorant making skills once the roster of classes was posted.

The backroom was an apothecary of sorts, where customers could order supplies, scenting with preferred essential oils. It wasn't just a natural store. It was an experience, an education, and was rapidly developing into a thriving community, before their doors even opened.

A portion of every dollar earned would go toward research. Their website offered an exact audit of every penny distributed as well as a detailed rationale of their standards. There was a logical plan for every aspect. And once they had their grand opening, the gears would be put into motion.

"Emma."

She turned from her laptop as Rarity called her name from the bedroom door. "What's up?"

Her friend sauntered into her room holding her purse. "You will see here, I have your purse and shoes. Please put them on."

"Are we going somewhere?"

"I feel slightly remiss that—as your maid of honor—I've overlooked a minor detail. I'd be more distraught if you—*the bride*—hadn't overlooked it as well."

"What?" She frowned, going over her mental checklist for the wedding. Everything was arranged.

Rarity scoffed. "You're getting married in less than a month and you don't have a *gown*."

Emma chuckled, trying to ignore the pinch in

her chest. It wasn't that she forgot. She thought about her wedding gown every day, thought about how much her first wedding gown had meant and how beautiful she looked in it, how much she loved that stupid dress—so much so she forgot she was supposed to be in love with the groom.

This time it was more about the guy. She shrugged. "It's just not that big of a deal to me now. I'll find something."

"Um…" Rarity sat on the edge of her desk. "I might be wrong here, but don't fancy dresses take, like, months to order and then you have to have them trimmed and fitted and stuff. Your wedding's in three and a half weeks, toots."

"I know." The anxiety over wearing a pretty dress with no boobs to fill it made her feel superficial and small, but she didn't want to explain herself to some snooty seamstress on Park Ave.

"Okay, I'm not sure what's going on here, but I'm going to need old Emma to come back for a few hours." She shut her laptop. "We're going to a little shop in Brooklyn. Put these shoes on. I have Riley's credit card. He's treating."

Knowing Rarity loathed dress shopping, Emma couldn't help but be impressed by her dedication to her duty as maid of honor. "We could just look online and take it to the seamstress around the corner when it comes in." That would be less painful.

"Not a chance. I know you, Emma. This is something you'll look back on with gratitude. You don't find perfect online. Put on the shoes.

We're not coming home until we've located the perfect gown."

The salon in Brooklyn was small and nothing like the fancy boutique her first gown had come from. The mannequins wore dated wigs and the carpet was a hideous shade of burgundy.

"Who told you about this place?" she mumbled as they scanned the showroom for human life.

"I have people," Rarity said, stepping to the counter and ringing the antique bell.

An older woman came from a door buried between racks of consignment prom dresses. "May I help you?"

"We need a gown," Rarity announced.

The woman smiled. "Are you the bride?"

"Not in this life." She nudged Emma forward. "Emma's the bride. I'm the maid of honor."

"Lovely to meet you. I'm Betty." She seemed to be the only person in the store and quite possibly the owner. Her fine silken hair was silver as a fox and her skin was translucent with age. "Congratulations on your engagement. When's the wedding?"

She fidgeted with her T-shirt. "September sixteenth."

"Of *this* year?"

"Yes."

"Oh." The woman fiddled with her earring as she took a quick scan of her inventory. "Well then, we have some work to do, don't we? Come with me."

Liking her optimism, they followed her

deeper into the salon as she explained which style gowns were hung where. "You two take a gander and I'll be back in a moment."

When they were alone she glanced at Rarity and snorted. "Seriously, where did you find this place?"

"I buy herbs from the Chinese place around the corner." She snickered. "I like her. She reminds me of the original Betty Boop."

They sorted through various gowns, none really sparking any deep affection. Betty returned with a tray of grapes and three glasses of wine. "I hope chardonnay's okay with you ladies. I'm all out of champagne."

"*Fan-shee,*" Rarity complimented in her Sean Connery accent as she took a sip. Betty was definitely creating a memorable experience.

"So," the woman lightly clapped her hands together. "Did you find anything you like?"

"Not yet."

She twisted her lips and perused the selection. "Well, you're going to need off the rack so we should start with your measurements and narrow the choices by size."

She retrieved a thin measuring tape and Emma asked, "Do you have a seamstress here?"

"That's me. I do it all, honey."

For some reason this eased Emma's stress.

"Let's get you into a slip and then we'll take your measurements. Sometimes the best way to find *the gown* is to try a bunch on first." She winked and whispered, "I say that about finding the right husband too. Go ahead and get down to your undergarments."

Breath jaggedly left her lungs as she nodded. Swallowing a hard lump in her throat, she walked behind the screen openly draped with a curtain. There wasn't much of a changing room. "Is anyone going to come in?"

"You two are my first customers this month, so I doubt it. There's a bell on the door, so we'll hear if anyone stops by."

Rarity sent her a reassuring grin. "It's just us girls, toots. No need to be self-conscious."

She nodded.

Betty selected various gowns and hung them on a nearby rack. Emma stepped out of her flip-flops and slid down her shorts. Taking a deep breath, she sluggishly lifted off her shirt.

Carrying back an armful of gowns, Betty said, "Now, some girls like a fuller gown, but September can still be warm—"

She paused, facing Emma's bare chest and tilted her head, a look of understanding and compassion quickly crossing her crystal blue eyes. Emma's chest tightened, but Betty barely flinched.

"You look to be about a size eight. We have lots of dresses that size. I think we can find something just perfect. Why don't you start with this one?"

Exhaling with relief, she took the heavy satin gown and Rarity helped her slide it over her shoulders. "You're doing great," she whispered.

The gown hit the floor and zipped up the

back. She turned and faced the triad of mirrors. *Not a chance.* The heavy beading at the chest left the loose material wilted and sad.

"Next!" Rarity called, pulling the zipper down without a second glance.

Betty continued to dive deep into the racks and dig up various gowns of all different cuts and styles. By the tenth gown, Emma was exhausted, frustrated, and in need of another glass of wine. Luckily, Betty was on top of her game and had plenty of Chardonnay.

"I have an idea," the woman said, as they took a breather, sitting in a pile of white satin and lace, sipping wine. She tapped a painted nail to her chin. "Where did that dress go?"

"What dress?" Rarity asked.

"It's an older style, from the sixties. A darling little gown. Oh, I could just picture you in it! Let me go look upstairs."

Betty left and Rarity said, "We might have to go somewhere else."

"Not today. I'm too tired." Plus, she really wanted to give Betty her business. The woman was determined to find something that fit and it didn't seem like her efforts were for the sake of a sale.

Rarity patted her knee. "We'll find it. Don't worry."

Betty returned with a white garment bag in her arms. "Do you believe I found it? I always loved this dress." She hung the bag on a hook and slowly lowered the zipper.

"It's short," Rarity observed.

"That was the style at the time. Women would wear dainty wrist gloves and short lace veils. Back then weddings were more about marrying the man of your dreams, less about the party and pomp."

Emma stood and touched the delicate fabric. Thin layers of chiffon flowed into a tea length skirt. The top was done in elegant plain lace, covering the shoulders as the actual bodice was cut simplistically straight across the chest. "Can I try it on?"

"I insist on it." Betty laughed, removing it from the hanger.

She fed the gown over her arms and fluffed the skirts. Emma stood and Rarity handed her a headband. "Try this on."

"And these." Betty slid two satin shoes under her feet.

She fit the plain silver band to her curls as Rarity clasped the pearl button at the base of her neck. Taking a deep breath, she turned.

I found it.

Her chest filled as she stared at the charmingly understated beauty in the mirror. Was that her?

"Oh…" Rarity and Betty sighed at once.

She couldn't take her eyes off her reflection. Her expanders gave her minimal shape, not enough to be mistaken for ordinary breasts, but in this dress, she was perfect. The lines and cut showcased her feminine figure, accentuating her hips and curves while disguising her lack of cleavage. She loved everything about it down to the ladylike way it highlighted her legs.

No other gown, not even the one in her closet at home, had ever made her feel so pretty. "I'll take it."

Betty smiled and folded her hands together. "Wonderful!"

CHAPTER 22

$\mathcal{R}$iley took another slow breath, waiting for his heart to stop racing. Fidgeting with his tie, he tugged at his collar and blotted away the sweat gathering at the back of his neck. This was why he preferred T-shirts.

"Riley, we need you over here."

Pulling at his gray lapels, he adjusted his purple tie and walked toward Joey at the foot of the Gapstow Bridge. The sky faded to pink as the backdrop of buildings gradually lit, creating a horizon of twinkling lights.

He shifted as his damn pants bunched awkwardly at the cuff. "Do I have a loose hem or something?" he asked, rotating his ankle.

"No worries, I have a needle and thread," Joey announced, dropping to his knee to examine the cuff.

Riley looked down. "Well, this is awkward."

"Not from my view." Joey winked and tapped

his shoe. "Cuffs fine." He stood. "Okay, the musicians are going to start when your guests are seated. Once Emma's ready on the other side, they'll shift into *Stand by Me.* The vocalist will be under that tree. You start to walk at the first line when you hear the word *night.* Take your time getting there, because Emma wants the entire song."

"Got it." He fussed with the knot of his tie some more. "Is this crooked?"

Joey tsked and swatted his hands away. "Straight men should *not* touch accessories. You're fine, darling. Once you see her all your worries will go away. Trust me."

He took a deep breath and tried to calm his nerves. He wasn't so much nervous as he was anxious. He'd waited a long time for this day. "Is she here yet?"

"We have her carefully hidden. Relax. Your only job is to walk when the vocalist says—"

"*Night.* Got it. Is my sister around?" It was difficult sharing his best *wo*-man with Emma.

"She's with your bride. Do you want me to get her?"

"Yeah." His heart continued to pound as Joey went in search of Rarity.

There was a long, low whistle. "Well, well, well, look at you."

He grinned as Rarity stepped closer, hands wedged casually in the pockets of her amethyst tuxedo slacks. Her hair was parted and slicked to the side, dapper and as cool as Dick Tracy on the scene of a crime.

"Look at me? Look at you. Should I be pissed your tux is cooler than mine?"

She laughed and adjusted his tie, which he'd messed with after Joey's warning not to touch it. His nerves quelled.

"You look beautiful, Rarity."

"Thanks, big brother. I feel pretty." She patted his chest and his anxiety eased some more. "You should see your blushing bride. Stunning."

"I bet. It's gonna be hard not to do her on the bridge."

"Ew." She tsked and took a step back. "So I guess you sent that invitation after all, the one to Mom and Dad."

His shoulders tensed. "Why, are they here?"

She nodded and whispered, "They're sitting next to Lexi's parents. I'm going to introduce them after the ceremony."

His brow lifted. "Really?"

"Yup. Life's too short to combat small mindedness. They can either accept me or not, but they'll never change me. I love Lexi too much to keep putting her second."

He squeezed her arm. "I'm proud of you, Rarity. That's really great."

"Rarity," Joey called. "The rest of the guests have arrived. We need you at the center of the bridge."

She gave him a wink. "I'll see you up there. Love you, Ri."

"I love you too, Rare."

Music started, just some soft background noise as the vocalist played with his microphone.

He'd often wondered if Emma remembered him holding her that time they danced in the rain, but now he knew she did. She said it was her weakest moment and his strength was the only thing that got her through. It seemed only right that the song be incorporated in their ceremony as they promised to stand together forever. He'd always stand by her. Always.

The guitar picked up the slow, recognizable beat and he drew in the first steady breath of the day. It was time. Calm washed over him as his feet moved at the precise lyric.

Twinkle lights and luminaries—not light sabers, but bags with little candles—lit his way. The vocalist sang promises to not be afraid and he wasn't. He was completely at peace. Soft rattles picked up the beat as he stepped onto the bridge and sensed her nearness, every step closer to her helping him breathe a little easier.

This was the first day since last August that he'd gone without seeing her. He would've never survived a lifetime of that. It was seven o'clock and he unbearably missed her.

Cresting the ivy covered bridge, his lips parted as he caught the first glimpse of her. She was, without a doubt, the loveliest creature to ever walk this earth.

The moment their eyes met, her smile turned from stunning to radiant. Her dad's hand tightened, slowing her steps. There was no anxiety left, only eagerness to hold her in his arms. His bride.

She looked amazing. Her dress showed her

sexy ankles and calves. It was simple, high-lighting her natural beauty rather than competing with it. Her flowers were deep purple and her curls were pinned back with a delicate veil.

Their guests waited in a small grouping of white chairs at the top of the bridge, his parents sitting stone-faced between Lexi's parents and Emma's mom. He didn't understand why their presence meant so much, but it did. He was glad Emma encouraged him to send the invitation. Behind them sat Jake and Emma's friend, Anna, with her new boyfriend.

Her father kissed her cheek and faced him. "Take care of my baby."

He nodded, breathing in her familiar scent. "Always."

She smiled as he took her hands, bringing her fingers to his lips so he could place a kiss there. "You're breathtaking."

"You're very handsome," she whispered.

He leaned close as the song finished. "I think the wedding planner was flirting with me."

She giggled. "I don't doubt it. You're very sexy."

"I've got my sexy pants on," he joked.

"Good, because I've got my dirty girl panties on."

He groaned, as his sexy pants got a little tighter. "You're killing me."

She snickered and the minister stepped forward. "We're gathered here this evening to witness the union of Emma and Riley…"

He stared into her eyes, as her vivacity

breathed life into his soul. His Emma. He wasn't sure what he'd done to deserve a love as pure and unrefined as theirs. Everything about their relationship humbled him.

"...and now Riley and Emma will exchange vows they've written as they promise their lives to one another. Riley."

He squeezed her hands and smiled nervously. "Emma, you stole my heart with a look, teased me with a laugh, and changed my life with a kiss. Today, I promise that I'll never ask for my heart back. It belongs to you. You're everything I am. You're the air I breathe, the rhythm of my soul, the song to my laughter, and the purpose to my day. Without you, my life would be bleak, because joy only exists when I can share it with you. I promise to love you as deeply as a man can love and every day I'll look for ways to take that love deeper still. You're more than the other half of my soul. You're my heart. And as such, I will love, honor, and cherish you for all the days of my life."

He glanced at Rarity who swept away a tear and handed him the ring. Emma removed her lace glove, her hands slightly trembling as he slid the band onto her ring finger. She squeezed his hands.

"Riley," she sighed and swallowed. "You're the angel that guards me in the night. You're the friend that makes me laugh when I need it most and let's me cry when that's all that can be done. Your endless energy and unbreakable spirit gives me strength when I'm weak and leads me home when I'm lost. In the darkest of nights, you're always the brightest star. I love you. I promise to be a good wife and never give you less than you deserve. I will *always* respect you, honor you, and treasure every moment we're blessed enough to share. I promise to love you for the rest of my life."

She took the ring from his sister and slid it onto his finger.

"By the power vested in me and the state of New York, I now pronounce you husband and wife. You may kiss your bride."

He tugged her into his arms and planted a kiss right on her sweet mouth as everyone clapped and cheered. Dipping her back, he whispered. "You're mine now. Forever."

"And ever," she whispered back, kissing him deeply.

"I present to you, Mr. and Mrs. Riley Lockhart!"

The musicians started again, this time doing a delightful acoustic rendition of *Love and Marriage.*

Emma frowned. "What is this?"

He shrugged. "You got to pick the processional song so I picked the recessional. Marriage is full of compromise, cakes."

"Enough kissing, you two. I need some hugs," Rarity interrupted, wrapping her arms around them and bouncing with happiness. "I love you two idiots."

"Riley." They broke apart as his parents approached.

"I'm glad you guys made it," he greeted. "You remember Emma, my wife."

His mother looked at Emma for a long moment, not missing a bit of the changes in her appearance, he was sure. "Congratulations, Emma." Her words took obvious effort.

His dad tilted his head and glanced back at Riley. Facing Emma he held out his hand. "Welcome to the family, my dear. I think you've made a wonderful impression on my son."

She shook his hand. "Thank you, but he's the one that's made an impression on me."

"Mom, Dad." They turned as Rarity stood beside Lexi, her dark hickory shoulders showing under her purple gown. "This is Lexi Bardel… my girlfriend. I've been meaning to introduce you since we started dating two years ago. Lexi, this is my mom and dad, Sophia and Oliver Lockhart."

His mother's face paled and he wasn't sure what was stressing her out the most, Emma's transformation, the fact that her daughter was gay, or that she was in love with a stunning black woman. Perhaps it was a combination of everything. Either way, she'd definitely be ordering a cocktail with dinner if they made it that far. Riley smiled widely, loving every awkward moment, immeasurably proud of his sister.

"It's a pleasure to meet you," Lexi nodded.

"Ladies and gentlemen," Joey called. "If you'd please take your seats. The bride and groom have decided to share their first dance as husband and wife at the park."

Where was Emma? He scanned the area and found her speaking to her parents. *"Woman!* I need you."

Grinning, she walked to him and he held out his hand as the music started. Her fingers laced with his. If ever there was a song written for him and his wife, it was Pearl Jam's *Just Breathe.*

He pulled her close and held her, a complete sense of contentment washing over him as he hummed in her ear and breathed against the softness of her neck. His eyes closed, the intimate way her body fit against his overtaking his senses as the rest of the world faded away and their hearts beat as one.

Everything he needed was in his arms. All he had to do was breathe and bask in the gifts he'd been given and he found a contentment he'd never dreamed.

Just breathe.

There were uncountable moments of stillness infringed by the pressures of life. Some days they lost their balance and some days they stood strong, grounded in what mattered most in this world. Sometimes the world crashed down on one person yet kept spinning for everyone else. If anything, the human soul was resilient.

Emma once told him she dreamed of being a princess dressed in pretty little ribbons, tied up in bows wearing tiny pearls pinned in a row. But the day she celebrated six months cancer free she told him glass slippers break and she'd much rather run and play. Live.

And that they did. She was so alive in everything she did and every day she enjoyed.

Some might call her a victim, but she'd never wear that label to him. She was so much more than a statistic or a survivor. To him, she was and would always be, his hero.

LA FIN

BACKMATTER

Never miss another book release!
Click here to sign up for Lydia Michaels'
Newsletter.

Follow Lydia Michaels on Instagram and
Facebook!
Instagram @lydia_michaels_books
Facebook @LydiaMichaels

Billionaire Romance
Falling In | Sacrifice of the Pawn | Calamity
Rayne

Small Town Romance
Wake My Heart | The Best Man | Love Me Nots |
Pining For You | Almost Priest

Emotional Favorites

Dark Psychological Thriller & Tortured Hero Romance
(TRIGGER WARNING)
Hurt

Non-Fiction Books for Writers
Write 10K in a Day: Avoid Burnout

About the Author

Lydia Michaels is the award winning and bestselling author of more than forty titles, a certified life coach, and transformational speaker. She is the consecutive winner of the 2018 & 2019 *Author of the Year Award* from *Happenings Media,* as well as the recipient of the 2014 *Best Author Award* from the *Courier Times.* She has been featured in *USA Today, Romantic Times Magazine, Love & Lace,* and more. As the host and founder of the *East Coast Author Convention,* the *Behind the Keys Author Retreat,* and *Read Between the Wines,* she continues to celebrate her growing love for readers and romance novels around the world.

In 2021, Michaels released the groundbreaking, non-fiction series, **Write 10K in a Day,** to commemorate her career in the publishing industry. She looks forward to many more years of exploring both fiction and non-fiction writing, teaching about the craft, and learning from the others in the author community.

Lydia is happily married to her childhood sweetheart. Some of her favorite things include the scent of paperback books, listening to her husband play piano, escaping to her coastal home at the Jersey Shore, cheap wine, *Game of Thrones,* coffee, and kilts. She hopes to meet you soon at one of her many upcoming events.

Other Titles by Lydia Michaels
Wake My Heart
The Best Man
Love Me Nots
Pining For You
My Funny Valentine
Falling In: Surrender Trilogy 1
Breaking Out: Surrender Trilogy 2
Coming Home: Surrender Trilogy 3
Sacrifice of the Pawn: Billionaire Romance
Queen of the Knight: Billionaire Romance
Original Sin
Dark Exodus
Calamity Rayne: Gets a Life
Calamity Rayne: Back Again
La Vie en Rose
Breaking Perfect
FREE! - Blind
Untied
Almost Priest
Beautiful Distraction
Irish Rogue
British Professor
Broken Man
Controlled Chaos
Hard Fix
Intentional Risk
Hurt
Sugar
Simple Man
Protégé
Forfeit
Lost Together

BACKMATTER

Atonement
First Comes Love
If I Fall
Something Borrowed
Write 10K in a Day

A NOTE FROM THE AUTHOR

Dear Readers,

I want to first thank you for reading my work. Your love for my characters brings me immeasurable happiness and I hope you enjoyed meeting Riley and Emma. When I started writing La Vie en Rose {Life in Pink}, it had nothing to do with cancer. Emma's condition was as much a shock to me as it was to her. I'm still not sure who the story belongs to, Emma or Riley, but I'd like to give it to all those who have been in their shoes. My life and views were forever changed after writing this story.

I'd like to acknowledge the countless women out there who have faced this horrible disease. If you have a story online (or one a relative wrote), I likely read it. You are *all* my heroes. To the women that blog and vlog, documenting their highs and lows so the next person doesn't feel so alone or scared, you are the true definition of brave. You are all a part of Emma and I hope you recognized yourselves in her unconditional beauty and unbreakable spirit. You're an inspiration to all.

To my dear friends Regina Hunter and Lisa Cody, you are the true Riley's of the world. Your endless love and stoic strength brings hope to those that need it most. Jack, you'll forever own a piece of my heart (#Action4Jackson). And to the amazing @TheAnncredible, though we've never met, I feel as if we're old friends. Your journey is an inspiration to many and your beautiful spirit captures so much of what it means to be alive. I believe when I wrote Anna's character, I was thinking of you. And thank you to The Rose Peddlers, who tirelessly promoted this story in their free time.

Beyond this note, readers can find links pertaining to the subject matter of La Vie en Rose. If you enjoyed this story, please leave a review. I'd love to hear your thoughts! I can also be contacted at Lydia@LydiaMichaelsBooks.com
Thank you for reading!

Love,
Lydia

www.CharityNavigator.org **Charity Navigator** works to guide intelligent giving. Their site offers detailed reports on various charities so that donors clearly understand how their generosity will be distributed.

www.bcrfcure.org **The Breast Cancer Research Foundation** is a non-profit organization dedicated to achieving prevention and a cure for breast cancer through critical funding. Founded in 1993, BCRF holds an A+ rating from Charity Watch and a 4 out of 4 Star rating from Charity Navigator.

www.LBBC.org **Living Beyond Breast Cancer** provides programs and services to people whose lives have been impacted by breast cancer.

www.cleaningforareason.org **Cleaning for a Reason** provides free house cleaning for women undergoing treatment for any kind of cancer.

www.locksoflove.org **Locks of Love** accepts donations of human hair with the intention of making wigs for children undergoing medical treatments that cause them to lose their hair.

9 781957 573250